# BRENDAN OF KILRUSH

By

Michael J. Schneider

Ink Smith Publishing
www.ink-smith.com

ISBN: 978-1-939156-50-1

Ink Smith Publishing
P.O Box 1086
Glendora CA

BRENDAN OF KILRUSH

"God purposely chose what the world considers nonsense
in order to shame the wise, and he chose what the world
considers weak in order to shame the powerful." (1 Corinthians 1:26)

# CHAPTER 1

Brendan poked a stick into the pile of coals. As he did so, the light gray ash fell away, exposing the yellow-red glow which reassured him adequate heat continued to radiate from this pile for his purpose. The wind behind him snatched up some of the ashes as he did so, transporting them toward the red ball of the sun sinking into the sea far beyond him. The wind felt good on the back of his head. It tossed his tangled mass of bronze hair about his shoulders and toward his face. The hair didn't quite match the lighter tint of facial hair just becoming visible below his nose and on his sun-tanned cheeks near and just below his ears.

As the wind passed his ears, they sensed something: a sound out of resonance with this pastoral environment in the year of Our Lord 812. Often Brendan would recognize wisps of voices as they drifted up from the village on the river below; but something was different. The faint sound he sensed more than heard was both familiar and alarming; enough so that he decided to abandon his fine catch of salmon, now roasting over the coals, and the sheep he tended and head toward the village. Brendan knew he risked his master's lash if caught abandoning the sheep; but something in the wind-born signal compelled him toward the village.

Brendan relied heavily on his staff for mobility. His right leg was immobile below the knee. The ankle and toes were locked since birth. When he was younger, some of the other village children teased him by telling him that he had been lucky that St. Patrick had brought Christianity to their land or surely his parents would have left him to die on the hillside. As the distance between Brendan and the village diminished, the signal on the wind strengthened.

Moving still closer, he recognized it as a voice. It was not just any voice but a familiar voice. It belonged to Kaileen!

Brendan bent his direction toward the sound of her voice. He had a special fondness for Kaileen and he knew something was wrong. To hear her from such a distance meant she was screaming. He must hurry. Why wasn't he born with two good legs like the other people in his village? He now slowed as he came upon that portion of the trail which wound through limestone outcroppings. Here he could easily stumble on any of the many gray stones protruding through the ground surface at random. A small hare suddenly jumped up, scurried a short distance down the path in front of him and disappeared into the brush on the side of the trail.

After passing through a dense clump of conifers, Brendan viewed the village from a distance. It looked as though the whole village was burning! Dark plumes of smoke rose from several dozen locations and coalesced into a large single cloud hovering over the small community. What could have caused so many fires? The question bewildered him. He had to get down there—fast! He pressed on, throwing his cloak behind his shoulders to hasten his movement.

By the time Brendan reached the outskirts of the village, the smoke had thinned, dispersed by a strong breeze moving in from the west. Where there had once been thatched-roof homes, now he could only see a few unburned poles and remnants of walls scattered here and there across the patch of land where the village once stood. Brendan then began to notice the corpses. Men who only yesterday sold their grain, cattle, sheep, and other goods in the town, the man who made things of iron, the man who formed bronze bowls and goblets, all these lay dead, their eyes staring blankly into the sky. The dirt around the bodies was dampened near the points where heads were split, limbs severed or bodies pierced.

Brendan spotted the remnants of a cooking fire. He walked over to it. A pot of stew still boiled over the smoking pit. Brendan reached down and lifted the wooden spoon from the pot scooping some of the meat and vegetables from the broth. He gobbled down the contents of the spoon, savoring each morsel. Starved, he was about to dip in for a second spoonful, when he heard Kaileen scream in the distance. *Kaileen, yes, where was she? In fact, where were any of the women and girls of the village?* He decided eating would have to wait until he found Kaileen. He last saw her yesterday morning. She'd asked him what he'd thought of her new tunic. Oh, and what a tunic it was! Bright dyed green linen ran across each shoulder and down the side of the body. Between these the portion which covered the main part of the front and back contained bright multicolored designs on a black background. Surely there wasn't a more fanciful tunic in the entire Shannon Valley. As beautiful as the tunic was, however, it couldn't compare to Kaileen herself. Brendan could picture her lovely sun-browned face framed by bangs of red brown hair across her forehead with matching locks falling below her shoulders on either side of her face.

*Kaileen, yes, he must find out why she was screaming.* The food would have to wait. Instinctively he searched around for a weapon. In the hands of a slain villager, he spotted a sickle. The man had obviously died trying to fight off his assailant. Brendan moved to the corpse; and pried the sickle from the dead man's grip. He tucked it into the rope fastened about his own waist, then moved in the direction he'd last heard Kaileen's screams.

As Brendan reached the edge of the village, he could see down to the banks of the Shannon. The first things he saw were the ships. He had never seen anything like them before. They were long, three or four times as long as any boat he had ever seen on the banks before. There were two of them. Each had a tall mast in the center with ropes running from the top of the mast to the sides of the ship. Between the two ships on the beach, Brendan saw many men form a cirlce around a large fire. The evening breeze blew the noise of their revelry to Brendan from Shannon. Brendan darted behind a bush of heather. The heather and tall grass could conceal him if he tried to move closer; so he decided to move as close to these strange men as he could. Slowly, he crept forward on hands and knees. He carefully moved among the brush, stones, reeds and grass, trying to disturb as few of these as possible, striving not to betray his presence by any sound.

He ran out of cover about ten yards from the boisterous group. Brendan decided to be content to observe from the last concealing bushes on the fringe of the opening. Brendan scanned the scene before him. These were strange beastly creatures, like nothing he'd ever seen before. Most had yellow hair, long, down to their shoulders. Their facial hair, equally as long, mixed with that protruding from under their metal helmets that the two were indistinguishable. Those helmets, many had horns protruding from each. Brendan wondered *what kind of men had horns?* Then he remembered Father Sweeney, who said Sunday Mass in the burnt village Brendan had just left. *Hadn't Father Sweeny spoken of devils as "horned beasts?"* A chill raced through Brendan's body. How could he, a mortal, fight the powers of Hell? He prayed silently to the Virgin Mary. The prayer made him feel better. Somehow he sensed now that these were only men, and men could be defeated. The question now was, how?

Brendan pondered this question as he continued to study the scene before him. To the right of the fire he spotted Kaileen. She sat on the ground with a group of about twelve women, some trying to comfort crying babies. It appeared all of these women were tied to a rope staked into the ground. The ones with children had only one hand fastened. The women without children had both hands tied. Most of the captors were eating and drinking, talking boisterously in a tongue strange to Brendan. A couple of spits alongside the fire contained pigs, undoubtedly stolen from the village, roasting over coals. Now and then, one of the strange men would walk over to the fire, pull a dagger from a scabbard on his waistband, slice off a strip of meat from one of the pigs and return to his place in the sand.

Brendan studied everything about these strangers. They all wore some kind of short tunic. The tunic only reached to mid-thigh, but wore some sort of trouser-like garment that covered each leg separately. Some of the tunics appeared to be woven from iron thread. Each man wore about his waist and over his shoulder a massive leather belt with a sword in scabbard attached. Here and there, scattered around the circle, were javelins with accompanying wooden shields, standing upright as though they had sprouted from the sand. As Brendan surveyed the mob, he looked for some weakness, some way to get Kaileen away from these men.

Darkness descended rapidly. "Good," Brendan thought. Brendan had keen night vision, sharpened by spending most of his nights in the pasture with the sheep. As the sky lost its light, an idea brightened in Brendan's head. The spark of an idea grew into a roaring flame within Brendan's head, much like the bonfire before him on the beach. With satisfaction, Brendan watched one of the barbarians stand before the crowd and begin to talk in the strange language. The man standing was obviously a storyteller, judging from the way all the others gathered about him. Soon his was the only voice audible around the great fire.

Seizing the opportunity, Brendan backed into the brush. He unbuttoned the brooch that fastened his cloak and flipped the cloak onto the ground. Rapidly he piled dry grass and twigs onto the cloak. Silently he compacted them with his hands and knees so he could carry as much as the cloak would hold. He then fastened the four corners of the cloak with his brooch and began to crawl toward the leftmost of the two ships. Both ships were partially beached with their bows resting on the shore. Staying in the shadows he made his way, dragging the bundle, to the bow of the first ship. The bow rose too high to climb over it at this point so he first threw the bundle over the bow. Next, he entered the cold water and swam to a point where he could reach the gunwale and pull himself over.

Performing this maneuver landed him abruptly on one of the hard wooden benches used by the crew. While he had made little noise, his left hip and upper thigh smarted where he'd contacted the bench. He crawled over the benches to the bow of the ship and located the cloak. Swinging one leg over a bench at a time, he made his way aft toward the main mast and the sail.

It was dark enough now that Brendan felt it safe to climb on to the main yardarm containing the massive sail. Pulling his knife from his belt, he shredded a large area of the wadmal fabric of the sail. Next, he pulled the grass and brush from his cloak. Brendan mixed the grass and brush with the fabric so that it would ignite the sail. Finally, he built a fire on the sail with dried grass which he ignited with a couple of strikes of his trusty flint stone against the steel of his knife blade. The sparks from the impact of the flint against the steel fell into a special bit of lamb's wool Brendan kept for that purpose. When he blew on the smoking embers in the wool, a small flame arose. He touched the flame to the dry grass. The fire spread along the sail so fast that Brendan nearly got burned before he dismounted from the yardarm. In a flash, he grabbed his cloak and dropped into the water on the side opposite the one where he had climbed aboard. He first swam to the port side of the second ship. Then he made his way toward shore alongside this ship. The warriors on the shore would soon notice the fire aboard the first ship and Brendan needed to remain concealed. For the moment, the shadow of the second ship would hide him; but Brendan knew he must make it to the brush on shore before the angry mob came storming down the beach.

Luck was with Brendan. He reached the safety of a salt marsh just as the first of the barbarians spotted the fire on the ship. Moments later, the gang on the beach was rushing to the ships as Brendan crawled into the marsh. Brendan made his way through the marsh, then back up the beach toward the fire the barbarians had just abandoned. Moments later, he reached a spot just opposite where the women were, trying desperately to free themselves from the leather thongs that prevented their escape.

Cautiously Brendan looked about. *Good, just as he'd hoped.* All the strange seamen had gone to the ships leaving the captives unguarded. He slipped from the cover of the brush and went to Kaileen first. With his knife he quickly slashed the leather thongs which bound her hands. He handed her the knife and instructed:

"Go to the other end and start cutting them loose."

Kaileen said nothing, but nodded acknowledgment and rushed for the other end. Brendan then pulled the sickle from the belt about his waist and set to work on the bonds of the woman closest to him. As he cut, he gave them the order:

"When you get loose, run in different directions. If we spread out, I don't think they'll try to follow all of us."

The women all nodded that they understood. Then, one by one, as they were freed, they disappeared into the bush, running in different directions as instructed. Kaileen cut the next to last captive free as Brendan was working on the last one. Instead of disappearing, she spoke to Brendan:

"I'm going to stay with you," she insisted. Then she continued: "With that bad leg of yours, you may need help."

The last thing Brendan was going to do was argue with Kaileen if she wanted to stay with him. He smiled and said, "OK, let's go."

As Brendan moved toward the brush, Kaileen said, "Wait."

Brendan then watched as Kaileen dashed toward the javelins and shields. She quickly snatched two javelins and rushed back to Brendan.

"We might find these useful," she announced.

With that, they disappeared into the brush. As they made their way through the bushes, brambles scratched their ankles and tore their clothing. Brendan didn't like trying to make his way through such thick brush in the darkness but he felt they must get as far from the strange sea warriors as possible. In the darkness, Brendan found his way by feel. He knew that to get away from the beach they must travel upward. He felt his way up the side of the Shannon Valley, noting that as long as they were climbing, they had to be moving away from the ships and the raiders. Brendan also resisted the temptation to move to the thinner brush or to follow any trails. He knew their pursuers would be more likely to spot them if he and Kaileen didn't stick to the heavy brush. Kaileen followed close behind Brendan. They each carried a javelin. Brendan found his useful for climbing but hard to manipulate in the brush. He didn't want to leave it; he might need it later to fight the bloody barbarians.

Brendan and Kaileen came to the edge of the brush they'd been traveling in. Ahead, they could see a silhouette of the ruins of the village which Brendan had been through earlier. The sweet aroma of the stew he'd tasted earlier drifted to his nostrils. The smell invoked pangs of hunger.

"I wish we could take time to eat that stew," Brendan whispered to Kaileen.

"I know where we can get some food we can carry with us," Kaileen answered.

Brendan listened to the sounds in the wind for a moment. Since he heard no voices approaching, his hunger prodded him to the decision.

"Let's find it quickly, then," he urged Kaileen.

She led the way, leaving Brendan hobbling to catch up with her. She stopped at the site of a burned down hut. Using the tip of the javelin, she parted the ashes along the edge where a circular wall had stood only the day before. After parting the ashes, she pried up several boards, burned and blackened on the topside. She reached into a pit and began pulling things out. In the darkness, Brendan could only make out something in the shape of a loaf of bread and a skin-covered flask. She also pulled out a large sack with straps. Kaileen quickly put the items she'd retrieved from the hole in the ground into the pack. As Kaileen was fastening the sack on her back, Brendan heard the sound of voices approaching. The seamen must be coming to look for them, he thought. He grabbed Kaileen's arm.

"We need to get going, I think they're looking for us," he said.

Kaileen needed no further prodding. She stood up and grabbed the javelin. Brendan led her into brush northeast of town. The voices grew louder as they began climb the side of the hill. The path wound through a forest of conifer trees that would obscure their movement. The sea raiders would not know of it and would have to search the area on the outskirts of the town to find it.

After traveling for a couple of hours, Brendan noticed he no longer heard the voices. He looked at Kaileen. She stooped badly under the burden of the pack.

"There's a place I know, not too far away. I call it 'fortress in the rocks.' We can rest there. I don't think they know which way we went. Those butchering pigs won't be able to pick up our trail 'til morning. Do you want to stop there and sleep till sunrise?" He asked Kaileen.

"Yes, I'm exhausted," she answered.

Kaileen then shifted the pack on her shoulders.

"Let me take that for awhile," Brendan offered and continued, "I don't think they're following us now. We don't need to move as fast."

"Thank you," Kaileen cooed as she slipped her arms out of the straps.

She then helped Brendan into it, and they continued on. About an hour later, Brendan spotted a large outcropping of limestone.

"Up there," he pointed to the rocks.

A few moments later they finished the steep climb and reached the rocks. Not visible from below was a natural crater formed by the rocks, which, indeed, made it appear to be a fortress. Brendan and Kaileen climbed down into the crater. He slipped the pack off and placed it under a rock overhang for Kaileen.

"Rest your pretty red head on this," he instructed.

Kaileen said nothing; she just smiled at Brendan and laid her head on it. Brendan then unhooked his cloak and started to lay it on top of her, but she shook her head.

"No, you keep it. Mine will keep me warm enough."

She smiled gently at him for a second time. Being alone with Kaileen for the first time, Brendan longed to talk to her, but fatigue paralyzed his body. He found a pile of dirt to use as a pillow and fell fast asleep.

The sun was nearly midway to its noon zenith when it struck Brendan. As he reached his hand to shade his eyes, a shadow blocked the sun. He lowered his hand to find himself staring at a heavily muscled body, armed with the same type of sword as the sea raiders.

# CHAPTER 2

A pulse of fear electrified Brendan. Instinctively, he reached for his javelin, but stopped. He recognized that face. It wasn't a butchering sea raider. It was Dungal! His only friend in the world, that is, unless he could now count Kaileen as a friend. Dungal was mute. Most of the people around these parts considered him an idiot. Dungal survived by going from farm to farm for his meals. Most everyone pitied him and considered it an act of Christian charity to feed him or provide clothing. Dungal, nevertheless, often repaid them by performing some task involving heavy labor like digging a new latrine pit or weeding a garden. Sometimes he just performed. Dungal was an acrobat. How, when, and where Dungal had learned such moves, Brendan had no idea. As he thought about Dungal's abilities, Dungal did a flip with his knees tucked into his chest from the rock he'd been standing on above and landed a few feet in front of Brendan. The impact of the landing, although scarcely audible, was enough to wake up Kaileen.

"Aieeee," screeched Kaileen.

Then she too recognized the long, swarthy, face with dark brown hair and thin beard to match.

"You, where did you come from?" she protested, her dignity clearly offended.

Dungal made several motions with his hands and arms in answer to her questions. Brendan understood him. The two of them had spent many days together. They had learned to communicate well. Brendan, unlike many of the other people who knew Dungal, also knew he understood every word you said.

He just wasn't able to speak. Brendan learned to read and understand nearly all of Dungal's gestures. Right now he just told Brendan and Kaileen that he had come from the burnt village.

"Where did you get the sword?" Brendan asked.

Dungal smiled, clearly pleased that Brendan had asked that question. Dungal launched into a series of gestures to tell the tale. Brendan translated the motions into words as Dungal continued so that he could confirm that he correctly translated the story, and share the story with Kaileen.

"You came upon the village at sunrise?" Brendan asked and paused as Dungal nodded his head to confirm Brendan's interpretation. Then, as Dungal continued, Brendan narrated the story out loud.

"You found the strange seamen passed out from drinking too much of the stolen Irish beer. There were a couple of sentries on guard but you didn't see them at first. You started looking around the beach for food or other valuables you could take. You didn't feel like it was stealing because they apparently had ravaged the village. May Father Sweeney forgive you."

Dungal paused and looked down as though ashamed for wanting to steal from the sea raiders.

"Considering what they did to the village, I don't see how Father Sweeney could accuse you of any sin," Brendan answered him.

Brendan knew that Dungal revered Father Sweeney. Dungal would walk ten miles to get to Father Sweeney's Mass on Sunday. Brendan watched the smile return to Dungal's face when he explained that Father Sweeney would probably not subject Dungal to a harsh penance.

"Now get on with the story," Brendan urged impatiently.

Dungal continued his pantomime, with Brendan translating.

"The sentries spotted you. They started yelling in some language you didn't understand. That woke the others up. The only place to run was toward the ships. You climbed on board one with a burnt sail. The sailors were almost to the ship. You got an idea. You cut one of the rigging ropes loose where it attached to the sail; but it was still attached to the top of the mast. You waited for the sailors to climb aboard the ship. When they were all either on board the ship or about to climb aboard, you climbed up on the side of the ship and swung around them on the rope and landed in the sand on the shore behind them. You ran. They pursued, but you were faster. After a night of drinking, most of them ran out of breath and stopped pursuing after a while. One of the sentries would not give up. You led him on a merry chase. After a while you found a spot where you were out of his sight for a moment. You ducked into the brush. He came running up.

He stopped to look around for you. When his back was to you, you jumped him and got your arms around his neck. You strangled him until he passed out. Then you took his sword and scabbard and ran to make your escape while he was still unconscious."

When Brendan finished the translation, Dungal lifted the scabbard with sword up in a gesture of pride at his accomplishment. Brendan smiled back then looked at Kaileen. She stood with her hands on her hips and a look of contempt on her lovely face.

"Would you be expecting me to believe a wild story like that?" she said smartly.

"Why not," Brendan replied, "Our escape was nearly as unbelievable."

"Oh, I suppose you're right," Kaileen answered reluctantly. Then she added:

"Don't you think we should be on our way? I don't want those swine to catch me again."

Brendan paused to listen for a moment. Then he answered.

"I don't hear any sound of them. I think we've time enough for breakfast. I'm starving and we may have to travel many miles before sundown."

Dungal nodded anxiously. Apparently he was hungry also.

"Oh, you boys. I've never known either of you that you weren't hungry."

With that, Kaileen dug into the knapsack and brought out a loaf of bread. She unwrapped the linen covering, broke the bread in half and wrapped half of it back up, placing it back in the pack. She broke the remaining half loaf into three roughly equal pieces, and handed Brendan and Dungal each a piece.

Dungal snatched the offered bread from her outstretched hand, and began to eat it eagerly.

"If you will be good enough till all is ready, I do have more," Kaileen snapped.

Dungal stopped eating, looking ashamed.

"Brendan, may I borrow your knife?" Kaileen continued.

Brendan slid the knife from its homemade sheath, and handed it, hilt first to Kaileen. She then produced a round of cheese from the pack, unwrapped it and cut three thick slices from it. These she also distributed to Dungal and Brendan, who both waited patiently for her to give them permission to start eating. She reached in the pack a third time and withdrew the flask she had taken from the hole the previous night.

"I'll pass this around, but try to take only a couple of swallows. We want it to last," she instructed.

Brendan and Dungal then started to work on their bread and cheese, but Kaileen interrupted again.

"Aren't you forgetting something?" she prodded.

"And what would that be?" Brendan answered her question with a question.

"The blessing!" Kaileen answered indignantly.

"Oh," Brendan said and bowed his head. Dungal followed his lead.

Kaileen made the sign of the cross and spoke:

"Bless us, O Lord, and these thy gifts which we are about to receive from thy bounty, through Christ our Lord."

"Amen," Brendan answered. Dungal nodded his "Amen."

They ate quickly and in silence. Brendan noted that the bread was the kind made with honey which he loved. The cheese was equally delicious but his slice seemed like the tiniest morsel as it was gone too soon. The flask contained beer but it hadn't been properly aged and was bitter. It wasn't hard to limit his consumption of it. Dungal finished first, followed by Brendan. Dungal made several gestures to Brendan indicating he would check the trail behind them while Kaileen was finishing her meal. Brendan watched as he nimbly scaled the side of the rock fortress and disappeared. When he was out of sight, Kaileen spoke up.

"What shall we do now?" she asked.

"What do you mean?" Brenden responded.

"I mean we have no plan. I don't know where my mother is. She wasn't in the village when those strange men attacked. She had gone to attend to a sick lady on a farm a day's travel to the north. I don't know the location. She told me to expect her to be gone a fortnight. I'm afraid she may try to return to the village with the barbarians still there. Do you think we can find her?"

Brendan thought a moment. He knew little of his parents. His mother had died giving him birth. His father died when a plague ravaged the land when he was ten. He knew what it was like to live without parents and expected that Kaileen might not see her mother again, but he wanted to sound hopeful.

"I think so. When Dungal gets back we'll head north. My master's house is northwest from here. It's not too far out of the way, so we'll stop there first. Maybe he'll know something that will help us. I should warn him about the sea warriors anyway."

"Oh, I hope we find mom. What was yours like, Brendan?"

"She died giving me birth, Kaileen."

"I'm sorry, I lost my dad when I was very little also," Kaileen said sympathetically.

"How?"

"The chief of the Dal Cais pressed him into service when he made war against the Ui Fiachrach. Dad was killed in battle."

"Did he want to fight the Ui Fiachrach?" Brendan asked.

"No, but all men under the protection of the Dal Cais must render service as a soldier when asked as part of their tribute. You're nearly old enough to incur that obligation; but with your bad leg, I doubt you'll be asked."

Brendan felt offended that he somehow wasn't good enough to serve the Dal Cais as a soldier. Nevertheless, he had often heard his master refer to their chief as a "blood sucking leech" because of the tribute in sheep his master had to pay each year after the new lambs were suckled. Brendan wasn't sure he'd like to serve this chief.

"I guess not. But I suppose he will call for Dungal one of these days," Brendan responded.

"I doubt that."

"Why?"

"Because he can't speak!" When Kaileen spoke these words she shook back her long red hair and fixed her dark brown eyes so intensely on Brendan's that he nearly missed hearing the words she spoke.

"Why should that make a difference?" he asked. He knew the answer; but didn't want to disturb the aura of intimate passion emanating from Kaileen.

"Because no one can communicate with him except you," Kaileen answered, exasperated.

"They could if they took the time. Dungal expresses himself quite well. You just have to spend some time with him."

"Well, I doubt the warriors of the Dal Cais will be willing to do that."

"It's their loss then. Dungal is about four years older than me, and strong, probably the match of anyone in the Dal Cais tribe." Brendan felt good boasting about his friend.

"By the way, where did he come from? No one in the village knows much about him. They say he just showed up at Mass one Sunday a few years ago and stayed."

"He came down with Father Sweeney from the north when his parents died of the plague five or six years ago. Since he was old enough to live without them, no one offered to take him in. He's been a wanderer since, but mostly sticks around here."

"He seems to hold Father Sweeney in high regard," Kaileen noted.

"That he does. It may be because Father Sweeney knows it's tough losing both parents. Maybe that's why Dungal and I get along so well together. At least you still have your mother."

"I hope so, but I don't know what we'll do now that our seamstress shop was burned down. Making and mending clothes was our whole living. The raiders stole what gold and valuables we'd accumulated. We have nothing to use as money to buy supplies to reopen the shop."

"Well, let's take things one at a time. First, let's find your mother. Say look at that." Brendan pointed to three little hares which had come out of the shadows to munch at a patch of grass along the edge of the rocks.

"They're cute," Kaileen smiled back at Brendan. "Do you like living outdoors?"

"It has its advantages I guess. I often wake up at those times of the night when the stars are so thick in the skies that they are like clouds. Also, no one bothers me, and most of the animals are friendly, except the wolf of course. Even the wolf would be friendly, I think, if my master would give him a sheep now and then. You know, one of the old ones."

"I should hope so," Kaileen responded, then continued, "I hate to think you would want to feed a sweet little lamb to a wolf."

"I wouldn't."

Sensing that this talk of the natural food chain might be offending Kaileen, Brendan decided to change the subject of their conversation.

"What happened yesterday?" he asked.

"The day started normal enough, I guess, but some fishermen coming up from the river spoke of strange vessels with long oars and sailing masts moving up the river. The men aboard the ships must have noticed our cooking fires and spotted the village huts. Most of the people turned out to watch the strange ships as they approached. The ships turned and headed for the shore below the town. They came in fast and slid right upon the beach, where you saw them last night. As they landed, warriors with swords, javelins and axes pulled shields from their mountings on the sides of the ships. They jumped over the sides and rushed ashore toward the village. Some of the women of the village ran for their huts, others, mostly those with children, grabbed the kids and ran for the countryside. They were the smart ones. I went to our hut to get our valuables; but that was a mistake. I ran out the front entrance and straight into one of the massive blond pigs. He dropped his javelin and grabbed me by the hair. I screamed in pain; but that was a mistake too. Another one of the barbarians heard him, turned and saw me struggling with the first. He rushed over and held my arms behind my back, forcing me to drop the valuables. They lashed my wrists together and the first warrior slung me over his shoulder, grabbed my bag and took me to the beach where you found me. By that time, other women were being carried down to the beach also. They pulled a rope from the ship, staked it in the ground, and tied us to it. Then they went back and set fire to the village. There were few men in the village at the time and I'm afraid they were all killed."

"I think they were. All those I saw when I passed through were dead," Brendan confirmed. Then he asked:

"Did you learn anything about these men? Maybe we can figure out how to defeat them."

"No, they spoke in a strange language. There was one man though, I think they called him Hakon. At least they raised their cups and weapons and shouted that word as this man passed as though paying homage to him."

"What did this "Hakon" look like?" Brendan asked.

"He's a huge man. Incredibly strong. I saw him throw one of the sailors who got drunk and said something he didn't like. He picked the man up over his head and sent him sailing at least ten paces. He had a hideous face. Long scraggly hair that reached below his shoulders and with a beard nearly as long, both are dirty yellow and tangled, like a horses tail that was left unbrushed. He eats and drinks like a pig."

"Do you think he's human or some kind of devil?" Brendan asked.

"He has the shape of a human; but acts like a beast. Didn't Father Sweeney say devils can take on all kinds of forms?"

"Yes."

"Then I think he's a devil!" Kaileen exclaimed.

"But the others seem to be human. Dungal defeated one, remember?"

"If you believe his story," Kaileen snipped.

"He had the sword to prove it," Brendan reminded her.

"That's true," Kaileen conceded.

The motion of a shadow on the rock drew Brendan's attention from Kaileen. He looked up to see Dungal scrambling down the rocks into the crater. Dungal was clearly agitated. He motioned to the direction he'd just come. He showed two fingers and touched his sword to indicate two of the barbarians approached.

"We'd better get out of here," Brendan announced.

Dungal shook head indicating he disagreed. Then he made a motion to his temple to indicate he had a better idea.

"OK, what is it?" Brendan urged.

# CHAPTER 3

Dungal indicated that Brendan and Kaileen should start down the trail as though the barbarians were not around. He motioned that they should not make any effort to conceal themselves from the raiders. He, Dungal, would follow behind and take care of the rest. He insisted that they hurry though; the barbarians were not far behind.

Kaileen quickly re-packed the pack.

"Let me carry that," Brendan offered.

"OK, but you must let me help you on the trail," Kaileen insisted.

Brendan was thankful for Kaileen's offer. Climbing out of the crater wasn't a big problem. He had strong arms; but once they were on the trail, he found he could travel a little faster with his arm around Kaileen's shoulder. They moved down the trail, Kaileen holding a javelin in her left hand and he carrying one in his right. They had gone about 200 paces down the trail when he heard a shout from behind. He and Kaileen turned to see the two barbarians. Both men carried shields. One shield was painted yellow and black, a black cross on a yellow background. The other had a picture of a red boar's head painted on a white background. One man carried a javelin, the other, a battle ax. Both wore chainmail armor shirts and iron helmets with a protective nose piece.

"Get behind me," Brendan ordered Kaileen.

She did as Brendan instructed. Brendan readied the javelin. He wasn't going to throw it. The strangers were too well covered with armor. He knew that if these two wanted to take Kaileen, they would have to kill him first. Brendan concentrated on the throat of the warrior on the left. He felt he could successfully

16

thrust the javelin through the warrior's throat. He didn't even consider what the other warrior might do.

The warrior on the left drew back his javelin as though preparing to throw. Dungal suddenly appeared and grabbed the javelin from behind, turning the warrior around with a mighty pull. The motion threw the barbarian off balance and he tripped over his own feet and fell flat on his face. In a long swinging motion, Dungal struck the barbarian's helmet with the edge of his sword and knocked it off. Then, with a mighty second swing, Dungal whacked the back of the fallen warrior's head with the flat edge of his sword, rendering him unconscious. The second warrior took a swing at Dungal with his battle ax. Dungal adroitly ducked the blade, leaving the warrior to slice the air. Before the warrior could strike again, Dungal thrust both legs sideways, one behind the warrior's knees and one across his thighs in front. Dungal's body, now almost horizontal, twisted toward the barbarian, his sword arm smacking the warrior in the chest. The effect of the movement was to throw the barbarian completely off his feet backwards. The impact of his head against the hard earth stunned the warrior long enough for Dungal to pull this warrior's helmet off and smack him unconscious with the broad side of his sword.

Everything happened so fast that Brendan hadn't had time to assist Dungal. He now moved toward him. Dungal, seeing him approach, made signs to Brendan indicating that they should search the two unconscious men before they woke up. Brendan undid the strap holding the scabbard and removed the sword from one of the barbarians. While doing this he noted that the barbarian had another belt from which hung a small leather pouch. He unbuckled the belt and pulled off the pouch. In the pouch were bits of gold and silver as well as some coins made from these metals. Brendan had never owned any gold or silver; but he had seen his master receive it when he sold sheep. He knew his master and others held these metals in high regard. He tied the pouch to his own belt. Likewise he strapped the sword and scabbard over his shoulder. He wanted to take the shield also, but was afraid carrying it would slow them down too much. He glanced over to see that Dungal had made similar finds. Brendan noticed, to his amusement, that Dungal strapped on the second sword. He now proudly wore two of them. Dungal then strung the battle ax from his belt, stood up, and motioned that they should be on their way.

Brendan nodded his approval. Then they went back to Kaileen.

"Let's head for my master's," Brendan suggested. "It's that way," he added pointing to the northwest.

"OK, but let's hurry, before they wake up," Kaileen answered.

"Oh, I don't think they'll follow us. I don't think they'll want to encounter Dungal again unarmed." Brendan said as he smiled at Dungal who nodded his agreement.

"Nevertheless, the farther from these heathens we get, the better I'll like it," Kaileen snapped, "Let's be off."

With that they turned to the northwest and disappeared into a woody thicket. Brendan led the way, since he was used to living in the outdoors and finding his way from one place to another. He thought it best to avoid using any well worn trails, just in case the barbarians should try to follow them. Kaileen followed behind Brendan, and Dungal followed her turning from time to time to see if they were being followed. Kaileen again offered to help Brendan; but it was too difficult to walk side by side in the woods.

They moved deeper into the woods. The oak and ash trees provided a cool respite from the noonday sun. The brush was thick with holly, whitethorn, blackthorn spindle, guelder rose, briars and smaller plants. As the sun began it's descent from the midday zenith, Brenden discovered a small spring. Following the sound of dripping water he led his companions to a small clearing where water dribbled down a series of moss covered rocks. Brendan found a spot where the water fell from an overhanging rock. He sat on a rock, cupped his hands, and held them under the narrow thread of water. He waited patiently for the water to pool up in his hands and drank the liquid down.

"Ah, this is cool and sweet," he sighed, "It must come from under the earth. Try some."

Both Kaileen and Dungal didn't need a second invitation. Dungal allowed Kaileen to go first then drank his fill.

"I think we should follow these rocks for a while. They seem to lead down this draw. Perhaps we'll find a stream below." Brendan suggested.

"How will that help us?" Kailen asked with a skeptical tone.

"It might lead us to a bigger stream where we can fish for our supper. I don't think you have much bread and cheese left do you?"

"Ok, but I don't want us to get lost or delay too much. I want to find mother, remember?" Kaileen answered.

"I understand," Brendan started to answer, and then he took a look at the surrounding landscape and continued. "We will still be heading in the same general direction. If we start to deviate too much, I promise we'll forget searching for a stream."

"OK, Brendan; but I'm trusting you to be honest with me."

"I will. Promise."

Brendan looked at Dungal who shrugged as though any path they followed was all right with him. With that, Brendan began to pick his way down the rocks, through the ferns. The moss made the rocks slippery and Brendan fell several times during the first thousand paces they traveled. By that time they had passed several side draws that were tributary to the one they followed. Each of these contributed small amounts of water so that by now they were following a stream several inches deep.

"You were right about finding a stream, but are we still headed northwest?" Kaileen asked.

"Pretty much. If this stream leads where I think it does, we may soon find the traveling a little easier. I may also have a surprise for you."

"What kind of a surprise?" Kaileen asked impatiently.

"Now if I told you it wouldn't be a surprise would it?" Brendan teased.

"Oh, you're a devil you are!" Kaileen said with a pout.

Brendan noted the pout made Kaileen especially charming. He smiled at her as a gesture that he had her best interests at heart. He then glanced at Dungal. Dungal made his eyes glance sideways in their sockets in Kaileen's direction and motioned with his lips that resembled a kiss. He was trying to tease Brendan about being Kaileen's lover. Brendan impulsively looked for something non-lethal to throw at Dungal; but decided not to because he'd have to explain the action to Kaileen. She noticed he was distracted, however.

"Something wrong?" she asked.

"No, nothing wrong, ah, I just had trouble understanding one of Dungal's gestures."

As he made the statement he looked toward Dungal. Kaileen naturally looked the same direction. Dungal looked as though he could burst out laughing. Kaileen gave Brendan a puzzled look and shrugged her shoulders. Brendan turned and continued to follow the stream, anxious to divert Kaileen's attention before she could ask any embarrassing questions. As the sun began to drop in the sky, Brendan observed with satisfaction that the stream they were following began to deepen. Now, here and there, the streamlined body of a salmon darted from the shadows out to midstream and back. As he, Kaileen, and Dungal went on further, the fish began to break the surface from time to time to snatch an unsuspecting fly. Brendan hurt from the prolonged walk on the rocky stream shore, so he decided to make the suggestion.

"Why don't we find a place to spend the night near here? The fish look like they are biting and we have little other food."

"It looks like quite awhile before dark; and I'd rather go farther; but if you want to stop we can." Kalieen answered. Brendan could feel the reluctance in her voice.

"We'll go a little further; but I think we should stop at the first place that looks good to spend the night. Right Dungal?"

With this response Brendan looked to Dungal for approval. Dungal nodded eagerly. Brendan was sure he was anxious to get at those fish. After traveling another 100 paces or so they spotted a nice flat area of streambank with a small clearing, surrounded by trees on three sides.

"Let's spend the night over there," Brendan proposed.

"If you insist," Kaileen answered.

Dungal nodded his approval also. They strode over to it and unburdened themselves of the pack, swords, and javelins.

"If you boys are going fishing, I'm going to look around and see if I can find some wild berries," Kaileen announced and disappeared into the brush. Dungal took the captured battle ax and cut two ash saplings. He stripped off the branches. Brendan instructed him to look for some vine to use as string. In the meantime, Brendan removed a pouch from his belt. In it he had several leaders made from sheep's intestine with hooks he'd crafted from bone. To these he had fastened bits of feather with thread to create an artificial fly. When Dungal returned with a couple of lengths of wild grapevine, they fastened the vines to the poles and the leaders to the vine. Afterwards, they stepped into the cold water of the creek and spread out. Brendan noted that Dungal threw a fly loop as well as any one he had seen.

The fish hit their lines with a vengeance. They quickly caught a dozen fish, Brendan caught five and Dungal seven.

"I'll clean the fish, if you'll start a fire to cook," Brendan proposed. Dungal nodded his approval and set about gathering firewood. Brendan skillfully gutted and scaled each of the fish and rinsed them clean in the stream. By the time he'd completed this task, Dungal had a small roaring fire going. They only had to wait a while for it to burn down enough to provide them coals to cook their catch of salmon. Brendan listened carefully to the sounds of the forest. It bothered him that he didn't hear anything unusual. He thought that surely Kaileen should be making some sort of noise. He decided to get a second opinion. He spoke to Dungal:

"Do you think I should look for Kaileen?"

Dungal shrugged, indicating he didn't think Brendan should be so concerned. Brendan wasn't so sure. He cut green branches to use as spits to roast the fish. Everything was ready but the fire. It was still burning too strongly. The thought of Kaileen being alone in the woods still nagged at him. He finally shouldn't stand it any longer.

"Dungal, I'm going to look for Kaileen. Will you start cooking the fish when the fire burns down?" he asked.

Dungal nodded his approval, and motioned with his hand for Brendan to go. Brendan headed into the bush in the direction he'd last seen Kaileen. He hobbled about thirty paces and called:

"Kaileen?"

Brendan walked about another fifty paces and called again. He walked about 100 paces more and called a third time. This time he heard a faint:

"Brendan?"

Relieved to hear Kaileen's voice he walked another fifty paces toward it. He called her name again. This time, Kaileen issued an irritated response.

"Brendan, stay where you," she ordered.

"Why?" Brendan demanded.

"Never mind. Just stay where you are. I'll be there in a minute."

Brendan obeyed. Moments later, he heard the crunching of brush that signaled Kaileen's approach. He focused on the woods in the direction of the noise. As the shapely figure of Kaileen appeared, he noticed her crimson hair clinging, soaking wet, to each side of her head. Her multicolored tunic, however, was dry.

"What happened to you?" Brendan asked, perplexed.

"If you must know, I was taking a bath," Kaileen snapped back.

"Is that why you didn't want me to come closer?"

"Yes, I needed time to get dressed," she explained.

Brendan noted an attractive blush washed over her face as she explained. Her embarrassment pleased him.

"But I thought you were looking for berries?" he asked.

"Well, I was," she began to answer demurely. "But, I saw this deep pool of clear water and I just couldn't resist."

"Well I got worried when I hadn't heard from you for so long," Brendan scolded her.

"You sound like my mother, Brendan!"

"Well, I rescued you, so I feel responsible for your safety," Brendan answered her.

"By the way, why did you risk being caught and probably killed to free me and the other women?"

"I didn't want them to take you, Kaileen."

"And why would that be now?" she pressed, smiling coyly.

Brendan now felt embarrassed. He could think of nothing to say that would sound sincere, but the truth.

"I really like you, Kaileen," he answered as she took hold of his left arm.

Although Brendan enjoyed the pressure of her hands on his arm, the tone of her voice disappointed him. It made him think that she liked him as a brother; but not with the special magic he felt for her.

"Hmmm, what's that delicious smell?" Kaileen asked.

"Dungal must be cooking the fish now. Are you hungry?"

"Famished!"

To Brendan's surprise, Kaileen ate a full one third share of the fish. He'd always thought women had smaller appetites than men. Four fish had filled him up, and Kaileen and Dungal had eaten the same number. When they were finished eating, the sun was down and daylight rapidly fading.

"I guess we'd better settle for the night," Brendan announced. "Would you like my cloak?" he asked Kaileen.

"No, Brendan, I'll be just fine if I can use the pack for a pillow again."

With that, she cleared a spot of twigs and brush. She placed the pack on the ground, fussed with it a little bit and laid her head on it. She pulled her cloak about her and said, "Good night."

"Good night," Brendan answered.

Dungan slapped both hands together, turned his head sideways and touched his head to his hands in a gesture that meant the same.

"Good night to you too, Dungal," Kaileen said, reading Dungal's gesture.

"Well, Dungal, I guess we'd better get some sleep also."

Dungal shook his head in disagreement.

"What do you mean?"

Dungal went on to indicate that they should take turns standing watch just in case the sea warriors might be about. Brendan agreed. Dungan motioned to ask Brendan whether he wanted the first watch or second. Brendan said he'd go first. Dungal indicated he'd take over when Brendan could no longer stay awake and expected Brendan to do the same for him. Brendan watched as Dungal settled down for the night. He made himself a bed of branches, and lay the captured sword alongside within easy reach. Brendan offered Dungal his cloak, since he had none of his own. Dungal accepted it, using it for a blanket. A moment later, Dungal was asleep.

Brendan sat on the ground and poked at the burning embers of the fire. He had nothing better to do, so he thought he'd build up the fire a little. Without his cloak, he was beginning to feel a little chilly, and figured it couldn't hurt to keep it going till morning. He scrounged for a few dried branches and put them on the fire. Brendan was careful not to build up the fire too much. He didn't want to wake Kaileen or Dungal and worried still about someone "out there" spotting them. After rekindling the fire he sat and looked at the sky. The night was clear and the stars plentiful. He was staring at the constellation Sagittarius and wondering what made the lights in the sky when he heard the gentle melody of Kaileen's voice.

"Want some company?" she asked.

Startled, Brendan turned to look at her. She held her cloak tightly wrapped about her. The firelight gave her face an angelic glow.

"Sure, but why aren't you sleeping? Tomorrow is likely to be a long day."

"Oh, I was asleep but woke up again. I'm having a little trouble getting back to sleep. By the way, what are you doing up?"

"Oh, Dungal and I thought it best if the two of us took turns standing watch throughout the night." Brendan answered.

"Why?"

"Just in case we have some unwelcome visitors," Brendan answered her.

"You mean the barbarians?"

"Yes"

"Why didn't you ask me to watch for a while?"

"I guess the thought never crossed our minds, what with you being a girl and all."

Kaileen huffed and slammed her hands on her hips.

"I do have ears and eyes," she snapped.

"Yes, and very pretty eyes they are." Brendan had the words out of his mouth almost before he realized what he said. He'd been mesmerized by the reflections of the fire in the pupils of her eyes.

"That's very flattering, Brendan, but I'm trying to make the point that you don't need to treat me like I'm helpless."

"OK, do you want to take over the first watch?"

"Well... Okay, did you want to go to sleep right away?"

Brendan sensed a tone of loneliness in Kaileen's voice. Although he welcomed the opportunity to sleep right then, he also saw an opportunity to build a closer relationship with Kaileen.

"I'd like to sit with you for a little while."

Kaileen smiled the kind of smile that told Brendan she wanted him to stay with her. Then she asked:

"Do you think we will find my mother soon?"

"I don't know for sure, but my master has a lot of hands working for him. They travel a lot herding his flocks. Chances are good one of them has seen or heard something and told the master. By the way, what will you do when you find her?"

"I don't know. I mean I haven't given it any thought. I don't think it would be safe to try to go back and rebuild where we were before; but mom may feel differently."

"I think you should try to find a chieftain to sponsor you. That way you'll be under his protection."

"I guess you're right, but mom and I like being independent. It will be tough to have to serve a master." Kaileen answered.

"You and your mother must have done well making garments," Brendan suggested.

"We weren't wanting for any of the basic creature comforts, I guess; but we weren't rich."

"Do you ever think of getting married?"

"Oh, I've only seen sixteen years, don't be marrying me off yet, young Brendan. I'm not sure I'd take to being married. As I told you before, I like me independence."

"Then there's no one courting you right now?"

"No."

Brendan sighed slightly, relieved that Kaileen had no current suitor. Kaileen must have sensed his feelings, however, because she smiled like a sister ready to tease her brother about having a girlfriend and said:

"Would you be wanting the position?"

"What position?"

"My suitor of course!"

Kaileen had bared Brendan's innermost feelings and now seemed to relish the embarrassment he was feeling. He looked away, staring into the flickering flames of the campfire.

"Well, I, uh, I uh, well yes, I guess so!"

"You guess! I'll not have my suitors be guessing." Kaileen teased him mercilessly.

"Oh, Brendan, I'll keep you mind when the time comes for me to be thinking about suitors; but for now we have more important concerns."

"You mean locating your mother?"

"Yes, I'm really worried that those filthy heathens got their hands on her."

With the last statement Kaileen's face turned somber. Involuntary tears appeared in the corners of her eyes. Then, as though embarrassed to let Brendan see her show emotion, she buried her face in her hands. Brendan couldn't think what to do next. Instinctively he moved along side her and put his arm around her shoulder. To his utter surprise she turned and buried her face in his shoulder and sobbed uncontrollably for a moment. Then, almost as quickly, she backed away. She wiped the tears from her eyes with her cloak, took a deep breath, and spoke in her normal tone of voice.

"Sorry, I didn't mean to let my emotions get the upper hand."

"Not a problem, I only wish I had some comfort to offer," Brendan replied.

"Go ahead and sleep now, Brendan, I'll be fine and we all need as much rest as we can get." With these words Kaileen pulled a little away from Brendan.

"Okay, wake me up when you need to sleep," he answered.

Brendan found a relatively flat spot under a large ash tree and stretched out on the ground. He was a little chilly without his cloak, but he remembered he'd spent many a night in the pasture with no cloak until his master's wife took pity on him one day and gave him the one he now wore. She cautioned him not to let her husband know where he had gotten it. He stretched out on his back, took a deep breath, and exhaled. This action so relaxed him that before he could repeat it he was asleep.

He dreamed he and Kaileen were alone in the pasture with his master's flock. It was a sunny day. He was lying on his back chewing on a lone strand of grass and sheltering his eyes from the sun. Kaileen, with the wind tossing her scarlet locks about her sun-kissed face, knelt down next to him. She bent over, her lips getting closer and closer, but just as she was close enough to kiss him she grabbed both shoulders and began to shake violently.

"Brendan, Brendan, wake up," she cried.

Brendan woke from the dream. It was still night, but Kaileen was kneeling alongside him shaking him violently. He tried to focus his eyes on her face, but the darkness obscured it.

"What do you want?" Brendan asked groggily.

"I hear someone coming," she whispered.

# CHAPTER 4

Brendan sat straight up. He cautioned Kaileen to silence by putting his index finger to his lips. He listened carefully for a moment. Sure enough, he heard branches scraping. Keeping his eyes fixed on the brush from where he'd heard the noise, he slowly and silently moved toward Dungal to wake him up. He was just about to reach over and wake Dungal when a mother wolf came out of the bush with two cubs close behind. She stopped for a moment to stare at Kaileen and Brendan. Then she snorted and disappeared back into the brush.

"Weren't those cubs cute?" Kaileen cooed.

"Well I might think so, if they hadn't interrupted possibly the best dream I will ever have in my life."

"What was it about?" Kaileen asked, exploding with curiosity.

"Never mind," Brendan started. "Why don't you sleep now?" he continued.

"Not telling, huh, must be embarrassing. Did it involve a girl?" Kaileen taunted.

"I said never mind," Brendan repeated emphatically.

"So it did involve a girl," Kaileen wouldn't give up.

"Go to sleep, Kaileen," Brendan ordered.

"Was she pretty?" Kaileen asked mercilessly.

"Yes, the prettiest. Will that satisfy you? Now go to sleep."

"Was it me Brendan?"

"If you must know, yes," Brendan shot back.

"Okay, I guess I've tortured you enough. Good night."

"Good night," Brendan gasped, glad she finally decided to stop nagging him.

The rest of the night went smoothly. When Brendan got to the point where he could hardly keep his eyes open, he woke Dungal up. After a short spell of grogginess, Dungal signaled for Brendan to go to sleep. Dungal, in turn, woke Brendan up again to stand watch shortly before dawn. As daylight slowly illuminated the forest, Brendan felt a strong sense of relief. There was a lot greater chance of spotting one's enemies in the daylight. He looked over at Kaileen and Dungal. Both were still fast asleep in the shadows cast by the trees and rocks about them. He decided to catch breakfast. By the time the sunlight caused Kaileen, then Dungal, to stir, Brendan had caught another dozen fish. Again they devoured Brendan's catch, leaving little waste. They washed their faces and hands in the icy stream water and resumed following the stream in its downhill course. By the time the sun was half way to the midday zenith, the trio had reached a point where they no longer heard the rush of water. In fact, the water surface soon was obscured by dense growth of water loving plants, including sedges and mosses. Travel was getting more and more difficult. Brendan and Dungal each took turns hacking at the dense wetland growth with the captured Viking swords. They had to take turns cutting at the growth because the work was so exhausting that neither could keep it up for long. In the hope of finding thinner brush, Brendan led the party into deeper and deeper water.

"Do you know where you are going?" Kaileen fussed.

"Not exactly, but do you want to go back where we've been?"

"No."

"Then trust me. From the feel of the bottom, we should see open water soon."

"Then what?" Kaileen asked.

"Then we might be able to tell where we are?" Brendan snarled. He'd just run into a spider web, and was frantically trying to clean it from his face and hair.

"Okay, you needn't be raising your voice to me, Brendan!" Kaileen shot back.

A few more hacks of the sword and Brendan broke through to open water and looked back to Kaileen and Dungal. He noted they stood in a tunnel carved in the living growth. He stood for a moment as they came abreast of him. Then all three looked over the shimmering surface of a small lake. On the West end of the lake loomed the silhouette of a large structure.

"It's the mill!" Brendan exclaimed.

"What mill?" Kaileen asked.

"The one where my master has his corn ground into meal. My master's house is not too far from there."

Then Brendan looked to the sky.

"With luck we should be there shortly after midday," he announced.

Dungal nodded his pleasure at the news. Brendan then led them around the pond, staying about waist deep in water to avoid the heavy brush in the shallows. As they neared the mill, the brush along shore began to thin out and finally gave way to tall grass where the timber had been once harvested to build the mill and the dam that created the mill pond. They moved on to dry land once more.

"Would there be any one at the mill?" Kaileen asked.

Nearly as soon as she got these words out, Brendan heard voices coming from the direction of the mill.

"Let's see who's over there," Kaileen suggested.

"What do you think, Dungal?"

Dungal put his hands to his heads in the symbol of horns.

"You're right. The sea barbarians might be over there."

Then Dungal pointed first at Kaileen then at Brendan and then at the ground. Then he crouched down and spread the grass.

"Dungal wants to scout it out first. He wants us to stay here until he gives the signal to come to him." Brendan explained to Kaileen; then he turned to Dungal.

"Go ahead. We'll wait here."

After Brendan's entreaty, Dungal disappeared into the tall grass and weeds lining a cart trail to the mill. Brendan turned to Kaileen.

"Let's get where we can see Dungal's signal" Brendan instructed. Then he led Kaileen to the edge of the brush which paralleled the trail. He sat down on the grass; then patted the ground next to him.

"Why don't you sit down and relax. Dungal is both cautious and thorough. It will probably take awhile."

Kaileen sat beside him. They talked together for a long while in low voices, with Brendan poking his head from time to time beyond the grass edge to look down at the mill for Dungal's signal. Kaileen spoke mostly of her mother, confessing times when she thought her mother stupid or overbearing. Clearly she felt guiltly for any angry words or thoughts that had passed between the two of them. Brendan, at a loss for words to comfort her, breathed a sigh of relief when he finally spotted Dungal waving at him in front of the mill.

"Come on," he said as he grabbed Kaileen's arm, pulling her to her feet.

They moved down the cart path as quickly as Brendan's bad leg would allow. Dungal didn't stay outside the mill; but quickly disappeared back inside. This was a peculiar move for Dungal. Brendan wondered what would have drawn him back inside.

When Brendan and Kaileen reached the two storied building, he could hear moaning and a comforting voice from inside. The voices came from the upper story which housed the millstone. Kaileen led the way up the steps to the entrance to the millstone. Pulling back the door made of rough hewn timbers, the sight they saw explained Dungal's haste to go back inside. Before them lay Father Sweeney on a bed constructed of straw and a couple of deerskins. He moaned and retched from side to side in agony. Brendan could see where a barbarian's ax had left an ugly crease on the left side of the priest's skull. Blood matted the graying hair around the wound. The miller, a man of 40 or 50 years, with broad shoulders and nearly as broad a stomach, knelt beside Father Sweeney's temple, dipping a rag into a wooden bowl of water, wiping the priest's temple and rinsing the cloth again. In this position the miller, whose long hair and scraggly beard bespoke of rough manners, now seemed to tend to the priest with the gentlest of movements. Dungal busied himself by stuffing additional straw under the deerskin to make the hastily constructed bed more comfortable.

"Father Sweeney!" Kaileen cried when she saw him.

A mixture of fear and rage raced through Brendan's body at the sight. "The barbarians must be responsible for this!" he exclaimed.

"I saw him in the village early the day of the attack. I guess I just never thought about it until now." Kaileen responded.

"Aye, someone tried to kill him for sure," the miller began. "He's in a bad way. Might not live through the night. Still, he's a strong man, had to have been to travel this far by himself after a blow like that. I found him this morning near the water sluice. He'd fallen face first into it. Like to have drowned if I hadn't seen him. What manner of devil did this to him?" the miller continued.

"Oh, I don't think they're devils. Dungal here defeated two of them that tried to attack us on the trail. See, we carry their captured weapons. Devils are supernatural, so Father Sweeney says. What need have they of weapons?"

"Ah, but surely they must be devils to attack a priest," the miller interrupted Brendan.

"They're heathens to be sure; vicious without a doubt, but they're wild and dangerous as a wolf is dangerous, and, like the wolf, can be overcome. Dungal here has shown Kaileen and I that it is so." Brendan boasted of his friend.

"This lad who cannot speak?" the miller asked incredulously.

"Yes, Kaileen and I saw him knock out two of them."

"Well I'll be..." the miller mused.

Brendan looked at Kaileen, then again at Father Sweeney

"I guess the question is: What to do next?" he said, hoping someone in the group would have the perfect answer.

"Well Father Sweeney is going nowhere for awhile if he's to survive that wound. I can hide the two of us if necessary. Those raiders probably will be happy with stealing the bit of grain I have stored and move on. I'm not sure I can hide the lot of you."

"I'd like to move on to try to find mother," Kaileen interjected.

"And I think we should make for my master's house. What do you say Dungal?" Brendan asked.

Dungal motioned that he would prefer to stay until Father Sweeney got better.

"Okay, Dungal," Brendan started and continued.

"The trail leading to the north from the mill forks about half a day's journey from here. The left fork leads to my master's rath. Kaileen and I will head that way. If you decide to join us later, you might be able to catch us."

Dungal stood up, clasped Brendan's arm with his, and patted Brendan's shoulder, a farewell gesture meant to wish Brendan good luck on the journey. Dungal started to make the same motion to Kaileen; but she reached around him with both arms and hugged him.

"Thanks for all your help," she said.

Brendan felt an irritating pulse of jealously when he saw the warm parting gesture she gave Dungal. The miller, attending to Father Sweeney's wound, stopped suddenly. He stood up and walked toward Kaileen and Brendan.

"Ah, where's my hospitality? I can give you a bit of bread and cheese, and a flask of beer for the road. Follow me."

They followed him along the perimeter of the mill house, looking at the massive millstone in the center. The miller stopped at a spot beside the wall, gave a board a rap, and it dropped down to a position perpendicular to the wall. Behind it were several shelves containing things such as sacks of flour, flasks, and a tub of butter. From one of the shelves, the miller pulled half a loaf of bread and turned to the two of them.

"Have you a place for this?" he asked.

Kaileen pulled the sack from her shoulders and opened it. The miller dropped the flask in, followed by a round of cheese and the bread. As Kaileen tightened the drawstrings and lifted the pack back on her back, the miller said.

"That should do you for a little while."

"Thank you very much," Kaileen responded.

"Thank you," Brendan followed.

They then followed the miller to the door where they had entered and left. Outside, the sun was high in the sky and a gentle breeze blew in from the west.

"Looks like a good day for a walk," Kaileen announced.

\*\*\*\*

Brendan first spotted his master's rath shortly before sundown. The day's walk had been uneventful. After the trials of the previous two days, Brendan welcomed the gentle sounds of the birds and animals scurrying through the grass of the meadows and the brush of the forest.

The master's rath was unmistakable. The master liked to do everything in a big way. A twenty foot high earthen dike wrapped about five acres of land upon which the master's house and several servants' houses stood. From the high ground in the distance, the dike appeared as a large egg with a hole in the sharp end where a log pole gate allowed people and herds access to the security of the ringed fort. Within the earthen enclosure, stone walls partitioned the egg shaped fort into four separate areas. The one nearest the entrance gate was the largest and the master penned his cattle there when the threat of cattle rustling was the greatest. It was not unknown for men from other tribes to try to increase their herds at his master's expense. Often the young men sought grants of land from their kings by stealing cattle and arguing they had livestock to support. The king, for his part, might grant the land in exchange for the best bull or cow and a promised tribute of a new calf each year after weaning.

In the next partition were the wattle huts of the servants, many of whom doubled as warriors when the time came to defend the master's property. In the third partition were a couple of stone houses with thatched roofs belonging to the master's daughters and their husbands. The master had not as yet sired a male son, so it was likely each of the daughters would inherit half of the master's estate. Finally in the last of the four partitions, lay the master's house. It was the grandest, with limestone walls neatly fitted together by the master and one of his sons-in-law, both skilled in the art of stone masonry. The walls were higher than the other houses and a wood post skeleton supported a thatched roof.

"Ah, here we are," he announced to Kaileen.

"Does that all belong to your master?" she responded.

"Yes, indeed."

"It's such a grand place. He must be quite prosperous," Kaileen said excitedly.

"Yes, he has a wealth of cattle, sheep, pigs and corn to feed them; but is stingy to a fault. I've heard that one of his daughters was nearly left a spinster because he didn't want to provide his prospective son-in-law with a proper dowry."

"Oh, I pity you, Brendan, to have to work for such a black-hearted man," Kaileen cooed sympathetically.

Brendan led Kaileen down the hillside path and across a bridge of green ash poles that provided access to the main gate. The bridge spanned the large ditch surrounding the rath. The ditch supplemented the embankment by providing a barrier to attack, particularly in the spring when it nearly filled with water. This time of year, however, only small ponds of water, randomly scattered, remained. Brendan and Kaileen spotted a few swans on the surface of one of the ponds of water as they crossed the bridge.

The gate was open wide and no guard posted at the gate. Noting this, Brendan remarked.

"Evidently my master has no news of the raiders yet."

"Why's that?" she asked.

"The gate is open and no guards posted. If my master had heard, he likely would have men posted on the gate, ready to shut it."

"That makes sense. Are we going directly to your master's house?" Kaileen responded.

"Yes, why?"

"I thought I ought to make myself more presentable first. Is there a well nearby?" she asked.

"You look lovely; but if you feel you need to wash your face and hands, there's a common well near the center of the rath." Brendan responded.

"Thank you, I'd feel better if I did. We've come a good distance today you know."

The two of them stopped at the well. Brendan lowered the wooden bucket and drew water for Kaileen. She washed her face and hands, then began to comb the long red locks of her hair. Normally, watching a woman comb her hair would have tried Brendan's patience; but Kaileen ran the comb through her hair with such graceful, sensual strokes, that the scene struck Brendan as a work of living art. It was a scene to enjoy and savor. Kaileen, sensing his wistful stare, turned her head sideways and, continuing to draw the comb through her hair, smiled at Brendan.

"What are you looking at?" she asked.

"I, I was just waiting for you to finish."

"Haven't you ever seen a girl comb her hair before?" she needled him.

"No, I guess you're the first. I have no sisters and I spend most of my time with sheep."

Kaileen huffed. "I guess I'll just have to get used to you staring then."

She put her comb back in a small purse which hung from her belt and stood up.

"Shall we meet the master?" she asked.

They walked past the last stone partition wall and up to the master's door. Brendan leaned his captured javelin against the wall. Then he unbuckled the belt carrying the sword in its scabbard and removed it from his shoulder, laying it on the ground alongside the javelin. He knew his master banned weapons in his house. He knocked on the door. To his surprise, his master's wife, Mugain, opened the door.

"Brendan!" she exclaimed when she saw him. Then she reached out, grabbed him with both arms and pulled him to her in a tight embrace. Brendan gasped for breath as he felt Mugain's biceps hard against his shoulders and her breasts against his chest. She had a hug that could squeeze the wind out of a full grown bull. Then she spotted Kaileen.

"Ah, Brendan, where did the likes of you find such a lovely colleen as this?"

As Mugain relaxed her grip, Brendan regained his breath enough to say: "The answer to that is part of the news I need to tell the master."

"Well he's out back, looking after a cow that developed a limp. But never mind him for the moment. You two look as if you could use a good meal. Am I right?"

Brendan hesitated. He looked for a moment at the motherly face of Mugain. She was still an attractive woman in spite of the fact she must be forty plus years old and had to live with the likes of Gall, her hard-nosed husband. Her deep brown, nearly black, hair was tied back off her ears and shoulders by a fine linen scarf. She wore a long purple dress which appeared to be made of linen with a white apron, neatly tied in back. On each forearm, she wore separate sleeves of washed linen, pulled over her dress. The extra sleeves and apron meant she had been busy cooking or doing other housework.

"Oh, I know Gall has a rule about the feeding of servants in his house; but he'll be busy with the cow for a while and there's more than plenty for him and the two of you." Mugain encouraged him.

"Well, if you insist," Brendan began.

"Of course I insist. I'm the mistress of this house. I never mess in me husband's business and I don't tolerate his interfering in the running of my house. Come on, take a seat at the table."

Mugain pointed to a table and two benches in the kitchen opposite a steaming cauldron in the fireplace. When Brendan slid onto the bench he noted how smooth the wood felt. He rubbed his hand on the table and felt the same smoothness. Gall and Mugain must have used this kitchen set for many years for it to have been worn so smooth. Kaileen sat on the bench opposite Brendan, which prompted Mugain to ask:

"Now how long have you two been traveling together?"

"A couple of days," Brendan answered.

"And you're not to the point of sitting next to each other, tsk, tsk..." Mugain muttered; she spoke to Kaileen.

"I don't mean to embarrass you, miss; but Brendan here's a good lad, you can trust he'll be the gentleman with you."

Brendan watched with delight as a red flush appeared on Kaileen's freckled face. He was glad to have Mugain plead his cause with Kaileen.

"Well enough of that. Let me get you some stew," Mugain said and headed for the cupboard. She pulled two wooden bowls off the shelves and ladled a heaping portion of stew from the cauldron into each bowl. She placed the bowls in front of Brendan and Kaileen. Returning to the cupboard, she brought back two wooden spoons, a loaf of bread, a knife, and a small wooden tub of butter.

"Did I forget anything?" she started to ask then answered her own question. "Oh, drinks. How about a cup of aged beer? I made it myself, aged it especially for my husband's taste."

"That would be fine, thanks," Brendan answered.

"If it's no trouble, I'd prefer water. We drank mostly beer this past day." Kaileen answered.

"No trouble at all."

Mugain then disappeared into the dark part of the kitchen. When she reappeared, she carried two bronze drinking cups and placed them on the table in front of Brendan and Kaileen. Brendan sipped his, noticing he tasted not beer, but the sweet taste of water. He whispered to Kaileen.

"Did you get water?"

She quickly sipped from her cup and shook her head. Then she set her cup down, sliding it toward Brendan, who slid his toward her. Mugain, who had returned to the kitchen, was none the wiser. Brendan tasted his stew. It was hot so he held a spoonful in the air, blowing on it to speed the cooling. Finally, he tasted it. The stew was wonderful! He couldn't remember the last time he'd tasted beef. He wasn't sure what vegetables were in the pot, but the flavor of beef permeated everything and that was fine with him. Mugain returned with a cup in her hand and sat on the bench alongside Kaileen.

"This is really good," Brendan mumbled, forgetting to swallow before he spoke.

"Thank you," Mugain answered and said, "Now tell me the story you promised me."

Brendan told her the complete story of the raid on the village, the warrior's pursuit on the trail and finding Father Sweeney at the mill. When he told of finding Kaileen tied up on the beach, Mugain put her arm around Kaileen in a comforting gesture, "Oh, you poor dear."

When Brendan finished the story, Mugain spoke.

"You will have to tell all of this to Gall as soon as we are finished here. He will likely want to herd the cattle into the rath and prepare for battle. I hope he has enough men to defend this place."

When they finished eating, Mugain led Brendan and Kaileen out the back door and into the yard. Gall, a tall man, with a massive chest and large stomach protruding over the web belt which gathered his tunic, was finished with the cow and was washing his hands and arms in a bucket. He finished by splashing water across his sun-bronzed face and mopped his face and gray-streaked black beard with the arm of his tunic. When he saw Mugain approaching with Brendan and Kaileen, he stood up straight, placed his hands on his hips in a lordly fashion, and spoke.

"What have we here, good wife?"

"Brendan has returned with important news," Mugain answered.

"And what of this girl?"

"She's part of the reason for Brendan's return; but I'll let him tell the story."

So Brendan told the story for the second time that evening. As he told it, he noticed anger filling Gall's face. When he was done, Gall burst out.

"And you left the flock I entrusted to you to the barbarians and the wolves?"

"Sorry sir, but Kaileen needed help," Brendan answered.

"She's a fine healthy girl; but I don't need a maid servant and she won't replace the fifty odd head of sheep you abandoned!"

"What was I to do?" Brendan began his protest. "We had the sea warriors fast on our tracks. Why, if it hadn't been for Dungal, we might not even be here to warn you of them."

"You shouldn't have left the flock in the first place. I thought I taught you that minding the flock was the most important thing you could do."

"Gall, aren't you being a bit hard on the boy? After all, he rescued this maiden. Wouldn't you do as much for me?" Mugain fired the words at her husband.

"That's different. I'm bound to you by the vows. She's no kin to him, and he abandoned my flock before he knew she was in trouble." Gall snarled back at his wife.

"You're a harsh man, Gall" Mugain answered him.

"Well I'm not seeing you complaining about the fine house you have, the meat for the pot, and the fine linens to wear. Would you have all of this if I made a practice of casting off my livestock?"

Brendan decided he'd better say something quick.

"Sir, I'll go back and find the sheep."

"I'll not be sending you, a cripple, back alone to gather the flocks with foreign warriors on the prowl. You wouldn't stand a chance. As it is, I'll have to send half a dozen armed herdsmen to see if they can recover the flock. You're no longer of any use to me Brendan. You've passed 16 years. Time to make it on your own. I'll have Mugain give you food and drink enough for a fortnight and then you'll leave."

Brendan felt his heart sink in his body. Stunned, anger welled up within him. Had the javelin been within reach, he could easily have hurled it at Gall. Choking with emotion he turned toward the rear door of the house, then, hesitating, turned toward Kaileen.

"Kaileen?"

She, in turn, looked at Gall.

"Sir, have you heard anything of a woman traveling in these parts?" she asked.

"No, why?" Gall responded curtly.

"My mother was gone at the time of the raid on our village of Kilrush, and I haven't seen her since."

"I have heard of no such traveler; but the herdsman may know of her. I'm sending runners out tonight to order them into the rath with their herds. When they are gathered in the morning, I will ask if they know anything. Regardless, you are welcome to remain as my wife's maid servant. I will ask one of my daughters to find you a place to sleep." Gall replied.

"You will not! If she's to be my maid servant, she will stay under our roof. She may sleep in our room tonight. Tomorrow you build her a room of her own." Mugain issued a fiery retort.

"And where am I to sleep?" Gall seethed.

"There's room a plenty beyond our bedroom, a night without your snoring can surely do me no harm."

"Nor you kneeing me in the ribs," Gall countered before he realized he'd just consented to the sleeping arrangements.

"And what about Brendan?" Mugain pleaded.

"He's on his own, I said," Gall thundered.

"Surely you won't turn the lad from the rath with nightfall coming will you?"

"Alright, he can stay 'til the morrow; but he'll stay in one of the stables." Gall conceded.

"Yes dear," Mugain cooed, apparently realizing she'd pushed her husband to his limit of tolerance and now sought to calm him down. Then she addressed Brendan.

"Come on, we'll find you a stall with no livestock."

Then, looking at Kaileen, she said, "Why don't you come with me. After we look after Brendan, we'll bed you down."

Brendan and Kaileen followed Mugain to a set of four stables. She pointed out an empty stall and said.

"I'll send Kaileen down here with a couple of blankets later."

"Oh, don't bother; I'm used to sleeping on the ground. The hay here will be a great improvement as it is." Brendan answered her.

"Well, wish Kaileen a good night now then," Mugain said with a wink.

"On second thought, if you have a spare blanket..."

"I'll see what we can do then," Mugain smiled back.

Brendan glanced at Kaileen. She had a disgusted look on her face. Apparently she was a little impatient with Mugain's attempts to promote a romance between the two of them.

After Mugain and Kaileen left, Brendan walked to the well. He wanted to pull off his tunic and pour a bucket of water over his head. But, since he was in a public place, he contented himself with washing his arms and dunking his head in the bucket. The cold water refreshed him. He returned to the stable to find Kaileen with a blanket folded over her arms.

"Mugain, she said I could call her Mugain in private, but mistress when her husband is about, sent these."

"Will you help me spread them out?" Brendan asked.

The two of them formed a bed from the hay with one blanket to hold the hay in place on the bottom and the other to cover Brendan. Kaileen even molded a pillow where Brendan chose to lay his head. When completed, they lay back staring at the thatched roof of the stable.

"Are you going to stay here?" Brendan asked.

"No, silly, I have to go back to the house."

"I don't mean in the stable. I mean will you stay and be Mugain's maid servant?" Brendan rephrased his question.

"I'd like to, since I've nowhere else to call home right now; but I must try to find mom."

"What do you plan to do?"

"I want to stay until Gall has assembled the herdsmen. One of them may know of her whereabouts. If they know nothing, I will stay here a few nights, then ask Mugain if she will allow me a fortnight to return to Kilrush to see if mom's there."

"What about the barbarians?" Brendan asked, puzzled.

"They burned the village. I don't think they would have done that if they had planned to stay permanently. Nevertheless, I will approach it carefully. I don't intend to be captured again. But I think mom will return there. She's likely there now. What will you do?"

"I plan to leave in the morning after Mugain gives me my fortnight of provisions. Gall doesn't want me here so I think I'll head north and see if I can find a chieftain or king who needs a herdsman."

"Well, I guess this is our last night together," Kaileen started. "Thank you for all you've done for me," she continued.

She leaned over and kissed Brendan on the cheek. Brendan reached for her to pull her closer so he could kiss her on the lips. Kaileen sprung to her feet, however, and backed away from Brendan.

"Ah, let's not be getting carried away. The kiss was just my way of wishing you well on your journey—nothing more. Anyway, I'd best be getting back to Mistress Mugain. She'll likely want to turn in for the night soon. Good night."

Kaileen then turned and scurried off in the direction of the master's house. Brendan watched her until the darkness swallowed her figure. Although he had spent many days in pastures with only sheep as companions, being alone never bothered him before. Now his spirit sank at the thought of being without Kaileen. He lay back down on his makeshift bed, and, after staring blankly toward the roof for a long time, fell asleep.

Brendan awoke the next morning to the sounds of men shouting as they herded cattle into the rath. After washing, he went to the master's house to get his provisions for the road. As he approached, Kaileen came out of the house and walked down to meet him.

"Mugain wants you to come to the back door," she said.

Together they walked around to the back of the house. Mugain was waiting with a stool and bowl of hot oatmeal.

"Here, eat this while I prepare you a sack for the road," she said.

Brendan sat and ate while Kaileen and Mugain went inside. Kaileen soon reappeared with a cup of apple cider.

"I'd like to walk you to the gate when you're ready to leave. Mugain said it was Okay," she said.

"Sure, I'd like that," Brendan answered.

Brendan finished the oatmeal. Kaileen took the cup, bowl and stool into the house. When she reappeared, Mugain was with her. Kaileen carried the makeshift knapsack she had born on the trail, slung across one shoulder. From the way Kaileen leaned, Brendan could tell Mugain had been more than generous with the provisions. He worried about toting the weight. Mugain spoke first.

"I'll say good-bye to you here. Kaileen will see you to the gate."

Mugain then hugged Brendan with both arms, holding him close and tight again. When she released the embrace, Brendan saw tears trickling down her face from the corners of her eyes.

"Take care, Brendan," she sniffed and ran for the house before her emotions exploded.

"What's with her?" Brendan asked Kaileen.

"She thinks of you like a son. It really hurts her to know you'll never return." Kaileen explained. "Are you ready for the pack?" Kaileen continued. She obviously wanted to change the subject.

"Let me put the sword on first," he answered her. Then he led Kaileen around to the front of the house where he had left the sword and javelin the night before. After Brendan strapped on the belt containing the sword in its scabbard, Kaileen lifted the knapsack onto Brendan's back. It was full but not quite as heavy as Brendan imagined it would be when saw Kaileen carrying it. Kaileen then handed him the javelin.

"Your spear, sir," she said with a mock curtsy.

"Thank you, my lady," Brendan replied, then turned and headed toward the gate. To his surprise, and delight, Kaileen slid her slender hand onto the crook of his left elbow. They walked in silence, working their way through the cattle as they went. When they reached the main gate, Brendan noted that, although it was open, Gall had posted two of the herdsmen, wearing helmets and breastplates and armed with both sword and spear as sentries, ready to close it at the first sign of trouble. They both nodded at Brendan. Apparently Gall had told them when and why he would be leaving. Brendan turned to Kaileen.

"I guess this is goodbye then," he said.

Kaileen leaned up and quickly kissed him on the lips. Brendan wasn't sure but it appeared her eyes were watery also. She backed down and said.

"If you come across my mother, be sure to tell her where I am."

"I will. I hope we meet again Kaileen."

"I do too, Brendan. Good bye."

With that statement, Kaileen quickly turned and scurried toward the master's house. Brendan hesitated for a moment, taking in the delightful motion of this most beautiful of God's creatures. About fifty paces from where he stood, she turned toward him again and waved. He waved back. Then he turned toward the bridge. Beyond it lay his future, a future now more uncertain than ever.

# CHAPTER 5

Brendan headed to the northeast. He'd heard stories of a king some distance in that direction who was rich in cattle. He felt it was his best chance of survival. The day dragged on. Walking with Kaileen and Dungal, he had hardly noticed time passing. Now the sun beat down relentlessly and the leg with the club foot ached constantly. As the day passed, he found himself taking more frequent breaks. Lack of motivation attacked his stamina, to the point that when he came upon the edge of a turlough, he decided to spend the night by the wetland; even though darkness would not be upon him for some time. He found a spot where the springy, short-cropped turf of grasses and sedges had been dried enough by the summer sun to provide a comfortable bed. He found an outcropping shelf of limestone to sit upon, sat down and unburdened himself of the pack, sword and javelin. Around him, he watched the flight of the Wigeons, White-fronted Geese and Whoper Swans as they busily sought food within the marsh.

*Food. Yes, he was ready to sample Mugain's goodies.* He had fasted the length of the day in the hope that he might stretch his supplies well beyond the fortnight promised. When he opened the pack, he was sure Mugain had given him at least a week's worth of food. There were loaves of dark bread, a small tub of butter, several rounds of cheese, dried beef, a couple of flasks of beer and one of apple cider, corn cakes, sausages, and cracked hazelnuts. He chose to have a supper of bread, sausage and beer with a corn cake for desert. As he ate he gazed at the sky, scarcely a cloud; it would be a clear night. Then he noticed something odd—silence.

Someone was close. The frogs had stopped croaking. The song birds were silent. The ducks and swans were swimming away from the shore. Brendan pulled his sword from its sheath and listened. He could now hear the rustling of brush from the direction which he had just come. Apparently someone was following the path he'd made to the turlough. His body trembled. He backed into the bush, pulling his pack with him. He tried to conceal himself. Brendan knew he couldn't outrun whoever it was and he didn't want to try to fight them. He hoped they might just pass by him. He waited and listened as the sounds became more audible. Then it occurred to him that if someone were actually tracking him, they would see that the trail ended. Brendan prepared to attack. He was determined to strike a killing blow with his first strike. The sun, descending the sky, now dimly outlined a silhouette of a body. Brendan hesitated. He could see the figure wore no helmet, yet walked with a spear. Finally, Brendan, posed to strike, saw a face. It was a familiar face.

"Dungal!" he shouted.

Dungal dashed from the trees and clasped Brendan's arm.

"How did you get here?" Brendan asked.

"He came with me," a second familiar voiced called from the bush.

"Kaileen! What brings you here?" Brendan asked, astonished.

Kaileen looked at Dungal then asked.

"Do you want to tell him or shall I?"

Dungal smiled and pointed his finger at her.

"Ok, if you insist," she replied. Then she continued.

"Shortly after your departure this morning, Dungal and the miller showed up at the gate to Gall's rath bearing Father Sweeney on a litter they made. Father Sweeney is doing a little better and the miller thought it wise to move him to a place that offered more protection from the barbarians than the mill.

"But we left them just yesterday, how did they make the journey so quickly?" Brendan asked.

"They traveled all night. Of course all within the rath know and revere Father Sweeney, so Gall dare not turn him away." Kaileen continued.

"But what of you? Why did you leave?"

"Oh Brendan, I just can't stay in one place until I find out what happened to mother. Dungal was willing to escort me; and Mugain said I could return whenever I was ready to stay." Kaileen answered him.

"So you want to search for your mother. I was planning to head northeast. I thought maybe one of the chieftains or kings in the interior would be in need of a herdsman or shepherd. Do you think we might find your mother up there?" Brendan asked.

"Actually I'd like to go back to Kilrush," Kaileen answered him. Her voice was gentle and sweet, obviously she was trying to persuade him.

"Back there?"

"Yes, I think the barbarians will be gone now and it's been three days since the raid. Mom is likely to have returned or will return shortly. I think I stand the best chance of finding her there." Kaileen explained.

"What say you, Dungal?" Brendan asked.

Dungal touched his chest with his hand and pointed to Kaileen in a gesture which indicated he would go where she wanted. Brendan thought for a moment and said.

"Well, I'll probably use up the rest of the food Mugain gave me making the return trip. I'd rather hoped I'd find new employment before they ran out."

Then Brendan looked into Kaileen's eyes. The big brown pupils pleaded with him to go with her. Right now Dungal and Kaileen were Brendan's whole world.

"Okay, we'll go back to Kilrush," Brendan answered and extended his right hand toward Dungal, palm down. Dungal responded by placing his right hand on top of Brendan's. Kaileen placed her's on top of their hands to show she was one with them.

"But let's camp here now and leave at daylight," Brendan proposed.

Dungal nodded that he agreed and Kaileen said, "Okay. By the way, Mugain loaded us down with food and drink also."

They ate supper, especially enjoying Mugain's sausages. The next morning, they were on the road at dawn. The next two and one half days passed without incident. When they reached the mill again, they went through it to see if the miller had returned yet. He hadn't. They were now nearing the village. So far, the only thing unusual was that they hadn't encountered anyone on the trail between the mill and Kilrush. The path was well worn, a sign that it normally was well traveled.

"I think we'd better get off the trail," Brendan recommended.

"Why's that?" Kaileen asked.

"If the sea raiders are still around Kilrush they may spot us on the trail from a good distance away. They may also have the trail staked out, waiting for unsuspecting travelers" Brendan answered.

Dungal nodded to indicate he agreed with Brendan. Dungal then led them into the brush. Their progress slowed, but by sundown they reached the edge of the formerly thriving village. Dungal pointed to Brendan, then Kaileen, then the ground. Then he pointed at his own eyes with two fingers and made a circular motion.

"You want us to stay here while you have a look around?" Brendan asked out loud to confirm he understood Dungal's meaning.

Dungal nodded "Yes," then disappeared through the brush.

"Do you think he'll be all right?" Kaileen whispered.

"You've seen him in action. Unless he is greatly outnumbered, he should be fine."

Although he said this to reassure her, he worried about Dungal too. The longer Dungal remained gone, the more he worried. In fact Brendan was about to ready to search for him when Dungal reappeared at the exact same location where he'd exited the bush. He put both hands with index fingers extended to his forehead to simulate horns and the shook his head. This meant he saw no sign of the barbarians. Dungal then led the way out of the bush and into the burned-out village. Brendan immediately noticed that none of the dead bodies remained.

"Someone has disposed of the bodies," he remarked.

"So I notice. Could the sea raiders have done it?" Kaileen asked.

"Somehow I can't picture them making the effort to do that. Perhaps some of the women who used to live here returned and buried them," Brendan answered.

Sure enough, when they reached the far side of the village, they saw eighteen neatly ordered mounds of dirt. On each mound lay a cross formed from stones. Brendan believed the graves further indicated the barbarians didn't do the burial. Obviously someone wanted to see they were given a Christian burial.

"Let's go to my place," Kaileen urged. When they got to the remains of her hut, Kaileen immediately noticed the underground storage chamber was open and empty.

"Didn't I close this before we left?" she asked Brendan.

"I don't remember for sure, we were in such a hurry when we left," Brendan answered her.

"I think mom might have been here," Kaileen said excitedly.

"I wouldn't jump to conclusions," Brendan said, "Anyone could have found that spot; even the barbarians."

"True, but I just have this feeling she's been here."

"Well, what should we do now?" Brendan asked.

Dungal rubbed his stomach.

"Okay, let's eat," Brendan laughed.

44

By the time they had finished eating, it was nearly dark so they decided to stay in the burned-out village for the night. In fact, Kaileen wanted to spend the night in the ruins of her house. They decided to take turns standing watch so they wouldn't be taken by surprise if any of the sea raiders might be around. Kaileen volunteered for the first watch, followed by Dungal, leaving Brendan to handle pre-dawn.

After finding himself an inviting spot on the dirt floor of the former hut, Brendan cleared it of a few stray bits of charred wood, then stretched out under his cloak. He stared at the cloud of stars forming the Milky Way for a moment. This was the last image he remembered until he was awakened by Dungal's shaking. He sat up, rubbed the sleep from his eyes, and patted Dungal on the shoulder to let him know he was ready to take over the watch. Brendan stood up and stretched. He decided to move around a little to wake up. Then he heard a noise from the woods to his left. His heart raced as he reached for his javelin. Just as he was pondering whether to wake Dungal back up, a large buck came out of the trees. The buck crossed the open field between Brendan and the river, looked at Brendan briefly, and disappeared into the woods again to the right of the village. Brendan exhaled.

"Just a deer," he thought. Then he pondered how before the raid on the village he would have expected the deer or some other animal. The sound wouldn't have sent the chill of fear throughout his body. The scare did get the adrenaline pumping. He was certainly wide awake now. He decided to pass the time trying to figure out how people saw pictures in the stars. Father Sweeney had told them stories about how ancient people saw images of gods and folk heroes in the stars.

Brendan amused himself searching for the pictures in the stars until the stars began to dim as daylight approached. His eyelids were heavy now, and, although dawn was nearly upon him, he was trying hard to stay awake. He decided to walk to the bank of the river and back to keep awake. The path was a little rugged, but he was in no hurry. By the time he reached the waters edge, daylight was upon him. He could see hundreds of footprints in the dirt. He could also make out two trenches where the keels of the long ships had left their mark on the muddy shore. He looked for a moment upriver, mesmerized by the shallow ripples in the water which flowed down river toward the sea; then he turned to look downstream.

The scene downstream brought his blood to a full boil. Ships were headed up the river. Yes, they were the long ships. What was worse was there were not just two of them. Brendan paused for a moment to try to count them. He couldn't be sure, but it looked as though there might be as many as ten. Then it occurred to him that he was standing in the open. They could easily see him, if they hadn't spotted him already. He limped as quickly as he could toward the trail that led away from the beach. As soon as he could see the sleeping bodies of Dungal and Kaileen, he called out.

"Dungal, Kaileen, get up, get up."

He called twice more before they sat up, dreary eyed.

"What is it?" Kaileen asked.

"The sea raiders are rowing up the river. Looks like ten ships. We've got to get out of here."

"Ten ships?" Kaileen asked incredulously.

"That's what I count," Brendan answered.

Kaileen quickly tied up her pack. Dungal did the same with the one Mugain had given him and buckled on his sword. By the time Brendan reached them, Dungal had tied up Brendan's pack. As Brendan stepped into the remnant of Kaileen's hut, Dungal handed him the other sword. All three of them hoisted their packs on their backs. Dungal led them back toward the trail to the north and out of town. Just when they reached the point where the trail disappeared into the heather, Kaileen spoke.

"You know, maybe we should hide here and see if they come ashore first."

"Why? Right now we have a chance to put some distance between us and them. You remember I can't travel very fast. We can use a head start."

"Yes, but we don't know for sure they'll land here. And if they do, we should try to find out how many and in which direction they'll be traveling so we can warn people up ahead." Kaileen answered him.

"Why should we risk our lives or capture and maybe torture by these barbarians just so we can warn people?"

"Remember there are eighteen graves back there. Perhaps if my village had been warned, they could have escaped. Maybe Father Sweeney wouldn't be lying at the rath of Gall with a broken skull!" Kaileen scolded him.

At the mention of Father Sweeney, Dungal nodded eagerly, indicating he agreed with Kaileen.

"You too, Dungal? I guess I'm outnumbered." Brendan sighed, "I'd still like to know how we'll get away to warn anyone without them spotting us?"

"We'll stay here until the sea warriors have headed in whatever direction they choose to travel. We'll follow them until they bed down for the night. Then we'll slip away while they're asleep. If we're quiet enough, the sentries won't hear us. If we travel all night, we can get a big enough head start that we can stay ahead of them, if they should choose to travel in our direction." Kaileen explained.

"And what do we do once we're away?" Brendan pressed.

"I think we should try to find the chief of the Dal Cais?" Kaileen answered.

"Why him? His rath must be seven nights journey to the northeast."

"Yes, but I think he's the only one who can raise a large enough army to defeat these barbarians."

"But will he try?" Brendan asked.

"The Dalcaisians aren't going to stand for invaders killing the people who pay them tribute." Kaileen explained.

"Okay, let's find a place with a good view that's comfortable. We may have a long wait."

Dungal nodded that he understood and led them around the perimeter of the village until he found a large stone in the middle of a large group of oak trees with gorse providing cover at the lower levels. From this particular spot they could see both the burned-out village and the beach below. Brendan could see the prow of the first ship now. They quickly slipped off their packs and sat down upon the stone. At first it appeared that the ship would continue up the river. Brendan breathed a sighed of relief; but then the ship turned toward them. It was headed for the beach below. One after another, the ships, with oars giving them the appearance of large centipedes, turned and moved toward shore. Brendan could now hear the sporadic sounds of shouting voices drifting up from the river. The first ship slid up on the shore. The seamen began piling over the gunwales, with shields on one arm and either a javelin or battle ax in the other. Brendan counted thirty-two of these warriors as they rushed ashore. They moved directly toward the village. In fact, Brendan could swear they were headed directly toward him!

When they reached the village, they quickly passed through, looking all around them as they went. They all looked savage with their long scraggly hair and beards, leathery faces and wild eyes. Brendan looked at Kaileen. She was pale with fear. Serves her right, he thought. Staying here had been her idea. The warriors quickly disappeared into the brush on the north side of the village. Brendan could hear them thrashing around in the heather and gorse ground cover. He assumed they were looking for anybody who might want to oppose them. Then Brendan shivered with fear. Had they spotted him on the beach this morning? Were they looking for him?

Brendan comforted himself with the realization that they were searching the area beyond the burned out village. If they were looking for him, they apparently assumed he had gone inland by the fastest route possible. He was thankful they hadn't decided to do a broad search by spreading out along the nearly semicircular ring of forest which surrounded the village.

Brendan now turned his attention to the beach. One by one the rest of the long ships were beaching on the shore. As their crews got out they spread out along a long rope attached to the bow. They pulled the ships far enough on shore that the water couldn't float them away again. After securely beaching the boats they grabbed their weapons and shields and formed a large semicircle on the beach. It appeared they were awaiting a speech from their chief.

The breaking of brush and male voices speaking in a foreign tongue distracted Brendan's attention from the beach again. The first landing party was coming back. This group retraced their steps through the village and back to the beach. As they approached the other barbarians on the beach, Brendan saw one of the sea warriors step from the crowd on the beach and walk towards the returning group. He was a huge man, certainly six feet tall if he were lying where one could step off the distance. One member of the returning group of warriors stepped toward this man and pounded his own chest in a gesture of salute. They spoke momentarily. It appeared the man from the returning group was giving the huge blond-haired Viking some sort of report. The huge man, with a tunic of chainmail, drew his sword from his scabbard. He waved it in the air in a circular motion.

"That big man is Hakon, their leader," Kaileen whispered to Brendan.

Brendan shook his head to indicate he acknowledged. Then he watched as all the sea invaders gathered around their leader. The leader said something. The mob of barbarians cheered. The leader spoke again. Again a loud shout arose from the crowd. Brendan wished he could understand their language. Finally, their leader pointed with his sword in the direction of the burned out village. As he took his first steps in that direction, the warriors forming the portion of the circle in front of him parted to let him pass. As he walked through, the warriors began forming a line behind him shouting:

"Hakon, Hakon, Hakon..."

Hakon led most of the barbarians up the trail from the river bank toward the village. About thirty remained on the beach. Brendan figured the ones staying behind were there to guard the ships which numbered ten. When the sea warriors began passing through the village, Brendan started counting them. Five hundred sixty-nine was the count as the last disappeared into the brush to the north of the village. He then whispered in Kaileen's ear:

"What are we to do now? We've got 569 of the barbarians between us and the people we should warn on one side and another thirty on the beach likely to pounce on us if they see us move from this spot."

"Let's follow the 569," Kaileen suggested as though it was the simplest of tasks.

"Follow the 569?" Brendan repeated her words with an air of disbelief.

"Yes," she answered and then went on to explain, "They don't know we're behind them. If we're careful, we should be able to follow them until they camp for the night. They're not going to find much to loot before dark. Once they're asleep, we can get past them and warn our countrymen beyond of their approach. By nightfall, we should have a better idea of the direction they're heading anyway."

"I guess that makes sense; but what of the thirty some sailors on the beach?" Brendan replied.

"I think if we're quiet enough we can slip away without drawing their attention," Kaileen said with confidence.

"What do you think?" Brendan asked Dungal.

Dungal tapped his chest with his fist and pointed with two fingers to his eyes, then with his index finger to the trail where the barbarians had just disappeared.

"You say we should follow them; but let you lead, right?"

Dungal nodded affirmatively.

"Lead on," Brendan answered him and motioned toward the trail.

Brendan, Kaileen, and Dungal followed the barbarians the rest of the morning. It was not hard to follow the direction the barbarians traveled as they generally made plenty of noise; but since Brendan couldn't walk as fast as a normal human being, he, Dungal and Kaileen gradually lagged further and further behind. When midday came, they could no longer hear their quarry. Brendan began to worry that the barbarians might have stopped to eat lunch and the three of them might come upon them suddenly.

"Keep a sharp look out, Dungal," he whispered. "We need to make sure we see them before they spot us," Brendan continued.

Dungal answered by making a sign across his chest which meant "Don't worry about it."

Shortly after that, Brendan could hear the sounds of the sea raiders' voices again. They began to get louder and louder.

"They must have stopped," Brendan whispered to Dungal. "I'd like to know what they are doing; but be careful," he instructed Dungal.

Dungal nodded. As they moved forward, they took each step with deliberate care, sliding the twigs and leaves on the forest floor out of the way before placing weight on the advancing foot and being careful not to let the branches they bent out of their path make noise as they dragged on their packs and clothing. Soon they came to a point where the forest cover gave way to a large meadow. Ahead they could see the unruly mob sitting and lying about the hillside, much like cattle basking in the midday sun. The barbarians were talking, laughing, drinking and eating.

"We'll have to wait here until they move on," Brendan whispered to Dungal and Kaileen. "Why don't we sit and eat also?" he continued.

Both Kaileen and Dungal nodded their agreement. They helped each other remove their packs, and Brendan removed his. They shared a meal of bread, cheese, and dried beef. They enjoyed a long rest as the barbarians lingered, apparently in no hurry to continue their journey inland. With the open field ahead of them, Brendan knew he, Dungal and Kaileen stood an even greater chance of being spotted when the barbarians resumed their trek. This meant giving the sea raiders an even greater lead, which, of course, meant a greater likelihood of losing them later.

"What direction would you say they are traveling?" he asked Dungal.

Dungal picked up a twig and scratched two small circles in the dirt. He drew a line from one to the next. He pointed to the sun and to the two circles indicating the circles and the line represented the path of the sun from east to west. Then he drew a line from the middle of that line, at an angle to that line, above the line, and toward the circle which represented the eastern position of the sun.

"Northeast?" Brendan asked to confirm.

Dungal nodded to indicate Brendan was correct.

"Do you know who lives to the northeast?" Brendan asked Kaileen.

"There are several farmers, I think; but none who have constructed fortifications like Gall. They will probably seek the protection of King Finian who I've heard lives four or five night's journey further to the northeast."

"Do you think we should try to warn them?" Brendan asked.

"I don't think we stand much chance of reaching them before the barbarians. Anyway, any of them are likely to spot a group this large from a good ways off. Like I said, they will seek the assistance of the king. Most of the ones I've met complain enough about tribute to the king. They'll not be shy about demanding the king's protection."

50

"Okay, I guess we don't have to try to get past the barbarians for a while. I doubt we could anyway" Brendan responded.

Just then, they were interrupted by shouts as the sea raiders were cajoled by their leaders to rise and continue their march. Since they were in an area which had little cover to conceal them, the trio had to wait until the barbarians had nearly disappeared on the horizon before they tried to follow. Near mid-afternoon, they passed a farmstead. Smoke arose from the remains of a hut and stable which had been burned to the ground. At Kaileen's insistance, they searched an area several rods in diameter looking for bodies. All three of them were greatly relieved when they found none. Brendan knew the absence of bodies likely meant the inhabitants managed to escape before the raiders attacked. When the sun disappeared from view in the western sky, Brendan, Kaileen and Dungal found themselves approaching a forest again.

Dungal suddenly turned and motioned for them to take cover in the brush. He then disappeared for a short time and returned. He rubbed his stomach and pointed in the direction of the woods. Brendan whispered to Kaileen.

"Dungal said they've stopped to eat. Most likely they'll make camp for the night. We should probably try to get around them while it is still light enough for us to find our way without bumping into them."

Dungal nodded that he agreed. Kaileen took a deep breath and sighed.

"Well, what are we waiting for?" she said. "Be off with you," She continued, smiling and motioning for Dungal to turn around and lead the way.

Again they had to step ever so cautiously to avoid making a sound. Brendan's heart jumped when he spooked a grouse from its nesting place. The sudden flight of the bird appeared to go unnoticed by the barbarians however. Approaching closer and closer, the barbarians' voices increased in volume. Then the delicious smell of roasting beef drifted to Brendan's nostrils. Apparently the sea raiders had profited from their raid on the farm. The aroma enticed Brendan; he daydreamed of a rack of beef ribs being slowly roasted over the orange-red coals of a fire, juice dripping into the coals, emitting a hiss as it impacted with the hot embers. This thought distracted Brendan enough that he didn't see the dry twig he stepped on until it made a clearly audible snap. Brendan, Dungal and Kaileen froze, hoping the barbarians were making enough of their own noise, they hadn't noticed—no such luck. First they heard a shout which sounded like a command. Next, they heard the brush breaking as the barbarian's footsteps approached.

# CHAPTER 6

Brendan, Kaileen and Dungal all hugged the ground. Brendan knew their only chance was to stay concealed and hope the barbarians now approaching didn't see any of them. The crunch of brush grew louder. The barbarians were headed directly at them. In a moment Brendan could see two black forms moving through the brush, swords and shields readied to deal with whatever they found. A few more steps and they would stumble upon him or Dungal, Brendan thought.

Just then the brush rustled behind Brendan. He was able to turn his head enough to see the familiar tail of a deer disappearing into the brush. The two approaching barbarians stopped and laughed. Then they turned around and headed back the way they had come. The deer had saved all of them.

When the barbarians were out of sight, Dungal crept through the brush on his feet, keeping low to stay concealed. Brendan followed, but, with his bad leg, found it hard to move in this position. Kaileen followed him, as nimbly as Dungal. Twilight was falling fast now. Being silent in the brush became more and more difficult as their surroundings were slowly enveloped in darkness. After what seemed liked an agonizingly long time, they came out of the forest into a meadow. A crescent moon provided modest illumination. Brendan looked around. All he could see were dark outlines of the shrubs where they arose above the grass here and there. Dungal stopped, waved at Brendan and extended his arm in a sweeping motion, indicating he wanted to know which direction to go.

Brendan looked at the stars. He located two groups of constellations. One he knew to be in the north sky and one in the east. He turned so he faced the direction midway between the two of them; he pointed with his index finger.

"That way, Dungal," he directed.

Dungal nodded and set off in the direction Brendan chose.

****

As the first light of the sun slowly illuminated the sky, Brendan found they were crossing a valley. A low cloud of mist blanketed the area, giving a feeling of dampness all around and an air heavy with moisture at each breath. The vegetation consisted of gorse and grass with an occasional struggling oak tree. Brendan longed to lie down in the grass and sleep the rest of the day and through the next night. He knew he couldn't though. They were ahead of the barbarians now but not by much. Ahead he could see a crooked string of ash trees below that likely hid a stream. *Ah, water; at least he could look forward to cooling his feet.*

"Looks like we've water up ahead," he announced to Kaileen.

"Good, I'd love to splash some water on my face," she responded.

With the image of rushing water in his mind, Brendan moved with renewed vigor. They quickly traversed the open land and arrived at the fringe of the forest. They could hear rush of water within. Entering the woods they descended quickly to the bank of the stream. Brendan pulled off his shoes and stepped in, then turned and faced upstream. He bent over, cupped his hands and scooped up water to his face. He took a long drink. Ah, it was sweet water. Then he washed his face. The water was cool, but not particularly cold. Nevertheless, it washed the previous night's weariness from his body. Kaileen was soon alongside him, following nearly the same ritual. He looked back to the bank for Dungal. Dungal stood there motionless. On either side of him stood sea raiders, their spearheads positioned inches from Dungal's throat!

Brendan froze. He thought frantically. How could he make a move to free Dungal without ensuring these barbarians would immediately slay his friend? What happened next convinced him it was futile to try. From behind these two barbarians came another four. These stepped into the stream and seized Brendan and Kaileen by the upper arms and shoved them toward shore. Brendan stumbled and fell face first into the flowing stream. He felt a mighty hand grasp the neck of his tunic and thrust him toward the streambank. He landed alongside his shoes and quickly slid them on. The barbarian closest to him grabbed him by the shoulder of his tunic and pulled him to his feet. The barbarian then grabbed the strap of the belt which held the sword in its scabbard which Brendan had strapped across his chest. He unbuckled it and took the scabbard with sword, throwing it over his left shoulder so that he now wore scabbards on both sides of his body. He then saw the two who seized Kaileen, forcing her up on the bank. He turned to look at Dungal again. Dungal had been disarmed also. Behind Dungal and Dungal's captors were another half a dozen of these warriors. Had the horde of the sea raiders caught up with them already?

The warrior closest to Brendan said something in his foreign tongue. One of those guarding Dungan responded:

"Hakon"

"I think they are going to take us to Hakon," Kaileen blurted.

One of the two men guarding Dungal motioned with the spear for Dungal to turn around. The other prodded Dungal in the back with the point of his javelin, indicating he should move back up the stream bank in the direction they had come earlier. The barbarians apparently were confident they had the upper hand, as they didn't take the time to bind the hands of any of them.

As they climbed backed into the open field, Brendan glanced behind him. Kaileen and four barbarians followed. Eight were ahead, one just in front, looking back periodically, two guarding Dungal and five ahead of them. Brendan, Kaileen and Dungal were outnumbered twelve to three.

The barbarian behind Brendan kept pushing, causing him to stumble. The sea raider cared little that Brendan had a club foot and could not travel at the same speed as the rest of the party. When Brendan went down for the third time, the barbarian in front of him turned. When he saw Brendan on the ground, he drew back his javelin in preparation to thrust into Brendan's chest. The commotion attracted Dungal's attention, however, who responded by pulling the withdrawn javelin from its owner's hand. The perplexed sea raider turned only to meet the spearhead as Dungal thrust it into his thigh. Like lighting, Dungal quickly withdrew the spear and thrust it toward the neck of the barbarian immediately behind Brendan. The barbarian countered by raising his shield to deflect the blow. Dungal spun around on one foot, leaped high in the air, thrusting his right foot into the side of the barbarian's head, sending him downhill in an involuntary cartwheel.

The other three rushed up from behind to come to the aid of their fallen companion. As they did so, they ignored Kaileen, leaving her behind—big mistake. She jumped on the back of the one closest to her and threw her arms around his neck, causing him to gasp frantically for a breath of air which she was equally determined to refuse him. She expertly positioned her forearms behind his shoulder blades so that all he could do was claw at her hands. Upon seeing this, Brendan sprung from the ground toward the barbarian closest to him. He aimed his head at the man's chin, seeking to butt him like a billy goat. Brendan's aim was accurate. The sea raider's chin absorbed the full force of Brendan's head butt and the raider fell to the ground unconscious.

The remaining barbarian in the rear guard now vacillated between assisting the companion being choked by Kaileen or directing his attention to Brendan. He started to draw his sword from its sheath, but, before he complete the move, Dungal came sailing through the air, his legs split apart. Dungal's left leg caught the back of the barbarian's neck. The right caught the front, right under the chin. With a twisting movement, he threw the barbarian off his feet, crashing head first, backwards into the ground. This barbarian struck the ground dazed and unable to retaliate, just as the one went down with Kaileen on his back. Kaileen released her arms when she realized he had passed out from want of air. Dungal and Kaileen sprung to their feet. Dungal snatched the sword from the dazed sea raider and motioned for Kaileen and Brendan to head for cover. Brendan nodded he understood; but he didn't want to leave Dungal alone to fight eight of them— at least seven of which were still healthy and charging toward them at the moment.

Brendan spied a javelin in the grass. He hurled it with all his might toward the lead barbarian now running back down the hill towards them. The javelin pierced the sea raider's throat and he fell, the momentum of his forward motion causing him to roll down hill. The other barbarians were running too fast and too close to the one who fell. The first two stumbled and fell over the body with the next two falling over them. The last two sought to avoid the pileup by leaping over it, however they failed to jump high enough to clear the heap and came crashing down on the other side. Dungal signaled to Brendan they should split up by drawing both outstretched arms together and spreading them apart again. Brendan nodded he understood, and limped toward Kaileen.

"Dungal wants us to split up," he said. "You and I will go one way. He will go another."

"Okay, just a minute," she answered. Then Kaileen rolled the barbarian she'd subdued over and grabbed his sword. "We may need this," she continued.

"This way," Brendan shouted as he pointed at the shortest distance to the woods.

As Kaileen and Brendan disappeared into the woods they noticed Dungal sprinting as fast as he could for a point in the woods further downstream.

Brendan didn't want to wait long enough to see how many of the barbarians would follow Dungal and how many would pursue Kaileen and himself. He followed Kaileen down into the thicket of underbrush under the forest of ash and oak trees. As they moved into the woods, he could hear shouts from the barbarians weakening. Apparently most, if not all, had chosen to pursue Dungal. He and Kaileen pressed on however. A couple of hundred feet later, they stopped to listen. Brendan heard the telltale sounds of brush breaking which meant someone was pursuing them.

Kaileen grabbed Brendan's head and pulled it close so she could whisper right into his ear.

"With your bad leg, I don't think we can stay ahead of them. If we stop and stay perfectly silent, they may pass us by."

Brendan nodded he agreed. He then very slowly and silently crouched down until he was sitting on the ground. Kaileen followed, scarcely making a sound. It felt good to sit. Brendan was thankful for the chance to rest. He could hear the crunching of twigs as their pursuers approached. Then there was silence. Apparently the sea raiders were waiting to hear noise from Kaileen and himself to guide them in their pursuit. A moment later, the crunch resumed. The noise grew stronger as they approached. Kaileen put her arm around Brendan's waist and held him tight, while leaning her head on his shoulder. Moments later, Brendan could see the silhouettes of two figures in the heather, in the field of vision which lay directly ahead. They stopped again.

Brendan and Kaileen both held their breath, fearing their pursurers might hear them breathe. The two silhouettes remained motionless. Brendan felt like his lungs would cave in. Then, to his relief, the two barbarians began to move on. Both Kaileen and Brendan exhaled together. A few moments later, the silhouettes faded as the barbarians moved on.

"That was close," Kaileen whispered in Brendan's ear.

Brendan just nodded. He was afraid even whispering might betray their position. To relieve his tension and pass the time, Brendan massaged the trapezius muscle on the left side of Kaileen's neck with his left hand. Kaileen responded by massaging the same muscle on both sides of Brendan's neck. Brendan nearly went limp as the tension dissipated from his body. Kaileen's strong but gentle hands created a heavenly feeling. While moments earlier he'd been anxious to get up and be on his way, he now wanted this sensation to continue without end. A little later, however, Kaileen, apparently tiring from massaging his neck, stopped and whispered.

"I think we can get going now."

"Okay, but I wonder which way?" Brendan answered.

"Why don't we try to head downstream a little? Maybe that way we'll be able to cross it without the sea raiders spotting us." Kaileen suggested.

"Then what?" Brendan asked.

"Then we continue our journey to the northeast. We've got to get to someone who can put together an army to stop these barbarians."

Brendan, with Kaileen close behind, slowly picked his way through the brush. By the number of spider webs he encountered on the way to the stream, he could tell no one had passed this way for some time. The undergrowth provided cover all the way to the stream bank. Trees on both banks of the stream also arched over the water, creating a living arch with their branches. Brendan decided it was as protected a spot as any they would find to cross the stream.

When he stepped into water he was shocked by the cold. He hadn't bothered to take off his shoes. If he had to move fast, he didn't want to have to take time to put them back on. When he reached the middle, the water was up to mid-chest. He hoped it didn't get any higher. He looked at Kaileen. Fortunately she stood nearly as tall as he was so the water reached about the same height on her. The creek bottom began to slope uphill again, to Brendan's relief. He shivered as the air hit the soaked portion of his body. They climbed high up the next bank. Then Brendan decided to sit and listen for a minute. Satisfied he heard no sounds of barbarian movement, he continued up the side of the valley. They had to fight their way through a dense growth of holly, whitethorn, blackthorn spindle, guelder rose and briars. Brendan tried to cut through it with the captured barbarian's sword; but the barbarian apparantly had been lax in keeping it sharp. By the time they came upon a trail, Brendan's hands and forearms were filled with dozens of small cuts and scratches from rose thorns and briars.

Not wishing to fight the brush any longer, Brendan decided to follow the trail for awhile. Compared to cutting his way through brush, the trail beckoned as a swift means of travel. It was also wide enough that Kaileen could walk alongside him. She spoke in a low voice.

"I wonder what happened to Dungal?"

"Dungal is very fast. If he got a head start, which it appears he did, they're either still chasing him or they've given up trying. I don't see how men wearing body armor could possibly have caught up to him." Brendan answered her.

"Do you think we'll ever see him again?" Kaileen asked.

"Oh, he'll find us if he's a mind to."

Travelling along the trail was so much easier, it was almost pleasurable. Brendan's clothes were almost dry again. His shoes of untanned hide, which he had made himself, were still quite wet, but that didn't bother him. The sunrays poked through the canopy of trees like dozens of separate beams of light. The birds were singing again. A short distance ahead a hare scurried along the trail then ducked into the under growth.

"I hate to leave this trail; but we will have to do so soon if we are to continuue to the northeast," Brendan said to Kaileen.

"Why's that?"

"It appears to head downstream, parallelling the creek, which flows mostly west," Brendan answered her.

"That's too bad. It is so much easier following the trail... what's that?"

Brendan stopped. He could hear voices coming from the direction they had just traveled. They were too far away for him to recognize any words. Since the only other people he knew were around were the sea raiders, he had to assume it was them.

"I think it's the barbarians," he said. "They must have found this trail."

"What should we do now?" Kaileen asked.

"It looks like we have three choices: first we can continue on this trail and hope we can stay ahead of them, or second, we can try go overland again; but we risk them hearing us in the brush and we will travel much slower; and third, we can hide and wait till they pass, then we could follow the trail upstream and to the east."

"I like option three best." Kaileen told him.

"Sounds good to me," Brendan answered, "You see that holly bush up there?"

Kaileen looked to the direction Brendan pointed with his outstretched arm. "Yes."

"I think it will hide both of us. Let's climb up there."

"Okay."

Brendan and Kaileen scrambled up the hill as quickly as Brendan's leg would allow. Brendan dripped with sweat from the exertion as they reached the bush. They ducked behind the holly shrub just as the first of the sea warriors became visible on the trail below. As they watched, four barbarians silently passed by on the trail below. Brendan was sure they were part of the scouting party who'd captured them earlier. He involuntarily held his breath, worried they might hear him exhale. When they were out of sight, the air compressed in his lungs burst out in a long pulse.

"Whew. I think if we wait a few minutes, it should be safe to climb down to the trail again." Brendan whispered to Kaileen.

She nodded and she reached out and took Brendan's left hand in hers, rubbing it to reassure him. A few minutes later, the sounds of birds chirping and the beat of their wings told Brendan it was safe to move about again. As he stood and began to move downhill, Kaileen took his arm and placed it on her shoulder to assist him in the descent. They had progressed about half the distance to the trail when it happened. Kaileen apparently set her foot down on a loose stone and one foot slid out from under her. The additional weight from Brendan relying on her for support conspired with gravity to send the both of them rolling down the hill. Kaileen let out an involuntary shriek as they tumbled, rolling alternately over and under each other until Brendan came to rest on the dirt path, cheek to cheek with Kaileen on top of him. He lay for a moment, enjoying the delightful pressure of Kaileen's cheek against his. Kaileen, however quickly scrambled to her feet.

"Sorry about that," she said, vigorously brushing the dust from her body.

"Don't worry about it. Nothing damaged. How about you?" Brendan answered.

Kaileen looked particularly sensuous with her hair mussed up and the odd bit of twig and leaf dispersed in it like carefully placed decorations. Brendan paused to take in the lovely image before him. Kaileen, apparently sensing the reason for his stare, prodded.

"Are you going to lie there all day? We need to be on our way. And what are you looking at?"

Brendan slowly rose to his feet. He searched for words to express how lovely he thought she looked and was about to deliver what he considered a witty response when the sound of rapid footsteps behind him distracted him. He spun around to see a dirty blond bearded figure charging at him, javelin pointing at Brendan's throat. Brendan grabbed the hilt of the sword in his scabbard; but before he could draw the weighty weapon from it, the four sea raiders had him surrounded. With javelins pointed at his neck and chest, Brendan let the sword slide back into his scabbard. One of the sea raiders grabbed Brendan's sword and pulled it out again. Then, apparently recognizing that Brendan wore a scabbard crafted by the race of sea raiders, he motioned for Brendan to remove it.

As Brendan unbuckled the belt, it suddenly occurred to him that all the raiders had their attention on him. This prompted him to shout: "Run, Kaileen!"

With Brendan's prompting, Kaileen shed her pack and darted down the trail to the east. Two of Brendan's captors gave chase. Kaileen, however, had enough of a head start and was apparently capable of outrunning her heavily armed pursuers. Brendan glanced over his shoulder to see Kaileen with the warriors in pursuit disappear down the trail. In response to Brendan's action, the two captors seized him by the arms and shoulders and forced him face down into the dirt. Brendan coughed and spit in an effort to clear the dust from his nose and throat. The barbarians lashed his hands together behind his back with a leather strap. Then they lifted Brendan to his feet. The barbarian with the dirty blond beard said something to him he didn't understand and jabbed Brendan with the tip of his javelin indicating Brendan should start walking along the trail to the east also. Sometime later, Brendan spotted two bodies sprawled on the hillside next to the trail. As Brendan and his two captors approached, the two figures ahead sprung to their feet. Brendan now recognized them as the two who chased Kaileen earlier. Apparently Kaileen had managed to run them to exhaustion and still escape.

When Brendan and his captors reached these two barbarians, the four warriors exchanged a lot of words. Even though Brendan couldn't understand the language, he was sure his two captors were ribbing the other two about losing a girl! Brendan smiled at the thought that Kaileen had managed to elude these two. The barbarian, seeing the expression of pleasure on Brendan's face, slapped him hard on the side of the face; then prodded Brendan to move on.

They walked until the sun began to drop low in the sky. Brendan noted that the barbarians had successfully retraced the route they had traveled across the creek and were now coming upon the meadow where Dungal, Kaileen and himself had escaped the sea warriors before. A feeling of sadness permeated Brendan's body when he thought of Kaileen and Dungal.

Although he was glad they were free, he missed having friends at his side. Brendan thought of Kaileen's lovely round face and delicate pink lips. Just as he formed this mental image, he was shocked back to the sense of current place and time by a painful blow on his right shoulder. This was followed the swish and thud of rocks sailing into the tall grass and shrubs. Brendan turned to his right only to see a hail of stones coming at them from that direction. This was followed by the most blood curdling scream Brendan had ever heard.

# CHAPTER 7

All four of Brendan's captors raised their shields and turned in the direction of the scream. One scream followed another, each increasing in volume. Through the space between two of the sea warriors, Brendan could see a dozen or so white shields moving towards him as their bearers advanced, stopping every several steps to sling another round of rocks at the party of sea warriors. The barbarians were clearly being attacked; but Brendan couldn't identify the attackers. He knew they were his countrymen from the white linen tunics and trousers they wore. Then Brendan noticed the sea warrior's attention was fixed on the approaching Irish warriors. This was his chance. He slowly backed away from the barbarians. They paid no attention to Brendan's escape attempt. The two warriors without javelins drew their swords. An Irish spear flew toward one of them, but he adroitly deflected it with his shield.

Brendan fled further, seeking more distance from his captors; but eventually curiosity got the better of him and he turned to watch the fight. The four barbarians were fighting madly now. Standing back to back to prevent being struck from the rear, they thrust at their attackers with javelins and slashed with their broadswords. One of the barbarians split the wicker shield of his Irish attacker and dropped him with a second blow to the head. While he was doing this, however, another Irishman managed to pierce his side with a spear. The barbarian turned and began to attack his new assailant as though nothing had happened to him. The Irishman held his small round shield up to ward off the blows, backing away and extracting his spear from the sea warrior's body. A couple more swings and the sea warrior fell face down in the grass.

The remaining three continued to fight, surrounded now by the linen clad Irish warriors, each wearing a brightly dyed cloak—red, blue, green, all the colors of the rainbow seemed to be represented. A cloud of white dust formed as the sea warrior's blows thudded against the shields of the Irish soldiers. The second of the barbarians fell, then was quickly dispatched from his worldly woes by the thrust of an Irish spear through his throat. This one was followed by a third, struck on the skull from behind by an Irish battle ax. Now alone, the Irish soldiers fell upon the remaining Barbarian. They knocked him from his feet. Brendan lost sight of this barbarian under the pile of Irish warriors for a moment. The Irish captors then stood their prey back on his feet, relieved of armor, helmet, shield and weapons which his captors distributed among themselves as souvenirs. The barbarian, face and arms bloodied by the skirmish, had his hands trussed and bound behind his back like Brendan. The invaders vanquished, a short, but powerful looking Irish soldier turned toward Brendan.

"Come here, lad," he ordered.

Brendan hobbled over to this man.

"And who would you be?" the Irish soldier asked.

Brendan looked over the man before answering. The sweat of battle caused the linen of his tunic to cling to his chest revealing the large, plate-shaped outline of his pectoral muscles underneath. A dark curly beard protruded outward from his face at a smart angle, and short-cropped curly hair was visible where not covered by his leather battle cap. Between beard and hair, Brendan could see little of his face, noticing only his piercing dark brown eyes.

"I'm, I'm... Brendan, I was born near a village some call Kilrush," Brendan stammered.

"Ah, ye need not be afraid of us, me lad," the dark-haired soldier replied, "Unless, of course, you be a cattle rustler, my master has no use for them," he continued.

"No sir, I used to be a herder, but I've never stolen another man's property," Brendan answered.

"Good! What say we release you from your bondage?" the soldier replied.

"Thank you. May I ask your name sir?"

"You may, my lad. My name is Kilian; I am a knight in the service of Finian, King of the land that surrounds you. Colgu, Dicuil, undo this boy's hands. The rest of you relieve the dear departed of their wordly valuables, and give them a proper burial; but bury our fallen brother first."

As Colgu and Dicuil went to work on Brendan's bonds, Kilian asked.

"What puts you in this place at this time; and what can you tell me about these four we've just vanquished?" Kilian pressed.

"They are raiders from the sea. Several nights ago they attacked Kilrush. They killed all the men there except Father Sweeney, who they nearly killed but left for dead. They seized the women and bound them; for what purpose I don't know. One girl, Kaileen, was among them. She was a friend so I found a way to release her as well as the other women. We've been on the run ever since from the barbarians. Oh, by the way, have you seen anything of a girl about my age?"

"Possibly, could you describe her?" Kilian responded.

"Well, she's sixteen years, beautiful hair, about the color of a beech tree leaf in autumn, reaching to her breasts. She has gentle brown eyes, the type that can see into your soul; and the sweetest pink lips..." Brendan started to answer.

"Ah, it sounds like the young colleen has captured your heart," Kilian interrupted, then continued. "We did run across such a girl a short while ago. She told us of your capture and begged our assistance."

Then Kilian put two fingers to his teeth an issued a shrill whistle. Brendan saw a solitary figure rise from the grass in the distance. As it moved toward them, he immediately recognized Kaileen.

"Kaileen!" he shouted, thrilled to be reunited.

Kaileen waved her hand over her head in recognition. As she approached, Kilian continued:

"My lads and I have been patrolling this area. Some of the lads from other tribes like to steal my master's cattle. King Finian has us patrol to discourage such activities. Anyway, the young lass, Kaileen right? stumbled upon us after she escaped the barbarians. She begged our help and led us here. Do you know if there are others of these foreigners about?"

"We counted 569 embarking inland from the ship, most of these I suspect are still somewhere between us and the great river now." Brendan answered.

"Five hundred sixty-nine! Ah, we'd best not dally around here. We need to tell King Finian. He'll need to raise an army to defend his kingdom. Be quick with those bodies, lads," Kilian replied. Then, just as Kaileen came astride Brendan, he turned to the two of them and continued.

"I'm going to have to order a forced march straight for Dun-Finian, the King's rath. I must insist the two of you accompany us. The King will want to question you at length about these barbarians. Can you keep up with us, young miss?"

"Sure, but Brendan here can't. One of his legs is lame from birth. We promise we'll follow you though; but we may arrive as much as a day later." Kaileen explained.

Brendan spoke to Kaileen: "You go with them, I'll follow alone. There's no need us both risk being captured again."

"Now if I leave you to your own wits, you'll be captured for sure," Kaileen fired back. "You need a thinking person to assist you, Brendan," she continued.

"There's no need for you to be lagging behind," Kilian broke in. Then he motioned to two of the soldiers who were pushing the last of the dirt into one of the shallow graves.

"You two, come here. And bring two of the captured shields as well as the barbarian's spears," Kilian ordered.

The two men did as instructed. When they stood before Kilian, he continued:

"Make a litter of these. You know how."

Brendan watched as the two soldiers ran the javelins through the arm straps of the shields, leaving the convex surfaces of the shields facing the sky. Kilian looked at Brendan and continued:

"When we leave, climb upon this. My men will transport you, so you'll have no problem keeping up with us. Now let's have the prayers for our fallen countryman."

Kaileen and Brendan joined the soldiers in a circle around the grave of the soldier killed by the barbarians. Kilian made a short speech.

"May God receive the soul of our brother Ailil. He fought with courage against the heathen foe. Ailil asked not much of this world, a cup of mead and the kiss of a lovely colleen now and then were his only pleasures. He served his king well these past five years."

After these words, each of the soldiers solemnly grabbed a fistful of dirt and threw it into the grave. Kilian spoke again.

"Lads, fill Ailil's grave quickly. We best be on our way."

Following this command, each of the foot soldiers set about filling in the hole. A couple of them scupped dirt with wedges of wood sliced from a nearby tree. Others just kicked in the soil. When the entire hole was filled, they mounded the dirt in the shape of a half cylinder and mounted a cross made of two stout oak branches lashed together with vine on one end. Compared to the three barbarian graves, Ailil's suggested it bore the body of a man of noble birth.

"Let's be off," Killian ordered. Then he pointed to two of the soldiers and continued.

"You two. Strap our captive to the back end of the litter. We might as well get a bit of work out of him. We'll each take turns on the front end."

The two soldiers fashioned a yoke from some leather straps and hung one and about the sea warrior's neck, then one of the soldiers handed his shield to his partner and picked up the front end.

"Hop on, Master Brendan, and we'll be off," Kilian ordered.

Brendan climbed upon one shield and stretched his legs, resting his feet on the other one. With Kilian in the lead, and Kaileen following Brendan's litter, the party set off on the trail into the woods, heading northeast once again. The soldiers moved fast, almost jogging along the trail. Brendan looked back at Kaileen. She seemed to have no trouble keeping up with them.

\*\*\*\*

Two nights passed and near noon on the day following, Brendan caught his first glimpse of Dun-Finian. In the distance, it looked like a great hat dropped by an ancient mythological god upon the land. Two concentric rings of earth surrounded a large mound of earth in the center. As the party approached closer, Brendan could see that a large building occupied the top of the center mound.

"What is on top of that mound?" he asked, pointing at the building.

"Ah, that that would be the house of King Finian," Kilian began. "Before you, is Dun-Finian, the great rath of King Finian," he continued.

As they approached the fortress, Brendan beheld a great field of standing stones, randomly scattered, like so many frozen soldiers before the rath.

"What are those?" he asked.

"King Finian had those stones hauled and erected to discourage the sudden onrush of an attacking army," the soldier bearing the front of his litter replied.

Moments later, the column of soldiers, Brendan and Kaileen included, snaked their way through the tortuous path of stone guardians. A short distance in, Kilian stopped short.

"I think we'd best blindfold our captive. He shouldn't become too knowledgeable about the entrance to Dun-Finian. Master Brendan can walk in from here anyway."

Brendan slid off the makeshift litter. Two of the soldiers then took the sea warrior in hand and cut off part of the sleeve of the barbarian's garment to make a blindfold. Once the blindfold was in place, Kilian continued to lead them along the twisted path. The path led to a small green field between the stone sentries and the open timber gate in the earthen dike of the rath. As they crossed this field, Brendan observed several dozen young men, some about his age, but most a little older, tumbling, doing hand stands, cartwheels and other stunts while a large man stood with his hands on his hips barking commands.

"What's going on?" Brendan asked the soldier in front of him.

"They're new recruits for King's bodyguard. The Master of the Sword is putting them through their agility exercises. A soldier's got to be flexible. If he's not nimble, he's likely to be cut down," the soldier explained.

The sentry on the gate brought his hand to his chest in a smart salute as Kilian approached him.

"Top o' the morning, Captain," the sentry greeted.

"Good day to you too, Shamus," Kilian answered him.

As Brendan passed through the gate in the outer dike, Kaileen came up astride him, pulling on his left arm.

"Tis a grand place it is," she said in a quiet voice.

"Yes it is," Brendan responded.

Brendan looked ahead. Before them was a second dike, rising another six to eight feet higher than the first. To his left and right between the two dikes, Brendan could see nothing but murky water, except for the dry strip of land upon which they walked. They passed through a second gate. Two sentries snapped to attention and saluted as they passed through. A few paces on the other side of the gateway, a lad about Brendan's age came running toward them. He stopped in front of Captain Kilian, sweat dripping from his brow.

"Message from the King, sir," he panted.

"Take a moment to catch your breath then let's have it," Kilian ordered.

Brendan watched as the boy inhaled deeply and expelled the air.

"The King grants an immediate audience with the Captain, sir," he gasped.

Kilian turned to his men.

"It appears the King summons me immediately. Show our stranger to an underground cell and keep the Master Brendan and Miss Kaileen with you. I shall return as soon as possible."

"No, I mean the King wishes to see the entire party, sir. He spotted your arrival and noted the number in your party had increased. He also noted your men bore someone on a litter. The King is anxious for a report, sir."

"Very well, take us to the King," Kilian ordered.

Kilian and his men, the captured barbarian, Kaileen and Brendan all followed the boy. On the other side of the second embankment, Brendan noticed the many timber dwellings arranged along the concentric land between the second earthen dike and the mound supporting the king's residence before him.

The houses appeared as large mushrooms tossed by some giant upon the ground, with wall of white plaster and conical roofs of straw.

"I wonder who lives in these houses?" Brendan queried Kaileen.

"These houses belong to the servants who attend the king. They house the wives and children of his personal bodyguard, the royal cooks, the historian, and others." One of the soldiers interrupted, overhearing Brendan.

"And that would be the king's residence, atop the hill before us?" Brendan asked the soldier. Before him Brendan could now see a path of flagstone steps spiraling around a large hill upon which sat what surely must be the King's residence.

"That be it," the soldier answered.

"Oooh, it's so magnificent, Brendan," Kaileen cooed.

"Yes, I'll bet you could put six of the servants' houses in it," Brendan marveled out loud.

"And the colors," Kaileen started, "They're so beautiful!"

Brendan noted that, in contrast to the white walls of the lower residences, the king's two story residence had lower walls of brillant green and upper ones of sunburst yellow with the exposed timber post and beams being painted a deep brown. The north, south, east and west of the residence were marked by red, orange, blue and purple flags, blowing in the breeze. Kilian led them up the flagstone steps which were adorned with moss in the areas not subject to heavy foot traffic. For Brandon it was a tedious climb, but one where he moved nearly as fast as the others because the act of climbing slowed them down. The trail finally terminated on a level green, bordered by semicircular rows of flowers on each side and before them were two massive doors of rough hewn oak with a man on each side, shields on arm at the ready and hands on their sword hilts. Upon seeing Kilian they snapped to attention, throwing a hand to their chest in salute. After saluting, each man grabbed a handle and pulled a leaf of the double door open for Captain Kilian to enter.

Once inside, Brendan was struck with awe. In the center of the room was the biggest fireplace he had ever seen, constructed in a circular shape on native limestone. Before the fireplace sat a lone man eating what appeared to be a rack of lamb's ribs at the head of a long table which Brendan estimated could easily seat ten warriors each side. Forming two large, nearly complete semicircles, concentric with the fireplace were interior partitions. Each semicircular partition had four openings in it, with a curtain to cover the opening. One of the openings to Brendan's right had the curtain drawn, revealing a bed within.

Captain Kilian then turned to the two soldiers escorting the barbarian prisoner.

"Take him outside until I call you," he ordered.

Then, looking at Brendan and Kaileen, he said, "Wait here till I call you."

After giving the order, the Captain removed his leather helmet and approached the man at the head of the table. Brendan saw the man only casually look at the approaching Captain. Brendan could make out little of the man's facial features from a distance. He had long red hair, probably once brillant but now subdued by a large amount of gray and a great bushy beard. He wore a deep purple tunic from which protruded two massive forearms. When the Captain was only a couple of seats from the head of the table, the man set down the rib bone he'd been gnawing, took a sip from a golden goblet and spoke.

"Let's hear of your trip," the man demanded.

"Sire, I bring news of an invasion to your kingdom," Captain Kilian began.

"Invasion! What tribe has dared to challenge King Finian?" the man shouted.

"They are not of Ireland, sire, they are foreigners, coming here in massive ships, killing our kinsmen, and taking our women to be their slaves. My men and I freed these two youths from a small party of them. We managed to take one prisoner but I'm afraid we lost Ailil. We buried him where he was slain."

"Ah that's a grand loss, I'll go to see his mother later," the man said, "Bid the youths come forward."

Captain Kilian motioned to Brendan and Kaileen. Timidly they walked forward until they were alongside Captain Kilian.

"Brendan, Kaileen, I'd like to present you to King Finian," Kilian said.

Brendan was at a loss for words but Kaileen did a short curtesy, and answered.

"Pleased to meet you sire."

"Yes, me too," the words stumbled out of Brendan's mouth.

"Relax, sit down. You too, captain. Colgu, come here." King Finian bellowed.

A lean old man wearing a leather apron over a coarse linen tunic appeared, coming from behind the fireplace.

"You called, sire?" Colgu asked.

"Bring food and drink for these three," King Finian ordered.

"But sire I only prepared enough for your midday meal," the servant protested.

"Search the pantry then! I'm sure you can find something: bread, cheese, whatever you can find. Just don't keep them waiting."

As Colgu disappeared into the shadows, King Finian spoke again.

"Oh Colgu's a loyal cook; but at times I think the Lord slighted him when he passed out the brains. While we're waiting, who wants to talk first about these barbarians?"

"I would, sire," Kaileen blurted.

"Well let's hear from you, miss," the king entreated.

Kaileen went on to tell the story, starting from the attack and sacking of Kilrush right up to their arrival at Dun Finian. Brendan saw a frown form in the wrinkles on the king's face as Kaileen spoke of the numbers of barbarians who disembarked from the ships. When Kaileen was finished, the King pushed back in his seat and sighed. He appeared about to speak when Colgu arrived with a large tray. He set copper goblets before each of them and filled each with ale. Following, he set a round of cheese within easy reach of all of them, provided a round of bread for each with knives and small containers of butter and honey.

"That will be all, Colgu," King Finian said. "Captain Kilian, I want you to send runners to all the tribal chiefs. Tell them King Finian requires his tribute of soldiers seven nights from this day at Dun Finian."

"Yes, sire, may I have your leave to do so now?" Captain Kilian asked.

King Finian was about to speak when the outer door opened and one of Kilian's soldier's ran in.

"Sir, the barbarian's escaped," the soldier announced, his chest heaving.

"Sire, I must attend to this straight away. That barbarian knows the way to Dun Finian. If he finds his way back to the others of his race, he'll lead them directly here no doubt." Captain Kilian hurriedly explained.

"Go then," the king answered.

Brendan and Kaileen watched in shock as Captain Kilian and the soldier rushed out the door. The voice of King Finian broke the spell of the moment.

"And now, what should we do with you two?"

This time Brendan responded first, an idea blossoming in his mind.

"Sire, I'm a trained herdsman, if you need help with your sheep or cattle."

"I don't keep sheep myself. I've tenants that bring me one in tribute when I request it. I do have a cattle herd. Yes, I might be able to use you there. Mostly likely we'll have to press some of the regular herdsmen into service as soldiers to meet this barbarian threat. When we've finished eating, I'll have one of my guards take you to the head herdsman."

The king then looked directly at Kaileen.

"Now, my dear, what about you?"

"Well, sire, my mother and I had a small shop making clothes; but the sea warriors burned our place. My mother was away at the time and Brendan and I have been so busy running from the sea warriors that we haven't had time to search for her. I'd like to find her again."

King Finian put his mighty hand to his chin and pondered a moment. Then he replied.

"With these barbarians running about, I think it's best you remain here for a while; but I'll have my runners spread the word that you're here and ask about the whereabouts of your mother. Guards!"

When the king hollered the last two words, the doors opened and the two guards Brendan had seen earlier rushed in. Even before they reached the king he started shouting orders.

"You," King Finian said as he pointed to the guard on his right, "Fetch my daughter."

"And you," the king pointed to the other guard, "Tell Captain Kilian to see me before he sends runners to the other chiefs."

Both guards beat their chests in a hasty salute, stood about face, and ran out, slamming the great doors shut behind them. The king looked at Kaileen again,

"What is your mother's name, and what does she look like?" the king asked.

"Her name is Cummie, and she's very beautiful," Kaileen responded.

"Well she may be that, but I'll need a little more of a description. I don't want to give my soldiers an excuse to bring in every beautiful woman in the kingdom."

Kaileen giggled a little. Brendan was glad to see she could relax enough to laugh.

"She's nearly as tall as Captain Kilian, has a very slender build, hair the color of your beard that falls halfway down her back, a lean face that belies her forty years and gentle blue eyes. The last time I saw her she wore a purple dress with white trim about the hem and sleeve ends and a black hooded cloak," Kaileen responded.

"Ah, that's much better," King Finian responded. "Now, how would you feel about becoming a handmaiden to my daughter?"

"I'd be honored, sire," Kaileen responded.

"Then so it will be."

Just as King Finian completed this last statement, one leaf of the great oak door and a solitary figure entered again. It was Captain Kilian. He strode briskly to King Finian. Brendan saw sweat dripping from his brow, and Kilian breathed laboriously. Before the captain could utter a word, King Finian spoke.

"What of the barbarian?" he asked.

"I've got your soldiers looking for him but I'm concerned about our chances of catching him again; he had a pretty good head start."

"How'd he get loose?" the king demanded.

"My men were lax in checking his bonds. Apparently he worked his hands free from the leather thongs that bound him. He waited until one of the men was distracted momentarily by a pretty maiden passing by. The barbarian then struck the other with his fist. The guard he struck was stunned long enough for the barbarian to snatch his sword from its scabbard. The barbarian then gave each guard a blow to the head with the sword. Their helmets saved them from death; but both were knocked unconscious. One of your door guards was nearby and gave chase, but the barbarian disappeared into the brush on the side of the hill. The guard returned to get help to search the rath."

"And the two men who were guarding him, how are they?" the king asked.

"In a lot of pain. Your physician is attending to them. He thinks they have a better than even chance of recovering."

"I hope they do. Call off the search. We can't waste the time or manpower searching for that one barbarian. Just alert all the guards to be on the lookout for him. Right now we need to get those runners dispatched. Round them up and bring them here. I want to instruct them personally," King Finian ordered.

"Yes, sire," Captain Kilian answered, then turned smartly and jogged for the door.

When the Captain was gone, the king turned to Kaileen.

"We'll get the word out on your mother. If she's roaming about my kingdom, I'm sure we'll locate her."

Before the king could continue, one of the heavy doors leaves opened again. In walked the most beautiful lady Brendan had ever seen.

# CHAPTER 8

"You sent for me, Daddy?" she asked.

As she strode across the room, Brendan scanned her from head to foot. She wore a white lace shawl over her shoulder length hair. She had wide, sensual eyebrows that matched her golden hair and gave a sense of mystery to her eyes. She wore a long purple dress which tightly hugged her upper body—slim, superbly sculpted. Below the waist, the fullness of the dress obscured the rest of her form.

"Yes, dear, I want you to meet your new handmaiden," the king replied, gesturing with his hand toward Kaileen.

Kaileen stood up.

"Pleased to meet you, ma'am," Kaileen greeted.

"Oh, call me Failend," the king's daughter insisted, "And please sit down."

Failand took the seat at her father's right hand, formerly occupied by Captain Kilian and directly across from Kaileen.

"Your new handmaiden is Kaileen and this is Brendan. He rescued Kaileen from slavery to some seafaring barbarians, and is largely responsible for her being here today. I've offered him a position as a herdsman," the king explained.

"How gallant," Failend said, enticing his undivided attention with her smile.

"That I'm a herdsman?" Brendan asked.

"No, that you saved Kaileen," Failend answered.

Brendan thought the words rolled from her lips like bubbling water down the rocks of a waterfall—clear, lively, and refreshing.

"Oh," he responded.

She so captivated him that he couldn't think of anything intelligent to say. Fortunately, a loud banging on the outside door distracted everyone at the table.

"Enter," the king bellowed.

The door opened and a young soldier, quite out of breath, ran forward and bowed before King Finian.

"Sire, is Captain Kilian about?" he panted.

"No, he went to attend to a matter of a runaway prisoner," the king explained, "But if you bear an important message for the Captain, let's hear it."

"Sire, we've captured the prisoner!" the soldier exclaimed, his chest swelled with pride.

"Let's have him in here, then," the king ordered.

"Aye, sir."

The soldier then beat his chest in a hasty salute, stood about face, and ran for the entrance doors. A moment later the heavy doors opened wide. With the brightness of the daylight behind them, Brendan could only make out three silhouettes at first. As the three men advanced toward the king, Brendan saw that two soldiers were escorting a man, hands and ankles cuffed in chains, between them. The man had his head down, in an apparent gesture of defeat. Brendan recognized something familar about the man; but he was sure the prisoner was not the barbarian captured on the trail. Something was wrong. For one thing, the clothes were not like the barbarian's; but the clothes did look familiar. Then the prisoner's head lifted. Immediately, Brendan recognized the bearded face as the prisoner's frown melted into a smile as his eyes met Brendan's. The prisoner was Dungal!

"Sire, this man's a friend of mine!" Brendan blurted spontaneously.

"You say this is not one of the barbarians?" the king bellowed at Brendan.

"But we spotted him in the woods beyond the gate to the rath," one of the soldiers protested, "He would not answer any questions we put to him. He didn't seem to understand us. We were sure he was the foreigner."

"He can't speak sire. He's been dumb since birth, but can make his thoughts known with gestures. If you unshackle him, you may ask him what you will and I will interpret his answers for you."

"Remove the chains," King Finian ordered.

The two soldiers removed both the wrist and ankle shackles. Dungal rubbed both wrists in a sign of relief.

"Ask him why he was in the woods beyond my rath," the king ordered.

"Begging your pardon, sire," Brendan started. "He understands you quite well. He only needs me to interpret his answers."

"Well get on with it then," King Finian said impatiently.

Brendan stood up and turned toward Dungal. "Answer the king," he ordered.

Dungal began gesturing, with Brendan interpreting for the king.

"After we split up, I ran into the woods with the barbarians in pursuit. They are too fat and heavily burdened with armor. I ran for a long time. After a while, they gave up; but I kept going to put some distance between me and them. When I was sure I'd lost them, I headed to the northeast, for the reputation of the great King Finian for generosity is known by even those as far away as Kilrush. I thought I might find someone who'd hire me here."

"And what kind of work can a dumb man do?" King Finian asked.

"Dungal can do many things. You'd be amazed, sire," Brendan answered.

Dungal made a slashing gesture with his hand, as though wielding a sword.

"He'd like to serve in your army," Brendan translated.

"A soldier?" the king responded.

"Yes, sire. Dungal is very strong and agile. I've seen him in action against the barbarians. He fights like three men!"

"You may have a high opinion of your friend, but my soldiers need to be able to communicate with each other. I can't use him as a soldier."

"How about as a herdsman? That way I can be around to interpret for him if necessary." Brendan suggested.

The king thought a moment, stroking the beard on his chin as he pondered. Then he answered.

"Very well, he can work with you, Brendan. That way, he can replace one of my herdsmen. I can use the man he replaces in my army."

The king then looked at the guards.

"One of you lead these two to my cattle herd. Inform two of my herdsman that their king requires them for military service" the king ordered.

"Father, can't we give Dungal something to eat first? He looks so hungry!" Failend interrupted.

Brendan looked to Failend. He thought he saw an unusal gleam in her eye. Was she attracted to Dungal? Perhaps. She surely didn't look at him that way. Brendan felt a pang of jealousy. She turned to look at Dungal. In the profile view, Failend's upturned nose made her look delightfully perky. Brendan wanted her for himself. She was a princess though. Herdsmen, even the best of herdsmen, couldn't hope to court a princess. Still, Brendan harbored a hope some upheaval in society would make it possible.

"Ah, my daughter, you're as generous as a saint with your father's victuals. Very well, sit your self down, young man, and we'll feed you."

"You may sit next to me," Failend entreated.

"Yo, Colgu," the king hollered.

When Colgu appeared the king ordered him to bring bread, cheese, and beer for Dungal. Brendan really felt jealous now. He couldn't help but picture Dungal and Failend sitting side by side as king and queen. For the first time in his life, it struck Brendan that Dungal, properly groomed and dressed could easily be taken for nobility.

**\*\*\*\***

Brendan pushed the sheepskin cover back and sat up. He rubbed his head vigorously with both hands, to brush the straw from his hair. He surveyed his surroundings. Next to him, buried under another sheepskin robe, Dungal continued to sleep. They were surrounded by the wicker walls of a crudely constructed shelter. Brendan then remembered where he was. After they'd eaten with King Finian, his daughter, and Kaileen, the soldiers had led them to the pasture where King Finian's cattle grazed. The soldiers introduced them to Feargus, the foreman or master of the herdsmen. Feargus, an older man, with light brown stringy hair streaked with gray, scowled at the thought of giving up two of his best herdsman for the king's army. Feargus appeared to be made of leather. He wore some type of cowskin trousers, a sleeveless leather shirt and a sheepskin cloak. Feargus had skin so taut and weathered that Brendan could scarcely distinguish it from the leather Feargus wore.

Feargus didn't appear too pleased when he discovered two of his best herdsmen were being replaced by a boy with a club foot and a man who couldn't talk. After the soldiers left, Feargus spent the rest of the afternoon walking Brendan and Dungal around the pasture. Feargus would stop from time to time to point out one of the herd, describing some peculiar characteristic about that animal. It was if he knew each of the animals as well as a father knows his children.

Finally, he led Brendan and Dungal to the hut they now slept in. Feargus and the herdsmen had built several of these on the periphery of each of the pastures where they grazed the king's cattle. As Feargus put it: "There's no reason not to enjoy the comfort of shelter from the wind and rain." Before they settled for the night, Brendan and Dungal split up the night watch. Dungal took the first watch; but, Brendan, making the mistake of staying in the comfort of the hut during his watch, had fallen asleep. He decided he'd better get up and count the cattle. He hoped none had wandered off or been snatched by rustlers during the night. He stood up and stretched to get the blood circulating to his extremities. He grabbed his cloak and threw it about his shoulders. He left the hut and began to walk around the herd, counting as he went. A morning fog hung above the meadow grass. Brendan pondered how peaceful it seemed compared to the events of the past several days. Still the image of Failend burned in his mind—and there was Kaileen. Was he ever to be close to either one of them again? He wished that once, just one time, that he could touch Failend's gentle lips with his.

A strange sound punctured this thought. Actually it was only strange because he'd rarely heard it in the pasture where he tended sheep. It was the sound of hoofbeats. Hoofbeats meant horses and, to Brendan, horses meant nobility. Most people around Kilrush were too poor to own horses. A few of the more wealthy farmers had draft horses, but generally oxen pulled the plows and carts. Brendan turned to face the wind, for the wind seemed to be carrying the sound of the hoofs toward him. Coming out of the woods now were two horses; one was without a rider. On the other horse, there appeared to be two riders. From the current distance, Brendan could make out two heads but could see only one body. A moment later the horses turned so Brendan could see them in profile. Two figures on one horse, a brilliant black one, appeared to be leading the second horse, a magnificent gray one.

Curious, Brendan started across the pasture toward them. As he got closer, both horses stopped. Brendan could now determine that both riders were women for they wore women's clothes. He noted that the second rider had apparently been grasping the first. The first woman swung her leg adeptly over the horse's withers and slid to the ground holding out her hand to assist the second rider in dismounting.

The two riders now had Brendan thoroughly entranced now so he moved closer. A few paces closer and he recognized them. It was the beautiful princess Failend with horse in hand and Kaileen.

When Brendan was within earshot, Kaileen spoke out excitedly.

"Hi."

"Hi," Brendan responded.

Apparently sensing Brendan's curiosity, Kaileen went on to explain.

"My lady, Failend, brought me to this meadow to teach me how to ride a horse."

"But I order you not to tell my father of this," Failend butted in, "He does not approve of me riding without a soldier escort, and he would never approve of me teaching a servant."

"Your secret's safe with me," Brendan answered, glad he now had something intimate to share with the beautiful Failend.

Failend helped Kaileen on to the gray horse and remounted herself. She looked magnificent sitting upon the black stallion. She, like Kaileen, rode bareback, legs astride the horses, their dresses rising to above their knees, showing off two shapely pairs of legs. Failend noticed Brendan staring and asked.

"What are you looking at?"

"The exquisite beauty of the Princess Failend, daughter of my master, King Finian," Brendan answered, hoping that he hadn't insulted Failend by gawking at her.

"Just so you remember my father is your master, young Brendan. Now if you'll excuse us, I'm going to get on with Kaileen's lesson."

With this statement, Failend tapped her horse with a small whip she carried in her hand and both horses moved off. As Kaileen passed Brendan on her horse, she stuck her tongue out at Brendan and whispered his words back at him.

"The exquisite beauty of the Princess Failend."

Brendan watched for a little while. Failend guided Kaileen's horse around the pasture for awhile first. Then she gave the reign to Kaileen and they began to ride at a walk, stopping every once in awhile to turn circles, first in one direction, then in the opposite. Then they would back the horses. When it appeared that Failend decided the lesson had gone on long enough, she and Kaileen disappeared into the woods, heading in the direction of the rath. Brendan went back to counting the cattle. It turned out he was one short on the count; but he found that one had wandered into the woods. Satisfied he hadn't lost any cattle by falling asleep on his first night, Brendan went back to see if Dungal was awake yet.

\*\*\*\*

The riding lessons continued every day but Sunday for many days after that. Brendan, often with Dungal, when Dungal woke early, delighted in watching the two of them. Once, when Failend was boosting Kaileen onto her horse, she thrust with such vigor that Kaileen went sailing over the back of the horse and into the dirt of the pasture on the other side. Kaileen sprung back up though, apparently unhurt. When Failend saw Kaileen was unhurt they giggled uncontrollably for awhile before continuing the lesson. Another time, when Failend decided to pick up the pace, Kaileen, unaccustomed to a horse trotting, bounced all over the horses back and finally off. Brendan thought he heard her horse laugh that time. On still another day, Kaileen's horse, cantering along, stopped suddenly at the edge of a stream, sending Kaileen sailing over his head and into the stream. She came out of the stream soaked, but unhurt. After several weeks, however, Brendan noticed she had gained considerable skill and was riding nearly as smoothly as Failend, her instructor.

In the meantime, the countryside was buzzing with activity. Every day new men arrived at Dun Finian to join the King's army. Some told stories of the barbarians attacking farms to the west, even looting a monastery. Since few of these stories were eyewitness reports, no one knew exactly what the truth was. The one truth everyone shared was that the barbarians hadn't been spotted near Dun Finian. As the new recruits for the army trained for future action against the sea warriors on the green outside the rath, one could hear the thud of wood swords against shields, and see a cloud of white dust around the practice field. Meanwhile, patrols of armed soldiers—scouts or escorts for civilians—streamed in and out of the rath. Brendan and Dungal saw these activities when they returned to the rath on Sundays to attend Mass and get new provisions for the coming week. Each time they found a few soldiers, relaxing about the well or waiting in line with Brendan and Dungal for rations, who were more than willing to tell tales of their patrols. None of the soldiers they talked to had actually made contact with sea raiders, however. They had found weapons, and other items discarded by the barbarians. They had also found some burned out farmsteads. The soldiers had been under orders not to patrol areas more than six nights journey from Dun Finian. The King was worried about spreading his forces too thin.

As the days passed, the fear of an attack on Dun Finian subsided. Brendan figured that, even if the captured barbarian made it back to the rest of the invading sea raiders, they preferred attacking monks and isolated settlements to assaulting the rath of King Finian. Brendan felt safe; but he also felt sympathy for Kaileen, for there had been no news from the returning soldiers of a woman fitting her mother's description. The main talk now was of the King leading an expedition to find and engage the barbarians in combat in order to drive them back to the sea.

Such was the situation this morning when Brendan awoke. Dungal had drawn the second watch that night, so Brendan hadn't fallen asleep on duty again. In fact, he thought with pride, he hadn't fallen asleep on duty since that first night. Brendan glanced at the sky. The sun was well up. Oh no! If he didn't hurry, he was going to miss his favorite entertainment: watching Kaileen's riding lesson.

He threw back the sheepskin and headed for the part of the pasture where Failend and Kaileen usually made their morning appearance. By the time he got there, Failend and Kaileen were galloping along, side by side, apparently racing each other. Dungal sat on the side of the downhill slope watching the action. By the time Brendan sat down alongside Dungal, the girls had changed direction and were heading toward them. They came at a gallop, slowing down only when they were very close. Then Failend slid off her horse and walked toward Brendan and Dungal, leading her horse. Following Failend's example, Kaileen slid off her horse executing the same quality of dismount and walked her sleek gray steed alongside Failend.

"What do you think of my pupil now?" Failend asked.

"She looks really good," Brendan responded.

"I'm talking about her riding," Failend teased.

"That's what I meant," Brendan protested, his face burned.

"Are you sure?" Failend shot back. She knew she'd embarrassed him and seemed to sport in teasing Brendan.

"I wish I could ride like that," Brendan answered, anxious to divert Failend.

It worked. Failend stroked her chin with her thumb and forefinger in a thoughtful gesture, and then she spoke:

"You know you could. Why don't I teach you?" she said.

"But what would your father say? A princess teaching a common herdsman?"

"Oh, Daddy doesn't have to know. He wouldn't be too happy with me for teaching my maidservant either."

"Great, when can we start?" Brendan asked.

"You can have your first lesson right now. Kaileen, loan him your horse." Failend ordered.

Kaileen handed him the rein to her horse. Brendan took the rein in his right hand and rubbed the horse's muzzle with his left. Kaileen then handed over the guide rod.

"Have fun," she said, smirking with anticipation.

Brendan then looked at the horse's withers. Failend instructed Brendan.

"To mount you must spring from the ground and slide over the horse's back, using your hands to help lift you."

Failend demonstrated by mounting her horse. Her full skirt spreading with the motion, allowing her to settle with one leg on each side of the horse's back. Brendan delighted that, once mounted on the horse; the delicate white skin of her legs was exposed from knee to ankle.

"Now you try," she coaxed.

Brendan put both hands on his horse's withers, duplicating Failend's motion. He jumped, using his good leg as a spring; he barely left the ground. He tried again. This time his stomach contacted the horse's back about halfway up the barrel of the horse. The horse reacted by moving his hind quarters a step sideways, and Brendan slid back to the ground.

"Try to transfer your weight to your arms," Failend instructed.

With these words, Brendan felt a tap on his shoulder. He turned to see it was Dungal. Dungal motioned for Brendan to hand him the guide rod and rein. Brendan complied. Dungal pointed at a spot on the ground indicating Brendan should stand there. Brendan moved back to the spot. Dungal then swung himself on the horse with the same ease as Failend.

"Great, Dungal, where did you learn to mount like that?" Failend shouted.

As Dungal started to motion to answer her in sign language, he inadvertently tapped the horse on the ear with the guide rod. Spooked, the horse kicked up both hind legs. Dungal sailed over the horse's head on to the ground, landing headfirst, but adroitly rolling onto his back in a somersault. Failend giggled. Dungal sprung to his feet. He brushed himself off, and smiled back at Failend. He enjoyed amusing her. Failend continued.

"I think you need to learn more about horses than just mounting them. Help Brendan on the horse then come over here. You can double up with me and I'll give you both a lesson."

Dungal handed Brendan the guide rod then stood with his back to the horse. He clasped his hands together so that his fingers interlocked and nodded to Brendan. Brendan put his left foot in Dungal's hands. With the strong thrust provided by Dungal, Brendan easily mounted the horse. He positioned himself on the horse's back, trying to imitate Failend's posture. Dungal walked toward Failend. As he came up on her, she slid off her horse. She handed her guide rod to Dungal.

"You mount first. Then give me your arm," Failend instructed.

Dungal followed her orders. When he was on top of her horse, he extended his powerful left arm down to her. She took it and sailed up behind him, appearing for a moment like a fairy sailing through the air. The horse stirred momentarily as Failend settled down behind Dungal.

"Whoa, Midnight," she spoke to the horse, calling the stallion by name. Then she instructed Dungal.

"Keep a firm hand on the reins. You have to let him know you're in charge. Now give him a light tap on the side with the guide rod. We'll pull up alongside Brendan."

It took a little while for Dungal to maneuver the horse alongside Brendan. Once they were abreast, Failend told Brendan to give her the rein.

"Since this is your first time, you should concentrate on getting the feel of the horse. We'll just walk around the pasture for a while."

Brendan was amazed that she could balance herself behind Dungal and still lead his horse. As his horse began to walk, Brendan could feel the motion of the horse's muscles under his thighs. This was so much easier than walking on his bad leg. He definitely could get used to this! Still, he was by himself, while Dungal had the beautiful Failend behind him! After walking the horses in a great circle, Failend decided to pick up the pace. As the horses began to trot, Brendan began to bounce all over the horses back. Failend looking back at him smiled and said:

"Try to balance yourself, Brendan. Use your thighs to hold your position. Lean back."

Brendan tried to follow her advice; but couldn't seem to keep from bouncing. Several times he came close to falling off, and was relieved when she slowed things down to a walk again. He couldn't help but be jealous of Dungal, however. First he didn't seem to be having trouble riding. Second, he had Failend snuggled behind him, her lips inches from his ears when she instructed him. A small breeze tossed her golden hair forward alongside Dungal's face. Then they came to a stop. Failend reined in Brendan's horse to bring it up alongside hers.

"You ready to try it on your own?" she asked Brendan.

"Sure."

Failend tossed him the rein. Then she went on.

"We'll walk around the pasture again. Just walk. Ready?" Failend asked.

"Okay," Brendan answered her.

Brendan saw Dungal tap Midnight in the flanks with the whip and Dungal and Failend began to move away from him. Brendan made the same movement with his whip; but nothing happened. He repeated the movement. Still nothing happened. Angry now, he struck with all his might. His horse bolted and took off. From a dead stop the horse quickly moved to a full gallop. Brendan miraculously managed to keep from falling when the horse bolted. He now hugged the horse's mane as they tore through the air. From behind, he could hear Failend's voice but couldn't make out what she was saying. Brendan pulled back on the rein, trying to get the horse to slow down. The horse, however, didn't seem to care. Brendan glanced behind. He saw Dungal slide to the ground as Failend took charge of her horse. But she was so far back. How could she possible catch up to him? Brendan looked back over the horse's head. They were fast approaching a grove of trees. He tried in vain to get the horse to turn with the guide rod. The horse didn't respond. The distance between Brendan and the trees was much less than the distance Failend had to travel to catch him. There was no way she reach him before his horse carried him into the looming dense thicket!

# CHAPTER 9

Brendan ducked down alongside his horse's neck as it plunged into the trees. Branches tore at his arms and legs. Next, a thick limb struck Brendan on the forehead, knocking him loose from his mount. Surprisingly, the impact upon the ground hurt much less than the blow of the limb on his forehead. Brendan rolled over on his back, writhing in pain from wound to the head and feeling sick to his stomach. He held his head with his hand. He didn't want to get up but didn't want to lie still either. The pain so overpowered his senses that he didn't hear Failend approach. The next thing he knew, he felt the fine fabric of Failend's dress as she knelt behind him and rested his head against her thighs. He then felt the soothing stroke of her hands against his temple.

"Are you okay, Brendan?" she asked.

"I, I feel terrible," Brendan answered.

"Try to rest here a minute while I get water."

With that, Failend laid Brendan's head gently on the ground. A few moments later, she again placed his head in her lap and dabbed at his head wound with a cold, wet cloth. The cool sensation made Brendan feel better. As he relaxed, the throbbing became a little less intense; but Failend's soothing touch was the best medicine.

"Oh, poor Brendan," she cooed, "What have I done to you?"

"You, you, didn't do anything. It was that, that... horse!"

"Ah, but I should have remembered he has such a hard mouth. He's hard to stop when he gets excited about something."

"Tell me," Brendan managed a bit of sarcasm, then he thought better and continued, "But I'm the one who wanted to learn to ride. I still do. Will you give me another chance?" he asked.

"Sure, Brendan," she said soothingly, "Not today though. I think you need a little time to recover first. Besides, I better be getting back to the stable soon or father may come looking for me. Let's gather up the horses and get back to Kaileen and Dungal."

"Do you think we can find my horse?" Brendan asked.

"No problem. He's down at the stream having a drink. I saw him there when I went to wet my skirt to put on your forehead. He didn't travel far after he wiped you off his back. Come on now."

Failend then lifted on Brendan's shoulders. When he sat up, Failend sprung to her feet. She extended her hand to Brendan to help him up. He took it, enjoying the delightful sensation of her hand in his. Once on his feet he stood for a moment. He could see that the hem of Failend's dress was soaked with water and stained with his blood. A short feeling of dizziness washed across him. He staggered.

"Can you walk all right?" Failend asked.

"I'm a little dizzy," Brendan answered.

"Here. Put your hand on my shoulder," she answered. Then she took Brendan's right hand and placed it on her shoulder.

"That better?" she asked

"Much," Brendan answered. He was suddenly glad that the incident, painful though it was, had taken place. Under what other circumstances could he have presumed to put his arm around this beautiful princess?

She led him through the brush. When they found the creek, both horses were munching on some tree leaves as though nothing unusual had happened. Midnight looked at Failend, stomped her foot and snorted.

"Wait here a minute, Brendan," Failend ordered, then walked alone toward the horses. They paid her little attention as she gathered in their reins. Compliantly, they followed her as she returned to Brendan. She handed Brendan the rein for the horse he'd been riding.

"This is Pooka," she said.

"We've met before," Brendan joked.

"You'll get to know him a lot better. Come on. Let's go find Dungal and Kaileen. We'll walk these guy's to give them a little rest."

They started for the forest edge. Brendan glanced at Failend. Her smartly upturned nose added an exceptional perkiness to her otherwise marvelous face. She sensed his stare. She turned and smiled.

"You look as though you have something on your mind," she commented.

Brendan, too embarrassed to tell her that he'd been infatuated by her face, answered with a question.

"I suppose, I mean being a princess and all, you probably have lots of suitors among the knights and nobles loyal to the king?"

"Well, there are a few. Why the interest?"

"I wondered what kind of man you would like," Brendan answered, he flushed with embarrassment.

Failend turned toward him with girlish smirk on her face.

"Hmmm, let's see. I like a strong man, a handsome man," she began.

"Dungal's a strong man," Brendan interrupted, feeling inadequate.

"And handsome too," Failend added.

"You're attracted to Dungal?" Brendan asked.

"If I tell you, promise you won't tell him?"

"I promise."

"Yes, he's very handsome and has the skills of a great warrior. I've never seen anyone so swift and agile."

"Yes, I've seen him in action against the sea warriors," Brendan commented. Then he blurted out the next question:

"Would you marry him?"

"No. I mean I can't. My father would never approve of such a marriage. Dungal is dumb and has no property to bring to the marriage. I will be expected to marry no less than a king of a tuath."

"I thought being a princess you would be free to choose anyone you liked."

"Most people have that misconception of royalty," Failend added grimly.

"Then Dungal, Kaileen, and I have more choice in who we marry than you do, don't we?"

"That's right, Brendan."

"Except I can't marry you," Brendan responded.

"Right again," Failend answered. Her eyes met his for a moment. Brendan couldn't be sure, but it appeared they were on the verge of tears. She continued.

"But you and Dungal can be my friends. I need good friends, Brendan. A princess can never be sure of people that purport to be her friends. There are so many who just want favors from my father. They seek my friendship as a means to influence my father or to gain some secret information they can use against him."

"But why do you trust me? Or Dungal for that matter?" Brendan asked.

"Have you ever heard of women's intuition?"

"No."

"Well it's kind of an internal feeling, special to women. Anyway, I sense that you and Dungal are honest with me. You don't have any covert political ambitions, no secret desires…"

"Except maybe one," Brendan interrupted.

"That's what I mean. You're even honest about your feelings toward me."

Failend smiled, then reached over and messed up Brendan's hair.

"What's up with you two?" Kaileen's voice broke in. Then she noticed the bump on his forehead, partially crusted over with a new scab. "What happened?"

"I had a close encounter with a tree limb," Brendan answered her.

"It looks like it hurts," Kaileen responded.

"It's better than it was awhile ago."

"Kaileen, you and I need to be off," Failend said.

Failend mounted Midnight and Kaileen swung up on Pooka. Brendan marveled at how effortlessly Kaileen mounted. Failend had taught her well. He wondered if he'd ever be able to ride like that. When Failend and Kaileen were nearly out of sight Dungal motioned with his hands, tracing the shape of a female figure.

"You want to tell me something about one of the girls. Which one?"

Dungal simulated two mounted figures with his fingers.

"The one you rode with, Failend?" Brendan asked.

Dungal nodded "Yes."

"What about her?"

Dungal put a hand to his heart.

"You're in love with her?"

Dungal nodded his agreement.

"Well forget it. A princess can't be in love with the likes of us."

Dungal spread his arms downward in a motion indicating he was asking "Why?"

"Because we're not chiefs or kings of tuaths," Brendan explained.

Dungal shook his head indicating he didn't believe Brendan.

"You don't believe me. I've never lied to you. Why should I lie to you?" Brendan protested.

Dungal pointed at Brendan and put his hand on his heart again.

"You think I love her, so I won't tell you the truth, Right?"

Dungal nodded to indicate that was what he thought.

"Well, yeah, I like Failend, a lot; but I'm still telling you the truth," Brendan steamed.

Dungal still shook his head in disbelief. Then he tapped his chest with both palms, his hands formed into fists. He raised both arms and flexed his biceps. Then he slapped his thighs with his hands.

"Yes, I know you're much stronger and agile than I am; but you can't speak..."

Immediately Brendan knew he shouldn't have made that last statement. Dungal stomped, turned, and started to stride off in disgust. Brendan hurried to him and pleaded.

"Dungal, I didn't mean she won't marry you because you can't talk."

Brendan grabbed Dungal's arm as he spoke, hoping to get Dungal to look at him. Dungal responded with a mighty shove which sent Brendan reeling to the ground, but didn't turn at all. As Brendan got up he shouted after Dungal:

"I'm trying to tell you she can't marry either of us. We're common people who earn our meals in servitude to someone else. We've no land, no cattle, nothing we could offer a princess!"

Brendan protested in vain. Dungal just kept going. Brendan slowly moved in the same direction, but Dungal continued to move farther away. Brendan was sure he had lost his best friend. He thought back. In all the time he'd known Dungal, he couldn't remember a time when a cross word had passed between them. Now it didn't look like Dungal would ever speak to him again. Speak, yes, that's what caused the rift. Brendan spoke without thinking, pointing out that Dungal couldn't speak, yet Dungal spoke with his gestures well enough for Brendan to understand him. Brendan decided he could do nothing more but let Dungal cool down. Perhaps it was better that Dungal knew how he felt about Failend. Better now than—than what?

He didn't have any greater chance of winning Failend's favor. He was on the same par as Dungal, a common laborer with no real hope for a better future. Still he didn't want to give up hope. He thought back to the earlier events of the day. The horse; that might be the answer. If he could learn to ride, his club foot would be meaningless. But he didn't have a horse of his own or any prospects for getting one. Never mind, that would have to come later. First he must learn to ride. He continued to follow Dungal to the cattle herd, anxiously awaiting tomorrow's riding lesson with Failend.

During the next several days, the mornings passed much too quickly for Brendan and the rest of the day lasted much too long. Brendan looked forward to the arrival of Failend and Kaileen and the riding lesson which followed. After several days, Brendan was able to mount by himself. Compared to nimble Dungal and the elegant movement of Failend, Brendan was sure he looked clumsy but he was doing it on his own. Failend had taken it easy on him. After a short walk to get the feel of the horse, she would have Brendan practice using the reins with the guide rod to turn the horse and back up. Then she would speed up the pace. For the first couple of days she had him canter for awhile, since this movement was easier to master than the trot. Now she was trying to get Brendan to master the trot, saying this was essential for him to work as "one with the horse."

Dungal continued to be distant. By necessity, they shared the same shelter, ate together, and managed the cattle together, but Dungal's communications to Brendan were confined to only those essential to conduct the days business. Clearly Failend unknowingly had managed to create a rift between the two longtime friends. It didn't help that Failend continued to ride double with Dungal during their lessons. Dungal seemed to be mastering his mount just fine, Brendan thought. If Failend needed to be riding to instruct them, why couldn't she ride with him instead of Dungal some of the time?

With these thoughts in mind, Brendan, with Dungal not far off, scanned the pasture in the distance searching for some sign of the two lady equestrians. They were late, at least it seemed so. Perhaps he was just over-anxious. Brendan noted the sun's position in the sky. No, the girls were usually here before the sun had reached this height. Then two figures on horseback appeared in the distance from behind the trees surrounding the creek. A wave of hand from the lead rider confirmed the girls were now approaching. Brendan and Dungal both waved back.

When Failend and Kaileen drew close, Brendan could see Failend had two sacks straddling the horse in front of her. She looked particularly ravishing today. She wore a velvet silk tunic with gold braid about her wrists on the sleeves and around the collar. The wind gently lifted and caressed her delicate golden hair. Her face, now tanned from the days spent riding in the pasture, gleamed with a radiant smile. She swung her right leg to the left side of her horse and slid to the ground, the hem of her dress sliding momentarily midway up her thigh revealing pale white skin in contrast to the golden brown of her lower legs.

"Say, let's do something different today. You guys game?" she asked.

"Sure," Brendan answered, and Dungal nodded his approval.

"You two are awful easy. Suppose I asked you two to rub our backs for the next couple of hours? Anyway, I thought we would have a picnic." Failend continued.

"Is today a special day?" Brendan asked.

"Well yes and no," Failend started, then, a frown forming on her face, she continued.

"It's not a holiday; but it's to be our last day together for awhile."

"Why?" Brendan asked.

"A runner arrived last night with word that the barbarians have seized the rath of Gall. Gall, in an effort to save his family from being put to the sword, conspired with the leader of the barbarians to lead them here where he promised my father's wealth was worthy of plunder. My father says I must remain within the rath, starting tonight until the scourge of the sea warriors has been eliminated from his kingdom."

Brendan's heart fell. With Dungal mad at him, the morning appearance of Failend had been the only pleasure in his life. Failend seemed to sense this. She reached out with her hand and touched Brendan's cheek.

"Cheer up, big boy, let's make the most of the morning." She said, "I know a nice spot down by the creek. Double up with Kaileen. Dungal and I will lead you there."

When Failend spoke these words, Kaileen slid down from Pooka.

"You first," Kaileen instructed.

Brendan mounted. When he had positioned himself on the horse, Kaileen asked.

"Your arm please?"

Trying to follow Dungal's example, Brendan extended his arm down to Kaileen. She took it with both hands, and asked.

"Ready?"

"Yes."

"When I leap upward, you pull," she instructed.

Kaileen leaped, Brendan pulled, and Kaileen sailed up, landing into position behind Brendan with a gentle thump, the horse jolting slightly at the impact. Dungal and Failend mounted in similar fashion; but as they started for the woods, Brendan felt Kaileen's arm slide around his waist.

"Mind if I hold on?" she asked, in a low voice, her words settling sweetly on Brendan's ears.

"Not at all," Brendan answered; he realized he probably sounded too eager.

As they transitioned from walk to trot to canter, Kaileen snuggled closer to Brendan. Apparently she didn't trust riding double with Brendan as she did with Failend. She lacked the confidence of Failend who rode with both hands resting on her thighs. Brendan didn't mind, though, the gentle contact of Kaileen's body with his felt pleasant. As he rode though the woods, with Kaileen behind him, Brendan was reminded the she was largely responsible for him being here at this time. The more he contemplated their adventures together, the less he thought about Failend. Yes Failend was beautiful, but Kaileen was certainly her closest rival in that regard. Moreover, Kaileen was infinitely more approachable. She, like him, was of humble birth.

They came upon a clearing by the creek, formed largely by a large outcropping of a limestone boulder, leaving a large flat area by the creek. The ash trees spread their branches over the outcropping, creating a great natural canopy. The creek bubbled down a series of rapids, sparkling in the sunlight which found its way through the canopy. Failend announced.

"This is it."

Dungal then swung his leg over the horse's mane and slid off, followed by Failend. Brendan repeated Dungal's motion, except that he staggered a little as he contacted the earth. Kaileen followed in similar fashion; but, when she touched down, Pooka turned and stroked her in the back with his muzzle. The movement was forceful enough that Kaileen lost her balance and fell toward Brendan. He responded instinctively, catching her in his arms. For a moment he gazed into Kaileen's alluring eyes, all his senses taking in the sweet sensations of her presence. To his surprise she lingered for a moment in this position. Brendan felt a strong urge to kiss her.

"Pooka must think you two should be together," Failend's voice broke the spell of the moment. "He has a rascally spirit, you know," she continued.

"Sorry," Kaileen spoke to Brendan in a gentle voice as she pushed away.

"My pleasure," Brendan answered. He spoke in a low voice so only Kaileen could hear.

When they separated, Brendan looked over to see Failend's "all knowing" kind of smirk on her face.

"Tie Pooka to a branch where he can graze to keep him out of trouble, and let's have our picnic," Failend ordered.

Kaileen grasped Brendan's upper arm and tugged in the direction of Failend and Dungal.

"Let's go see what goodies my mistress brought," Kaileen entreated.

Kaileen assisted Failend in laying the food out and pouring the wine into separate wooden cups Failend had brought for that purpose. Brendan took a sip from one of the cups. The liquid had a delightfully refreshing taste, not bitter like the beer he was used to drinking.

"This is really good," he commented. "Where did you get it?"

"Father gets a dozen bottles from the monks who pilgrimage to Rome each year. He guards this treasure jealously, usually only bringing it out during the Christmas season.

"Won't he be angry when he finds a bottle missing?" Brendan asked.

"Oh, he'll forgive me. Especially now, when he knows I won't be able to enjoy my morning ride for a while. I'll just tell him Kaileen and I had it at a picnic."

The four of them enjoyed the good food. Brendan noted that even Dungal's spirit seemed to pick up a little, although he still seemed colder that he had in the past, before Failend came into their life. Afterwards they rode for a while, first doubled up, then Failend dismounted.

"Hop down and let's see how these two do on their own."

Kaileen complied. Failend spoke to Dungal and Brendan.

"Why don't you two ride a little on your own; but take it easy, I won't be able to help you if your horses decide to run away with you. I don't think Midnight will leave me by myself; but Pooka, he's a devil sometimes. He might take it in his mind to return to the rath whether you want to go or not. You'll have to use a firm hand with him."

Dungal prodded Midnight in the flank with the guide rod and headed up the hill, urging his horse into a canter. Brendan decided to follow him. Brendan was happy when the horse broke into a canter. Being on top of the horse, by himself, gave him a feeling of freedom he'd never known before. For once he could move as rapidly as Dungal, or any other man for that matter with two good legs. He urged Pooka forward, coming up alongside Dungal, who merely turned and glanced for a moment at Brendan. When they reached the top of the hill, Brendan, full of confidence now, shouted over to Dungal.

"I'll race you back."

Dungal turned and, for the first time in days, smiled back. He nodded his approval to Brendan, prodding Midnight at the same time. Brendan responded by prodding Pooka. In moments they were at full gallop heading back toward the girls. Pooka quickly closed the gap between the two of them; then overtook Dungal and Midnight. Pleased at his conquest, Brendan kept up the speed until he'd nearly reached the girls. He attempted to rein the horse back but Pooka wanted to keep on going. Pooka headed in the direction of the rath and there seemed nothing Brendan could do stop the horse. Brendan strained on the rein; but the horse continued to run. Panic pulsed through his body. If only he'd listened to Failend.

"Hang on, Brendan," Failend's voice seemed to materialize out of nowhere.

Brendan managed a glance over his shoulder to see Failend, on Midnight, closing on them. She came up alongside and moved ahead. As she moved to the front of Pooka, she leaned down alongside her horse's neck and snatched Pooka's bridle. Then, hanging on to the bridle, she pulled Pooka's head up toward her. This movement caused Pooka to falter. Brendan nearly sailed off over Pooka's head. He stopped himself by hugging Pooka's neck. Pooka began to slow down, finally stopping as Failend straightened up on Midnight's back. When Pooka had slowed to a trot, she released the bridle. Both horses slowed to a walk.

"What were my last words to you, Brendan of Kilrush?" Failend scolded.

"Something about taking it easy," Brendan answered, sheepishly.

"You boys. I should have known better to turn the two of you loose on your own."

"Sorry, it's just that for the first time in my life I've felt the equal to any other man. With my bad leg, I've never been able to keep up with other people before."

"Forgiven. I guess I understand," Failend began. "I wish I could continue to give you lessons; but that will have to wait until Dad drives the sea warriors back to where they came from."

"I'm going to miss you," Brendan blurted out.

"Is it me you're going to miss, or the feeling of power that riding gives you?"

"You," Brendan said with emphasis.

"But what about Kaileen?" Failend probed.

Brendan thought for a moment. He liked both girls; but was afraid that expressing any feeling he had for Kaileen would offend Failend. Failend solved his dilemma for him.

"You can't decide which of us you like best, can you?"

Brendan nodded to indicate she was right. He looked at Failend. She wore that "all knowing" engaging smirk again. Brendan felt the need to say something while he had Failend alone.

"I think you're the most beautiful woman I've ever seen."

"Thank you. You know you are the first man to ever tell me that?" Failend

"Really?" Brendan answered, astonished.

"Really," Failend confirmed. "Oh I get the feeling men are staring at me all the time when I'm in public, but you're the first one who's ever commented on my looks. Except my dad, of course."

"Well I know Dungal feels the same as I do," Brendan reassured her.

"Ah, so that's the reason the atmosphere's so frosty between you two of late," Failend commented with a wink.

"Yes, we both want you; but when I explained that neither of us can have you, Dungal thought I was lying because I want you for myself."

"Oh, Brendan, as I explained before, I can't ever marry either one of you; but I love you both equally. Can't we continue to be good friends?"

"Okay by me; but I think you should explain things to Dungal. Then maybe he won't be mad at me."

"Do you think I can?" Failend asked.

"Sure, he may not be able to speak; but he can hear real well. I'm sure he'll listen to you."

"Done then. What about Kaileen?"

"What about her?" Brendan answered her question with a question.

"Have you told her how you feel about her?"

"Why do you think I have any special feelings toward her?"

"I saw how the two you looked at each other down by the creek. I've only seen that look between a couple once before."

"When?" Brendan interrupted.

"That's how my father used to look at my mother—before she died," Failend answered.

"How did she die?" Brendan was both curious and anxious to get off the uncomfortable subject of his feelings for Kaileen.

Failend's face grew solemn. Brendan regretted asking the question. He didn't like the look of unhappiness he'd never seen on Failend before.

"She died giving birth to my little brother. My little brother died a few days later. The midwife said she thought he had come out of the womb too early. In a short span of time, my father lost both wife and the male heir to his kingship. I will inherit his kingdom, but I'd much rather have my mother back."

"I'm sorry." Brendan tried to console her.

"There's nothing to be done about it now. I miss her; but I still have my father. I just worry about him being killed in the upcoming battle with the barbarians."

"I think you're father's a great man. I'm sure the army he leads against the sea warriors will protect him, and I think they will be victorious."

"Thank you, Brendan; that helps. I will be glad when we can get together again."

Brendan and Failend had now arrived where they had left Kaileen and Dungal. Both dismounted. Then Failend spoke.

"Brendan, Kaileen, I'd like to talk to Dungal privately. I'm going to have him walk me part of the way back to the rath. I'll say good-bye to you now Brendan."

With these words she walked over and kissed him on the cheek.

"Hope to see you again soon," she said.

"Me too," Brendan answered.

Brendan could see rage in Dungal eyes; but Failend began to lead him off, as she did Midnight, heading across the pasture. After a few steps, Failend turned as though she'd just realized she'd forgotten something.

"Kaileen, why don't you meet me back at the rath. That way you can have a little time alone with Brendan too." Failend said, winking at Brendan.

"Now what was that all about?" Kaileen asked.

"Oh, Dungal thinks he's in love with Failend," she wants to explain to him why she can never marry him.

"And how would she be knowing that? What with him a mute and all." Kaileen asked.

"Well Dungal told me, in sign language, like you've seen, and I told her," Brendan explained.

"Is that the reason you and Dungal have been giving each other the icy stare?"

"Well, ah, yes," Brendan confessed.

"So you have the eye for the lovely princess Failend too?" Kaileen quizzed.

"Uh," Brendan started; but Kaileen jumped in.

"Admit it now. There wouldn't be the bad feelings between you and Dungal if you weren't desirous of the same thing."

"Okay, yes, I like her too," Brendan admitted.

"Well that sounds like a couple of young bucks. The two of you scrapping over a woman neither of you could ever possess. Brendan, I thought you had more sense about you," Kaileen chided.

"I guess you're right. It's kind of ridiculous, isn't it?"

"That it is, although, from here, the two of them look like lovers to me," Kaileen added.

Brendan looked at the two figures of Dungal and Failend receding in the distance. Kaileen was right. Failend was holding Dungal's hand now, her head turned toward Dungal as they walked, as though she didn't want to take her eyes off him. The pair stopped. Failend reached over with both hands and pulled Dungal's head toward her. Then she kissed him full on the lips. Dungal put both his arms around Failend and they held that embrace for a moment. Then Failend pushed herself away from Dungal and leaped on Midnight, riding toward the woods in the direction of the rath. Brendan burned with jealousy. She hadn't kissed him like that! Dungal turned and headed up the hill toward the cattle. Failend rode fast at first; then slowed down, apparently to give Midnight a rest.

"See what I mean?" Kaileen's voice floated across the air as though blown from some distance land, as Brendan stood staring at the receding figure of Failend on horseback. Then he realized Kaileen was speaking to him. He turned to look in her luscious brown eyes.

"I guess you're right," he conceded.

Then Brendan looked back at Failend in the distance. She was about to turn around the edge of the woods from where she and Kaileen had come earlier that morning. Suddenly, he saw half a dozen figures dart from the woods. Even though they were a long way off, Brendan recognized the silhouettes of the sea warriors. They quickly surrounded Failend's horse and dragged her off Midnight, slapping the horse on the rump to run it off. Then, as quickly as they had appeared, they disappeared with Failend into the woods.

"Oh, Brendan," Kaileen shrieked with terror, "We have to do something."

# CHAPTER 10

Brendan looked desperately in the direction he'd last seen Dungal. The lone figure was nearly out of sight and shouting distance. Apparently Dungal was unaware of what had just happened. Brendan thought for a second and turned to Kaileen.

"Get on your horse. Ride as fast as you can. Don't slow down for anything. You must get to King Finian and tell him what happened. I'm going to try to trail the sea warriors. I will leave a trail for the king's soldiers to follow. Tell King Finian that," Brendan ordered.

Kaileen leaped on Pooka. She was about to strike the horse with the guide rod, then hesitated. She held her arm out for Brendan.

"Hop on," she ordered. "I'll get you closer to where we saw them kidnap Failend."

Brendan took her arm and leaped with all his might. To his amazement he lighted behind Kaileen on Pooka's back on the first try. As quickly as he landed, they were off. As they neared the edge of the woods where they'd last seen Failend, Brendan spoke into her left ear.

"Slow down only a little here while I drop off. Then get out of here as fast as you can."

Kaileen nodded her agreement. Then, as Brendan felt the horse slow, he let go of Kaileen's waist and pushed off sideways. He landed hard on his left side, but rolled to dissipate some of the energy of the collision. He stood up and brushed himself off. Kaileen was looking back at him. He waved to let her know he was all right. She blew him a kiss, then turned away and urged Pooka to accelerate. Brendan headed for the woods.

Brendan spotted the place where the barbarians had entered the woods fairly easily. A large circle of broken brush indicated that Failend had put up quite a struggle. A discarded piece of leather thong suggested they had probably had to bind at least hands, perhaps her feet also, in order to transport her. Brendan could hear the sound of brush breaking in the far distance. Good, that meant they weren't too far away, he would probably lose the sound; they seemed to be moving fast. This was good too. It meant they would be careless and leave a trail easy for him to follow. With years of experience in finding errant sheep, locating a bunch of barbarians traveling with an unwilling woman shouldn't be too hard.

As Brendan followed their trail, he was careful to leave one of his own. Breaking branches, tying shocks of grass, laying arrows with sticks and rocks on the ground, Brendan left a trail behind that he felt any idiot could follow.

Before long, Brendan could no longer hear the sound of the barbarians breaking brush ahead of him. Still, they left a trail easy for him to follow. When they had crossed the creek, they left footprints in the mud. Further up the hill on the far side of the crossing, Brendan found a piece of purple silk from Failend's dress. This discovery brought a tear to his eye when he thought of the innocent and beautiful Failend in the clutches of those monsters. He just had to find her quickly, and help King Finian get her back.

By mid-afternoon, Brendan was picking up the sound of voices again. He moved forward more carefully now. He didn't want to stumble on the sea warriors' sentries by mistake. Looking carefully into the distance, he spotted a large form in the brush ahead. Okay, there was a sentry. Brendan wanted to get closer. He figured King Finian would need all the details he could supply. More importantly, Brendan needed to see Failend. He just had to know she was unhurt.

How to get around that sentry? The problem plagued him. Brendan searched the surroundings. He noted there was a large heather shrubry between the sentry and the area he appeared to be guarding. If he could get beyond that shrubry, he should be okay. The guard would be looking the other way then. He needed some way to divert the guard's attention.

Brendan spotted a large stone. That should do it. He slowly removed his slingshot from his waist. He reached over and picked up the stone and put in the sling. Now the most risky moment was at hand. The act of slinging to rock took a large motion. This increased the likelihood that the sentry might spot him. Brendan took a deep breath to calm his nerves, positioned himself so the rock would travel in the right direction, then wound up and let loose. All was good. The rock followed the planned trajectory and came crashing into the brush a good distance from the sentry. Brendan noted with amusement that the impact of the rock in the brush startled the sentry. Predictably, however, the sentry went to investigate the source of the noise. This gave Brendan the opportunity he needed. He moved as quickly as he could and managed to gain the cover of the heather shrub while the sentry was still searching for the source of the noise.

Crawling now, Brendan inched forward. Each movement had to be slow and meticulous. The thickness of the brush was both a blessing and a curse. The thickness provided cover but was difficult to move through without making noise. Steadily, he moved forward, parting one branch at a time, returning each branch by hand lest it snap back and betrays his position. As he drew closer, the sound of voices grew louder and more numerous. Pretty soon a clearing became visible. Brendan slid on his belly up to the base of a tree so that the tree trunk was on one side of his head and a branch of hazel on the other side. He now had a good view of the expanse of the clearing.

Every sea raider he'd seen disembark from the ships seemed to be there as well as Hakon their leader. Sitting on the ground, her hands bound and tied to a stake was the lovely Failend. Next to her, were two other women, one Brendan recognized as Mugain, Gall's wife. Her posture indicated she was in a state of great fatigue. The barbarians must have mistreated her badly. The other woman Brendan recognized to be Kaileen's mother, Cummie. Not only that, but alongside Hakon stood Father Sweeney and Gall, himself.

Brendan wanted desperately to get closer; but he had to content himself with trying to figure out what was going on from a distance. It looked like Gall said something to Father Sweeney and Father Sweeney said something to Hakon. Hakon then ordered his men to their feet and they formed a semi-circle in front of Hakon. Hakon shouted something. Then the barbarians formed a line with Gall in the center and started moving toward Brendan. They entered the woods, only a couple of dozen feet from where he lay. Brendan decided he must follow them. As the last man in the column entered the woods, Brendan glanced over at the sentry. The sentry waved at his comrades then looked off the other way.

It was a risk, but Brendan decided he wouldn't get a better chance. He decided to fall in behind the last of the barbarians; albeit far enough behind him that the barbarian tail man couldn't see him. Thirty or forty rods later, Brendan felt partial relief. The sentry hadn't spotted him, and he felt confident he couldn't now. All Brendan had to worry about was being detected by the barbarian patrol he was following. As time passed, this too became less of a worry. They easily outpaced Brendan and were getting further and further from him. Brendan had no trouble following them, however, as they left a trail easy to follow. He glanced at the sky through the forest canopy. It would be getting dark soon. *What was Hakon up to? He'd sent a party of twelve men with a lone Irishman in the direction of a formidable enemy, King Finian, in the evening hours. Surely twelve barbarians could not match the power of the force King Finian would have marching toward them at this moment. King Finian, yes, the king should probably be near where Failend had been captured.*

A few moments later, shouts from the trail ahead signaled a clash between the two opposing forces. Brendan hurried as fast as he could; disregarding the fact he was now making enough noise to compromise his own position. Soon he came upon the forest edge. He paused, holding back in the cover of the brush, choosing to take a chance to observe without being observed.

What a spectacle he saw before him. Gall stood in a circle of the twelve barbarians. They, in turn, were surrounded by an army of Irishmen, spears and shields at the ready, anxious to fall upon the sea warriors and dispatch them to the depths of hell. Likewise the barbarians stood, shields and javelins poised prepared to make their last stand against the Irishmen. In the middle, Gall shouted:

"King Finian, King Finian, I must speak with King Finian."

The ranks of the Irish soldiers parted. Between them, the mighty figure of King Finian strode, his left hand resting on the golden hilt of his sword which was sheathed in an ornately decorated bronze scabbard. The scabbard hung from a wide belt that lay across his massive chest under which the king wore a leather sleeveless shirt. The leather shirt, in turn, overlay a deep purple, knee length tunic. King Finian looked like the king of warriors.

"Who calls King Finian?" he bellowed.

"I bring a message from Hakon, King of Hafrsfjord," Gall answered.

"And who be you, who speak the native Irish, among these vile heathens?" King Finian demanded.

"I am Gall. I had a bit of land to the southwest of here, until these barbarians came, ran off my herds and flocks, and burned my residence. They have my wife and King Hakon says he will put her to the sword if I don't do his bidding."

"Ah, yes, Gall, you were always stingy with your tribute, I recall; but never mind that now. Have you news of my daughter, Failend?" the king asked.

"Yes, King Hakon has her. She is as yet unharmed. King Hakon proposes a trade." Gall answered.

"What does the Hakon require in trade?"

"A hundred rings of gold and the return of the girl who serves the Princess Failend."

"Kaileen?" King Finian responded, obviously puzzled, "She is of Irish birth. What claim does this Hakon have on her?"

"He claims her by right of conquest. His most loyal captain has taken a fancy for her."

"I will scrounge for 100 rings of gold to buy my daughter's freedom; but I'll not be handing over an Irish maiden to that heathen."

"King Hakon refuses to barter for any less than what he proposes," Gall responded.

"I suppose I will have to take her by force then. I'll start with the lot of you. Seize them," the king barked the order.

As the front ranks of his army rushed forward, the sea warriors tightened their circle. Gall shouted desperately.

"Do you want your daughter to die?"

"Halt" King Finian commanded.

The soldiers stopped dead in their tracks. They were so close to the barbarians, they could easily have struck killing blows.

"What do you mean?" the king demanded.

"King Hakon said to tell you, that if this party doesn't return, unscathed, he will put your daughter to the sword. In addition, he promised she would be slain if you make any attempt to rescue her," Gall explained.

"Very well. Captian Kilian," the King shouted.

The mass of men parted on Finian's right and Captain Kilian rushed forward, turned in front of King Finian and saluted.

"Take a couple of men, return to the rath, and bring back Kaileen. Mind you, don't distress the poor girl by telling her what has transpired here. Just tell her that her mistress requires her presence."

"Yes, sire." Kilian answered. Then he disappeared into the mass of armed men.

King Finian then looked toward Gall again.

"You tell the king of the heathens to bring my daughter here by this time tomorrow. I will have his blood money waiting."

"And the servant girl?" Gall asked.

"And the servant girl," the king replied somberly.

Brendan was dismayed to hear King Finian make such a devil's bargain, but then he realized Kaileen was only a servant while Failend was the King's only daughter. Brendan watched as Finian's soldiers parted to let the sea warriors retreat with Gall. Then Brendan ducked back into the brush and sought cover behind a holly bush. This negotiating party was coming straight at him. Brendan held his breath and wished his heart could stop beating until they passed. They were so close he could smell the stench of the barbarians. After what seemed an eternity, they had disappeared into the woods. Brendan decided he must talk to King Finian.

Brendan stood up and walked to the edge of the wood. He'd barely stepped out, when two of the King's soldiers seized him.

"I must see King Finian," Brendan protested.

"We'll let the captain decide that," one of the soldiers said gruffly.

They walked across the open pasture. Around him, Brendan saw the soldiers making camp for the night. The smell of wood smoke began to fill the air. Some of the soldiers were building fires to cook the evening meal. The two soldiers had marched Brendan about a hundred paces or so when he spotted the familiar face of King Finian.

"Sire!" he called out.

One of the soldiers shook Brendan.

"Hush, lad. No one addresses the king without the Captn's okay."

The king, however, looked their direction and spoke.

"Bring that boy to me," the king commanded.

"Looks like you get your wish," the soldier on his right said in a low voice.

When they reached King Finian, the king recognized Brendan. He dismissed the soldiers. The king then spoke to Brendan.

"Brendan, isn't it?"

"Yes, sire."

"Why aren't you tending my cattle?" the king queried.

"Sire, I've much to tell you, I saw Failend's abduction."

"Go on then, tell me what you know."

"Well, Kaileen and I were watching as Failend was riding toward home ..."

"And why was Kaileen not with Failend?" the king interrupted.

"Well she wanted to talk to Dungal privately before she rode for home, and ..."

"Now what would she be wanting to talk to him about? In fact, as I recall, he can't speak." King Finian steamed.

"Well he can listen real well. You see he thinks he's in love with Failend."

"In love, in love," King Finian roared. "My daughter and a deaf mute!"

"He's only mute sire, he can hear real well," Brendan pointed out.

"Regardless, how is it that my daughter is taking up with a dumb herdsman?"

"It wasn't her idea, I mean Dungal and I had an argument about Failend and she was just trying to straighten things out ..."

"And what was the nature of this argument?" the king interrupted again.

"It was over whether or not she could marry one of us. I told Dungal she could never marry common folk like us; but he thought I was just saying that because I wanted her for myself," Brendan explained.

"Well I hope she straightened him out, or I'll have to discharge the both of you. It's not right for either of you to become emotionally involved with a princess, much less the Daughter of Finian!"

"Yes, sire," Brendan acknowledged humbly.

"What more can you tell me of my daughter?"

"I followed the trail of the men who captured her. I know where they are holding her."

"Now that is useful, can you lead us to her?" the king asked.

"Yes sire, but Hakon has a large army, deep in the woods. Any approach by an army big enough to defeat his would surely be detected too far off to have any chance of getting to the women before he slays them." Brendan answered.

"Women?" King Finian asked.

"Yes, he also holds Cummie, Kaileen's mother and Mugain, wife of Gall. The three of them are tethered to stakes in the middle of the barbarian encampment. To reach them from any direction, you would have to fight through barbarians."

"So that's why Gall was so cooperative. He may be a scoundrel, but he loves Mugain. He probably is only cooperating to keep her from being harmed. We must find some way to defeat these barbarians!"

"Are you going to exchange Kaileen for Failend?" Brendan asked.

"No, but we may need Kaileen here to create some sort of ruse. That's why I sent for her. Would you be willing to lead a few of my men back to Hakon's camp at first light?" King Finian asked.

"Sire I could do it still tonight. The moon has been full lately. I think I can find my way."

"Even better. Let's go to my tent. I'll send for the men who'll accompany you. We need to plot strategy for tomorrow."

King Finian then put his hand on Brendan's shoulder in a fatherly gesture and led him toward a tent which appeared big enough to sleep a dozen men. Inside, two cots made from calfskins stretched over wooden frames sat parallel to each other with a table fashioned from spears and shields in between. On the makeshift table were two candles, a silver goblet, and a bronze pitcher. King Finian motioned toward one of the cots.

"Sit yourself down," he ordered.

Then King Finian called for the guard. Two soldiers, with spears in their hands, entered the tent.

"One of you get the cook." King Finian began; then he went on. "Tell him to bring food and drink for six to my tent."

"Yes, sire," one soldier saluted and disappeared through front flap of the tent. The king then addressed the remaining one.

"Fetch me Deicola and Manchan."

When the second soldier had disappeared, King Finian turned to Brendan and explained.

"Deicola is my primary strategist. I want him to go to the enemy's camp. If there's a way to free the captives and defeat the barbarians he'll be the best to plan it."

"Manchan is my master of the dagger. He can slip in, kill his prey, and leave with scarcely a sound. He'll be a good man for tonight's work, especially for neutralizing sentries," King Finian said.

"Sire, might I suggest adding Dungal to our party?" Brendan queried.

"Why?" the king asked.

"I've seen him fight. If we get in trouble, he'll be like having three extra soldiers along."

"But aren't the two of you at odds? Besides we'd have to locate him first," King Finian countered.

"Dungal will be loyal to the purpose, especially when he learns Failend is in danger..."

"But can you trust him to follow my man Manchan's orders and not do something foolish that will jeopardize the success of this mission?" The king interrupted.

"Yes, sire if he's told any breech of discipline is likely to have dire consequences for the princess. And you can find him over the next hill to the north." Brendan explained.

"It would be best if you went for him; but I want to hold counsel soon. We have no time to waste. How long to reach him and return?" King Finian asked.

"On foot, maybe two hours, by horse, perhaps within the hour."

"How is it you can ride a horse?" the king asked, bewildered.

"Failend taught us."

"Us?"

"She taught Dungal too," Brendan explained.

"I'll have to speak to me daughter about that," King Finian commented. Then he went to the flap of the tent, held it back, and shouted, "King's groom to the king's tent."

The King returned to his cot. "Can you and Dungal ride one horse?" he asked.

"Yes, sire." Brendan answered.

Just then a voice came from outside the tent.

"King's groom reporting as ordered, sire."

"Enter," the king bellowed back.

A ruddy, full bearded man dressed in a coarse wool tunic with horsehair rope about his waist entered. Brendan noted he really had the smell of horses about him.

"How may I serve my king this evening?" the groom asked.

"Take this lad and give him my personal mount. Then lead him to our defensive lines. Arrange a password with the sentry at the northern most outpost. He has business beyond the lines; but is under orders to return to his king within an hour."

"Yes, sire," the groom answered.

"Go with my groom," the king ordered.

Brendan got up and followed the groom out of the tent. Outside, the groom led Brendan up the hill. It was completely dark now, but the light of several fires illuminated the hillside. Brendan had no trouble following the groom up the hillside to where several horses stood, hobbled. As they walked up the hill Brendan suddenly thought that maybe he should have told the king he'd never ridden at night. The groom picked up a bridle and guide rod hanging from a tripod formed of spears and walked over to the biggest white horse Brendan had ever seen! The groom reached the rein of the bridle around the horse's neck, wrapping it around the horse's neck so that he had the horse under control. Then the groom slipped the bridle on and led the horse to Brendan. He handed the guide rod to Brendan.

"Mount up, lad, I'll lead you to the north outpost," the groom instructed.

Brendan had a little trouble mounting, upon sliding back to the ground after the first attempt, the groom commented.

"You sure you can ride boy?"

"Yes," Brendan replied curtly.

Prodded by the groom's remark, Brendan easily mounted on the second try. The groom led him through the dimly illuminated darkness past groups of soldiers gathered around campfires eating bowls of stew. Soon they reached the darkness of the outer boundary of the encampment. Brendan could see a lone guard walking several paces in one direction, then, turning, walking in the other direction. The groom waved as he approached, leading Brendan on the horse. The guard waved back and asked.

"What brings you here?"

"The king is sending this lad on a mission. He's to go out and return within the hour." The groom explained.

"Ah he'll be needing a password then," the guard commented.

"How about Nighthawk?" the groom suggested.

"Nighthawk it is then," the guard confirmed, then he went on, speaking directly to Brendan.

"Listen carefully. You must return at this point. When you approach, I will ask you to identify yourself. You say Nighthawk, nothing more. If you don't follow these directions explicitly, you're like as not to have a spear thrust through your heart. Understand?"

"Yes, sir."

"Then be off with you," the guard responded.

"The groom handed Brendan the rein. A slight touch of the guide rod was all it took to send his horse trotting into the night. Brendan went slowly at first, allowing his eyes to adjust to the darkness surrounding him. The moon provided enough light for Brendan to find his way across the now familiar pasture. Brendan brought the horse up to a canter. He hoped Dungal and the cattle hadn't moved too far from the location where they'd been grazing them. He rode forward for what seemed like more than half his allotted hour; but saw nothing. Dungal must have moved the herd! Even if he found Dungal now, he would be hard pressed to make it back in time. Should he turn around and return? Which was worse? Returning without Dungal or returning with him late? Then a speck of light in the distance caught Brendan's eye. Dungal's campfire no doubt. He turned the horse toward the light. As he closed on it it got bigger. Brendan urged the horse to a gallop.

It was a camp site all right. Brendan could recognize it as such a he rode closer. He saw no sign of Dungal though. When Brendan finally arrived, Dungal was no where in sight. A small fire burned brightly in front of a make shift lean-to. It was eerie. It appeared that Dungal must have been there only moments ago. As Brendan pondered what could have happened to his friend, a body came smashing into his from somewhere near his left rear. The momentum carried Brendan from his horse to the ground below.

# CHAPTER 11

They both impacted the ground simultaneously. The assailant had him in a choke hold. Brendan struggled to his feet, then, feeling for the assailant's head behind him, he grabbed the head with his right hand. Then Brendan threw both legs forward, sitting down hard, and bending at the waist. This movement threw his assailant forward, causing him to release his grip and somersaulting forward on the ground. As the assailant rolled from his back to his stomach and sprung to his feet, Brendan saw it was Dungal. Nearly as quickly, Dungal recognized Brendan and froze.

"Dungal, what are you doing?" Brendan protested.

Dungal cupped one hand to his ear, pointed to the horse, and stamped the ground indicating he'd heard the hoof beats at a distance. Then he scratched his head indicating he wondered why he heard hoof beats at night. He shook his head and folded his arms in a hugging motion, indicating he didn't think it could have been a friendly visit that time of night. Then he pointed to the darkness from which he had sprung and crouched down to his haunches indicating he'd waited in the shadows for the horse and rider to arrive. Then he put a hand over eyes and pointed to his back with the other to indicate he couldn't tell who the rider was because all he could see was his back.

"Okay, but I need you to come with me," Brendan responded, anxious to be on his way.

Dungal threw up his arm in a motion that asked "Why?"

"Failend's been kidnapped," Brendan started.

Dungal became fully animated. "When? By whom?" he signed.

"The sea warriors, earlier today; King Finian's preparing a plan to get her back. The king wants your help." Brendan fired back the answers.

Dungal pointed at Brendan, at himself and at the horse in three quick motions, indicating they should leave immediately.

"Let's go then," Brendan answered.

It took Brendan and Dungal a moment for them to find the guide rod since Brendan had dropped it when Dungal smashed into him. Once he had it, he mounted with Dungal swinging up behind. Finding their way back wasn't nearly as difficult. A short distance from Dungal's camp, Brendan could spot the fires of King Finian's camp, appearing like many distant stars on the low horizon in the distance. Brendan guided the horse toward the northernmost one with the hope that they would approach the encampment at the same point where he had left it earlier.

As they closed in on the campfires, fear pulsed through Brendan. He knew he was overdue. The trip had taken much longer than expected. He also didn't know for sure if he would enter where the sentry would recognize him. As these worries cycled through his head, he drifted into a trance. This was broken by a shout.

"Halt. Go no further. Identify yourself."

"Brend..." Brendan started to say, losing concentration by the shock of the voice in the dark. Then, horrified, he remembered the password.

"Nighthawk," he shouted, overcompensating.

"Pass," the sentry ordered.

Brendan inched the horse passed the sentry. He noticed as he passed, this was a different sentry. He wondered why the sentry had let him pass. *Never mind. He had to get to the king's tent as soon as possible.* He spotted it; but as he rode toward it the groom appeared from the darkness.

"I'll take the king's horse now," he said.

Dungal and Brendan dismounted. Brendan handed the rein and guide rod to the groom.

"This way," Brendan instructed as he led Dungal to the king's tent.

When they reached the tent, the guards immediately ushered them in. As Brendan passed under the tent flap, King Finian spoke.

"Where have you been?"

"It took longer than I thought. Forgive me, sire." Brendan answered.

"Never mind now. Just get over here. We've much to do, and not much time," King Finian ordered.

Beside the King were two men. One was tall and thin with shoulder length red hair, wearing a linen shirt over linen trousers. The shirt was gathered with a leather webbed belt, upon which hung a dagger and several pouches. King Finian introduced this man as Deicola, his master strategist. The other man wore deer skin clothing of much the same style as Deicola, but had a large sword in wooden sheath hanging from a wide belt which crossed his chest. He also wore a leather belt with a dagger hanging from it as well as several pouches and a neatly wound shank of rope. He had a leathery face, taunt and covered with what appeared to be a couple of days growth of whiskers. His right cheek bore the remnants of a large scar which bespoke a history of previous battles. The king pointed to this man and announced.

"Manchan, here, will be in charge of this mission. You may advise him. However, he will have the final say. You will obey him as you would your king."

"Yes, sire," Brendan and Deicola responded in unison. Dungal nodded his assent.

"Now," King Finian went on, "We need a plan to rescue my daughter, and defeat these barbarians; but my daughter's welfare must be foremost in your mind. For this reason, I'm sending Deicola with you and Dungal to do a reconnaissance of the barbarian forces. You must get in, learn as much as you can about them, and get out. You must get back here as soon as possible so we can plan our attack. But, most important you must not be caught. They may kill Failend if they discover any of you."

"Yes, sire," all joined in unison.

Then, speaking to Manchan, "Brendan here knows the way to the camp. Dungal can help you take out the guards—if necessary; but, mind you, avoid being discovered at all costs."

"We'd best be getting you a weapon, Dungal," Manchan said. "What do you fancy?"

Dungal pointed at the dagger on Manchan's belt. Manchan responded by calling for a guard. When the guard appeared, Manchan ordered him to get a dagger for Dungal and one for Brendan. He turned to Brendan.

"You'd best be armed also, just in case," he said.

The guard saluted and ducked back out under the tent flap.

"While you are waiting, take a little refreshment," the king entreated, motioning toward the table.

Brendan took one each of the slices of bread and cheese before them, and one of the goblets of ale. He'd barely had time to finish his bread and cheese before the guard reappeared with the weapons. Brendan gulped down his ale and wiped his mouth with his sleeve. Manchan handed him a dagger on a leather belt which he tied with thongs. Brendan strapped it on his right side, noticing that Dungal had done the same.

"By your leave, sire, we'll be off," Manchan addressed the king.

"Go," King Finian replied.

"Brendan, lead the way," Manchan commanded.

Brendan threw back the tent flap and led the small group into the night. When he entered the woods, he began to worry a little about finding his way. The moon which provided sufficient light to find his way across the pasture now seemed inadequate to illuminate the trail before him. The burden of the mission now weighed heavily upon his shoulders. Failend, Kaileen's mother, Mugain, Fr. Sweeney, and perhaps many of the soldiers might live or die, depending on the outcome of their mission. He had to find his way back there.

Several hours later, Brendan felt for sure he'd lost his direction. He pressed ahead. He was afraid to tell Manchan. He desperately hoped for some sign he was going in the right direction. Moving through the brush in the dimly lit forest was very slow going. Brendan had to do it almost by feel, searching for the path where the brush had been parted before. He was about to give up when heard a distant sound which, although faint, Brendan took to be human. It gave him hope though. He mentally fixed on the direction where he'd heard the sound and began making his way toward it. A few moments later, to Brendan's relief, he heard additional faint sounds drifting in the gentle night breeze. Brendan adjusted his course and pushed on. Voices were audible now; but not understandable. He was confident the sea warrior camp lay ahead. Yes, light was visible now from at least one fire. He turned to Manchan and whispered.

"I think we're nearing Hakon's camp now. We must be on the lookout for sentries."

Manchan first nodded that he understood and said, "We'll take it slow, and we'll all keep our eyes open. Go ahead, lead on."

Brendan dropped to his hands and knees to move forward. He knew he could be almost silent this way. He fixed his sight on the light from the fire. It grew as Brendan inched ever closer, until he could see that it was a great bonfire. Brendan was a little concerned that they'd spotted no guards yet. He was sure he'd led his party inside the barbarian's perimeter outposts. Then a cough from the darkness only a few feet away sent his heart racing. He'd led his party of four right to the guard. The next thing he sensed was hot breath right next to his left ear on which he heard two words: "Stay here." The words were Manchan's.

Manchan slid by Brendan in silence. A moment later, Brendan heard a grunt, followed by a crash, and a short period of thrashing in the brush, then silence again. Then Manchan crawled out of the brush ahead.

"I had to take him out," Manchan explained, then went on "We were so close, he'd likely have spotted us even if we tried to retreat. One of us should stay here to guard our path of retreat for now. After we do our reconnaissance of the camp, I will dress in the guards' clothes and armor. Hopefully, I can pass myself as one of them so they won't discover the missing guard."

"Isn't that extremely risky?" Deicola asked.

"I think it's our best chance. We must do everything we can to keep our visit here a secret." Manchan explained.

"Dungal can stay here to guard the path," Brendan suggested.

"Okay. You tell him to watch for other warriors. If anyone tries to come in behind us, he must find us immediately." Manchan instructed.

Brendan moved back, passed Deicola, to Manchan. He passed on Manchan's orders. Dungal nodded he understood. Brendan moved back to his position in the lead. He crawled down to the edge of the clearing he'd seen once earlier that day. A great fire burned in the center of the clearing. Around it, everyone slept, barbarian warriors with their heads resting on their helmets, Father Sweeney, Kaileen's mother, Mugain, Failend, and even Hakon. Only two warriors, tending the fire, were awake.

Deicola and Manchan crawled up on either side of Brendan. They took in the view; then Manchan whispered.

"It looks like only two are awake down there. It may be possible to take those two out, free the prisoners, and get out of here before any one wakes."

"I wouldn't advise it," Deicola answered, then explained. "We have a lot of open ground to cover, undetected. All one of those barbarians has to do is see us and start shouting to wake everyone up. Then where would we be? Surrounded by 150 more or less barbarians, with no way out. Besides, there may be others, beyond the fire on the far side in the brush where we can't see them from here."

"Yeah, I supposed you're right. I sure wish we could bring the king's daughter back with us, though." Manchan commented.

"Ah, the king would be pleased if we could do that to be sure," Deicola commented, and then he continued. "I've got an idea."

"What's that?" Manchan asked.

"Well, Kilian will likely have to attack the camp to free the hostages, right?" Deicola began.

"True," Manchan answered.

Michael J. Schneider

"The attack will result in a lot of confusion. We don't know how the barbarians will react. They may get to the hostages before we can. It would be good to have someone in the camp, familiar to the hostages, who can free them during the attack, and lead them out of harm's way," Deicola said.

Deicola and Manchan were both now looking at Brendan. Manchan asked, "What do you have in mind?"

"Suppose Brendan here were in the camp when the attack begins. He might free the hostages and lead them out," Deicola proposed.

"But how do we get him into camp and still have the freedom to free the others?" Manchan asked, appearing quite puzzled.

"He'll have to let himself be captured," Deicola responded.

"But how can he help anyone if he is a prisoner?" Manchan asked.

"He has to convince them he is of little threat. It helps that that he has a club foot. Most likely that fact alone will convince the barbarians he'll cause them no trouble," Deicola explained. Then he spoke to Brendan.

"In addition, Brendan you must act quite humble, and willing to serve the sea warriors. Are you willing to give it a try?"

Brendan contemplated for a moment. The thought of being alone, among all those barbarians scared him. He wished he could come up with some excuse to decline that would not make him appear to be a coward. Then he thought of Failend and Kaileen's mother, Cummie, and Mugain, who had shown him so much kindness. What would the barbarians do to them? He decided he had to do what he could to free them."

"Okay, I'll do it," Brendan agreed.

"I must warn you will be facing extreme danger. I can only speculate on how the sea warriors will react. They could decide to kill you on sight." Deicola explained.

"I understand, and I'm willing to do it; but I can use all the advice you can give," Brendan answered.

"Okay, let's get back to Dungal and work things out," Deicola suggested.

With Brendan leading, the three crawled back to the point where Dungal waited. Brendan announced their arrival by whispering,"Dungal, it's us."

A slight rustling of leaves and Dungal appeared walking crouched down. The four formed a small circle. Deicola outlined the plan.

"Dungal and I will return to King Finian. I will recommend that the king send part of his forces back here to attack the camp. Hakon will probably bring the bulk of his forces and Failend with him to meet the king and trade for Kaileen. I will recommend the king make the trade without incident. By the time

112

the trade is completed, the king's forces should have taken the camp here. Brendan you will need to free the hostages when the attack begins and lead them to a safe place here in the woods. Stay put until the king orders you out. We plan to follow Hakon back to the camp at a distance. When Hakon arrives, he should be trapped between the forces in the camp and those pursuing him from behind. He should be taken enough by surprise that we should be able to snatch Kaileen and send what's left of his forces running for the sea."

"But how am I going to be able to do all the things you expect of me?" Brendan interrupted.

"First, take your dagger and strap it to your thigh inside your tunic. You'll need it to cut the bonds of the hostages. We're counting that you will not appear to be any threat to these sea warriors, so they will not try to search you for weapons. Captain Kilian and I will lead the king's forces in the attack on the camp so we will coordinate with your activities in the barbarian camp. You will stay here with Manchan until we have returned. I will signal our return with a bird call. When you hear three chirps of a skylark with a short pause followed by three more chirps, we're back. Walk toward the camp and let the sentries catch you. More than likely they'll take you to Father Sweeney so they can question you. They'll need him to interpret. That's when we'll attack. You need to cut all the hostages loose—fast. Then get them out of there."

"But what if things don't go like you describe them?" Brendan asked.

"Hopefully, Manchan can assist you; but Hakon will likely relieve the guards on the outposts at dawn or very near then. I hope Manchan can pass for one of them long enough for us to pull this caper off. It will be difficult since he can't speak or understand their language."

"Just how will he avoid speaking?" Brendan asked.

"Oh, I've seen Manchan manage a conversation on a grunt and a nod when he's had too much of the whisky," Deicola answered with a chuckle. Then he continued, "If you're ready, Dungal and I'll be off."

"I, I, guess I'm ready," Brendan answered.

Dungal pointed to his chest, then to Brendan and clasped his hands together.

"Dungal wants to stay with me," Brendan translated.

"I want him to come with me. Should anything happen, there's a better chance one of us will get through to the king." Deicola explained.

Dungal shrugged his shoulders in a sign of resolve. Deicola saw this gesture and understood. He spoke to Dungal:

"Okay, let's go. Do you know the way?"

Dungal nodded, "Yes."

Dungal then disappeared into the bush with Deicola following.

When they'd gone, Manchan spoke to Brendan.

"It'll be some hours before we'll be called to do our duty. Why don't you lie down and get some rest. I'll awake you when it's time."

Brendan strapped the dagger to the inside of his left thigh. Then he tried to stretch out the best he could under the bushes. He thought he was too excited to sleep; but he was concentrating on an interesting cluster of stars when the next thing he knew there was a hand over his mouth and Manchan's voice was whispering for him to wake up. Brendan opened his eyes. The darkness of the night was giving away to the gray light of early dawn. When Brendan started to sit up, Manchan held him back.

"Easy, you remember where we are?" Manchan asked.

Brendan nodded. Manchan lifted his hand. Brendan sat up, still obscured by holly. Manchan was kneeling next to him. Then Manchan asked:

"You see that big ash tree over there?"

Brendan looked in the direction Manchan pointed. Scanning the forest for a moment, he was sure he spotted it.

"Yes."

"I've been watching it for sometime. There's another sentry over there. I want you to crawl about half way from here to there; then crawl far enough out so that you are outside of the defense perimeter. Watch for the sentry to look the other way for a moment, then stand up and walk toward the camp as though you were just passing through the woods looking for a stray cow or something," Manchan instructed.

"Then what?" Brendan asked anxiously.

"Then things should pretty much happen. Just act like the herdsman who's lost a cow. When King Finian's forces begin the attack, think of nothing but cutting the hostages loose and getting out of camp. Now off with you."

With this last urging from Manchan, Brendan began crawling through the forest understory. The ground cover was thick, and the going slow. Brendan felt as though the eyes and breath of a thousand men were on him, waiting for him to make the final move that signal them to assault the barbarians. He worried that he was taking too long, that they would launch the attack any minute, even if he were not in position to free the hostages. A little further, yes, now he was out far enough; but he couldn't see the sentry. He moved out a little further. He now spotted the sentry through the gorse and heather. He was pretty well

114

camouflaged by the brush also. A bird flew passed the sentry's right side distracting his attention for a moment.

Brendan stood up. Brendan looked straight in the direction of the camp, daring not to glance either in the direction of the sentry or Manchan. He took a dozen or more steps. He was beginning to wonder if he was going to be able to walk directly into the camp unopposed when he heard a deep voice bark:

"Stop!"

Brendan froze and looked at the massive figure of the barbarian, dirty blond hair and all, crashing through the woods toward him. The barbarian drew his sword from its sheath as he came. Brendan trembled. Would the barbarian take him captive or kill him where he stood?

# CHAPTER 12

The barbarian slapped his shoulder with the sword and pointed the sword in the direction of the camp.

"Gå," the barbarian ordered.

Brendan got the idea. He headed toward the camp. As they moved forward, Brendan heard his captor holler something once again he had no hope of translating. Then Manchan appeared from his hiding place and waved his sword at them in a sign of recognition to sea warrior holding him captive. To Brendan's surprise, Manchan didn't join them. Of course, a guard wouldn't leave his post, unless ordered, or he needed to assist the guard now marching him in, which he clearly didn't. Besides, the chances of the barbarians discovering Manchan's true identity increased if he was drawn into camp where he might be questioned.

As Brendan entered the camp, he noticed at once the absence of Failend, and Hakon was nowhere in sight. As they approached the fire, Father Sweeney rose from his seat on the ground where he had been eating a bowl of porridge. He staggered forward, obviously still suffering from the wounds he'd received at Kilrush and who knows what abuses since then. Apparently the barbarians were convinced he posed no threat for he was not bound. In contrast, both Cummie and Mugain had their hands bound and legs hobbled by leather straps. They sat with their backs toward Brendan until Father Sweeney arose. They turned sideways to look at the reason for Father Sweeney's attention being focused behind them. Mugain wore a light blue linen tunic, soiled and torn about the shoulders, indicating she struggled against her captors. When she first recognized Brendan, she started to smile. The smile quickly metamorphosed into

116

an expression of pain. Mugain's dark hair hung from her head in clumps of strands that gave her head the appearance of an inverted rag mop. Cummie, while her pink linen tunic showed not the evidence of battle with the barbarians, looked equally disheveled from the neck up. Her golden-red hair, usually kept in a myriad of curls about her head, now appeared kinked as sheep's wool. The face that Brendan remembered as always bearing a sympathetic smile now sagged under the burden of captivity and separation from Kaileen. One of the barbarians, covered with hides of deer and wolf stepped forward and shouted:

"Hvem vaere dere?"

"Use the Latin," Father Sweeney prodded him.

The sea warrior repeated "Who are you?" this time in Latin. Father Sweeney translated the Latin to Gaelic.

"I am Brendan, a humble herdsman," Brendan responded.

This prompted the sea warrior to ask: "Who do you serve?"

"King Finian."

"Why are you here?" the barbarian asked. Brendan knew what the barbarian asked before Father Sweeney completed the translation.

"I lost a cow. The last I saw it, it ran into these woods." Brendan answered.

"And where might we find your king?" the sea warrior asked.

"About half a day's journey from here, in that direction," Brendan answered, pointing in the general direction to where King Finian's camp was located.

"My king has business with your king. You'll have to stay here until he returns. My king, King Hakon, will decide what's to become of you. Do you know this man here?" the barbarian leader asked.

"Yes, he's Father Sweeney who," Brendan caught himself. He was about to say, "Who you nearly killed," but he didn't want to remind the barbarian he'd had contact with them before.

"Who is he to you?" the sea warrior asked.

"He is our priest. The one who teaches us about Jesus Christ, his apostles, and the saints," Brendan answered. He noticed Father Sweeney's face beamed when he translated Brendan's words.

"You worship this Christ as a god, don't you? I've heard of him before, from earlier conquests."

"He is God," Brendan protested.

"We Vikings have our gods too, but I don't believe in them. They've never done me much good. Still King Hakon demands we offer sacrifice to the gods before each voyage. Never mind that now. If you stay with Father Sweeney and

117

don't try to run away, we won't have to bind you like these women, understand?"

"Yes," Brendan answered. He wondered when Finian's army would attack. It seemed like he'd been there much too long already. What were they waiting for?

"Do you know either of these women?" the Viking pressed.

Fear struck Brendan. He was afraid to say no lest the sea warrior sense he was lying. He didn't want to acknowledge he knew who they were either. If they knew Cummie was Kaileen's mother, they might torture her, or threaten to torture her to get Kaileen to do anything they wanted. He decided to stall.

"How is it that you speak Latin?" Brendan asked.

"Some of us have picked it up in our travels. It seems those who have valuables to hide know the language. We tend to seek those people out, for obvious reasons. Many appear to be these worshipers of this god you call Christ."

"He was man also," Brendan interrupted, hoping to draw the Viking leader into a religious debate to divert his attention from Mugain and Cummie.

"Never mind that. I asked you if you know these two woman?" The barbarian bellowed back.

"The dark-haired one, she is the wife of a former master," Brendan answered. He hoped he would not have to say anything about Kaileen's mother.

"And the other?" the Viking leader urged.

Brendan was about to say he'd seen her trading in the village or upon the road, just to appear sincere without divulging any more details when it happened. There was a rushing of branches and a stone struck the barbarian on the side of the head. It wasn't an incapacitating blow; but it stunned the leader long enough. Brendan pulled up his tunic and removed the dagger. He dove for the feet of Mugain. He sliced the leather thong of the hobble on her ankles.

"Take Father Sweeney and head that way," he ordered.

Brendan pointed to the woods where a wave of Irish warriors was washing down on the camp. Then he rolled to his right and slashed the bonds on Cummie's ankles. He stood up, and helped her to her feet. Fortunately, the Viking leader and the remaining barbarians in the camp were too busy falling into a battle formation to defend themselves against the onslaught of Finian's men. Brendan took hold of Cummie's bound hands and led her toward the woods, following behind Mugain and Father Sweeney.

"I'll free your hands once we get some distance between us and this camp," Brendan shouted.

As they moved into the woods; Irish soldiers passed by them on either side. Brendan felt some sense of relief that the soldiers were now between them and the barbarians; but knew Viking sentries might still be lurking about and posed a real danger. Brendan looked ahead. Mugain was behind Father Sweeney, urging him on. She glanced back from time to time to assure Brendan was following. After a several dozen paces, Brendan stopped for a moment and slit the leather thong binding Cummie's hands, just outside of the knot. They continued on, with Kaileen's mother working her hands free of the bindings as they moved.

"Oh, thank you, Brendan," she said, "I don't know what they might have done to us, if you hadn't freed us."

"Don't count yourself free of them yet," Brendan chided her.

"Do you know anything of my Kaileen?" Cummie asked.

"She's under King Finian's care," Brendan answered. He didn't want to tell Kaileen's mother that Hakon had proposed trading Failend for Kaileen.

"Good, but the king of those barbarians left early this morning with an Irish girl they captured, Mugain's husband and more than half his warriors. What do you suppose he intends to do with the girl and Mugain's husband?"

"The girl is Failend, King Finian's daughter. Hakon, the barbarian king, demands a ransom for her. Gall, Mugain's husband, is communicating the transfer terms," Brendan explained.

"Isn't King Finian worried that the attack on Hakon's camp will endanger his daughter?"

"King Finian is counting on King Hakon not learning of the attack on the camp until after Failend is returned. He plans to pursue Hakon at a distance after the ransom; then trap him when he returns to the camp. Hakon should be caught between the two forces of King Finian. The King will likely recover his ransom." Brendan explained.

"Well he is responsible for freeing me, and I'm grateful for that. But how is it that you are in the middle of this?"

"That's a long story; but it is because Gall dismissed me and I had to find a new master. King Finian took me as his herdsman."

"And Kaileen, do you know how she came to be at King Finian's estate?" Cummie asked.

"That is also a long tale; but we were fleeing these barbarians together after they attacked and burned Kilrush."

"Is she all right? Did they harm her?"

"No, she is okay, but your house is no more, nor is the village." Brendan confided.

"Father Sweeney told me about the village; but he could tell me nothing of Kaileen," Cummie explained.

"He was badly hurt by the barbarians. Kaileen and I came across him. We last left him with the miller near Kilrush."

"And that's where I came across him. He'd just recovered enough to travel. He told about the raid on Kilrush. A group of six of the barbarians found us at the mill. The miller tried to draw them away from us but one of the barbarians hurled a ·javelin at him. It caught the miller in the back and killed him. The barbarians then searched the mill and found us. They were about to kill Father Sweeney when one of them noticed the wooden cross he wears on his chest. Apparently they have had previous contact with priests and monks. They know the priests and monks speak Latin, so they are useful as interpreters. They took us to their king. The king questioned us briefly; but was preoccupied with assaulting Gall's rath. He took them by surprise. There was little Gall's men and family could do to defend themselves. Still they managed to fight the invaders off for half a day, forcing them to fight hut to hut, and killing at least one of the barbarians for each of them killed. Gall's daughters and their husbands were all killed in the fight. Gall himself might have been killed; but so many rushed upon him so quickly that that he couldn't fight back. They've threatened to kill Mugain if he doesn't do their bidding."

"Well that explains why Gall is so cooperative," Brendan began, "He tends to be a selfish scoundrel; but he loves Mugain very much."

"Are you taking me to Kaileen?" Cummie asked.

"I'm taking you to King Finian; but I'm sure he will see that you are reunited with Kaileen." Brendan answered.

"You sound hesitant, Brendan, what's wrong?" Cummie asked.

"Nothing, other than we're trying to escape a band of vicious barbarians," Brendan shot back.

"No, it has to do with Kaileen, what is it Brendan?"

"Hakon wants Kaileen as part of the ransom."

"He what? I mean how? Why? Why would he make such a request?" Cummie stammered. "What's Kaileen to him?" she continued.

"He captured her when he attacked Kilrush. I freed her. We've been on the run most of the time since," Brendan explained.

"Do you think King Finian will turn Kaileen over to these barbarians?" Cummie asked.

"He loves Failend as you love Kaileen. He sent soldiers back to the rath to bring Kaileen to the meeting place. I can't say for sure what he will do. I know he planned to free all hostages." Brendan continued.

"Do you think we can get to King Finian before he pays the ransom?" Cummie asked.

"Not likely, but King Finian may try to stall for time so that these forces now attacking his camp can move into position behind Hakon's forces."

"Then let's hurry."

"Sorry, mum, but I can only move so fast."

"Oh, I'm sorry, Brendan. I forgot about your bad leg."

Brendan looked ahead. Father Sweeney and Mugain had paused to wait for him to catch up with them. Father Sweeney was rubbing Mugain's shoulder in a gesture of comfort. It took only a few more moments for Brendan and Cummie to catch up to them. As Brendan approached, Mugain held out her bound hands to him.

"Can you do something about this?" she asked.

Brendan was suddenly aware that the dagger had never left his hands. He slit the leather strap binding her hands and quickly unraveled it for her. Mugain responded by placing her hands on either side of Brendan's face. Then she pulled his head straight toward her and kissed him hard in the lips. Then she threw both arms around him and hugged him so hard Brendan huffed as he involuntary expelled air from his lungs.

"Thank you, you wonderful boy," she beamed.

"I'm very grateful too, Brendan," Cummie added. "But would you lead us on to King Finian?" she continued.

"Yes, mum," Brendan answered.

Brendan took the lead; but the brush thinned for a while and Mugain came up on his right side. She grasped his upper arm and gave it a friendly shake. She continued walking alongside him and spoke as they walked.

"Oh, it's good to see you again. I worried about what happened to you when my husband turned you out. How's Kaileen?"

"She's doing okay. She's now a servant to King Finian's daughter, Failend," Brendan answered.

"You mean the girl we met in camp?" Mugain asked.

"Yes, that's her," Brendan answered.

"How did that barbarian manage to snatch her away from King Finian?" Mugain asked.

"She and Kaileen would ride in the pasture where I tend King Finian's cows. She had decided to ride back on her own. That's when the sea warriors, they call themselves Vikings, kidnapped her. They sprang from the woods and pulled her off her horse." Brendan recounted the incident.

"Where was her handmaiden when this happened?" Mugain asked.

"She was with me," Brendan answered.

"Is there something between you and Kaileen?" Mugain asked.

"Like what?" Brendan asked innocently.

"Like are you in love with her?" Mugain put the question to him bluntly.

"No, I mean, if you really must know, I think I'm in love with Failend."

"Ah, but she's of royal blood. There's no way you can marry her. Are you sure you don't feel the same toward Kaileen?" Mugain pressed.

"Well, maybe," Brendan hesitated.

"Ah, I thought as much. A mother can tell, you know," Mugain said with a wink.

"Do you suppose?" Brendan asked as he glanced back at Kaileen's mother.

"Ah, no. Not yet at least. Cummie doesn't know you as well as I do," Mugain answered as she squeezed his arm.

"I'm sorry to hear about your daughters, and their husbands," Brendan tried to console.

"You know of that? Yes, it pains me deeply; but they fought to their deaths alongside their husbands. It is more a comfort for a mother to know they are in the hands of angels instead of these devils as I was before your rescue," Mugain answered him.

"Where are you taking us?" Father Sweeney's voice came from behind.

"To King Finian. It is his soldiers who are now attacking the Viking camp," Brendan answered.

"I must thank him, and you, for our freedom," Father Sweeney continued.

"You may be a bit premature, Father, we're not out of the woods yet," Brendan shot back.

"A pun, eh, Brendan, well at least you're in good spirits. Lead on," Father Sweeney answered.

They trudged through the forest moving as quickly as Brendan's club foot would allow. After the long night, Brendan was exhausted and wished he could lie down and sleep. By noon Brendan began to hear noises from the brush ahead. In a few moments they would likely reach the edge of the woods he estimated. He stopped and motioned the others around him to stop.

"We need to watch out for Hakon's men," he whispered. "Be as quiet as you can."

Brendan had to slow down now. He quietly picked his way through the brush until at last he reached the edge of the wood. He now could see King Finian's forces forming a great semicircle in the field beyond. They stood, shields on arm, swords drawn or spears pointing at the sky, ready to be turned to the enemy. Just outside the forest edge stood Hakon's forces. Their swords were sheathed; but the sea warriors stood with the kind of confidence which said they felt superior to the army they faced across the vast field of uncut hay. Brendan could see King Finian with Diecola on his left and Captain Kilian on his right sitting on horseback just in front of his troops. Brendan looked for some sign of the Viking king; but there were too many of the sea warriors between him and where Brendan guessed King Hakon might be standing. One thing Brendan noticed was that he could see no sign of Kaileen among the Irish ranks. He couldn't see Failend either; but she might be near Hakon and out of his view. He wanted a better view.

"Follow me," Brendan whispered to the others.

Then he crawled through the bushes toward the area in line with the center of Hakon's forces. After a short time he spotted a Viking leaning against a tree. Close enough, he thought. He motioned to the others to settle back in the bushes. He could just make out the figure of Failend by looking between the legs of the sea warriors. The ground sloped downward in front of him to a depression then rose again, giving the high ground to Finian's army. It was Failend's dress flapping gently in the breeze that drew Brendan's attention to her. As he settled into place, he heard Mugain whisper in his ear.

"What do we do next?" she asked.

"We wait till they leave or for some kind of commotion," Brendan instructed. "If any kind of a disturbance breaks out, run for Finian's lines and don't look back."

Just then, Kaileen, with two soldiers on either side of her appeared on top of the hill. Then Brendan heard Gall's voice.

"The king wants you to send the girl down with two of your soldiers. He will send your daughter up with two of his men. They are to meet midway between you and King Hakon. If you try to cheat, King Hakon has given orders to his men to kill your daughter immediately. If you try to follow us after the exchange to rescue the girl, Kaileen, she will die. Do you understand?"

"I do," King Finian responded.

King Finian motioned to the two soldiers on top of the hill, raising his arm above his head and pointing first toward Kaileen, then toward the Viking lines. The two soldiers marched forward with Kaileen in step between them. As they moved down the hill, Brendan noted Kaileen walked erect and tall, hands free at her sides. She was going into captivity willingly, to secure the freedom of her mistress.

"No," Cummie squealed in the bushes behind Brendan.

"Shush," Brendan scolded her and explained.

"I'm sure King Finian has a plan to rescue her. Be patient or we'll blow his plan and possibly get Kaileen and Failend killed."

"Sorry," Cummie whispered.

Brendan turned back to watch the exchange again. He could now see Failend walking up the hill between her two Viking guards. Her hands were not visible, probably still tied in front of her. Brendan waited nervously as the two parties approached each other closer and closer. Finally they stopped within arms reach of each other. Failend stepped forward toward the two Irish soldiers. Kaileen made the same motion toward the Vikings. That's when chaos erupted! Kaileen pulled up her dress and jumped sideways at the Viking on her right. Suspended for a moment parallel to the ground, Kaileen shot one leg behind the Viking guard knees and the other up his thighs, twisting her body abruptly toward him. This motion had the effect of completely throwing the Viking onto his back. As Kaileen scrambled to her feet, she hollered.

"Run, Failend,

The other Viking drew his sword and attempted to decapitate Kaileen; but one of the Irish soldiers parried the blow. In the meantime, Failend was sprinting up the hill. The two Irish soldiers engaged the Vikings in close combat. Kaileen managed to regain her feet and started running up the hill, following Failend. The Viking and Irish armies rushed toward each other, screaming their battle cries at the top of their lungs. King Finian rode down the hill toward his daughter. Deicola and another officer rode to the lead the left and right flanks of the Irish army. King Hakon and a band of fifty or so rushed in a mighty wedge toward the center of the Irish lines. Brendan turned to the group behind him.

"Head for the top of the hill, now. Don't wait for me." Brendan commanded.

Father Sweeney, Cummie and Mugain sprung from the bushes and ran toward the battle fray. They headed to the left flank of the Viking ranks where the combatants were more spread out. Brendan followed them. A cloud of dust rose above the field as swords impacted the Irish shields, releasing chalk dust into the air. Through the dust, however, Brendan could see King Finian reach down and pull Failend up on his horse. Then the King jumped down to do battle as Failend rode for the top of the hill. King Hakon reached King Finian at the head of his rushing wedge of warriors. Two of the warriors immediately began to attack King Finian. With the Irish king,being engaged in mortal combat, King Hakon led the rest of the wedge of Vikings up the hill. Brendan now worried that they would overtake Kaileen who continued to scramble up the hill. Then a second horseman appeared. It was Dungal! He rode toward Kaileen—the Vikings were almost to her.

# CHAPTER 13

Just as Dungal reached down to grab Kaileen's outstretched arm, two of the barbarians grabbed her from behind. She grasped Dungal's forearm in desperation; but the gesture only served to pull him from the horse and into the horde of sea warriors. As the horse scrambled to get away from the commotion, the Vikings bound Kaileen and Dungal and began to retreat down the hill and toward the woods to the right. Brendan looked back to Father Sweeney.

Brendan now had a tough choice ahead. He could follow Father Sweeney and the others to the relative safety of King Finian's camp or follow King Hakon who now had his two best friends on earth captive. Brendan hoped the Irish soldiers would note King Hakon fleeing and pursue him. The fact of the matter was that, without the additional troops who attacked Hakon's camp, the Irish soldiers were outnumbered by the Vikings and the fighting was likely to continue for some time. Brendan made his decision. He would follow King Hakon and the group of Vikings now heading away from the left flank of the Irish battle lines. Brendan moved along the edge of the woods. He tried to stay in cover of the woods but not let the forest obscure his vision of the retreating party of Vikings with their two captives. Fortunately the barbarian party moved slowly, having to stop from time to time to fight their way through Irish warriors. This gave Brendan time to make progress along a path that would eventually intersect theirs. By the time the barbarians had crossed the depression and were heading into the woods, Brendan was close enough to follow them at a respectable distance. Brendan glanced back toward the fighting. There was no let up and no sign of anyone pursuing the contingent of Vikings now escaping into

126

the woods. Brendan would have to follow and look for his chance either to free them or to bring soldiers to assist him in freeing them. When the last of the Vikings disappeared into the woods, Brendan was only paces behind them.

\*\*\*\*

Several hours later, as Brendan continued to follow the Vikings, he determined they must be heading straight for the river and their ships. Brendan thought they would attempt to reach their camp; but they weren't going that way. Brendan had hoped they would head for their former camp. That way they would likely run into King Finian's soldiers who were returning from the assault on the camp.

Following the Vikings wasn't easy. Brendan couldn't hope to keep up with them. This was both a blessing and a curse. While it was hard to follow the trail, being so far behind them, Brendan knew the risk of discovery was a lot greater if he got too close to them. Brendan wondered why King Hakon had abandoned his forces both on the battlefield and at the Viking camp. Could it be he knew of the attack on the camp and knew Finian's forces were closing on both sides? It didn't matter. Hakon had both Kaileen and Dungal now and Brendan must find some way to help them escape. Why didn't they kill Dungal? That was another curious question. It would have been just as easy to slay him and leave him on the battlefield.

Brendan pondered these questions during the next two days journey as he followed the warriors. The Vikings stopped to sleep, something for which Brendan was very grateful, but made no campfires, lest it betray their presence. It gave Brendan pleasure to know they were the ones now on the run, that they were in fear of being pursued and killed or captured. If only Manchan and half a hundred of King Finian's men were with him now. They could rescue Kaileen, Dungal and destroy the remaining barbarians.

\*\*\*\*

By noon on the third day, Brendan recognized the familiar signs of the trail leading to the former village of Kilrush. He had only to worry about keeping his distance now. He was sure the Vikings would follow the trail to the beach. As he neared the beach, the smell of burning wood and roast rabbit filled his nostrils. It was then than Brendan realized he hadn't had a meal since the night King Finian sent him off with Deicola, Manchan, and Dungal to Hakon's camp. Some berries found along the trail and water from the streams he crossed was his only sustenance. He moved into the woods as he neared the ruins of Kilrush and worked his way down to the beach. Brendan found a good site in the rushes and settled down to observe. The Vikings had stopped to cook themselves lunch. Evidently they tired of eating uncooked food since they hadn't built fires to cook during their flight to the beach. Now, only a 100 feet or so from their ships, they decided to relax and enjoy a real meal. A dozen or so fires burned in a rough circle. Over each fire were spits containing salmon from the river or small game like rabbit or badger. The smell made Brendan's mouth water. The only trouble was that around each fire were anywhere from two to eight sea warriors. In the middle of this ring of fires Kaileen and Dungal sat, back to back, their hands and feet bound in iron shackles and chains. As a further precaution, the barbarians had fastened a chain from their foot irons to a stake in the ground. There wasn't much hope of freeing them.

Brendan turned his attention to the ships along the beach. He noted that King Hakon was directing a dozen of the Vikings busy removing items from the ships alongside the two in the center of the line of ships and loading them into the middle two. It appeared they were going to leave in the two center ships. King Hakon turned and shouted and another dozen left their fires and ran for the beach. The sudden departure left one of the fires vacant with a spit containing a roasting rabbit. This was almost too much temptation for Brendan to bear. Then he got an idea. He knew he couldn't free Kaileen and Dungal under the present conditions. Brendan looked around. Yes, it was possible to snitch the rabbit without being observed. He scurried from the rushes grabbed the spit containing the rabbit and darted back to the rushes. Turning around and sitting in silence for a moment to assure he hadn't been seen, Brendan breathed a deep sigh. The activity on the beach continued as it did before he stole the rabbit. Now for a decent meal.

Brendan ate every morsel of the rabbit, leaving only a pile of bare bones. His hunger satisfied, Brendan sat back and watched the activity, waiting for the next phase of his plan. Soon the work parties completed the loading of the ships and returned to their fires. When a group of three returned to the fire with the missing rabbit, they hollered; then looked around. One of the Vikings from a neighboring fire apparently made a crack offending the three Vikings without a lunch. These three drew their swords. The four Vikings sitting around the fire from which the wisecrack came reacted by drawing their swords also and soon a fight broke out. The rest of the barbarians ran to see the fight. Soon the spectators formed a large circle around the combatants. This was the effect

Brendan hoped for. He moved as quickly across the open beach as he could; heading for the closer of the two ships which the Vikings had recently loaded. As he crossed the open area, he was sure Kaileen spotted him, although she made no gesture to indicate she knew he was there.

Arriving at the ship, Brendan climbed up one of the ropes hanging over the side which the Vikings had been using to load cargo onto the ship. Once over the gunwale, he moved to the bow. From the bow he first glanced back toward the beach. King Hakon was in the process of breaking up the fight. As far as Brendan could tell, no one was seriously injured—too bad. Next Brendan looked back over the length of the ship. In the stern he saw a number of barrels tied together with ropes and half a dozen bundles covered with hides, deerskins and skins from other animals which Brendan didn't recognize. That looked a likely place to hide. He crawled over the benches where the barbarians would sit at their oars. When he reached the rear, he found an area near a bundle wrapped in skin. With his dagger, he cut the binding on the bundle and threw several of the parcels underneath overboard. Good, now he had enough room to get underneath and still be covered. He was also close to the water barrel should he need a drink. All he had to do was wait for his opportunity to free Kaileen and Dungal. Then a terrible thought crossed his mind. What if they were put on the other ship he saw being loaded? Well he would just have to hope that the two ships traveled together and an opportunity would present itself.

He didn't have to wait long for things to happen however. He had just discovered a stash of apples, and was lying back enjoying his second one, when noises emanating from the beach signaled that the Vikings were returning to the ships. He pulled the skin over himself, leaving just a crack open so he could watch what was going on. The Vikings came climbing over the side, grunting and belching and apparently joking with each other, although Brendan couldn't understand their speech. A couple of the sea warriors threw a net over the side. When they hauled it back on deck and opened it, the bodies of Kaileen and Dungal rolled out on the deck.

The barbarians took Kaileen forward and chained her to an iron eyebolt attached to the hull of the ship just inside the bow. Dungal they chained to one of the oars. A few moments more and the boarding of Vikings ended with King Hakon boarding last. He sat on a bench at the bow and barked several orders in succession. Following the command, the Vikings raised their oars. Dungal remained limp at his oar until the Viking at the oar behind Dungal struck him on the back of the neck with a whip. Dungal winced with pain; then began to row in rhythm with the others.

Brendan could feel the ship move backwards. Before long they were fully floating. A few more commands from Hakon, and the bow of the ship turned to the downstream direction. This was the first time Brendan had been on a ship. The motion of the ship in the current relaxed Brendan. Under other circumstances, this might actually have been enjoyable.

By nightfall, Brendan could hear the rush and fall of the waves as they approached the open sea. The ship undulated violently as they crossed the bar and entered the sea. The movement of the sun from the bow to the port side of the ship told Brendan they were changing directions again. They were apparently heading north.

King Hakon barked an order and one of the Vikings pulled in his oar and walked forward to where Kaileen lay chained. After a few words from the king, the barbarian unlocked Kaileen's shackles and started with her toward Brendan in the aft of the ship. They stopped only a couple of feet from Brendan. The Viking struck one of the kegs. The sweet smell of ale permeated Brendan's nostrils. The Viking reached under the seat and brought out a wooden pitcher. He filled the pitcher with ale and handed it to Kaileen and pointed down the aisle toward the bow. As Kaileen walked down the aisle, the Vikings on either side withdrew their oars and held out wooden cups for Kaileen to fill. In the meantime, the Viking walked toward the bundle that helped conceal Brendan. Brendan held his breath. To his relief, however, the barbarian pulled a sack out from under the bundle. He took the sack and walked forward, handing biscuits to each of the sailors. In the meantime, Kaileen came back to refill her pitcher. Brendan felt it was a good time to let her know he was onboard.

As she filled the pitcher, Brendan pulled back the tarp far enough to expose his face and whispered, "Hi."

Kaileen's eye's bulged immensely, then she smiled and whispered, "You!"

Someone then hollered from the forward part of the ship.

"I've got to go," Kaileen whispered.

She turned and walked back up the aisle to the point where she had left off filling cups. Brendan pulled the tarp back in place. The Viking who passed out the biscuits returned and pulled out another bag. This one contained strips of some sort of dried meat. He moved forward again. Kaileen was now returning to refill her pitcher. When she arrived at the barrel, Brendan pulled back the tarp.

"What are you doing there?" Kaileen asked.

"I'm looking for an opportunity to rescue you," Brendan answered.

"How are we going to get away from all these barbarians?" Kaileen asked in disbelief.

"I haven't figured that out yet; but there's got to be a way. I'm sure these barbarians will put into shore again."

"Anything I can do to help?" Kaileen asked.

"Serve these barbarians obediently. Try to gain their trust. It may be useful."

"I'll try, Brendan, but they make me sick to my stomach," Kaileen answered.

"I understand. Oh, there's one more thing. Try to think of a way to free Dungal. We don't want to leave him with these barbarians."

Just then another shout from the front meant Kaileen had to return to serving the crew. When she returned again, the Viking who distributed the food came back with her so Brendan couldn't talk to her. The Viking escorted her to the bow of the ship. He reached for the irons to lock her up again. The King said something and the Viking dropped the chains on the deck and he returned to his bench. Apparently the King would allow her to remain unshackled while they were at sea. Every other sailor now stored his oar and set about trying to make himself comfortable lying along side his bench. Before long it was too dark for Brendan to see much beyond the dark shapes of the ship. Brendan decided to make himself as comfortable as he could also. He stretched his legs between the bundle and the bulkhead of the ship. He reached under the tarp and pulled back a bag. It turned out to be the one with the dried meat in it. Brendan ate his fill and pushed it back out. He wondered if he should dare a drink of ale.

He decided it was dark enough to risk it. He felt around for the pitcher Kaileen had used to fill the Viking's mugs. He found it. Then he felt for the point on the keg where the cork plugged the previously tapped hole. He put the pitcher right up by the hole and pulled the cork. After a little of the liquor flowed into the pitcher, he replaced the cork. Brendan slid back under the tarp. He took a long draw on the ale. Ah, meat and drink, now all he needed was a beautiful woman. As if in response, Brendan heard Kaileen whisper.

"Brendan."

"Yes?" he answered.

"Don't show yourself. I'm going to lie down outside here," Kaileen responded.

"Okay, but how did you get back here?" Brendan asked.

"I asked King Hakon if I could sleep in the stern, away from the waves breaking over the bow. He doesn't speak our language, of course, but he seemed to understand since I added gestures." Kaileen explained.

"And he gave you permission?"

"Well he tossed me a deerskin and waved me back here."

"I wouldn't have believed it of that devil!" Brendan commented.

"Now at least we can try to plan an escape. Do you have any idea where we are going?" Kaileen asked.

"North, as well as I can guess. Probably returning to their homeland. I suspect King Finian is now hunting down and destroying the ones they left behind."

"Do you think we'll see him or Failend again? Failend was such a good friend. And I still must know what became of my mother."

"Oh, I think we'll see them again, but it may take some time. As to your mother, she should be safe in Finian's camp now," Brendan consoled her.

"What? You've seen her. Where? When?" Kaileen asked excitedly.

"Hakon had held her captive. I went with some of King Finian's soldiers and we freed her, Mugain, and Father Sweeney. They entered King Finian's camp during the battle where you were taken prisoner again." Brendan recounted the tale.

"Was she, is she all right?"

"Yes, she's just anxious to see you again."

"And I her," Kaileen sobbed, "How do you think we can get away from these demons?"

"I've been giving that some thought. It doesn't look like they have enough provisions for a long voyage. That means they will probably put into shore again. More than likely looking for some place to plunder. I expect our best chance for escape will be right after they leave the ships to raid for their supplies."

"But won't they leave Dungal and me in chains then?" Kaileen asked.

"Yes, but I have a couple of ideas about that also."

"Such as?" Kaileen asked.

"Well, first, chances are good they will leave the barbarian with the key to guard you," Brendan started.

"And?" Kaileen pushed.

"And do you think you could slip a dagger to Dungal?"

"Yes, but how will that help?"

"Dungal can use it to work on freeing himself from his chains. If you get it to him, he'll know how to use it best. It will help if Dungal is free when it comes time to overpower the guard," Brendan explained.

"Okay, pass me the dagger."

Brendan slid the dagger from the sheath on his thigh and passed it under the tarp to Kaileen. She held his hand with the dagger in it for a moment, rubbing it gently, then took the dagger from him.

"Brendan," she started again.

"Yes."

"What do you think they'll do to us if the escape plan fails?" Kaileen asked.

"They'll probably kill Dungal and me," Brendan answered somberly.

"And me?" Kaileen pressed.

"It looks like they want to force you to marry one of them."

"I'd rather they kill me too," Kaileen sobbed.

"Then we must escape. Now go to sleep. You will need to be rested for the days ahead."

"Good night, Brendan," Kaileen said gently.

"Good night, Kaileen."

The next day went relatively well. Brendan woke with the dawn. The smell of the sea was a shock to Brendan, having spent all his life inland. When he awoke, he looked to make sure all parts of his body were concealed. During the day he lifted the skin a little by the stern to let the gentle breeze of the sea purge the stale air of his hiding space. Kaileen made several trips back to his hiding spot getting drink for the sailors during the day; but spoke little to him, lest she might be noticed in the full light of day. The Vikings kept their rhythm at the oars by singing. Brendan, of course, understood none of the words, but from their tone, he imagined the songs boasted of Viking conquests, adventures and travels to far away lands. As dusk neared again, the singing subsided. Apparently the men were tiring at the oars. In addition, a steady wind began to blow from the southwest. In response, King Hakon ordered the sail raised and the men stowed their oars. As the wind filled the sail, the speed of the ship picked up; but the waves did also. The ship began to rise and dip with the passage of each wave. This additional movement jarred the keg of ale loose, sending it rolling forward on the deck. Two of the Vikings jumped up to save the barrel from smashing against the closest bench potentially destroying the barrel with the loss of its precious contents. They rolled the barrel back and set it up right again. One of the sailors picked up the rope which had held the barrel on place; then searching for a place to tie the barrel fast again, pulled back the skin covering Brendan.

# CHAPTER 14

Brendan held his breath, hoping that by some miracle they wouldn't see him. Today wasn't the day for miracles however.

"Hvem er der?" the Viking shouted as he drew his sword and put it to Brendan's throat.

Brendan involuntarily trembled as he looked into the fiery eyes of the scraggly-haired barbarian. The sea warrior looked as though he would run the sword through Brendan's throat just for pleasure. After an intense moment, Brendan's captor backed off and motioned for Brendan to stand up. Brendan complied. The Viking motioned for Brendan to move forward. Brendan climbed over the benches one by one, feeling every once in a while the point of the barbarian's sword at his back.

When they reached King Hakon in the bow, the Viking exchanged words with the king.

Brendan supposed that he was recounting the discovery at the stern of the ship. King Hakon looked at Brendan and asked: "Hvem er der?"

Brendan guessed at the meaning of the words and answered: "Brendan, herdsman."

The king didn't understand the Irish, so he asked another question in Latin. Brendan knew little Latin. "Dominus vobis cum," was the only phrase that came to mind. He'd said it often at Mass but he wasn't sure of its meaning. He just stared into the icy blue eyes of the king.

Hakon apparently was satisfied that there was little point in questioning the boy further as there was no one to translate. The king gave an order to the

134

barbarian guarding Brendan with sword drawn. The barbarian, in turn, grabbed Brendan by the scruff of his tunic and pushed him back toward the stern. Brendan began to climb over the benches, moving aft when the hand of the following barbarian halted him as he reached Dungal's bench. The Viking then motioned for Brendan to sit down by Dungal. Brendan complied. Then the barbarian tapped the oar with his sword indicating Brendan should assist Dungal in the rowing. Since they were under sail at the moment, Dungal had the oar resting on his lap with his arms, chained at the wrist, resting on top of it. Brendan's captor then returned to assist the other sailor in securing the provisions in the stern. When he'd left, Brendan spoke to Dungal in a low voice.

"Did you get the dagger from Kaileen?"

Dungal nodded, "Yes."

Dungal then moved his arms a little. He slid the dagger from up his sleeve into his right hand. Then he slid the point into the lock on the left wrist. He jiggled the dagger a little and gave his left wrist a twist. The left shackle separated. Dungal smiled; he refastened the lock on the shackle with his right hand so he could free himself whenever he wanted. The sea warriors evidently didn't consider Brendan much of a threat as they didn't shackle him. Now all they needed was a good opportunity to escape.

"I think the barbarians will have to put into shore for provisions soon. As near as I can tell they are not stocked for a long voyage. Perhaps we can escape then," Brendan said in a low voice.

Dungal just nodded he agreed. Just then, one of the Vikings shouted something and pointed to the northwest. Everyone on the ship turned to look. Just visible on the horizon was a silhouette, the shape of another ship. King Hakon shouted a series of orders and half a dozen of the crew sat about changing tack on the sail. Moments later the Viking ship was on an intercept course with the vessel in the distance.

As the interval shrunk between the Viking ship and its quarry, Brendan could make out two sails on the ship they were pursuing. Both were square shaped with one being about half the size of the other. The sails appeared to be skimming across the foam of the sea. When the Vikings' ship got much closer, Brendan could finally make out details of the nature of its hull. The skin of the hull was all leather, unlike the wood of the Viking ship. Sails of Irish linen, bearing the image of a giant boar's head stitched into the fabric, billowed full on the mast. The rust red fabric of the boar's head contrasted with white fabric of the background enhancing the image of the boar. One sail hung from a spar on a fifteen foot oak mast while the other appeared to hang from a thirty foot one. The length of the ship must have been nearly sixty feet, rivaling the length of the Viking ship.

As the Viking ship bore down on them, the sailors on the Irish ship struck the main sail and began to slow down. Brendan wondered why they made that move. Could it be that they looked upon the Viking ship as brethren of the sea and were preparing to conduct trade with these barbarians? The Vikings closed in as the Irish ship struck their second sail. The Vikings now changed tack again to turn their ship to come alongside the Irish one. Then the sea warriors struck their sail also. King Hakon ordered all to man the oars, using them to do the final maneuvering alongside the Irish vessel.

As the Viking ship slid up alongside the Irish ship, Brendan counted about a dozen of his countrymen on board, certainly no match for the fifty or sixty warriors on the Viking ship. The Vikings stowed their oars and moved toward the mast. Extending from the top of the mast were a dozen or so ropes. The Vikings began undoing these and swinging through the air, and landing on the Irish ship. As the Vikings swarmed aboard the Irish ship, the Irish sailors were so taken by surprise they froze in place. Two of the Viking boarders ran fore and aft to receive lines thrown over from the Viking ship. These they tied to the wicker skeleton that supported the leather hull of the Irish ship, effectively joining the two ships. Some of the Vikings drew their swords and held the crew at sword point while others searched the ship.

A short time later, one of the Vikings called for a line and cargo net. The Vikings loaded the booty they pirated from the Irish into the net and, as quickly as they had attacked, they returned to their home ship. The final move was to cast off the bow and stern lines, freeing the Vikings to raise their sail and continue on their way. Once under sail, King Hakon ordered his men to bring the contents of the ship they'd pirated before him.

To Brendan's surprise, the Vikings had obtained little booty. They brought forth two barrels of ale, one of biscuits, several sacks of corn meal and a vat of honey. Apparently the Irish ship was low on provisions, probably on its way back to its home port. Yet the Viking ship buzzed with excitement as the first of several dozen leather bags were brought before King Hakon. The king ordered the contents of one bag opened. Gold rings, bracelets, and necklaces splayed out on the floor. The Viking crew roared. The king ordered all the bags opened. All contained a similar type of jewelry, although more than half of it was in silver; but a very valuable treasure indeed.

The king ordered the treasure stowed in a storage space in the bow. Then the king ordered one of the captured ale kegs be struck and its contents distributed to all in celebration. Kaileen went back to get her pitcher. King Hakon said something to one of the sea warriors up front. That Viking grabbed Brendan and pushed him toward the stern of the ship. Brendan climbed over the benches, the Vikings following behind. When they got to the ale keg the Viking dug another pitcher out from behind the last bench he pulled the cork out of the ale keg and yellowish-brown liquid arched into the pitcher. He handed the pitcher to Brendan and grunted. Kaileen, who was just returning to refill hers, noticed Brendan's confusion and butted in.

"You're supposed to help me serve. I guess the king doesn't want his men to have to wait too long for their drinks," Kaileen explained

"Oh, now I understand," Brendan answered.

Together they made their way back to toward the front, filling the wooden cups in the outstretched hands as they went. As they returned to refill their pitchers, Brendan got an idea. As they reloaded the pitchers, Brendan posed it to Kaileen.

"You know, if we could get these barbarians drunk, we could probably escape," he said.

"Sure, but where are we going to escape to out here?" Kaileen chided him.

"I know, but if we were in sight of land, it might be an option."

"I suppose. Can Dungal swim?" Kaileen asked.

"Yes, he taught me in fact. We used to swim in the river near Kilrush in the summer."

"Well it's not the best of plans, but we can try it if we get desperate. I still think it best if we wait and see if they put into port," Kaileen continued.

"Okay," Brendan agreed.

They continued serving ale. As the sun began to approach the ocean in the western sky, Brendan and Kaileen were given the biscuits and honey to distribute. Kaileen passed out the biscuits and Brendan followed with the vat of honey. The Vikings dipped their biscuits in the honey and ate them eagerly. It appeared they had never had a taste of honey before! When they reached the king, darkness was nearly upon them; but Brendan could see a small light in the distance toward the northeast. King Hakon, noticing Brendan staring at something, turned to look also. The King saw the light also and began shouting to his men. They changed course and headed toward it. King Hakon waved Brendan and Kaileen off. They returned the remaining biscuits and honey to the stern. There they stopped to have a few for themselves.

"Are you thinking what I'm thinking?" Brendan asked as they ate.

"That we might escape tonight?" Kaileen quizzed.

"Yes, it appears the sea warriors may be putting into shore," Brendan continued.

"I'm certainly willing to try. I can't wait to get away from these monsters."

"Let's trying serving some more ale. We want whoever they leave to guard us to fall asleep." Brendan suggested.

"Okay, we'll give it a try. Say, you don't suppose they'll take us ashore with them do you?" Kaileen asked.

"Bite your lip," Brendan scolded her. "I can't see why they would want us ashore if they're planning a raid."

Brendan and Kaileen then filled their pitchers and started serving the barbarians. To their surprise, King Hakon made no movement to stop them, but he ordered them to stop when they completed the first round. Brendan returned to his seat alongside Dungal. Kaileen returned to the bow. As Brendan sat down near Dungal he asked.

"Kaileen and I want to try an escape tonight if we put into shore. Are you with us?"

Dungal nodded his approval.

As the ship drew closer to the speck of light, it began to separate into several lights. They were probably people using candles to travel about within a village. The moon, although only about a quarter full, provided enough light to indicate they were approaching an area with massive cliffs jutting above the sea. Brendan worried that the barbarians might think this area unsuitable to land the ship and would pass by in favor of finding a more favorable harbor. Just then, though, King Hakon gave the order to drop the sail and man the oars. Brendan joined Dungal in the steady rhythm of the oarsmen as they moved toward shore. The Vikings spent considerable time picking their way along the coast until they found an inlet with more gently sloping land. The lights they'd seen were gone now. The moonlight illuminated the landscape enough that Brendan could see the outline of a large ridge between them and where he'd last seen the lights. He supposed that the Vikings planned to climb the ridge and come down on the town from the other side.

As the ship neared shore, King Hakon ordered two of the Vikings to come to the bow. One of these came back and grabbed Brendan. He pushed Brendan toward the bow where the other Viking was just locking Kaileen into one end of a pair of shackles attached to the hull. They locked Brendan's right wrist into the other one. They went back for Dungal. They unlocked the shackle on one of his wrists, passed the iron bracelet through the ring which bound it to the oar and brought him to the bow. There they passed the loose bracelet through a similar ring on the bow across from Brendan and Kaileen, and locked it back on Dungal's wrist.

With their prisoners secured to the bow, the Vikings stowed their oars. The ship jerked silently in the night, indicating it had run aground. The sea warriors began piling over the side, splashing through the surf on the way to shore. Brendan watched as they disappeared into the darkness. Soon the ship was vacant except for the three prisoners and one Viking left to guard them. The Viking decided to help himself to some more ale while the others were away. As soon as the barbarian neared the stern of the ship, Brendan whispered to Dungal.

"Do you still have the dagger?"

Dungal answered by pulling it out and unlocking the bracelets on his wrist. Then he silently crawled across the deck to Brendan. Dungal worked a few moments with the bracelets on their wrists and they were free.

"Now how can we take out that guard?" Brendan whispered his thoughts out loud.

Dungal responded by striking his chest with one hand and pointing in aft direction. Then he pointed to the deck underneath the closest bench.

"You're going toward the rear and hide under a bench?" Brendan asked.

Dungal nodded "Yes."

"Then what?" Brendan pressed.

Dungal pointed at Brendan and Kaileen. He held both of his palms up and raised them slightly.

"You want us to stand up?" Kaileen asked this time.

Dungal smiled and nodded "Yes." Apparently he was pleased that Kaileen could understand him also. He then made a sweeping motion with both arms toward the starboard side of the ship.

"You want us to go over the side while the barbarian is watching us," Kaileen responded, obviously quite pleased with herself that she could understand Dungal.

Dungal beamed and nodded he agreed.

"Okay, let's do it," Brendan said nervously.

Brendan and Kaileen lay in the bow as though still shackled. They watched Dungal. First he carefully picked up a pair of the shackles, gathering up the chain quietly so they wouldn't make a sound. Then he began a tedious process of crawling over the benches one by one. First he would pop his head up just far enough to see over the bench. When he was convinced the barbarian's attention was diverted, he crawled over the bench, then repeated the process on the next one. When Dungal had made it approximately halfway to the rear, he waved his hand as a signal for Brendan and Kaileen to make their move.

"You ready?" Brendan asked Kaileen.

"How about you?" Kaileen answered with a question.

"Let's do it," Brendan said.

They both stood up and headed for the starboard side of the ship. They took no care to be quiet. The Viking spotted them almost as quickly as they stood up. The barbarian dropped the wooden mug of ale he'd just lifted to his lips and began leaping over the benches, dashing for Kaileen and Brendan. Kaileen looked at Brendan.

"Should we go over the side?" she asked.

"Yes, we'd better look like we're serious about leaving. I think Dungal can take care of the barbarian." Brendan answered.

As Brendan and Kaileen threw a leg over and straddled the gunwale, however, they hesitated. Dungal had just leaped upon the Barbarian from behind. He now had the barbarian in a choke hold, with the Viking clawing desperately to release the chain from around his neck.

A few moments later, the huge body crumpled to the floor. Dungal looked toward Brendan and waved. Brendan and Kaileen both swung their legs back into the ship.

"Is he? Is he dead?" Kaileen asked.

Dungal shook his head then placed his head on his hands sideways.

"He's just asleep," Brendan translated. "Let's get out of here."

"Wait, why don't we help ourselves to some of their food?" Kaileen suggested.

"Good idea, but what if he wakes up again?" Brendan answered, pointing to the sleeping sea warrior.

"Let's chain him up," Kaileen answered. "See if he has the key on him," she instructed.

Brendan and Dungal searched the Viking. Sure enough, they found a key hanging from a strip of rawhide around the sea warrior's neck. Brendan worked it off over the Viking's head. Then he and Dungal began the arduous task of moving the limp body to the bow. By the time they had him in place where they could chain his hands; sweat trickled profusely down the sides of Brendan's face. Brendan handed the key to Kaileen who placed the iron bracelets on the barbarian's hands and locked them shut. When they were done, the barbarian lay on his back, asleep, with each hand hanging from either side of the iron ring protruding from the bulkhead of the ship. He looked strangely comfortable for being in such an awkward position.

"Let's go get the food, now" Kaileen pressed.

Dungal and Kaileen raced ahead of Brendan to the rear of the ship. As Brendan followed, his right foot struck a sack under one of the benches. He heard a dull metallic clang—the treasure. He had a great idea. When he joined the others in the aft portion of the ship, he proposed it.

"Why don't we take as much of the treasure with us as we can carry?" Brendan asked.

"I don't think that's a good idea Brendan," Kaileen answered him.

"Why?"

"If we take any of their treasure, they'll chase after us for sure," Kaileen explained.

"Well it's not their treasure. They stole it from our countrymen. And who's to say they won't chase after us anyway. After all, they seem pretty determined to get their hands on you." Brendan shot back.

"The treasure will only slow us even more, Brendan. What good is the treasure to us if we become captives again?" Kaileen pleaded.

"That's true; but ..." another idea entered Brendan's head. "Suppose we could find a place not far from here to hide it. Then maybe we could come back and recover it some day."

"Brendan you're hopeless!" Kaileen exclaimed, then continued, "Okay we'll take as much as we can carry off the ship; but if we haven't found a suitable hiding place by the time we've traveled a thousand paces beyond the beach we drop the treasure wherever we are and don't look back at it, agreed?"

"Agreed."

Kaileen then loaded biscuits and dried venison into three of the drawstring bags she found and arranged two of them on Brendan and Dungal so that they would hang from their sides with the drawstring across their chests. She placed the third bag on herself. She found two empty flasks, filled them with ale, and placed one each in Brendan's and Dungal's bag.

"Now to the treasure," she entreated.

Kaileen did the same arrangement with the bags of treasure. Brendan noted immediately how much the treasure bag pulled him to one side. It was certainly much heavier than the food.

They moved to the bow of the ship. When Brendan climbed over the side and dropped to the beach, he found himself almost chest deep in water! It took a moment to recover from the shock of being immersed in the bone chilling waters. The food bag floated up to the water's surface; but the treasure bag pulled Brendan down. Maybe Kaileen was right, they shouldn't have tried to take the treasure ashore. As he moved to the firm sand of the beach, however, the water drained from the treasure bag, lightening his load a little and renewing his confidence.

Dungal took the lead as the trio moved up the beach and into the rocky hills of the ridge. This land had little brush cover. They would be out in the open for a long time. At night this wasn't a problem, but once the sun arose they would be visible from a long way off. It would be best to go as far as they could before dawn.

About two thirds of the way to the top of the ridge, something to the right caught Brendan's eye. A dark spot, it was a dark spot. Actually there were a lot of dark spots on the ridge, but this one was unusually dark. Brendan called to the others.

"Stop."

Kaileen turned around and answered, exasperated, "What is it Brendan?"

"I think I found something."

"Like what?"

"Maybe a cave," Brendan answered her.

"So?"

"So maybe we can hide the treasure," Brendan answered.

"Okay, Hey, Dungal, let's see what Brendan found."

Dungal stopped, turned and shuffled back down hill. By the time Dungal caught up to him, Brendan was at the dark spot he'd found. It was a cave alright. Brendan felt around inside it to try and determine its size.

"That's the cave?" Kaileen asked sarcastically.

"I think it's big enough. And there's lots of rocks around here we can use to cover it," Brendan replied.

"Okay, let's bury it," Kaileen said.

Kaileen seemed most anxious to unburden herself of the extra weight. Brendan put her sack in first, followed by his and then Dungal's. Giving a good shove, he found they all fit with a little room to spare. Kaileen and Dungal passed him stones rapidly and in no time Brendan had formed a natural looking pile of rocks which obscured their treasure. Brendan took a moment to locate three land marks and estimate his distance from them.

"What are you doing? We should be on our way," Kaileen pressed.

"Well, if we want to see our treasure again, I need to make a mental map of the area and find landmarks from which to locate it," Brendan explained.

"Okay, but hurry, we need to be on our way," Kaileen urged.

Brendan nodded. He spotted an island just off the coast, then there was the point where the ridge dropped off sharply to the sea and finally there was a rock shaped like a ram's head on the very top of the ridge. These should be good. He stood up.

"Let's go," he said.

They climbed the ridge in the dark. It was rough going. There were so many rocks cropping out of the ground, Brendan stumbled frequently. When the reached the top of the ridge they could see several blotches of light in the far distance.

"It looks like they're burning the village," Brendan commented.

"That's like those black-hearted villains," Kaileen sneered. "Do you think we can do anything to help the people in the village?"

"Just the three of us?" Brendan asked, then began to answer his own question, "I suppose we could bury the dead, look after the wounded..."

"You're right Brendan, remember how we found Father Sweeney," Kaileen gushed with emotion.

Brendan regretted his earlier words. He forgot Kaileen had seen her village burned right before her eyes. He would try to dissuade her with a practical argument.

"If we go there, we're liable to run into the barbarians on the way."

"We can move carefully. Remember they won't be looking for us until after they return to their ship."

"But shouldn't we try to get as far from the sea warriors as we can before dawn?" Brendan asked.

"Yes, but won't the barbarians think that's our plan also? I don't think they'll expect us to go to a village they've just attacked, and they have no other reason to return," Kaileen suggested.

Brendan decided he needed another opinion.

"Dungal, what say you? Do we go to the village the Vikings just attacked; or overland and try to escape them?

Dungal pondered for a moment. Then he pointed to the top of the ridge indicating they should go overland.

"Dungal!" Kaileen pleaded.

Dungal smiled and pointed toward the fires in the distance.

"See, the two of us want to go to the village," Kaileen effused.

"You win. Dungal, keep a sharp eye out for the barbarians. We don't want to run into them in the dark."

Dungal nodded vigorously, indicating he understood. They changed course and made for the fires still burning in the distance. Not long after that, the first refrains of a song reached Brendan's ears.

"They're coming, hide," he whispered.

Brendan, Kaileen and Dungal found a large limestone outcropping they could hide behind. The voices got louder and rowdier as they approached. Apparently they had helped themselves to large quantities of beer or ale in the village. As the barbarians passed by, they staggered and stumbled. In a moment, one came rolling down the hill past Brendan. He finally stopped hands and feet outstretched and face down in the dirt. Someone yelled from above. He pushed himself to his knees, shaking his head from side to side. Then he looked straight at Dungal, Brendan and Kaileen.

# CHAPTER 15

"Toke," a barbarian called from above.

The barbarian below Brendan shouted something back and started scrambling up the hill. Apparently he had not noticed them in the dark. Perhaps he was "blind drunk" as Brendan had once heard Father Sweeney describe someone in a sermon. Nevertheless, the barbarian rejoined the rest and moments later their drunken song trailed off in the distance again. The trio waited until they could no longer hear the barbarians, just to make sure, then Kaileen spoke up.

"We need to go."

Brendan and Dungal nodded agreement. They pushed on toward the fires in the distance. As time passed, the light from the fires dimmed. Apparently the flames could no longer find an abundance of fuel to consume. Brendan began to pick up the first smell of smoke. They were getting near the village. It was quite a while later, however, before they actually came upon the village. The first indication was sound of a woman sobbing. When Brendan, Kaileen, and Dungal reached her, she was kneeling on the ground cradling the head of her husband. Brendan studied the limp body attached to the head. None of the body parts moved, even the chest cavity was strangely still, and the man's eyes had the blank stare of the dead.

"I'm afraid he's dead mum, I'm sorry," Kaileen spoke consolingly.

The woman looked up. Tears trickled down the sides of her face.

"Who are you?" she asked as her eyes scanned Brendan, Dungal and Kaileen.

Brendan could see she was so steeped in grief that she showed no fear toward them.

"We come from the land of the Dalcassians, we were prisoners of the same barbarians who attacked your village and killed your husband." Brendan explained.

"But we've been told the Dalcassians are barbarians too. This is the land of the Ui Briuin. Those from the land of the Dalcassians are treated as enemies here." The woman sobbed.

"Surely you don't consider us the same as those men who did this?" Kaileen protested.

"Actually you are the first of the Dalcassians I've ever met. Would you help me?"

"What can we do?" Kaileen asked.

"Prepare a grave for my husband, and go to the monastery for a priest."

"We'll help you as much as we can, ah, er .." Brendan stammered, wondering how to address her.

"Uasal, my name is Uasal," the woman answered.

"But I must warn you," Brendan continued, "The barbarians, they call themselves Vikings, may come here searching for us. Their King, Hakon, seems adamant about keeping Kaileen here for himself."

"And no wonder. She's such a beautiful girl now, isn't she?"

"Yes," Brendan answered without hesitation. He couldn't help but look at Kaileen, who blushed a moment with embarrassment; then ordered.

"Brendan, go see if you can find something to dig the grave. Dungal, I need you to go for the priest." Kaileen ordered.

Then Kaileen turned to Uasal.

"Can you tell Dungal here how to find the priest. He's mute, but he can understand you real well, and he's smart."

Dungal smiled at Kaileen's last remark. Apparently no one had ever told him he was smart before. Brendan left while Uasal was giving Dungal directions to get to the monastery. He walked through the village. He counted thirteen wicker style homes smoldering. There was very little open flame; but the first light of a new day was upon them. Except for a half a dozen male corpses, the village was deserted. Apparently any women and children, with the exception of Uasal had gone into the nearby hills in search of sanctuary. Brendan remembered that he had seen no women among the reveling Vikings when they passed by, returning from this raid. Apparently they hadn't attempted to take any women captive here. The women had fared much better here than at Kilrush.

Dungal passed by him on his way into the hills in search of the priest. He waved; then continued on his way. Brendan found the blackened remains of a wooden pole. This must have been part of a wall at one time he thought. He picked it up and dropped it again immediately. His hand had touched a still smoldering coal on the log. Brendan examined the pole more carefully. The other end looked cold. He felt it cautiously this time. Yes, it was cold. Picking up the pole from that end, he vigorously beat out the smoldering embers on the other end. Then, using the pole, he began picking through the burned remnants of the buildings. Several cooking pots and iron spits later, Brendan found a shovel. This would do.

When he returned to where he'd left Kaileen and Uasal, he found that the two women had wrapped the body of Uasal's husband in a linen shroud, and were in the process of sewing it closed. Brendan now noticed that Uasal was quite young and pretty for a widow. She had dark hair, with a slight reddish tint which fell about her shoulders, long enough to reach nearly halfway to her waist. She wore a modest light brown lined tunic, drawn at the waist by wide belt or girdle knitted of wool and dyed blue. The triangle formed by the lines from the woman's shoulders to waist suggested she had a very slim waist. The overall impression was that she had a very attractive figure. It was fortunate the Vikings had raided at night. Had they seen this woman in the light of day, they surely would have taken her captive.

"Well don't just stand there gawking, Brendan, start digging. We need to have things ready when the priest comes," Kaileen scolded.

"Where?" Brendan asked.

"Where you are standing is good enough," Kaileen answered. "While you are at it, make it large enough to bury the other dead in the village."

"That big! It will take all day," Brendan protested.

"It will probably take most of the day for Dungal to return with the priest anyway, so get busy," Kalieen chided.

Brendan scratched an outline on the ground with the shovel; a rectangle he felt would accommodate all the bodies he'd seen if they were laid side by side. Then he began breaking the stony soil with the shovel, throwing the soil back to the outside of the rectangle. When Kaileen and Uasal finished enclosing Uasal's husband in the shroud, the two women dragged the body to edge of the grave where Brendan was working.

"We're going after the others," Kaileen announced.

Brendan nodded and continued digging. Some time later, Kaileen and Uasal returned, this time dragging a litter, made of several logs lashed together with several sheepskins stretched over it. On the front, Kaileen and Uasal shared a common yoke which they had made from a large leather strap which passed over their shoulders and attached to poles on either side of the two human beasts of burden. On the litter was the body of one of the men slain by the Vikings. The ladies unloaded the body from the litter, sliding it alongside Uasal's husband. Brendan was only about six inches deep into the grave so far.

"We're off for another," Kaileen announced; then she and Uasal left.

By mid afternoon, Brendan had reached the point where the grave was several inches over his head. Deep enough he thought. He pulled himself up the dirt wall and onto ground on the opposite side of the grave from the bodies Kaileen and Uasal had neatly lined up, ready for burial. He brushed himself off and looked back toward the village. He could see the girls coming again, this time without the litter. Instead, Uasal carried a water skin and Kaileen another bag. Both carried their burdens slung over their shoulders. Brendan sat himself down on the side of one the piles of dirt he'd just created with the contents of the grave. When the girls arrived, Kaileen spoke first.

"Uasal found us some food and she has fresh water from the well. Would you like something to eat or drink?"

"Drink please," Brendan said dryly. He'd been thirsty for some time but didn't want to stop digging to search for a drink. He wanted to get out of here. He expected the Vikings to come storming over the ridge again any minute.

Uasal slung the water skin off her shoulder and presented it to Brendan.

"Thanks," he said and uncorked the drinking spout. He took a long draw of the liquid. It tasted so good he couldn't help but drink swallow after swallow.

"Take it easy, you'll drown yourself," Kaileen scolded.

Brendan stopped and drew a deep breath.

"Would you like a corn cake and some cheese?" Uasal asked.

"Sure," Brendan answered. He suddenly realized he was hungry too.

Uasal took the deerskin bag from Kaileen's shoulder. She reached in, took out two corn cakes, and handed one each to Brendan and Kaileen. She then pulled out a small round of cheese. Withdrawing a knife from a sheath hanging from her girdle, she cut off two chunks and handed them to Kaileen and Brendan. The three sat on the dirt pile for several minutes in silence as Brendan and Kaileen enjoyed the food. Brendan noted that Uasal ate nothing. He assumed she was much too upset at the death of her husband to be hungry. Uasal finally broke the silence.

"How did you come to be here?" she asked.

Kaileen told the long story of the raid on Kilrush, her capture, Brendan rescuing her—all the events leading up to their discovery of Uasal early that morning. When she finished, Uasal commented.

"Oh, you've had the most horrifying experiences, haven't you? As soon as we bury my husband and the others, we must journey to the monastery. Perhaps we can work for the monks in exchange for food while we rebuild."

"I think Dungal, Kaileen and I would be willing to accompany you there; but we best not stay here." Brendan responded.

"Why?"

"I think the Vikings will come looking for us. We need to keep moving."

"Why would they spend so much effort looking for you?"

"They want Kaileen for one. Also we took some of their treasure from the ship. We buried it near the ocean. They'll want us to take them to it."

"Oh," Uasal commented with a understanding look.

"And I need to get back to mother," Kaileen added.

"Oh I understand that," Uasal began; then she continued. "I have no living family here anymore. My father and brother were both killed in one of King Donnechadh's wars of conquest. I don't even know who they were fighting. My mother died last year of the shaking disease. I had no one left but my husband."

"I'm sorry," Kaileen apologized.

"Could I go with the three of you? I just want to get away from this horrible place."

"I have no objection. Do you Brendan?" Kaileen passed the question to Brendan.

"I don't think it wise. I mean the three of us have been on the run for most of the past month. You said yourself the people here are hostile to people from other kingdoms. Then there's the Vikings. If they catch up to us..."

"Please," interrupted Uasal, then she continued. "I will face danger with you. It will be better than facing a life of loneliness."

"But I'm sure someone among your people will take you in, look after you," Brendan countered.

"Perhaps, in the spirit of charity they will do so; but many around here tend to exploit the needy by making them slave for their subsistence. I can't stay at the monastery. The monks have strict rules about single women staying there."

"I can understand that," Brendan blurted out without thinking.

"What did you mean by that?" Uasal asked with the air of a woman who'd been insulted.

"I mean a pretty widow like you is likely to be quite a distraction in a monastery," Brendan explained.

Then Brendan felt a sharp jab in the ribs from Kaileen. Apparently she strongly objected to Brendan's comments.

"Oh, I guess I understand," Uasal responded.

"But I would be glad to have you join us, if you don't mind the danger," Brendan continued.

"I'm sure you would, you lecher," Kaileen mumbled under her breath.

"What was that?" Uasal asked.

"I'm sure we'd all be glad to have you," Kaileen answered her.

"Thank you," Uasal responded.

Brendan shifted his gaze to the hill beyond the village where he'd last seen Dungal. He spotted two figures coming toward them. One strutted in the characteristic style of Dungal. The other seemed to have to hurry his steps to keep up with Dungal. As they approached closer, Brendan saw that the other man wore the coarse brown robe of a monk.

"Dungal and the priest approach," Brendan said pointing toward them.

Kaileen and Uasal busied themselves with tying up the bag of food, brushing the crumbs from their garments, and straightening their hair.

"I am going to look for a few wildflowers," Uasal announced.

She then scurried up the hill and began picking purple flowers from the heather. In the meantime, Dungal arrived with the monk. He was a short man, but exceedingly thin. Brendan thought he could ascertain all the bones of the monk's facial skeleton under the skin which was drawn tightly over it like leather over a drum's head. This man appeared to have fasted so much he couldn't possibly have any sins left to atone for.

"Let me introduce myself, I am Father Paul," he said.

"That doesn't sound like a very Irish name," Kaileen commented.

"The members of our order take the name of a saint when we take our final vows. I chose Saint Paul since he had to endure so many hardships. It helps me to be content with the more minor sufferings I have." Father Paul explained.

Father Paul looked from Brendan to Kaileen and then to the row of bodies on the other side of the open grave.

"What happened here?" he asked.

Kaileen pointed to Uasal gathering flowers. "She is from this village. Barbarians from the sea attacked and destroyed the village and killed those men. She lost her husband. He is among the dead you see. We, Dungal who sought you out, Brendan here and I were prisoners on their ship. We managed to escape while they were raiding this village."

"I could tell from your speech you were not from here. And, speaking of speech, Dungal here does a wonderful job communicating through his gestures. He convinced me I must come to attend to some dead. If you will come I will give them the last rites."

Father Paul then somberly moved to the bodies. He took a small copper vial from a pouch which hung from his belt and began anointing the bodies. Uasal, seeing the priest with the bodies, stopped picking flowers and returned to join Brendan and the others who were watching the priest perform his duty. When they got to her husband, the priest asked her to open the shroud so that he might anoint her husband's body. Kaileen assisted her. When the priest completed the anointing, they sewed the shroud closed again. Then the priest directed them to place the bodies in the grave. Brendan and Father Paul handed the bodies down to Dungal who laid them neatly side by side in the grave as they had been on the ground above. Uasal gently tossed the flowers into the grave, spreading them evenly across the bodies. Father Paul led them in a series of prayers for the dead, after which they filled the grave above the bodies with the dirt Brendan had removed earlier. When the hole was filled, they mounded the excess dirt on top. As a final touch, they laid stones on top of the dirt in the form of a cross. As they walked from the grave, Father Paul addressed them.

"What do you plan to do now?"

"I think we will all try to return to the land of King Finian; the place where Brendan, Dungal and I were captured. Uasal wants to come with us too," Kaileen answered.

"That's a long way," Father Paul began, "The shortest way is to make your way along the coast and cross the bay at Carna. I can give you a parchment to take with you that will tell monks there to transport you across the bay."

"How will we find these monks?" Brendan asked.

"You will have to be patient. They live on an island in the bay called Inishmore; but they come to the mainland at Carna to minister to the people there. You will have the best chance of meeting them on a Sunday. Just hang out near the bay and wait for them to come ashore."

"Then what?" Brendan asked.

"Then they'll take you across the bay to the mainland on the other side. I'll instruct them to do so in the parchment. Of course they may want to stop on their island first; but I'm sure that will only delay you a day or so. It will take you much longer on foot to go around the bay."

Brendan thanked the priest; then he spoke to Uasal.

"Are you sure you still want to come with us, even to a different land?" he asked.

"Yes," she answered.

"Well come now to the monastery. You can spend the night there. I'll see if the brothers can't part with a little of their daily bread to aid you in your journey," Father Paul continued.

They arrived at the monastery just in time for supper. To Brendan's surprise they had prepared enough to feed themselves as well as the four guests. Father Paul led his guests to a wattle-walled and thatched building that looked like a great beehive. Inside, Brendan counted five tables, each made of slabs of wood hewn from ash logs, not well finished. Of the five tables, the longest one was placed along the diameter of the circular dining hall. Parallel to it on either side were two shorter tables and parallel to these, closest to the outside wall were two that were shorter still. Brown-robed monks sat at all the tables; however Brendan noted sufficient space available for half a dozen more near one end of the long table in the middle.

"The brothers left us a place," Father Paul entreated as he led the foursome to the vacant part of the table.

They sat down. The other monks continued eating. Two monks got up from their seats and disappeared through a skin-draped doorway. The reentered a moment later and placed large rounds of bread in front of each of the guests as well as Father Paul. They disappeared again and came back with two large steaming bowls. On the third trip, the monks returned with wooden cups containing a hot liquid which Father Paul described as their own special herbal tea. Brendan took a sip and decided that it was the trace of mead in the hot liquid that gave it its real flavor. Father Paul said grace then cut a layer off the top of his great loaf of bread. Then he ladled some stew from the steaming bowl across the remainder of the round of bread, the bread itself forming a bowl. He spread butter on the slice he'd taken off the top and began to eat. Brendan and the others followed his example. It was a delicious venison stew. The monks must enjoy hunting as much as the general populous.

By the time they finished supper, most of the monks had cleared the dining hall. Father Paul then told them that Uasal and Kaileen could use his hut for the night. He and the monk who normally shared his hut would sleep in the dining hall with Brendan and Dungal. Father Paul then led the ladies to his hut, leaving Brendan and Dungal in the dining hall. A short time later, Father Paul returned with another monk. Both carried a couple of deer hides and wool blankets.

They gave a hide and blanket each to Brendan and Dungal.

"Here, you may use these to make yourself as comfortable as possible," Father Paul said.

"Do you think we should take turns standing watch?" Brendan asked.

"You mean because of the barbarians you call Vikings?" Father Paul asked.

"Yes."

"Don't worry, my son. Each night the monks of our order perform a nightly vigil. We take turns walking the grounds of the monastery, praying and meditating for a time. When one monk has finished he wakes another to do the same, then retires. Usually six to eight monks do the vigil from dark to dawn. I have instructed the ones scheduled to do the vigil tonight to give the alarm if they see or hear anything unusual," Father Paul explained.

Brendan felt safe with so many others about, and knowing that the monks were aware of the danger of attack. He found a smooth looking spot on the dirt floor. He spread his deerskin out first then lay on top of it and pulled the wool blanket over him. He looked at one of two candles which illuminated the room for a moment. The next thing he knew it was dawn and the monks were entering for breakfast.

After a breakfast of porridge, milk, bread and honey, the foursome thanked the monks for their hospitality and left the monastery. True to his promise, Father Paul handed Brendan a rolled parchment which the priest said provided the necessary introduction to monks who would ferry them across the bay at Carna. From the monastery, Father Paul had instructed them to travel west a short distance to where they would find a well traveled trail leading to the southeast.

As the beehive huts of the monastery began to shrink in the distance behind them, the uncertainty of the future began to weigh heavily on Brendan's mind. He decided to ask Kaileen and Dungal for advice.

"Kaileen," he began.

"Yes, Brendan," she answered.

"What plans do you have for the future?"

"I want to get back to mother most of all; but I would like to serve Failend again. She was more than a mistress to me. She was as close a friend as I've ever had. I miss her dreadfully," Kaileen explained.

"I guess you are in a hurry to get back to them," Brendan commented. Then he turned to Dungal.

"How about you?"

Dungal tapped his chest over his heart with his right hand and pointed to Kaileen.

"So you want to go back to Finian's kingdom too?" Brendan translated.

Dungal made a quick motion with both of his hands making the shape of an outline of the female form.

"A girl? Failend? You want to go back to Failend?" Brendan probed.

Dungal nodded that Brendan guessed correctly.

"Even though she can't marry you?" Brendan asked.

Dungal responded by placing the first two fingers of his right hand alongside the first two fingers of his left hand and shrugging his shoulders.

"So you think if the two of you are close to each other, anything can happen?" Brendan asked.

Dungal smiled and nodded. Brendan had to admire his confidence. Brendan pondered a moment; then decided to share the thought that had been nagging at him, since they buried the treasure.

"I think I might leave you to return to King Finian's land on your own."

"What? Brendan," Kaileen gasped, "What do you plan to do?"

"I'm going back for the treasure."

"But it's too dangerous to go back now. The Vikings likely will be close by. Besides, you can't carry it all by yourself," Kaileen protested.

"I'll take only what I can carry."

"But why not wait 'til a time when we all can safely return?" Kaileen asked.

"Because I've nothing to call my own. I've never in my life had anything to call my own. And, once we return to Finian's land, it will be such a long journey to return."

"But you would likely be killed by the barbarians. Look what they did to Uasal's husband," Kaileen said.

"And what kind of life do I look forward to with no land or money?" Brendan countered.

Kaileen's eyes lowered their glance away from Brendan, telling him she couldn't answer that question. Then she looked back at Brendan.

"Then I will go with you," Kaileen continued.

"No, Kaileen. You want to get back to your mother. You've been the prisoner of these barbarians twice. I want you to return to King Finian. Dungal will see the two of you back to Finian's kingdom. The three of you can travel much faster without me anyway. I really would rather do what I'm going to do alone. That way, I won't feel responsible for any harm that may come to any of you."

"So you've made up your mind?" Kaileen asked.

"Yes, I have."

Uasal stepped up and kissed Brendan on the cheek.

"Take care, young man, and thank you for tending to the burial of my husband."

Dungal extended his arm and Brendan clasped it firmly. Dungal pulled Brendan toward him and patted Brendan's shoulder with his other hand.

"Good-bye, Dungal," Brendan said.

It was now Kaileen's turn. She threw both arms around Brendan's neck and kissed him hard on the lips. She then backed off, and looked into his eyes for a moment. Brendan noticed several tears trickling down either side of her nose.

"Be careful to stay away from those barbarians. What do you plan to do after you get your treasure?" Kaileen asked as she backed away.

"I'll head for Finian's kingdom too. I should be wealthy enough to buy a piece of my own land then. Maybe a few of my own cows too."

"Ah, but you're the ambitious one, Brendan. Well, good luck then."

"Thank you," Brendan answered Kaileen. He then turned to the north, back in the direction of the Viking ship.

About a thousand paces later, Brendan looked back to the south. He could barely make out the tiny figures of his friends bobbing along the path in the distance. A pang of loneliness permeated his body. If fact, he felt lonelier than he had ever felt before. He had to face the dangers that lay ahead with neither Kaileen nor Dungal at his side. *Should he turn back to join them now?*

# CHAPTER 16

By the time the daylight began to fade from the sky, Brendan had reached the top of the ridge overlooking the bay. Secretly he'd hoped the Viking ship would be gone and he could get to the treasure without worrying about anyone seeing him. No such luck. The ship lay at the same spot on the beach where they left it two nights ago. Hiding behind a large limestone outcropping, Brendan surveyed the beach. He spotted two figures, milling about a speck of a fire on the beach in front of the ship, guards, no doubt. There was no other sign of human activity. The rest of the barbarians must be looking for their former captives.

Brendan looked for the landmarks he had memorized the night before last. From them he triangulated to the point where the treasure should be. He couldn't spot the pile of stones.

Brendan remembered that the angles and distances would look somewhat different from his current position than they did that night. After several more sighting attempts, he located a likely pile of rocks. Yes, that's probably it, he thought to himself. Still, he couldn't be sure until he got down to the pile. There were many limestone boulders and outcroppings between him and the rock pile. The temptation was great to work his way down the hill, darting from rock to rock until he reached his objective. He fought off the temptation to advance before dark. The hillside had little vegetation. He could easily be spotted as he moved from one boulder to another, even if the guards weren't actually watching the hill at the time.

Brendan spent the time waiting for darkness to fall memorizing plants, formations of grass, and rocks which framed the location of the rock pile. He

156

also repeatedly estimated the distance between him and the rock pile. He didn't want to overshoot or fall short in the darkness.

When, at last, he decided it was dark enough to go forward, Brendan scanned the hills around him. He wanted to convince himself he was the only two-legged creature roaming the hills. His eyes carefully panned the hillside to his right, in back, to the left and below. As he surveyed the hill above, he did a double-take. Did he catch some movement out of the corner of his eye? He stared at the suspect spot for a moment. No, there was no one there. Okay, it was time to go down.

Carefully feeling each step, he worked his way down the hill, moving from boulder to boulder in a zig zag pattern. When at last he reached the rock pile, he sighed with pride that he hadn't disturbed as much as a pebble on the way down. Laboriously, Brendan pulled stone after stone from the pile and carefully placed them to the side so as to not make any noise. As he worked anxiety gripped him. Surely by now he should be spotting at least a piece of one of the bags! Was this the wrong pile?

After removing two more stones, a leather draw thong dropped out. Brendan took a deep breath and let it out slowly. What a relief! Motivation restored, he returned to the task of removing the rest of the stones from the pile. Yes, all three bags were still there. Brendan sat back to rest a moment. He wiped a bead of perspiration from his forehead. As quickly as he did that, a hand clasped over his mouth with an arm following around his neck. He could feel two forearms pressed against his shoulder blades, so he couldn't turn to his left or right. Then he heard a familiar voice whisper.

"Brendan, it's us."

Nearly as quickly as he heard Kaileen, the two arms restraining him relaxed their grip. Brendan expelled the air from his lungs and turned to see the smiling faces of Dungal, Kaileen, and Uasal!

"What are you doing here?" Brendan asked.

"You don't think we would let you keep all that treasure to yourself?" Kaileen answered.

"Actually, it is because of Uasal that we returned," Kaileen explained.

"You see, as we were walking along the trail, Uasal started talking about her husband. She told me how he'd built himself his own boat, a leather-hulled curragh. They used to sail it together, fishing off the coast. She remembered that he kept it hidden because he didn't want to be pressured into loaning it to anyone. Some friends of his had gone to sea in a curragh he'd made once and never returned. He always felt guilty that he had loaned them the boat."

"So what connection is there between the boat and why you are here? This is still a very dangerous place to be right now," Brendan butted in.

"Don't you see? With the boat we can all escape together and take the treasure too!" Kaileen said excitedly.

"How far is it from here?" Brendan asked.

"Not far," Uasal answered. "It's in a cave near the ocean and the village where I used to live."

"Why didn't you mention this before?" Brendan asked.

"I was so overcome with grief at the death of my husband; it just didn't come to mind," Uasal explained.

"But none of us know how to sail," Brendan protested.

"I do," Uasal smiled, pushing her long hair back over her shoulders. "As long as you follow my orders without question, I think we can get to the same place the monks from Innismore would take us."

"Yes, mum," Brendan said with enthusiasm.

"We'd better quit dawdling about here," Kaileen snapped.

Kaileen then pulled one of the treasure sacks from the cave and handed it to Dungal. She pulled out the other two, handed one to Uasal and slung the remaining one over her shoulder.

"I can take one of those," Brendan said.

"I thought you might travel faster if you didn't have to carry so much weight," Kaileen explained.

"Okay, but if one of you get tired I'll spell you off," Brendan answered.

Dungal held his big bag toward Brendan, cracking a big smile with the movement.

"You're strong enough to handle your own," Brendan fired back.

"See if the coast is clear," Kaileen said, playfully slugging Brendan in the shoulder.

Brendan crawled up on the big boulder which obscured them from the guards on the beach. One of the barbarian guards below appeared to be asleep. The other paced a hundred feet or so in one direction up the beach, returned to his starting point then walked about the same distance the other way. It appeared to Brendan the guard was fighting off sleep. He scarcely looked toward the hills. Brendan scurried down from the rock to return to the others.

"I think we can go now; but leave one at time and stay spread apart and in the shadows until we're all over the ridge. Dungal why don't you take the lead? Uasal follow Dungal after he gets fifty feet or so ahead of you. Kaileen will follow you, and I'll follow her," Brendan instructed.

Dungal took off. Brendan crawled back up on the boulder to watch the beach as the others left one by one. The guard showed no sign that he was aware of Dungal, Uasal, and Kaileen moving up the hillside. When Kaileen was far enough up, Brendan left. He turned every fifty feet or so to look back toward the beach, taking his last look just before he dropped over the ridge, out of sight from the beach. Nothing appeared to have changed.

On the other side, Brendan rendezvoused with the others who were waiting for him. They continued their journey with Uasal in the lead since she was to lead them to the hiding place of the curragh. As the night wore on, fatigue tugged heavily at Brendan. He took turns carrying Uasal's and Kaileen's treasure bags. Brendan really didn't feel he was able to travel any faster when he wasn't carrying one of the bags. It was the foot that slowed him down.

By dawn, the stony coast lay visible before them. They slowly wound their way down the rocky outcroppings on their way to the sea.

"Over there," Uasal said excitedly, pointing to a cluster of rocks just off the shore.

"Good," Brendan answered her.

He was exhausted and looked forward to sitting down in a boat and letting the wind do all the work. Then, he sensed an odd sound. It was the sound of a human voice which the wind had dispersed so as to make unintelligible what it said. Instinctively, he looked over his shoulder to his left. He saw a line of several dozen barely visible figures standing still on the side of the hill in the distance. Fear raced through his body when he surmised who they were. The Vikings apparently were returning to their ships after scouring the area for Brendan, Dungal, and Kaileen.

At first Brendan thought the barbarians might not have noticed the party of four heading for the coast. No such luck. Brendan saw one of the sea warriors raise his javelin over his head and pointed toward them. Next, they started coming across the hillside.

"Vikings!" Brendan shouted.

Dungal, Kaileen, and Uasal stopped in their tracks and looked in the direction Brendan was pointing. Uasal then started down toward the sea again.

"Hurry," she said, "We can get to sea before they get here."

Uasal then disappeared with Dungal in between two of three large pillars of rock. By the time Brendan and Kaileen reached the same formation of rock, Uasal and Dungal reappeared pulling behind them a leather-hulled craft like the one the Vikings had attacked on the high seas.

"Lend a hand here," Uasal ordered.

"What should we do?" Kaileen asked.

"Get on either side near the stern. Throw your bags in. Grab the rope and help carry," Uasal continued.

Brendan hurried to the port side, Kaileen stayed on the starboard side. About a foot below the gunwales, a large diameter homespun rope ran the circumference of the ship. The ship was really too heavy to carry, but, lifting up on the rope made it easier to slide it across the sand to the water's edge. As they entered the water, the natural buoyancy began to take effect, making their task easier. Uasal then vaulted over the gunwale and shouted.

"Kaileen, get aboard and give me a hand. You two boys get this thing into the surf."

Kaileen followed Uasal's example and attempted to vault over the gunwale. Kaileen wasn't nearly as nimble as Uasal though. She hung from the gunwale sideways for a moment before pulling herself over and rolling into the boat. The additional weight caused the boat to sink lower, with the hull running aground in the sand. Brendan looked back toward the hill above the beach. The Vikings were coming down the hill now. It wouldn't be long before they were on the beach.

He strained on the rope. He looked ahead and saw Dungal straining also at the bow. He looked up to see that Kaileen and Uasal were trying to raise a sail from the main mast. Brendan prayed that they would get a boost from the wind. The breeze, however, seemed to come from the sea. How was the sail going to help them? Brendan glanced back at the beach. The first of the Vikings, King Hakon himself, was almost on the beach. Brendan looked back toward the bow. A large wave was coming toward shore.

"Dungal, wait until that wave hits, then lift and pull forward with all your might," Brendan shouted.

Dungal nodded. Then the wave hit. Brendan strained at his handhold on the rope. The wave broke over his head and drenched him; but the boat floated freely. They pulled forward into the surf. The water was up to Dungal's neck now.

"Dungal, come back to the stern," Brendan shouted.

Dungal released his grip on the bow and waded back until he was opposite Brendan on the starboard side. Brendan looked back toward the beach. The Vikings were on the beach now heading toward the water with the little curragh struggling to escape. On deck now, Usual and Kaileen were tugging at a rope to raise the cross spar up the main mast, the sail flopping in the breeze. Brendan looked back toward the beach. King Hakon and one of the other Vikings were splashing toward them now with the others at their heels. It would be only moments before they reach the boat! Meanwhile the water was now so deep, there was little point in staying in it.

"We've done all we can. Let's get in the boat Dungal," Brendan shouted.

The two rolled over the gunwales on opposite sides simultaneously. Brendan looked up to see the lovely faces of Uasal and Kaileen as they struggled with the rigging at the bottom corners of the square sail. Uasal noticed Brendan was now on board.

"And what are you lying there looking at? Give your girlfriend a hand securing that sail," she barked. Then she looked at Dungal.

"Start hauling up the spar of the forward mast. I'll help you set it in a moment," Uasal said.

Dungal sprung to his feet and darted for the forward mast. It was smaller than the main mast and Dungal had the spar raised in a matter of seconds. Uasal continued to adjust the rigging on her side of the ship. She took hold of it and shouted at Kaileen.

"Leave me some slack, but stand by to tighten on my command."

"Aye captain," Kaileen shouted back teasingly.

Uasal busied herself with the sails, adjusting the angle of the sail on the main mast. The sail began to billow and stretch on the riggings putting tension on the rope Brendan and Kaileen had just fastened. Brendan looked back toward the stern. The Vikings were in the water following them now. King Hakon was nearly in arm's reach of the stern. If he got a hold, he might provide enough drag to hold the ship back until the other Vikings could reach it. Brendan reached for the dagger he had strapped to his thigh.

"What are you doing, Brendan?" Kaileen asked.

"We may have an unwanted guest in a moment," Brendan explained pointing to the stern where the Vikings were nearly to the boat.

Kaileen shrieked. Apparently she had been too busy to notice how quickly the Vikings approached. As Brendan stepped toward the rear, dagger at the ready, he noticed the distance between the stern of the boat and Hakon began to increase. Somehow, Uasal had managed to get the boat to sail even though the wind seemed to be coming off the sea.

"Tighten up on that rigging," she shouted at Kaileen and Brendan.

Brendan went back to assist Kaileen. He pulled hard on the rope from the sail while Kaileen redid the knot which fastened the rope to the hull of the boat. Brendan looked to the rear again. The distance was now rapidly increasing between their curragh and the Vikings. As Brendan watched, the Vikings gave up the chase and headed toward shore.

"You did it, Uasal," he shouted exuberantly, "I could just kiss you!"

"I'll permit one, if you wish, but no more," Uasal replied.

Brendan rushed to her, threw his arms around her and kissed her full on the lips. He drew his head back and was about to repeat the action when Uasal reached up and put her hand on his mouth.

"I said just one, remember," she scolded, "Now get up forward. I'll be needing help with the other sail."

Brendan released Uasal and together they moved forward to set the sail there. Brendan glanced back at Kaileen. She stared back at Brendan as though she were ready to kill him. Her expression puzzled Brendan. Brendan shrugged and went to help Dungal and Uasal set the sail for the forward mast. He marveled at the change in Uasal's personality from grieving widow to captain of a sailing vessel. When they had set the forward sail, Uasal gave another round of orders.

"Dungal, stay and man the foresail. Brendan, stand by the mainsail to help Kaileen. I need to man the steering oar before we run up on one of these reefs."

Too late, even as she spoke, the little ship jerked. Uasal hurried aft and grabbed hold of the steering oar, turning the curragh to avoid further impact. Then she shouted.

"Brendan, go inspect the hull. See if there are any leaks."

Brendan headed for the bow on the port side where he thought the boat had impacted on the rock. Brendan saw a pool of water was forming in the bow. His eyes followed a stream of water flowing down the inside of the hull back to a foot long tear in the hide.

"We have a leak," Brendan shouted his discovery back to Uasal.

"You and Dungal start bailing the water out. There's buckets near the main mast. We'll have to wait until we're farther out to sea. I need to drop the sails and, if I do it now, we'll likely drift back to shore. I don't think we want to risk that, do we?" Uasal said sarcastically.

"No," Brendan answered her.

He went to the main mast and found two wooden buckets. He tossed one to Dungal who scooped up a bucketful of the intrusive seawater and threw it over the side. Brendan made his way forward and filled his bucket, handed it to Dungal who took it and handed the empty one to Brendan. Working steadily this way they were able to keep the pool of water in the bow from growing. As they worked, Brendan scanned the shore. He could see the mass of sea warriors climbing back up the ridge; apparently they were heading back to their ships. He wondered if they would attempt to try to catch them at sea. He shouted back to Uasal.

"Looks like they're leaving."

She turned and looked toward shore, then looked back at Brendan.

"Do you think they've given up on us?" Uasal asked.

"I don't know. We should have at least a half a day head start on them; but those big ships of theirs travel fast with the right wind. They may over take us, especially if we have to stop to repair the hull," Brendan answered.

"But would they want to try to catch us? I mean they must realize it would be difficult to overtake us. Why should they want to take the trouble?" Uasal asked.

"Well we have their treasure and Kaileen. I think they want to get both back," Brendan answered.

"I understand the interest in recovering the treasure; but what's the special interest in Kaileen?" Uasal asked.

"Well I think it's because she is an incredibly beautiful girl and young. I think King Hakon may want her for himself, or maybe it's just to save face among his crew since she's escaped twice now."

Uasal looked at Kaileen; then she continued.

"You're right, Brendan, she is pretty, I do believe she has a face that would launch a Viking ship."

"Stop it you two," Kaileen protested. "You make me feel like I'm a prize cow, something to be traded among men."

"Sorry, Kaileen," Uasal came back.

Uasal guided the ship out until the coast was barely in sight. Then she changed course to the direction she reckoned to be south with a slight easterly heading. She called Kaileen back to take the rudder, instructing her how to maintain course relative to the coast.

"Brendan, Dungal drop the main sail. I think I can do the patchwork with the foresail raised. That way we can make a little progress," Uasal ordered.

As Brendan and Dungal lowered the main sail, Uasal went to a small roll of oxhide, unrolled it and cut off a patch. In the meantime, the water began to rise in the bow again. Uasal continued to rummage about in her belongings on the boat. When Brendan and Dungal had successfully lowered and secured the main sail, Uasal told them to get back to bailing. They bailed frantically for a short time until they'd lowered the water level to where it had been before they'd attended to the sail.

"OK, gentlemen," Uasal began. "I have to go over the side to patch the leak. I want you to keep bailing, but toss the water over the opposite side. And don't look back to my side."

"Why's that?" Brendan asked.

"Because I have to take my clothes off before I go over. I expect you two to respect my dignity."

"Yes, mum," Brendan smiled at Dungal, and then they both turned away from Uasal.

"I saw those smirks. Kaileen, you keep an eye on these two. If one of them looks the wrong way, let me know. I'll throw him overboard personally," Uasal fired back.

A moment later, Brendan heard a splash. He and Dungal continued their bailing. Brendan wanted desperately to watch what Uasal was doing. Although the thought of seeing Uasal undressed excited him, he was also curious how she would fix the leak. As he waited, he could hear the sound of Uasal breaking the surface as she came up for air again and again. Then, when Brendan heard her break the surface again, he also heard her voice.

"Brendan."

"Yes?"

"I need your help," Uasal answered.

Brendan, his back still toward Uasal, asked, "What do you want me to do?"

"There's a small wooden crock by the oxhide I cut the patch from. Get it and bring it to me."

"Okay," Brendan answered.

He went to the center of the boat. He spotted the crock and headed back toward the bow.

On the way back he noticed that the seepage through the crack in the leather had greatly slowed. Around it he could see stitches, much like those he'd seen on clothing patches. Dungal bailed slowly now.

"I've got the crock, what now?" Brendan shouted to Uasal.

"You may hand it over the side to me. I'm in the water so I doubt you can see much."

Uasal was right When Brendan bent over the gunwale to hand her the crock, she was upright, treading water, holding on to the ship with one hand. The natural refraction of light in the ocean blurred the image of Uasal's body in the water. When he reached the crock to her, she said:

"Remove the top please and just hand me the jar."

Brendan did as she requested. When he took the top off, he saw it was filled with grease of some sort. He handed the jar to Uasal.

"Thank, you," she said as she took the jar from him. When Brendan hesitated, she continued. "Please turn away again...until I give you the OK."

Brendan did as he was told. Little water leaked into the ship now, so he and Dungal spent most of the wait staring into the vast expanse of ocean. Finally, a slightly tipping of the ship to the port indicated Uasal was reboarding. Brendan fought back the urge to look at her. A moment later he heard her voice.

"You two can turn around now," she said.

Brendan and Dungal turned around together. She was fully dressed again, only the wet hair clinging to the side of her face indicated she'd spent extended time in the ocean.

"Did these two behave themselves?" Uasal asked of Kaileen.

"Yes."

"Well it's comforting to know I can trust the two of you. It will be some days until we reach our destination and the quarters on this ship are cramped. Dungal, Brendan, raise the main sail again and let's get as much speed out of this ship as we can."

**\*\*\*\***

Several hours later, as the sun appeared to be sinking into the sea in the west, Uasal was confident enough she'd trained her crew that they could pair off during the night. To Brendan's surprise she paired Kaileen with Dungal and asked Brendan to assist her while Dungal and Kaileen slept. They had meal of dried venison, bread and honey from the provisions the monks had given them for their journey. After eating, Kaileen and Dungal asked to take the first watch. Uasal agreed. Uasal then spoke to Brendan.

"You can sleep in the bow or the stern near the main mast. I have only one deerskin for cover. It's big enough to share with you, if you promise to behave yourself."

Brendan pondered the dilemma. The wind off the ocean carried a mist that was beginning to give him a chill. Uasal, however was attractive, and the thought of sleeping next to her stirred feelings within for which he was ashamed. The decent thing to do would be to endure the night chill by himself. On the other hand, Uasal made the offer in full view and hearing of Kaileen and Dungal. The implication was clear. She would share the protection of the deerskin and nothing more.

"Okay, I accept both the offer and the condition," Brendan said.

"Good. Let's get some rest. I recommend we stay aft of the mast. It's usually the driest"

Uasal then unrolled the deerskin. She arranged the cargo so they had clear space on the wicker-like skeleton of ash laths, lashed together, which formed the frame on which the leather skin of the hull was stretched. She spread the ox hide patch material as a mat over the lath.

"Here, you lie on this. I think you'll find it more comfortable than sleeping directly on the ship's frame," Uasal explained.

"I think you should take it," Brendan began, "I've spent many a night sleeping on a rocky hillside."

"Ah, so you're the tough lad, are you? Well, suit yourself; but you can't change your mind once we lay down."

"I won't," Brendan reassured her.

"Well get yourself down here," Uasal ordered.

Uasal stretched out on the ox hide, adjusted the pack which served as her pillow and sat back up. She waited as Brendan lay down and shifted his body to a position he felt was comfortable. He thought maybe he should take Uasal up on her offer to use the mat. He was too proud to do that though. Uasal pulled the deerskin over the both of them until it was up to Brendan's chin.

"Good night, Brendan," she said gently.

"Good night, Uasal," Brendan responded.

"Thank you," she answered him.

Uasal was asleep just moments later. Brendan could tell by her gentle snoring. Brendan lay staring at the clouds of stars in the sky. The frame of the ship did bother him; but the creaking of the ship, the sound of the ocean as waves slapping against the hull, and the gentle swaying of the boat finally rocked him to sleep.

The next thing Brendan knew there was a gentle hand shaking his shoulder and Uasal's voice in his ear.

"Time to get up, Brendan. We have to change crews."

The last thing Brendan wanted to do was get up just then. It was warm and secure under the deerskin. He opened his eyes. Millions of stars filled the sky overhead! He sat up. The chill of the night sent a shiver through his body. In reaction, he rubbed both his arms with his hands.

"Come on Brendan," Uasal urged. "Your friends are anxious for their turn to sleep."

Brendan stood up. Uasal was already headed to take the rudder from Kaileen.

"What do you want me do?" he asked.

"Loosen the riggings on the mainsail and rotate it a little more to port. I'll tell you when you've turned it enough," Uasal instructed.

Brendan followed her instructions. It took several attempts to get it the way she wanted, and required he cross from one side of the ship to the other. He'd just crossed back to port side again and noticed Dungal and Kaileen were sound asleep under the protection of the deerskin. The appearance of them together roused a twinge of jealousy in him. Just then Uasal's voice broke the silence.

"That should hold for awhile. Would you like to steer the boat for awhile?"

Brendan carefully stepped to the rear of the ship. Uasal slid over so Brendan could take the rudder. When he sat down she instructed.

"See that group of stars over there that looks like a teapot? Guide the bow just a little to the left of that. Yes, that's right," she said.

"How did you learn to sail?" Brendan asked.

"Oh, my husband taught me. He liked to fish a lot. We spent a lot of time on the water. I guess that's the reason we only have one deerskin on board." Uasal spoke the words wistfully, staring into the sky, turning toward Brendan as she finished the last sentence.

Brendan could see tears rolling down her cheeks. Evidently his question reminded her of her slain husband.

"I'm sorry, I didn't mean to remind you..." he started.

"Oh don't worry about that, Brendan," she interrupted, "It's more important to have someone to talk to."

"Why's that?"

"It helps me to forget that I now face a life of loneliness."

"You're very beautiful, I'm sure some man will ask you to marry again," Brendan said.

"I don't think I could love another man."

"There's the convent then. You'll at least have plenty of other women to keep you company," Brendan proposed.

"Aye, that may be the answer. I'll certainly give it some consideration. How about you Brendan? Now that you have treasure, what do you plan to do?"

"I think I'd like to buy my own piece of land. It would be nice to raise my own sheep and cattle, instead of minding them for someone else," Brendan answered.

"And do you plan to do this alone?" Uasal pressed.

"Why not? I've been alone most of my life."

"Isn't Dungal your friend?" Uasal asked.

Brendan glanced over at his bearded friend asleep on the deck. Then he answered her.

"Oh, Dungal? He's a free spirit. He might want to work a bit of land sometime in the future; but I'm afraid he prefers to wander. Anyway he's in love with a princess right now. He's likely to want employment that keeps him close to her."

"And who is this princess?" Uasal asked. Her face took on a look of pleasure. Apparently the talk of romance between Dungal and a princess diverted her attention from her troubles.

"Failend, daughter of King Finian," Brendan answered.

"Is she pretty?"

"Very."

"I think she's charmed you too, hasn't she?"

"Well, yes; but I've resolved myself to the reality that she can't marry me. I'm afraid you can't convince Dungal of that. Failand seems to prefer Dungal anyway," Brendan explained.

"And how about Kaileen? I thought you two were a little closer than a couple of village neighbors," Uasal asked.

"Well, ah, she... I mean she's really pretty; and she's nice most of the time; but she and her mother were partners in a business before the sea warriors attacked. Kaileen's anxious to get back to her mother and wants to return to Failend."

"What's her connection with Failend?" Uasal asked.

"She was serving as Failend's maid servant; but the two of them became really close friends," Brendan explained.

"So how does that prevent you from wooing her?" Uasal asked.

"I guess it doesn't, but..."

"But what?" Uasal pressed him for details.

"I just don't know if I want to," Brendan answered her.

"Why not?"

"First, why would any woman want to marry someone with a defective leg like mine?"

"Some women might reject you because of that; but I don't think Kaileen would," Uasal commented. "What are the other reasons?"

"As I said before, Kaileen wants to be close to Failend. I guess that would make me uncomfortable," Brendan explained.

"In other words you are still infatuated with Failend."

"I guess so," Brendan confessed.

"Well you're still young. There's no need to committing to anything now," Uasal commented.

"I guess you're right. Who knows? I might find someone I like better than Failend or Kaileen," Brendan mused.

"You might very well indeed," Uasal said with a sly smile slightly upturning her lovely Irish lips.

# CHAPTER 17

The night passed quickly. Brendan spent most of it in conversation with Uasal. She had such a pleasing air about her. She drew out his innermost feelings and shared some of hers with him. When, at last, the rising flood of daylight woke both Dungal and Kaileen, Brendan was disappointed he could no longer share intimate conversation with Uasal. The wind shifted again and Uasal ordered her crew about setting new tack on the sails. Brendan scanned the ocean. First he looked west toward the endless expanse of sea, then to the southeast. Land was barely visible off the port bow. Then he looked to the stern, focusing for a moment on the smiling face of Uasal, her hair floating on the wind. As his eyes drifted beyond her to the sea behind, he noticed a speck, a dark speck, on the surface of the sea in the distance.

"What do you think that is?" he asked Uasal, pointing to the speck in the distance.

"A ship," she answered.

"Could it be the Vikings?" Kaileen asked.

"It's too far away to tell how big the ship might be," Uasal explained. Then she continued, "If it is the Viking ship, they are moving very fast to be that close already."

"Do you think they'll overtake us?" Kaileen pressed.

"Well, by rights, we should be able to outrun the size of ship that would transport so many men; but, since it's an alien craft, they may have a sailing technology more advanced than ours."

"What can we do?" Brendan asked.

"This craft is already making its best speed. We can get a little more out of her, by changing tack more often. It means manning the sails constantly, are you up for it?"

"Sure," Kaileen and Brendan said simultaneously with Dungal nodding his assent.

"Dungal you man the foresail, Brendan and Kaileen to the mainsail, stand by to follow my orders. We'll make this baby fly!" Uasal shouted enthuastically.

Brendan, Dungal and Kaileen scrambled to their posts. For hours they tugged at the rope rigging, tied and untied the knots, pulled the sails to reposition them, fighting the mighty power of the wind most of the time. Uasal was right though. With the constant changes she ordered, the curraugh seemed to plough through the water like a racing chariot. Uasal seemed to have a sixth sense about how to get the most out of the prevailing wind. By mid afternoon, Brendan, Kaileen and Dungal were exhausted both physically and emotionally. In spite of Uasal's superior seamanship and their hard work, the ship had continued to gain on them. Although the ship was too far away to make out enough details to ascertain it to be the Viking ship, the fact that it continued to follow them throughout the day was enough to convince them they were being pursued. They were closing in on the coast now. Uasal changed their course to run parallel to coast. The course change caused their speed to drop.

"Why are we changing course?" Brendan asked.

"The ship that's following us seems to be overtaking us, I'm looking for a place where we might gain the advantage over them or where can hide," Uasal explained.

"Why don't just put into shore and escape overland?" Kaileen asked. "We probably have a big enough lead on them now that we can lose them in the brush."

"You forget about Brendan. With his bad leg, we stand a better chance of keeping ahead of them on the water than on land. Also, if you look up the shoreline, you'll notice that there aren't many trees. It will be difficult to conceal ourselves if we don't find a place with more cover.

"What's your plan then?" Brendan asked.

"I think we should follow the coast for awhile. I think an opportunity will turn up," Uasal answered.

"I hope you're right," Kaileen responded, distressed.

"You remember I lost a husband," Uasal sought to console her, "I have no desire to be caught by these barbarians."

"I'm sorry," Kaileen answered her.

"Okay, but you can trust me, I'm your captain, remember?" Uasal smiled.

Brendan sensed that Uasal's smile had a charming effect on all of them. With a renewed vigor they set about coaxing all the speed they could out of the little curragh. The sea began to get rougher. Waves began to splash over the side with the result that Dungal had to divert his attention from the foresail to bailing water from the little ship. Brendan looked back at their pursuers. The rough water wasn't holding them back. Looking out to sea, Brendan could see the clouds forming into huge balls like smoke billowing above a great fire. It wouldn't be long before they'd have a storm to contend with too.

The winds began to build. The sea rose into enormous swells that threatened to engulf the boat. Kaileen had to help Dungal with the bailing. Brendan struggled to man the mainsail by himself. The ship was being tossed so much now that he could hardly stand up. Then he heard Uasal shouting.

"We can't fight this, let's take her in."

Uasal steered for the coast, ordering Brendan and Dungal to redirect the sails. Brendan and Dungal had to double team both sails which tried desperately to tear the rigging ropes from their hands. By the time Uasal told them they had the right tack, both of them were exhausted. The effort was worthwhile. The wind, now mostly at their backs, sent the small ship almost skimming across the water surface toward shore. They were essentially surfing ahead of a great wave building behind them. The increase in speed sent adrenaline coursing through Brendan's body. He'd never traveled this fast before in his life and it was thrilling in spite of the circumstances. Nevertheless, they were approaching the shore fast, prompting Brendan to ask.

"What'll happen if we hit the beach traveling this fast?"

"I plan to turn and slow down a little before we hit the beach," Uasal said. Then, eyeing something in the distance off the starboard bow, she shouted at Brendan and Dungal.

"Back on the mainsail, I've got an idea."

Back they went to the riggings. A few moments later, they were heading at about a forty-five degree angle to the coastline. Then Brendan saw it. They were approaching an estuary where a river entered the sea. Uasal had them headed for the river. Like as not, if the strength of the wind held, they could sail right up the river.

"Are we headed for the river?" Brendan asked.

"That we are, Love," Uasal answered.

Brendan wondered why she called him "Love." He liked it, of course, but he wondered why. Perhaps, in the excitement of the moment, she thought she was sailing with her husband again. Never mind, a more important question came to mind.

"Do you think they can follow us upriver?" he asked.

"Brendan, my village was on a river, remember?" Kaileen remarked.

"Yes, but that's a much larger river compared to the one we're approaching. I wonder if the Vikings can navigate this river," Brendan explained.

"I would expect we have the advantage," Uasal answered, then went on. "But I also thought we could outrun them on the open sea."

Brendan looked back. The ship that had been following had changed course and was still following. The sea got a little rougher as they crossed over the submerged sandbar at the mouth of the river. Moments later, the curragh slowed a little as it met the downstream current of the river. The wave they'd been riding dissipated as they entered the river's mouth. Now rocks and grasses covered shore both to port and starboard as Uasal steered to keep the little curragh in the middle of the river channel. The wind was nearly as strong as at sea but the water they traveled on much calmer. Although traveling at a slower pace, they sailed steadily upriver, the land beginning to grow higher above the river banks as the distance from the river mouth increased. Close to them, however, on either side of the ship, lay the marshes of the river's flood plain. Great reeds in the marshes bent before the wind, pointing upstream as thought an invisible force were telling them the direction to travel.

The storm was now beginning to overtake them. Great droplets of rain were followed by a steady pour. Brendan and the others soon became thoroughly drenched. The winds began to raise havoc by continually changing direction.

"Brendan, Dungal, drop the sails," Uasal ordered as she turned the small craft into the reeds. By the time Brendan and Dungal had stowed the sails, the bow was plowing into the rushes.

"There's two oars below the repair material. Dig them out," Uasal ordered.

Brendan and Dungal rolled back the repair leather and found two small oars.

"Take the oars and keep paddling, I'll guide the ship from here," Uasal instructed.

They did as she told them. It was difficult paddling in the rushes; but they continued to make forward progress until a silent forward jerk indicated they'd struck ground.

"Everybody over the side," Uasal ordered. "We'll have to wade the rest of the way."

Brendan climbed over the side near midship on the starboard side. Kaileen followed at the bow. Uasal and Dungal climbed out on the port side. Brendan felt the cold, slimy mud ooze between his toes. Taking hold of the rope that ran the perimeter of the boat, the four of them dragged it along the surface of the water toward shore. Brendan noticed Kaileen was having trouble guiding the boat through the reeds. She turned toward Brendan.

"Can you come here and help me break a path?" she asked.

Brendan moved forward and began breaking a path through the reeds. Kaileen followed directly behind. The three of them appeared to have no problem moving the boat with Brendan clearing a path through the water. It wasn't long before they were dragging the craft onto dry land.

"We'll leave the boat here in the rushes," Uasal said. "I think it will be hidden enough that no one can see it from the river."

"Yeah, I think you're right," Brendan responded. "You know, in this storm, we can probably get across these barren hills, without being seen too," he continued.

"I think you're right. Let's do it," Uasal commented.

Uasal climbed in the boat and distributed the food and treasure. Brendan and Dungal got the largest bags of treasures, while Kaileen took the smaller one and Uasal packed the food. Once they had lashed them to their shoulders, they began to climb the rocky slope before them.

The ground, slippery after being saturated with rain, made the climb twice as difficult. Darkness was nearly upon them as they reached a long plateau of grassland. They all paused a moment and looked back toward the river. In the distance Brendan could make out the square sail of the Viking ship on the river.

"I guess it was them following us," he commented.

"We'd better get further inland before they spot us," Kaileen added.

"Okay, let's go," Uasal urged.

The storm was now easing up. Just before darkness fully blanketed them, they came upon a formation of ragged rocks. They stood fifteen to twenty feet in height, looking like a natural castle.

"Let's stay here for the night," Kaileen suggested.

Brendan, exhausted, said "Yes" enthusiastically.

No one disagreed. Even Dungal nodded his agreement. Dungal, although thoroughly drenched like the others, looked refreshed as though he thrived on the strenuous activity they'd just been through. The little group dumped their packs and huddled together for a meal of cold venison jerky, bread and a little beer.

"I wish we could build a fire," Brendan said, "But any light can be seen from a long distance at night and that will surely give us away."

"Well we could all huddle together for warmth, if you don't mind getting close?" Uasal suggested, smiling mischievously.

"That would be lovely," Brendan remarked smartly, "But I suggest one of us stand watch for the barbarians."

"You're right about that," Kaileen shivered as she spoke. "I don't want them dropping in on us in the middle of the night."

Brendan looked at Dungal.

"Do you want the first watch, or shall I take it?" Brendan asked.

Dungal tapped himself on the chest.

"Okay, you wake me up when you're ready for me to take over," Brendan responded.

"Now we ladies can do a watch too, you know," Kaileen snapped.

Uasal nodded she agreed.

"Okay, if you don't mind losing a little sleep," Brendan answered her.

"Do you think I want to sleep next to the likes of you or Dungal all night?" Kaileen joked.

After that remark, they settled down for the night. Brendan wound up in the middle with Kaileen on his right and Uasal on his left, huddled on the ground beneath their cloaks. He stared at the sky for a moment and thought about how he spent most nights of his life alone in the pasture. Now he had a beautiful woman on either side of him. With this pleasant thought he fell asleep. He started to dream he was back at King Finian's great house. There was a party going on, only it was a strange party. King Finian sat on a magnificent waxed oak throne. On either side of him stood Captain Kilian and Manchan. A little off to the right of King Finian, a group of musicians played a lively tune on harp, horn, trumpet and timpan. To the king's left, stood Failend and Uasal. Brendan was dancing with Kaileen; in spite of the fact there was no way he could dance with his club foot. After a few rounds about the floor, he released Kaileen and took up Uasal in his arms. A few times about the floor with Uasal and it was Failend's turn. As he took her in his arms, she closed her eyes and drifted toward him, lips at the ready. Brendan was about to meet her with his when he felt Dungal's strong grip on his shoulder, pulling him away. Brendan shrugged his hand off, but it returned and started to shake him. Then everything went dark for a moment. He opened his eyes. The dark image of Dungal was over him, upside down, that is, Dungal was kneeling behind him, bent over Brendan's head.

Brendan caught a glimpse of the stars in the sky and then remembered where he was.

"My watch?" Brendan asked, noting Kaileen and Uasal were both sound asleep.

Dungal shook his head to say "no", then snarled with his teeth and pointed to one of the separations in the stones. Brendan saw something move and then a pair of white teeth snarled at him about two feet off the ground.

"Wolves!" Brendan exclaimed. "How many do you think there are?"

Dungal opened and closed both fists rapidly indicating he estimated at least twenty. This was bad news. If there were that many wolves this close to humans, they either must be very hungry or just figured there were enough of them that they could overpower the humans. Either possibility was enough to send shivers down Brendan's spine. When he minded the sheep, he always had a fire that burned through the night. If wolves came around the flock, he could fashion a torch and chase them off. If they built a fire here and now, they might easily be spotted by the Vikings. Brendan weighed the options in his mind then decided to get a second opinion.

"Do you think we should build a fire, Dungal?"

Dungal put his fingers on either side of his head to symbolize the horns on a Viking helmet. Then Brendan continued.

"You're right. A fire could give us away, if they are where they can see it; but right now these wolves are here, and, I think, ready to attack. Maybe if we built it close to that big rock."

Dungal shrugged, meaning he didn't have a better idea. Brendan thought they might try driving them off with sticks and stones; but that could provoke an attack. Anyway, they'd likely end up making so much noise that they would still give their position away.

"Let's build the fire and chance it," Brendan said.

Fortunately there was enough brush around them to feed the fire, so they didn't have to try to go beyond their stone fortress to seek fuel. In a few moments, Brendan had a good blaze going. As the light illuminated the inside of their little fortress, Brendan could see many of the wolves milling around near the woods beyond the stones. The wolves appeared to want to attack, but they feared the humans enough, especially those with fire. Still, they could see the two sleeping humans on the ground. Could it be they were waiting for fatigue to overtake Brendan and Dungal so they would have four easy prey?

Brendan had no trouble staying awake. The fear of having to defend themselves against a wolf pack kept the adrenaline surging through his body.

Brendan hoped the wolves would give up and seek other prey. They didn't seem to budge; but continued their ominous pacing back and forth beyond the stones. It suddenly struck Brendan they were trapped. If they tried to go back toward the river, they risked being caught by the Vikings. To get away from the Vikings they needed to enter the woods beyond the rocks; but the wolves stood between them and the woods.

Brendan stared at the face of one of the wolves. It snarled back defiantly; but then suddenly raised its head and howled at the sky. After that, it turned and ran off. The brush rustled with the sound of other members of the pack following. Could it be Brendan scared the lead wolf by staring at it? Then a twig snapped among the brush from somewhere below them on the river side. Dungal put his fingers to his temple in his characteristic symbol for the Vikings.

"Right Dungal, the Vikings must have seen light from the fire. I imagine the wolves heard or, more likely, smelled them approaching. We'd better wake the girls."

Brendan shook Kaileen and Dungal woke Uasal. The darkness was beginning to fade into daylight.

"Wa, What's up?" Kaileen groaned.

"Shhh, I think the Vikings approach," Brendan answered.

"Oh, Brendan, if they know where we are now, they're already too close. How will we stay ahead of them?" Kaileen pleaded.

Brendan thought a minute. Then he spoke.

"Dungal, you, Kaileen, and Uasal go on without me. I know the three of you can stay ahead of them if you don't have me to slow you down."

"Dungal shook his head, pointed at Brendan then at himself and clasped both hands together, meaning he refused to abandon his friend."

"Thanks, Dungal, but we have the women to worry about. We don't want the Vikings to capture them..."

Dungal nodded he agreed. Then Kaileen burst out.

"Don't worry about us, Brendan. I think we should all stay together."

"Well, we're wasting valuable time arguing," Brendan responded. "I've got a few ideas on how to slow those barbarians down. Dungal grab the girls and go, Brendan ordered."

Dungal followed Brendan's order literally. He grabbed both Kaileen and Uasal by the arm just below their shoulders and started to escort them toward the woods. Both shook loose of his grip.

"OK, we'll go," but were not leaving these valuables for the Vikings," Kaileen responded.

Kaileen hoisted her pack on her shoulders. Uasal and Dungal did the same. Dungal pointed at Brendan's pack, then at himself.

"Yeah, take mine with you too, if you can handle it. It will help me not to have to carry it," Brendan answered him.

Dungal swung Brendan's pack up so now he had a bag on each shoulder. Kaileen rushed to Brendan and kissed him full on the lips, but didn't linger.

"Take care, Brendan," she said.

"My turn," Uasal said.

Then she came up to Brendan, took him by the shoulders, pulled him to her and kissed him. To Brendan, her kiss was as sweetly pleasurable as Kaileen's.

"I appreciate being called a 'girl' again," Uasal said with a coy smile. "It's been a long time."

Brendan watched for a moment as the trio disappeared beyond the rocks and into the trees. *Now to business, he thought.* He'd had his eye on a great boulder resting precariously on a large rock outcropping. It was large enough to splinter a Viking ship into small pieces if it could be launched on top of it. Although that would be an impossible task, Brendan fantasized about the havoc he might cause by rolling it down on an approaching army of them. He crawled out on the flat rock alongside the boulder. He stayed flat against the rock to keep a low profile. Peering over the edge, he first saw some movement in the bushes. This was followed by glimpses of the sea warrior's helmets and a brief view of a body or two, trudging up the incline. The time was ripe. If he waited too long, the boulder would likely land and roll harmlessly behind the approaching party. Brendan wedged his body between a large upright rock and the boulder. His back was against the upright rock and he placed both feet on the boulder. This left him in a bent up position, so that if he attempted to straighten out, he would be placing the maximum force he could on the boulder. Flattening his back against the upright stone, he pushed with his feet. Brendan strained with all his might but it seemed the boulder wouldn't budge. Brendan relaxed his muscles to catch his breath. As he relaxed, the boulder tipped back toward him. Quickly he thrust again. He could feel the boulder move a little on the forward thrust. Again, Brendan strained as a follow through on the forward thrust until he had to take another rest. Again the boulder tipped back toward him, only more this time. Brendan now became concerned the boulder would go the wrong way and crush him. Below he heard the rustle of brush as the Vikings closed in. Brendan strained again. This time the boulder gave way and rolled off the edge of its rocky rest. Branches snapped and the ground rumbled as the boulder rolled down the hillside. Shouts and screams followed, along with the unmistakable sound of King Hakon's voice shouting orders.

Brendan would have given half the gold they'd taken from the Vikings to know what damage the great boulder had inflicted upon them; but now was not the time to stick around and satisfy his curiosity. Brendan headed off the way Dungal had gone with the girls. Brendan couldn't take the time to try and follow their trail. He'd just have to trust to luck that he would eventually catch up to them. The important thing now was to slow the advancing sea warriors. As Brendan limped along, his eyes darted from side to side, looking for something else he could use to thwart the barbarians.

A bee buzzed by Brendan's ear. Brendan paid little notice until a second, and then a third passed. He looked around. To his right he saw several swarming around a tall snag of a tree. The tree looked as though it had been dead for decades. It bore no upper branches, just stood with its jagged top pointing to the sky. It was large, and, judging by the number of bees swarming about it, probably contained thousands of them inside. That gave Brendan an idea. He went over to inspect it. About half way up the side of the tree was a large knot hole. Yes, Brendan thought it just might work. After all, the wood looked thoroughly rotten. Brendan searched until he found a large downed branch he could use for a pole. He broke off the unneeded branches from the larger stem. Then he shoved the smaller end into the knot hole until it would go no further. Then, using the pole as a lever, he pushed a little on the large end until he heard a crack. He looked up on the decayed trunk to see a large crack running almost from the top to the bottom. Brendan then looked for something to use as rope. He found some briar and was about to splice some of it together when he spotted wild grapevine. Brendan dragged a length of it out and cut it off at its base. He then dug strand after strand from the brush. The grapevine was flexible enough he could tie the vines end to end. He tied the end of the first vine to the end of the pole he'd wedged into the knot hole. Brendan then started working his way from the tree crag, tying vine to vine, making his natural rope longer and longer. By the time he'd gone about thirty feet from the rotten tree trunk, he had only a couple of lengths of vine left. He could now also hear the barbarians moving through the brush.

Brendan tied the last pieces of vine together.  As he was doing this, he could start to see the dark silhouettes of their bodies in the foliage. In a moment they would be visible; but so would Brendan. For his plan to work this time, Brendan figured he would have to show himself. The moment had to be just right though. Brendan lay low, waiting. The Vikings were picking their way through the trees now slowly. They were probably looking for newly broken branches among the foliage or footprints which indicated Brendan had passed that way previously.

Brendan's body shook with fear as they approached. He fought it. He had to be patient he reminded himself. Then, as he watched, they started to turn a different direction from a path that would lead them past the rotten tree stump. He stood up, purposely making noise as he did to attract attention then he heard:

"Blikk!"

They had spotted him. Brendan moved away, slowly, laboriously, trying to act as though he was hurt. He needed to delay his departure until the right moment; but didn't want to raise suspicion. At last, two barbarians at the lead of the rest reached the stump. Brendan pulled with all his might. The stump split apart spewing forth a swarm of angry bees. Brendan could see the two lead Vikings swatting madly and running both right and left away from the stump to try to escape the onslaught of stingers.

Again, Brendan would have liked to watch the attack of the killer bees; but knew every moment mattered if he wanted to stay ahead of the Vikings. He pushed on through the woods. A thousand paces or so later he came out upon a great grassy field. There would be no cover for several miles at least. Once the Vikings shook themselves free of the bees and spotted him in the open field, it would be a foot race between Brendan and the barbarians!

Brendan headed off toward the top of the grassy hill. He hoped he would find cover of some kind on the far side of the hill; but the top was so far off, the sea warriors could easily overtake him long before he could reach it. Brendan thought of reentering the woods he just left. He might slip by them and head toward the river again. The barbarians wouldn't expect that. Brendan turned to reenter when something to his left caught his eye.

# CHAPTER 18

Three horses were grazing, twenty or so feet away from Brendan. If he could catch one, he could easily escape these barbarians. One horse was almost completely black with a white splotch on his muzzle and three white socks. The next one was roan with a black tail and four black socks. The last was a gorgeous gray steed with white specks strewn about on the gray background like so many stars in the sky. The horse was sleek with a slender barrel that sloped up toward its hindquarters. He looked as though he could outrun any horse that grazed on Irish turf. The gray it would be; but how to catch him? Brendan thought on what he could use for a bridle. Some vine would do nicely; but he would have to venture back into the wood for that. He could use the rope that gird his waist but then he'd have nothing to carry his purse containing his fire starting paraphernalia, needles and fishing line that he needed for survival. Instead he took out his dagger and cut off the narrow hem of his tunic. Then he searched around and found a stick suitable for use as a guide rod. Now he had the hard part: catching the horse.

Brendan thought he'd act as though he wanted the roan. He thought that way the gray horse might pay little attention to him. As Brendan moved toward the roan horse, the horse turned its head toward him. Then the horse trotted forward a little. The gray horse only looked up a moment. Then he returned to grazing. Brendan moved toward the roan again. Again, the roan trotted away from Brendan. The gray horse was behind Brendan now. Brendan took a couple of steps backward. Then he glanced slightly over his right shoulder. He was nearly in reaching distance of his quarry. He moved back a few steps more. He sensed he'd startled the gray horse because it raised its head and seemed ready to run away. Brendan quickly ran his right hand under the horse's neck, throwing the loose end of the cut off garment hem over the horse's neck and grabbing with the other hand. He now had the gray horse under his control. Brendan fashioned a bridle from the garment and mounted. The horse reared once; but Brendan managed to stay on. The horse was testing this new rider. Using the branch as guide rod, he turned the horse toward the hill.

About halfway up the hill, Brendan turned to look back. He could see the Vikings emerging from the woods. He urged his horse to a gallop. Glancing back again, Brendan could see two of the Vikings had mounted the two remaining horses. It looked like Brendan just lost his advantage. Oh well, he was still way ahead of them and he would bet his horse could outrun theirs.

When Brendan reached the top of the hill, he allowed his horse to slow to a canter. Brendan was worried about wearing the horse out. He looked below him. The long barren slope below did eventually lead into a brush covered gully. Brendan decided to head for the cover. He let the horse pick his own speed descending the hill as a precaution against the horse stumbling. Brendan knew the slower pace might give the Vikings a chance to catch up; but he didn't want to risk causing his horse to break a leg on the slope.

Entering the forest, Brendan followed a deer trail. A short time later, he heard the sound of breaking brush in the distance behind him. The Vikings were closing in. Brendan had to duck suddenly as his horse went under a branch, oblivious to the fact he had a rider on his back. This gave Brendan an idea. He rode back and took hold of the end of the branch. Backing the horse up a little, the branch bent easily. Brendan looked for a place to hide. Yes, there was a large clump of bushes. Brendan was split emotionally. Half of his inner conscious said he should just keep running. The other half compelled him to stay there and try his idea. His horse was still breathing hard. Brendan hoped he would calm down before the others arrived. He could hear the cracking of branches on the forest floor now.

Brendan took hold of the branch and backed his horse up behind the cover of the bushes. The branch got harder and harder to hold as he bent it back. Finally, Brendan reached the point that he could bend it no more. He waited and hoped he wouldn't have to hold it long. He heard one of the barbarian's mounts whinny in the distance. Brendan reached over and patted his horse on the muzzle with his spare hand, hoping this would distract his horse from neighing in response. It worked. The gray horse only snorted a little.

The Vikings were getting close. Brendan could see them through the leaves. The lead rider was King Hakon himself. Patiently, Brendan waited for the king to reach just the right position. Swoosh, the branch went. Brendan glanced their way momentarily. During the quick glimpse, he noted that the branch had swept King Hakon off his horse and into the one following him. This, in turn, caused the second horse to rear casting off the second barbarian.

Brendan rode back and scooped up the rein from the horse King Hakon had been riding. The king had been stunned. He started to his feet when he saw Brendan; but by that time Brendan had his horse and was darting back into the brush along the deer trail. It wasn't easy to control the gray horse he was riding and lead the roan horse the king had been riding. Brendan strained to do so for as long as he could. He wished he could have taken both horses; but the two Vikings would now either have to ride double or only one pursue on horseback. If they rode double it should slow them down enough that Brendan could stay ahead of them. If not, Brendan now had only one of them to contend with.

The deer path led to an open hill again. Brendan dropped the rein of the horse he'd been leading. He kicked his mount into a faster pace, hoping he could over top the hill before any pursuers could see him. Just before he went over the top, he saw the single figure of King Hakon, emerging on horseback from the woods. Well it was him against the king of the Vikings now. Brendan hoped he'd picked the better horse.

On the other side of the ridge, Brendan turned his horse to run parallel with the ridge for a while. The beautiful gray horse dropped its head and ran as though he delighted in running. The grass was tall here and swished as Brendan's horse ran through it. Brendan hoped it might obscure him enough to throw King Hakon off; but that was not the case. When Brendan glanced back toward the ridge, he could see the king had just topped the ridge and was in fast pursuit. Brendan turned and urged his mount on. All of a sudden, the gray horse darted sideways, nearly throwing Brendan off, and, over the edge of cliff where he might have fallen 200 to 300 feet to his death.

This gave Brendan another idea. He turned his gray horse to face the oncoming barbarian king. Brendan rode toward him, pointing the branch he used as guide rod toward his adversary like a lance. As they closed, Brendan could see King Hakon draw his sword. The two combatants sped toward each other. Brendan pointed his "lance" at the king's throat. King Hakon appeared unthreatened, his sword bearing hand dangling at his side. When the horses were almost nose to nose, the king shifted his horse so it passed on Brendan's left instead of the right. At the same time, he made a mighty swipe with his sword.

Brendan almost didn't duck in time. He felt the wind of the passing sword raise several hairs on his head.

Brendan turned his gray mount, heading back toward King Hakon. This time he decided he wouldn't point his makeshift guide rod. The king had turned and was heading back toward Brendan now. The king was now facing the wrong way for Brendan's plan to work. Brendan also wanted to make sure the king was really worked up. Brendan tried to fix his eyes on the King as they rode the collision course together again. This time, Brendan raised the branch into the lance position only when Hakon was almost against him. The king however parried the branch away with his sword, cutting the end of it off as he did. Seeing this, King Hakon let out a malicious laugh as he turned his horse to go at Brendan again.

Brendan decided now was the time. Instead of turning the gray steed to face the king, Brendan headed for the cliff. He hurried to reach it before King Hakon could get too close. As he neared the edge, he turned the gray horse to face Hakon again, raising the shortened branch as if to defend himself. King Hakon bore down on Brendan, a visible sneer on his face. Just before the king's horse reached his, Brendan kicked his gray mount, moving away to the side. King Hakon's mount suddenly sensed the presence of the cliff and veered to the right. The momentum of the approach, together with the element of surprise combined to send the unprepared Viking monarch sailing and screaming into the air, off the cliff.

Brendan walked his gray horse to the edge of the cliff. Below, on the ground, he could see the lifeless body of the dead barbarian. Above, the black horse with white splotches grazed calmly on grass as though nothing had happened. Then, a moment later, the horse whinnied as though recognizing an old friend. Brendan looked around. Coming down from the top of the ridge was the roan horse Brendan had turned loose earlier. It came running toward Brendan, apparently anxious to rejoin his grazing partners. Brendan decided that the barbarians might still want to pursue him, so he must take the horses with him, even though they belonged to someone else.

The black horse came up alongside the roan. Each snorted in recognition of the other. Brendan slid off his mount and walked over to the two horses, leading his gray mount as he went. Both horses had bridles fashioned from ropes. He tied the two bridles together and remounted. To the right, the great grassy hillside sloped downward into a valley and then rose again. Brendan decided to head for the top of the far hill. He figured he could see a long way from the top of the hill and maybe regain his bearings there. He'd been so obsessed with escape from the sea warriors that he'd become disoriented.

When Brendan reached the top of the great hill, he looked back to the way he'd come. He couldn't see far enough to see either the sea or the river. He did see a band of two dozen or so of the barbarians descending the side of the ridge in the distance. Would they discover the body of their dead king? What would they do then if they did? Would they come looking for him or return to their ships? Brendan felt confident now that they couldn't catch him. The horse gave Brendan a freedom of movement he'd never experienced before. Hunger was beginning to gnaw at Brendan's stomach. At the bottom of this hill, in the direction Brendan had been heading, there appeared to be a pond or lake. It looked like a good place to water the horses and maybe catch a fish or two.

Brendan was surprised at the size of the lake when he reached it. From a distance, many trees tended to obscure it. Up close, you could see the surface of the lake extended some 1000 feet in diameter, although much of it appeared to be shallow, with reeds and rushes rising above the milky water surface. Brendan led the horses down to the lake where they all drank heavily. Brendan noted the earth around him had been trampled bare and contained deer, horse, sheep and cow prints in addition to many other native animals. The spot must have been a favorite watering hole. Like as not, he might run into other herdsmen. Brendan took out his fishing line and started looking along shore for a suitable branch to use as a pole. As he headed back into the brush, he found himself looking at the pointed end of six spears.

Holding the six spears on Brendan, were six very hungry looking men. All wore clothes fashioned from skins of animals, most notably deer, fox and badger. All wore scraggly beards and had uncombed hair. Apparently, they, like Brendan, spent most of their lives in the wild. The strongest looking of the bunch, a man only slightly taller than Brendan, maybe a little heavier, and with wild eyes, looked to either side at his companions; then spoke.

"Looks like we've captured a horse thief."

"Yeah, yeah," the others said in concurrence.

"What are you talking about?" Brendan asked.

"Bind his hands," the leader of the group ordered, ignoring Brendan's question.

Instead, one man on each side of Brendan grabbed his arms. They forced his hands together behind his back and lashed them together with some sort of rope.

"But I only took the horses to escape from barbarian sea warriors who were after me," Brendan protested.

"Don't waste your breath on me. You can tell all to the chief. Let's go," the ringleader responded. They escorted Brendan back to the water's edge to gather up the horses. As Brendan limped through the soft earth; he heard the voice of the leader again.

"What's wrong with you, boy?"

"I've got a bad leg. I was born with it," Brendan sneered.

"Put him up on that horse we saw him riding," the leader ordered.

Brendan felt two hands on each arm shove him towards the gray horse. When they reached it, one of his guards held him by the shoulders as the other stood, back to the horse and locked his fingers together, palms up, making a step for Brendan's foot.

"Up with you, lad," he ordered.

Brendan placed his right foot in the man's hands, bounded and swung his left leg over the horse's back. It was difficult to balance himself with his hands tied behind his back; but he managed to wiggle into a comfortable position. One of the motley looking herdsmen took the rein of Brendan's horse. Then two more took the reins from the other two horses and fell in behind him. The leader and the other two herdsmen lead the way. Brendan was surprised to see that none of the other herdsmen mounted the two extra horses.

The group followed the perimeter of the lake until they reached a point where the lake narrowed down to a waterfall. A bridge, well constructed of oak and ash timbers, spanned the out fall of the lake. A thousand feet beyond the bridge on the far side lay a large round stockade, fashioned from ash logs, carved to a point on the top. A double gate, made of the same logs, was opened and they entered. Inside were three circular houses, with outer walls made of upright poles in the same fashion as the fort, but with thatched roofs. On the inside of the outer perimeter wall of the fort, Brendan could see a number of little huts which appeared to sprout from the main wall of the fort.

They led Brendan to just outside the largest building in the center of the fort. The leader ordered Brendan to get down. Then he shouted toward the entrance of the building.

"Fergus of Creegh to see Chief Aidan."

A grizzly man, with gray beard and hair to match, came bursting out of building with a goblet in his hand. Brendan guessed the man must have seen sixty years at least. He staggered out, giving Brendan the impression he bore some pain that made it difficult for him to walk. Aidan then threw back a purple cloak, revealing a bright green linen tunic over white linen trousers with gold embroidered about the neck and sleeves.

"For what reason do you disturb my dinner?" Aidan shouted.

"We've captured a horse thief," Fergus explained.

"Bring him here," Aiden ordered.

Two of the herdsmen took Brendan by the upper arm and brought him to face Aiden.

"Who are you?" Aiden asked.

"My name is Brendan. I come from an area some call Kilrush. There used to be a village there..." Brendan started.

"How did you get here, and why did you steal my horses?" Aiden demanded.

"I was captured by Vikings, sea warriors from some alien land. I managed to escape them when they put ashore north of here. I have a bad leg. The Vikings were chasing me. When I saw your horses, I took one to escape the barbarians. I managed to get the other two away from the Vikings after a battle with their king."

Aiden laughed, then continued, "I've heard the bards tell tales of alien invasions before; but this is the first I've heard of an alien abduction"

"But it's true," Brendan protested. "As we speak, they may be on their way here. These men are vicious killers. They burned the little village at Kilrush and destroyed another north of here."

"We've seen no sign of these barbarians. Are you sure you're not making this up?"

"It's true I tell you, although their king is dead now, so they may return to their ship and leave."

"How did their king die?" Aiden asked skeptically.

"He was chasing me on one of your horses and it threw him off a cliff," Brendan explained.

"That sounds like a pretty fantastic story," Aiden commented.

"I swear it's the truth sir," Brendan answered.

Aiden took a sip from his goblet and bowed his head in thought for a moment.

"Fergus, take two men and check out that great cliff to the north of here, see if you see any sign of these aliens."

"Yes Chief," Fergus responded. Then he turned and pointed to two of the men whom had been in the party which brought Brendan to the fort.

"You and you, come with me," he ordered.

Fergus then left with the two men he'd selected. Aiden then looked at Brendan again.

"You know we punish horse thieves severely here," Aiden continued.

Aiden stopped, took another sip from the goblet, and went on.

"Looks like you may be our guest for awhile, at least until I can decide if you're telling the truth. Do you promise not to try to escape?"

"Yes, ah, er, Chief?" Brendan responded.

"You may call me Chief," Aiden answered. Then he addressed the two men guarding Brendan.

"Undo his hands; but stay with him," he directed.

Then Aiden turned back to Brendan. "You like lamb stew?"

"Yes, Chief," Brendan answered enthusiastically.

"Let's go have dinner," Aiden entreated, nodding to the two guards to escort Brendan into the house.

Brendan was led to a long wooden table near a round stone hearth in the center of the room. On it, a large bronze caldron steamed. A woman, gray haired, but perhaps as much as ten years younger than Aiden, attended the fire in the hearth. Aiden identified her as his wife's sister whom he had taken in after the death of her husband and whom had chosen to stay after the death of Aiden's wife. Aiden ordered her to bring bread, mead, and bowls of stew for everyone. The two guards sat down at the table on either side of Brendan. Aidan sat at one end. When the food was placed before Brendan, he ate ravenously. Aidan noticed this and commented.

"It looks as though you haven't eaten in a long time."

"Not such a tasty meal as this, to be sure," Brendan commented.

"You must tell us how you came to be here," Aiden entreated.

Brendan told the whole story, from the time he first freed Kaileen from the Vikings to his capture by Chief Aiden's men. When he finished, Aiden commented.

"Either that's the grandest tale ever told in this house, or you've been through quite an adventure. So you know King Finian eh?"

"Yes Chief," Brendan replied.

"He and I've been rivals for many a year now. Every year he wagers a prize cow against one of mine at the great fair at Kilkee, and every year I've lost the bet. Just once before I die, I'd like to beat him." Aiden continued, completing the last sentence in a wistful tone.

"What do you wager on?" Brendan asked.

"A horse race, one of mine against his. I used to ride against him in the race; but a couple of years ago, my horse fell and rolled on me. I broke my hip and it didn't mend right. I can't even mount a horse without a lot of help," Aiden explained.

"Why don't you have one of your men ride for you?" Brendan suggested.

"I tried that the years since my hip broke; but none of my servants can properly handle a horse. Worse, none of them really has a heart to learn the skill. A horse has a personality, like a human being, it takes the right man to get a horse to perform his best." Aidan explained.

"I'll bet that gray horse of yours could outrun any horse King Finian could put up against him, with the right rider of course," Brendan boasted.

"Oh, you think so now, and I suppose you think you're just the man to ride him," Aiden snarled.

"The horse is a fast horse, to be sure; but I've not been riding a full season yet," Brendan pointed out.

"Ah, but you love the horse don't ye lad? I can see it in your eyes."

"True enough," Brendan said sadly.

"Tell you what. You win that race for me, and I'll forgive you for taking my horses."

"I only took your horses to save my life, Chief," Brendan protested, then continued. "And I wouldn't feel right about racing against King Finian. After all, his men saved me and my friends from the evil barbarians, and King Finian gave me work when my master had turned me out."

"Suppose I told you that you could keep the gray horse if you win?" Aiden proposed.

"Such a fine horse, ah, but sure you wouldn't want to lose a prize like that?"

"T'would be worth it to beat Finian in the race it would; but don't be counting the horse yours until you've won it," Aiden reminded him.

"Yes, Chief," Brendan humbly replied.

"Are you agreed to race the horse for me then?"

"When is the race?" Brendan asked.

"Four nights from now. If we leave at sunrise, we can make Kilkee by sundown tomorrow. That'll give us a couple of days for you to get the feel of the course. I hope Finian doesn't come early. If he sees I have a lad riding he might not be of the mind to wager," Aiden commented.

"But what about the barbarians? There is a chance they might attack here," Brendan asked.

"We'll know by morning if they're about. The lads I sent out to scout around will find them if they be out there. Unless it looks like an attack is imminent, you and I can go to the fair. I'll leave all my lads behind. They're the best you'll find when it comes to a fight," Aiden said with confidence.

"If you say so, Chief."

"I say so. I'll have my sister her fix you up a bed in the house here. You look as thought you could use a good night's rest. And I'll set her about finding you some decent clothes. Those you're wearing are a ragged as a begger's."

Aiden then sent the two guards away. He gave orders to his sister concerning the bed and cloths. She made a bed in the same room as the hearth with a mat of reeds and straw covered by a deerskin with a wool blanket for Brendan to cover himself. She took some measurements on Brendan; then disappeared into another room, leaving Brendan alone with Chief Aiden. They talked a long time with Aiden doing most of the talking and Brendan listening. It wasn't hard to listen though, for Aiden told of many of his exploits as a youth, including cattle raids against King Finian. King Finian, of course, retaliated with the result that, over the years none really gained any advantage, so they made a pact to respect each others livestock. Finally the mead had its tranquilizing effect on them and they agreed to call it a night. Brendan marveled at the soft sensation of the bed he lay on. He was asleep almost as soon as he threw the blanket over him.

"Wake up lad," Aiden's voice barked. "We've got to be off soon."

Brendan sat up. From the light streaming in from the window Brendan deduced day had broken.

"There's a well behind the house if you want to wash up a bit. And here, try these on for size," Aiden said as he tossed a bundle to Brendan.

Brendan got up and headed for the door.

"Be quick about it too, if you want a bit of breakfast before we leave."

Brendan went to the well and washed his face and hands. Then he went back to the house and changed into the new clothes. There were light brown trousers and a fine purple tunic with a bright red cloak to throw about the shoulders. Brendan had only known men of wealth to wear such finery. Aiden came limping in from outside. He looked Brendan up and down and commented.

"Ah isn't it the fine gentleman you are now."

"Yes, I wonder where she found such fine clothes on such short notice?"

"I believe they belonged to her husband, God rest his soul. He was about your height, but a much wider man. I suspect my sister had to take them in a bit to fit you," Aiden explained.

190

Just then Aiden's sister-in-law entered and Brendan thanked her. She said nothing, just smiled deeply and bowed.

"Well let's have a bit of breakfast and be off," Aiden burst out.

They had a large breakfast of sausage, eggs and dark bread, washed down with fresh milk. It didn't take Brendan long to eat his fill. He couldn't remember a time when he'd had a more satisfying meal. When he finally set his fork down, the chief spoke.

"Well if you had your fill, let's be off."

"What news of the barbarians?" Brendan asked.

"Ah yes, the Vikings as you call them," Aiden began. "My men did see them. They were carrying a dead man, I presume that king, back towards the river to the north. I don't think we need fear an attack. My men counted only twenty of them. My lads can muster twice that number among the neighboring landowners if it looks like they'll attack. Right now the lads are spreading the word among the neighbors. With everyone alerted, any move they make will get back to my men. I doubt they'll return this way. More than likely, with their king dead, they'll be fighting among themselves over who's to take charge."

"I hope you're right," Brendan commented.

"Trust an old man."

With that comment, Aiden lead Brendan out the door where he beheld one of the most magnificent sights he'd ever seen.

# CHAPTER 19

Brendan couldn't decide if it was a chariot or a cart. A polished oak carriage rested on a single axle. The carriage was shaped predominately like a chariot with sides that curved down and to the rear. On top at the front was a finely crafted oak seat with a polished bronze rail around it. A footrest was attached a little below the seat, made of the same fine polished oak and attached with bronze fittings. Ornamental wood carving decorated all the edges along the outside of the carriage and a large boar head had been carved on each of the two side panels. The wheels had bronze instead of wooden spokes, although the outer rim was constructed of an oak rim with iron tires in the usual style of the times. Two powerful chestnut geldings were hitched to the front and the beautiful gray horse, wearing a halter, was tied to the back.

"What do you call that?" Brendan asked.

"I like to call it Isaiah's chariot because it goes so fast I often think the wind might set it on fire. I had to make some accommodations though since I can no longer stand for long periods of time," Aiden explained.

"You ought to challenge King Finian to a chariot race instead," Brendan suggested.

"I've tried; but once he saw this baby, he'd have nothing of it. He's got nothing that will compare to it," Aiden explained. "Come on, hop up on the seat. We've got to be off."

Brendan climbed into the seat on the left side. Aiden followed on the right side, taking up the reins. He pulled a whip from its holder on the right side, cracked it, and they were off. Brendan anticipated that Aiden would run the horse full out for awhile to impress him; but Aiden was content with a lively trot. Brendan marveled at how the seat seemed to absorb the bumps and dips of the road. Surely this vehicle was a masterpiece of transportation!

The sun was getting low in the sky as they arrived at the fairgrounds of Kilkee. Aiden chose to make camp in a clearing in the hawthorn and ash trees on the perimeter.

"Why not join the others?" Brendan asked.

"Ah they'll be making revelry all the night through over there. We need to get our sleep if we're to be in top form on racing day," Aiden explained.

"Have we need of a fire?" Brendan asked.

"Ah, we might want for a bit of warmth and light. Why don't you make a wee one."

Brendan gathered downed timber and built a small fire. They warmed their bread by it so that when they put butter on the bread it soaked in, making a delicious companion to the dried venison jerky and raw turnips. To wash things down, however, Aiden produced a bottle of aged red wine, which he said had come from the land of the Franks.

"You'll find many such a delicacy at a fair like this, although the cost may be quite dear," Aiden explained.

They finished the bottle and settled down for the night. Although the noise born by the wind from the fair kept Brendan awake for awhile, sleep finally overtook him. He was awakened the next morning by the sweet smell of smoked bacon. Aiden was cooking it on a flat stone he'd apparently heated for the purpose. Eyeing Brendan he said,

"Well it's about time. I was about to wake you up; but I've seen the salted pork has done the job."

"Smells good," Brendan responded.

"Get up and have breakfast. Afterwards, we'll visit the fair and look over the race course. It's especially good to have a thorough knowledge of the course."

Brendan enjoyed his fill of bacon and flat cakes cooked on the rock. He didn't recognize the type of wheat used in the cakes; but it had a delightfully novel taste. After they'd eaten, Brendan helped hitch up the team and they headed for the fair.

They passed livestock pens first, where farmers had brought their cattle, pigs, sheep, chickens and goats for sale or trade. Right then, in a central arena, a man was parading a beautiful chestnut mare around a circle of enthusiastic bidders. After the arena came the stalls where clowns, jugglers, fire eaters, and acrobats performed, stopping now and then to encourage the crowd to reward their efforts with small gold or silver token rings. Following these were three sided tents where one could purchase all manner of food and drink. They passed booths where local seamstresses as well as foreign tailors sold clothes of many sizes, shapes, and all the colors of the rainbow - sometimes within a single garment. There were also booths containing jewelry of gold and silver, brass and bronze cookware, and many other products produced by skilled artisans. As they passed one of the jewelry booths, a man came running out from the booth hollering.

"Gentlemen, gentlemen, stop a while. We have many fine gifts for your wives."

"We don't have wives," Aiden hollered back.

"Then we have rings, braclets, and necklaces sure to win you one," the man answered, undaunted.

Aiden turned to Brendan. "These hawkers are merciless," he said. "They'll pull almost any kind of trick to separate you from your gold or other valuables. Be cautious around them."

"Thanks for the advice. Maybe being poor has its advantages in this place." Brendan commented.

"Perhaps, but means going hungry too," Aiden philosophized.

"Where are we headed?" Brendan asked.

"I think we'll try out the race course. It will be good to give Gray Streak the feel of the course."

"So Gray Streak's his name, is it?" Brendan asked.

"Appropriate, don't you think?"

"Sure."

They rode on past the last of the craftsmen's booths, and came to a pair of poles set in the ground. The poles were set about a hundred feet apart with two parallel ropes fastened between them at the top. Between the two ropes hung letters made of wadmal fabric that spelled out "Finish Line". Passing between the poles, Aiden explained that this gate served as both the starting and finishing point of the race. They followed a well worn trail nearly as wide as the gate where the soil was sandy, not unlike a beach. The brush on either side of the path was short and the ground undulated ahead of them. As they rode along in the chariot they came to a line of bushes which Aiden drove around, explaining that Brendan and Gray Streak would have to jump the bushes. Aiden instructed Brendan to give Gray Streak his "head" at this point and the horse would do the rest. Next they came to narrow pond, which Aiden instructed Brendan to treat like another row of bushes.

They continued, with Aiden pointing the rest of the hazards along the course which Gray Streak would be expected to negotiate. When they reached a great sycamore tree standing all by itself, Aiden explained this was the turn around point where Brendan was to head back to the finish line.

"Now mind you there'll be judges here to make sure none of the riders turn back short of this tree," Aiden cautioned.

When they'd returned to the starting gate, Aiden instructed Brendan to untie Gray Streak and ride him through the course.

"Take it at a canter first trip," Aiden instructed. "The horse needs to learn the course too."

Brendan untied Gray Streak and mounted. The horse wore a specially crafted leather bridle. Aiden had given him a special bronze guide rod. Brendan walked Gray Streak to the gate and took off. Gray Streak accelerated quickly to a canter and Brendan found he had to hold the horse back from breaking into a gallop. He remembered Aiden's instructions about giving the horse his "head." The first time they came to water, however, the horse stopped short, sending Brendan over his head and into the pond. Nothing was hurt but his pride - especially since it soaked and muddied his new clothes. Just before the next water hazard, he nudged Gray Streak into a gallop so the horse was moving too fast to stop at the water's edge like before. It worked. Gray Streak cleared the breadth of the water as gracefully as he cleared the height of the bushes.

They ran the course half a dozen times, resting Gray streak for a short time in between. When at last, the horse began to show signs of more lasting fatigue, Aiden announced.

"That's enough work for today. Give Gray Streak a proper rub down and we'll visit the fair," Aiden ordered.

After Brendan finished rubbing down the horse, Aiden drove to just outside the arena where Brendan had seen the horses being paraded for sale earlier. He parked the chariot there and they walked around the fair. Aiden treated Brendan to several different foreign delicacies from the food booths. They made their selections based on the smell of the food. When Brendan pressed Aiden to tell him what they were eating, he told Brendan it was better if he didn't know. Aiden purchased a bottle of wine and suggested they go watch the games.

Returning to the arena, they found a javelin throwing contest underway. Brendan and Aiden found seats in the wooden stands. The javelin contest was followed by a trick riding contest. As Brendan sat in the stands, sharing the bottle of wine with Aiden, he marveled to the point of jealously at the tricks the riders performed. They rode hanging sideways, facing the horse's rear, standing straight up, one lad even did it standing on his hands.

"I wish I could ride like that," Brendan remarked.

"You may very well some day my boy," Aiden mused.

"You really think so?"

"Anything's possible."

After the horse riding were wrestling matches which continued until darkness began to fall. Then Aiden stood up.

"We'd best find our camp for the night. You need a healthy rest. The race is only two nights away."

They camped at the same location as the previous night. The next day passed pretty much the same. Brendan rode Gray Streak as fast as he could this day. The horse sailed through the course on every run. Finally, Aiden stepped in.

"That's enough for today. I want Gray Streak fully rested for tomorrow. How do you feel?"

"Unbeatable," Brendan replied.

"Well don't be getting a big head. It'll be different tomorrow. You'll be crowded in with thirty or more other horses. Some of the lads will be of a mind to win any way they can, so be on guard against dirty tricks," Aiden warned.

"Like what?" Brendan asked.

"Like trying to cut your rein, kick you off, or bumping your horse to cause it to stumble."

"Can't they be disqualified for that?" Brendan asked.

"That they can; but the judges often miss it or let it pass as a prank to be expected by any contestant," Aiden explained.

"But it isn't fair!" Brendan protested.

"Neither is you being born with a club foot or me breakin my hip in my prime," Aiden added. "Give Gray Streak a rubdown and let's go find some foreign beer to sample."

After a second evening of merriment and another night on the perimeter of the fair, Brendan actually awoke before Aiden the next morning. Brendan remembered Aiden had sampled double the amount of foreign beer he had. Perhaps that was the reason for him sleeping so long. The crackling of the breakfast fire finally woke Aiden though and they had a light breakfast of flat cakes with honey, washed down with milk obtained from one of the prize cows at the fair. As Brendan cleaned up and put out the campfire, he asked Aiden.

"Are we off to the race now?"

"That's not 'til later this morning. First, we've got to find that King Finian of yours. I'd need to make my bet with him," Aiden answered.

"Do you think he came this year?" Brendan asked.

"Oh, he'll be here, to be sure. I suspect he's down at the track inspecting the competition. Let's go."

Brendan joined Aiden in his chariot. Aiden drove past the many booths of the fair to the area outside the starting gate of the race. There were many horses there now. Most were tied to stakes outside tents where apparently their owners had spent the night. Many of the horses neighed and stomped their forehooves in restless anticipation. Aiden drove his chariot along the large crescent shaped group of competitors. Brendan stared intently looking for some sign of King Finian, hoping that Failend might have accompanied him. When, at last, they came to the last of the group, Brendan's spirit sagged with disappointment. Then a familiar voice boomed from behind them.

"Are you ready for some horse racing?" King Finian asked.

Brendan turned. There, mounted on horseback were King Finian and Failend, side by side. Failend's lovely golden hair was neatly trussed behind her neck, emphasizing the elegant shape of her chin and giving the impression of nobility. On mounts behind King Finian, Brendan recognized the personages of Deicola and Manchan. Behind those two, were two other mounted soldiers. Apparently, the king was prepared to deal with trouble of any kind. Aiden who had turned at the same time as Brendan, now spoke.

"And who is the angel who graces King Finian's presence?"

"I'd like to present my daughter, Failend," King Finian responded.

"Pleased to meet you sir," Failend greeted.

"The pleasure is mine young lady," Aiden answered, then turned to King Finian. "It's hard to believe a man of your looks could have sired such a beautiful creature. Her mother must have been twice this lovely."

King Finian snickered and answered: "Ah, Aiden, you do have the tongue for exagerating; but I'll not be tricked into comparing my daughter to her dear departed mother. Now where may I ask, did you find that lad?"

"My men came across him riding one of my mounts and leading the other two. I thought they caught a horse thief; but this lad told a tale of fleeing from some 'sea warriors.'" Aiden responded.

"He's telling the truth on that account, you can be sure. My men did battle with them seven or eight nights ago. A nasty lot they are. They even kidnapped my daughter!"

"You don't say!" Aiden said, clearly astonished.

"Your lad, Brendan, in fact, played no small part in freeing her from the clutches of the vile heathens."

"You mean the lad's a hero?" Aiden asked.

"My daughter and I do owe him a great deal," King Finian answered. Then, looking at Brendan, he asked.

"But what of the girl, Kaileen? And that partner of yours?"

"Kaileen, Dungal? When last I saw them they were headed toward Dun Finian with a young widow, Uasal. Surely they'd have arrived by now," Brendan answered, worry welling within.

"We left three nights ago for the fair. They may have arrived after our departure. Captain Kilian will look to their needs, I assure you," King Finian responded.

This didn't reassure Brendan; but there was nothing he could do about it at the moment.

"Aiden, shall we have a drink and talk of a wager?" King Finian changed the subject.

"Aye that we should; but I prefer to discuss business alone," Aiden responded.

"Oh, I'm sure my men can find some way to amuse themselves. As to Failend," King Finian began.

"Could Brendan show me the fair, Daddy?"

"I suppose there's no harm in that. Just make sure you are back in time for the great race, understand?"

"Yes, father," Failend answered demurely.

She dismounted and handed the rein of her horse to Manchan. Seeing this, Brendan got out of the chariot and walked towards her. King Finian then took a small purse from his belt. He poured some of the contents into his hand.

"Here's a few Bunne-do-ats for you, Failend. Don't spend it all in one place," The king instructed.

Failend went to her father and he dropped the items into her cupped hands. The king and his escort rode off followed by Aiden. When Failend returned to Brendan, she took a purse from her belt and dropped the small, gold, open rings with buttons on the ends into the purse. Then she took Brendan's left arm just above the elbow.

"Shall we be off, too? Oh, Brendan you tell must me everything that's happened since I saw you last."

Brendan told the whole story. When he got to the part about the death of King Hakon, Failend remarked.

"Do you think that means we'll be rid of these barbarians?"

"I certainly hope so. With the ones your father's army killed, their numbers are greatly reduced and their King is dead; but still they are a fierce lot. I don't know," Brendan responded.

"Well, we'll not concern ourselves with them today," Failend smiled, then continued. "Oh, here's a spear throwing contest. Want to enter?"

"Failend, I've no training on the spear. I can't compete against the champions around here," Brendan protested.

"Then I'll enter," Failend said as she shook Brendan's arm and snickered.

The contest area consisted of a large semicircle of stones laid on the ground, beyond which lay a large open field where the grass had been mowed so that you could see where the spears landed. To one side of the circle, a fat man with a round face, dressed in a dark brown tunic stood shouting.

"Step right up, step right up. One Bunne-do-at will get you five, one Bunne-do-at will get you five; just throw your spear the furthest. Too many winners today. I'm going broke. Take your chance before I run out of gold."

"Failend, this is a waste of money. Do you really think you can win a contest like this? Just look at the other contestants."

Brendan was referring to the group of men who had gathered. All of them carried their own spears and all bore the posture of professional soldiers.

"Oh, it will be fun. Just watch," Failend said as she pulled Brendan toward the fat hawker who now was saying:

"Only nine contestants, we need one more. Who'll be number ten? Easy money folks."

"I'll be number ten," Failend addressed the fat man.

"Your boyfriend wants to try his luck then," the fat man responded.

"No, I want to try my luck," Failend corrected him. "But I need to borrow a spear."

"I have a fine selection of used spears. Look 'em over. Take your pick. Only two Bunne-do-ats each," the fat man said.

Failend looked at spears. She picked each up, looked down the shaft and felt the weight in her hand.

"Two Bunne-do-ats each. It's not likely the lot of them are worth two Bunne-do-ats. You know stealing's against the Fifth Commandment don't you?" Failend scolded the fat man.

"OK, since the lady's at a disadvantage in the contest, I'll make you a special price: one Bunne-do-at."

"You'll be needing to confess this deal to the priest; but one Bunne-do-at it is," Failend answered.

Failend then selected one of the spears, paid the fat man, and walked to the forward most point of the semicircle.

"Ladies first?" she asked with a captivating smile.

The other men, who had been waiting for the last contestant, smirked and made a show of backing off to allow her room. Failend threw her spear. Brendan was surprised at the distance it traveled. The other contestants followed. One by one they attempted to best Failend's throw. In the end, two did. Even though Failend came in third, winning nothing, she came to Brendan beaming after retrieving her newly purchased spear.

"Why are you so happy after losing the contest?" Brendan asked.

"I had fun. Just looking at the faces of those men when I made my throw was worth the cost of entering the contest," she said. "Here, something for you to remember me by." Failend answered, handing Brendan the spear.

"Thank you; but I hope we are never again so distant from each other that I need an object to remind me of you." Brendan answered as he took the spear from her.

"That's sweet Brendan; but you'll not be wooing me again will you?"

"I would, if I thought my chances were as good as the chance of you winning that spear throwing contest."

Failend rubbed Brendan's head, mussing up his hair.

"Oh you. Lets go see what other delights this fair has," she said as she grabbed his arm again.

Brendan relished in the rush that Failend's playful attention brought on. They went on, arm in arm, enjoying the sights, sounds, and smells of the fair. They stopped to watch jugglers, fire swallowers, and acrobats. Then they came to a small amphitheater where a man stood in front of a small crowd reciting what seemed to be some sort of story.

"Oh, a teller of tales," Failend said excitedly. "Let's stop here for a bit," she entreated.

They took seats in the amphitheater. Brendan was immediately drawn into the story. It was about a fabled Irish hero who took part in a great cattle raid and did things that were scarcely believable. The speaker was a fantastic storyteller, modulating the tone and volume of his voice, and pausing at just the right times for the maximum effect. Brendan was spellbound and quite disappointed when the story finally came to an end.

"So you enjoyed the story then?" Failend asked, bringing Brendan back into the present.

"Yes, how could you tell?" Brendan asked.

"I made a few comments to you during the story; but you took no notice of that," Failend said.

"Oh, I'm sorry," Brendan answered.

"Don't worry about it," Failend responded, then went on. "I think you're the first man I met who enjoys attending a recitation. How do you feel about music?"

"I like it I guess, although I've not heard much. A few women singing at work or hymns in church."

"There's some musicians a little farther along, let's go listen to them." Failend offered.

They walked another thousand feet and came upon another amphitheater carved in the natural limestone outcroppings of the hillside. At the foot of the amphitheater was a wooden stage. On the stage a small group of musicians: harpers, pipers, fiddlers and timpanists were playing a lively tune. Failend led Brendan to one of the stone step-seats where they listened as the group went through several pieces. Like the recitation, Brendan was drawn into the music. He was disappointed when Failend stood up and threw a Bunne-do-at in tribute on the stage.

"The race will be beginning soon, Brendan. We must get back to the starting gate." She said.

"Okay."

Brendan stood up reluctantly; but once Failend took his arm, he was again caught up in the pleasure of walking with her. They moved directly this time, not stopping to take in any more exhibits or contests. Brendan also noticed many people were moving in the same direction. Apparently the races would be drawing a good crowd.

When they neared the gate, they had to push their way through the crowd searching for King Finian and Aiden. Suddenly a hand grabbed Brendan' right arm.

"Over this way, and hurry. Most of the riders are already mounted," Aiden's voice came from behind.

Brendan looked at Failend. He couldn't just abandon her in this crowd.

"Bring the girl with you. Her father is near your mount."

Brendan, with Failend in tow, followed Aiden as he cleared a path through the crowd. They soon came to Aiden's magnificent chariot. Gray Streak was bridled and ready to be mounted. The horse snorted at the sight of Brendan as if to scold him for being late. Brendan couldn't explain why, but the horse radiated victory. Brendan felt the horse had made up his mind to win this race whether Brendan came along for the ride or not. He turned to Failend.

"I've promised to ride in the race for Aiden. I hope I will make you proud since you were responsible for my learning to ride."

"Oh, I'm sure you'll do fine Brendan, Good luck." Failend answered him.

"Will you meet me here again after the race?" Brendan asked.

"Sure, Brendan, now off with you."

"The lady's right. Get to the lineup at the gate, and mind what I told you about some of the lads not playing fair," Aiden commanded.

Brendan mounted Gray Streak, turned the horse and nudged his mount to the starting gate. There must have been two dozen horses standing abreast in a long line. Many snorted or pawed the ground in restless anticipation. Brendan's stomach began to tighten as he approached the line and stress seized him. He pulled his horse alongside a beautiful coal black horse, whose rider sneered at Brendan in an attempt to intimidate him. A moment later, a lean, warrior-looking rider pulled up alongside Brendan on a chestnut stallion. Following him, another rider came into line riding a magnificent white horse. The race master was climbing now into a small tower lashed from logs and ropes. On the ground, to Brendan's left, were several trumpet players. In front of the horses, two men were busy stretching out a long rope along the ground.

"Riders bring your mounts to the rope, but mind you don't cross it or you're disqualified," the man in the tower shouted.

Brendan brought Gray Streak to the rope; then glanced to his left to see if any new contestants had arrived. In fact, there was a new one, a very familiar new one. It was Failend riding Midnight.

# CHAPTER 20

The sight of Failend hit Brendan like a bucket of cold water first thing in the morning. Up to now, the ability of the other riders in the race had been of little concern to Brendan, because Brendan knew nothing of them. Likewise, he knew little of the speed of their horses. This ignorance allowed Brendan to feel an air of confidence. He felt that he and Gray Streak had just as good a chance of winning the contest as any of them. Failend's entry into the race changed everything. Brendan knew she rode like the very wind itself. She'd be the one to beat.

"Attention riders," the man in the tower began.

Brendan listened as the man outlined the course and ended by announcing that the race would begin with a blast from the trumpets. Brendan glanced again at Failend. She looked straight ahead, apparently focused on the race course.

"Ta da, ta da, ta da.... ta da," the trumpets sounded.

Brendan was stunned to the point that all the other horses left the starting line ahead of him. Gray Streak decided not to wait for the master's command and chased after the others, nearly leaving Brendan behind. Brendan snapped out of his initial shock and bent low along Gray Streak's neck. To Brendan's surprise, he didn't need to urge the horse. Gray Streak sprinted forward. In a few moments they began passing other riders.

Gray Streak cleared the first water hazard with the grace of a wild deer. Brendan noticed several riders were thrown at this point. Well, that lessened the odds; but Brendan was now in the middle of a great wedge of horse flesh, with Failend moving toward the lead, her magnificent gown flapping in the breeze. The second water hazard approached. Brendan relaxed, trying to become one with Gray Streak. The strategy worked. Gray streak cleared the obstacle with ease, even though it claimed several more riders.

Failend was in the lead now, as they approached a steep hill. Gray Streak seemed to relish climbing, powering his way past horse after horse. As they came on top of a sparsely vegetated plateau, Brendan began to pass the coal black horse he'd been alongside at the start of the race. As Gray Streak drew up alongside, the rider of the coal black horse glanced over at Brendan. Suddenly he struck out at Brendan with his guide rod, the point of which lacerated Brendan's cheek, drawing blood. This action enraged Brendan. He nudged Gray Streak closer to the rider who had just struck him. As Brendan anticipated, the rider struck again. This time, however, Brendan was prepared. He grabbed the rod with his right hand and jerked hard. The rider, caught off guard, came sailing back toward Brendan. Brendan released his grip on the rod, allowing the man to fall from the coal black horse.

"That should teach you some sportsmanship," Brendan muttered.

The racers were now approaching the great sycamore that marked the turn around point. Failend had increased her lead to two horse lengths ahead of her closest pursuer. Brendan had six horses to pass to catch up to her. Rounding the sycamore, one of the horses stumbled and went down. A moment later, they came to the steep hill. Three of the contestants slowed their pace as they descended the hill. To Brendan's surprise, Gray Streak didn't. He easily passed those three and was now catching up to the first of the final two between him and Failend. They came up on a low stone wall. The horse ahead of Brendan cleared the wall, but stumbled momentarily on the far side, giving Gray Streak, who sailed over the wall like a bird on wing, the opportunity to move into third place.

The second place horse began to tire, allowing Brendan and Gray Streak to overtake him. Now Brendan had only to challenge Failend for the lead. He hoped Gray Streak had enough left in him. Gray Streak seemed to have an insatiable desire for victory; for he began to narrow the gap between him and the lead horse. They were approaching a water hazard now where the horses would have to jump water followed by a row of shrub. Brendan was a little to the right and only a horse's length behind Failend now. Failend's horse started to enter the water a little before leaping into the air to clear the bushes. As a result, Midnight slipped, falling into the bush and sending Failend headlong over it into the dust on the other side.

As Failend sailed through the air, without horse, Gray Streak neatly cleared the obstacle. Worried, Brendan glanced back to see Failend get to her feet and slap the dust from her dress in disgust. Brendan could clearly win now.

An urge then struck Brendan, irrational though it was, but Brendan acted on it. Midnight jumped the bushes without his rider and continued toward the finish line. Brendan turned Gray Streak around and headed back to Failend. He had to hurry; two riders were fast closing on the obstacle. He shouted ahead to Failend

"Take my arm and mount behind me."

Failend did as instructed and they turned for the finish line just as the next contestant started to clear the bushes. Brendan felt the delightful sensation of Failend's arms around his waist. Then he heard her voice in his ear.

"What are you up to, Brendan?"

"If we catch up to Midnight, do you think you can mount him on the run?" Brendan asked her.

"Yes," Failend answered.

"Be ready, then," Brendan shouted back.

Without Failend on his back, Midnight began to relax his pace. This allowed Gray Streak, even with the extra weight of Failend, to overtake him. Brendan brought Gray Streak up on the left side of Midnight. As he did he felt Failend's arms release their grip and then she no longer was behind him. Next thing he knew she was riding abreast of him, shouting.

"See if you can beat me now!"

The gate marking the finish line was now in sight. Brendan knew he dare not look behind to see who was following, lest it might cause Gray Streak to even slightly reduce speed. Gray Streak and Midnight were neck and neck now, scrambling toward the finish line. For all practical purposes, there was only one person racing against him.

Neck and neck they continued toward the finish line. Just seconds before they crossed, Gray Streak made up his mind that today was his day and produced one last burst of speed, propelling him across the finish line half a horse length ahead of Midnight. Brendan had won.

Brendan let Gray Streak coast to a walk. He did not want to risk causing any injury to this magnificent animal. When Gray Streak finally slowed to a walk, Brendan dismounted. Even though they had traveled well beyond the crowd gathered by the gate, Gray Streak was badly lathered and Brendan felt he needed to relieve the horse of his weight. It didn't matter, the crowd raced toward him now on foot. As they pressed around him, cheering, Brendan felt hands lift him up so the next thing he knew he was riding on top of the crowd, Gray Streak's rein in hand, toward the gate he had passed under only moments ago.

When, at last, the crowd set him down at the gate, Aiden rushed up shook his hand vigorously and threw his hand around Brendan's shoulder.

"You did it, my boy, you did it. How many years have I waited for this day?" Aiden shouted euphorically.

The crowd parted a little to make way for the Master of the Race who had climbed down from the tower he'd occupied during the race. Behind him walked a very beautiful red haired girl of some seventeen to eighteen years. She was dressed in a bright green gown with white lace around her collar and sleeves. Alongside her walked a boy of about seven years carrying a satin pillow with a gold chain and medal on it. She stopped in front of Brendan and waited while Master of the Race made his speech.

"As Master of the Race I have the honor to present to...?"

"Brendan... of Kilrush," Brendan answered. Immediately he thought that sounded a little pretentious, as though he owned property there.

"Brendan, I present to you the champion's medal for first place."

The lovely red-haired girl then took the medal from the pillow. She stepped up to Brendan and placed it over his head, arranging it neatly around his neck. She kissed him on the lips and the crowd roared their approval. With a slight blush the girl backed up and stood by the boy with the pillow. Brendan sensed that she was embarrassed to kiss a stranger in front of so many people. Aiden burst through the crowd. He shook Brendan's right hand and patted him on the shoulder.

"Well done my lad. This is the happiest day of my life. I finally beat King Finian, although I wish it was himself that had been riding in the race," Aiden lauded.

"And what did you win?" Brendan asked.

"A fine young bull, the pick of the spring calving season some two years past. 'Twill make a fine addition to my herd," Aiden answered.

"Congratulations," the voice of King Finian boomed.

Brendan heard it even before King Finian emerged from the crowd. Brendan turned to see the crowd part, allowing the monarch and his daughter to pass. King Finian offered his hand, which Brendan grasped.

"I never thought a herdsman could outride the daughter of Finian. Where did you learn to ride?"

Brendan coughed and hesitated, not wanting to betray Failend to her father. Failend saved him.

"Kaileen and I taught Brendan and Dungal, in the pasture near home," she explained.

King Finian's face grew grim as he scolded her.

"Oh, I remember now. By the way, it's not your place to be teaching the hired hands to ride horses. What need of a herdsman for a horse to perform his work? Who ever heard of chasing cows on horseback?"

"In Brendan's case, I mean with his bad leg and all, he could do his job much better," Failend pleaded.

"I'll not be supplying my herdsmen with horses," the king replied, his nostrils flaring as he did.

"There's no need to provide me one. I have my own now," Brendan boasted.

"What do mean?" King Finian and Failend asked simultaneously.

"Gray Streak, the gray horse I rode, is now mine," Brendan explained.

As if to signal his agreement, Gray Streak snorted and pushed Brendan in the back with his muzzle.

"Aye, the boy's right. That was the deal we made," Aiden added.

"And are you still of a mind to herd cows for King Finian?" King Finian asked.

"Yes sire, if you will have me back," Brendan answered.

"You may return. Failend and I will leave for Dun Finian this afternoon. Do you wish to ride with us?" King Finian asked.

Brendan looked at Aiden. He felt he should escort Aiden back to his home before setting off for Dun Finian. On the other hand, he was anxious to learn if Uasal, Kaileen and Dungal had reached the safety of King Finian's estate. Aiden seemed to sense the indecision in Brendan and spoke up.

"Don't worry about me, Brendan. I've not far to go and I've traveled the way many times alone."

"And now, how about a good meal before we're off?" King Finian proposed. Then he continued, "Aiden, how about I, the vanquished, treat my old rival to a rack of ribs?"

"I'll not contest that offer," Aiden snapped back.

"Good, I know a woman here at the fair. What she can do with meat. She makes lambs ribs so delicious and tender that you have to take care not to eat the bones with the meat!" King Finian boasted.

"You don't say?" Aiden answered. Brendan thought Aiden to be salivating in anticipation. Then he spoke to Brendan.

"You go on with the king. I'll get me cart and follow."

Brendan, Aiden, Failend, King Finian, Deicola and Manchan all enjoyed a filling meal of roast lambs ribs, cabbage and bread, washed down with adequate quantities of beer. By mid afternoon, they bid farewell to Aiden after escorting him to the edge of the fair. King Finian promised he'd have the bull delivered within a fortnight. In fact, he might even have Brendan deliver the bull. When they parted, Failend and her father rode in the lead, followed by Manchan and Deicola with Brendan behind them on Gray Streak, leading a pack horse which carried supplies for the king and his entourage. They rode until nearly sundown, when King Finian gave the order to make camp. Brendan then helped raise a tent for the king and Failend, gathered wood and built a fire. Deicola disappeared into the heather for a time. When he returned he had the carcasses of two rabbits and a badger.

"We eat well tonight," Deicola announced.

Brendan enjoyed his portion of rabbit; but found the badger only moderately palatable. The King produced a couple of bottles of wine purchased at the fair. These they passed around until the bottles were empty. As the fire began to die down, King Finian spoke.

"Brendan, you must tell us of your adventures since last we saw you at Dun Finian," the king ordered.

Brendan told the story, leaving out the part about taking the treasure from the Vikings. Brendan wasn't sure how the king would react to that. Anyway, it was probably best not to let it be known too widely that they'd acquired the treasure. As he told the story, he noticed that all listened intently, as though he were telling a story of the legendary Irish folk heroes. When he was done, King Finian made no other comment than to announce he and Failend would be going to bed. When the king and Failend disappeared inside the tent, Brendan, Deicola, and Manchan drew straws for the first watch. Brendan won.

Deicola and Manchan, used to the rigors of a soldiering way of life, had constructed beds of reeds and small leafy sprigs, and, spreading rawhide below, and their cloaks above them were soon fast asleep. As the gentle sound of snoring brought serenity to the night, Brendan looked at the sky. The moon hadn't risen yet, so the sky was full of stars. Brendan stared at them, wondering if anyone would ever be able to go up there and find out what kept them in the night sky. He heard a slight shuffle behind him. He turned to see the slender figure of Failend standing beside and slightly behind him.

"I thought you were asleep," Brendan said.

"Oh, I'm a little restless," Failend answered him.

"How about your father?" Brendan asked as he stood up.

"Oh, he's quite asleep. I'm sure you can hear him snoring," Failend answered. "Brendan?" she continued.

"Yes."

"Why did you come back for me after I fell off Midnight today?"

"I wanted to make sure you had a fair chance to win," Brendan answered her.

Failend smiled a coy little smile. She looked to the ground in front of her and back to Brendan.

"Would you have done that for any of the other riders?" she pressed.

Brendan pondered the question for a long moment. Then he answered, "No."

"Why not?"

Brendan thought again. There was no use trying to hide the truth.

"Because none of them are as pretty as you," he answered.

"I thought it might be something like that. You really care for me, don't you?"

"Ah, yes," Brendan answered nervously.

"I suppose I should show you some sign of gratitude for your sportsmanship," Failend teased.

"That's not necessary."

Failend moved close, very close to Brendan. She put both her forearms on his shoulders, clasping her fingers behind his neck. Her eyes looked directly into his.

"I will grant you permission to kiss me—in reward for your sense of fair play," she said.

Brendan thought to tease her by refusing the reward; but the sweet smell of her, combined with the inviting eyes and tempting lips was too much to resist. He leaned forward until his lips met hers. The gentle touch was titillating. Her arms tightened around his neck. Brendan responded by placing his arms around her, one around her waist and the other behind her shoulders. He held the position until she pulled away to take a breath.

"Do you feel adequately rewarded?" she asked.

"More than adequately," Brendan answered, caught up in the euphoria of her kiss.

"Since you are not greedy, I think you should be rewarded for that too. What do you think?"

Brendan answered her question by drawing her to him and kissing her again. After another delightfully warm moment, Failend pulled away again.

"You know this is impossible, don't you?" Failend said.

"What's impossible?" Brendan asked, perplexed?

"I can't love you, Brendan."

Michael J. Schneider

"Why not?"

"Because I'm a princess, and you're…"

"Just a herdsman." Brendan finished the sentence for her.

"Yes, I believe we had this talk before." Failend continued.

"You said I couldn't marry you; but I don't see how a feeling of love can be confined by a difference in social position," Brendan countered.

"It's just that I've always believed I'd love the man I married."

"Do you think your father might allow me to marry you if my fortune changed?"

"What do you mean?" Failend quizzed.

"If I became a man of property, a land owner."

"You aspire to a dream, not reality, I'm afraid my dear Brendan. Most land is held in common. The chiefs assign the land to tenants. It is rare for individuals to own land and tenants are usually allowed only to pass the land they farm to their heirs," Failend explained.

"But there are some individual or family owners of land are there not? How do they get their land?" Brendan asked.

"Most inherit their property. From time to time, a king may make a grant of land to some individual for some special service rendered," Failend continued.

"Has your father ever made such a grant?"

"Not to my knowledge."

"Then there's hope I might merit such a grant," Brendan suggested.

"Oh you are a dreamer!" Failend said staring wistfully into his eyes.

"Well it's not impossible. Some time ago would you have believed I would ever own such a fine horse as Gray Streak?"

"No, I, I, guess not."

"Well, why don't we see what the future brings. After all," Brendan hesitated. He wasn't sure he should tell her about the treasure.

"After all, what?" she pressed him.

"My fortune may change, I plan to be a landowner, which should make me a noble in your father's eyes," Brendan explained.

"That is possible, but the chance of that happening is pretty remote," Failend reiterated.

"Why don't you let me take that chance? Will you give me time before accepting someone else's proposal of marriage?" Brendan asked.

"I will give you until the Feast of St. Brigid two years hence. My desirability as a wife will decrease with age, and the pressure from my father to marry will likely increase. I can't promise anything beyond that time."

210

"Fair enough. That gives me more than two years to achieve noble status. I can't ask for more than that. Will we be able to see each other at Dun Finian?"

"We'll have to be discreet. If father gets wind of the pact we just made, he'll banish you from the kingdom; then there will be no hope," Failend explained.

"Okay, discretion's the plan," Brendan said as he leaned forward to kiss her.

Failend put her finger to his lips to stop him, commenting: "This must be the last time for tonight. I must return to the tent. I'm afraid father or one of the others might wake up and see us. After all, what we've been doing here isn't very discreet is it?"

Brendan relished the smirk on Failend's face as she asked the question. He didn't answer though, just pulled her close into a passionate embrace. When they broke again, Failend headed back to the tent. Brendan sat back down. During the next hours, the images of the encounter with Failend preoccupied his mind. He was too excited to sleep. Before he knew it, the first light of dawn began to dispel the darkness surrounding him. Fatigue gushed through him. He woke Deicola and lay down to catch what little rest he could before King Finian awoke.

Although it seemed like he'd barely closed his eyes, the sun was well up in the sky when he heard the whispered voice of Failend.

"Brendan, love, it's time to get up. The king awaits."

"You're much to gentle, my lady," boomed the voice of Manchan. "Give him a sound shake."

That wasn't necessary. Brendan sat up at the sound of Manchan's voice.

"You need to get up lad," Manchan continued. "The king is ready to depart."

Brendan stood up and looked around. The tent was gone. Apparently everything had been packed up.

"Pack away your bedding and let's be off," King Finian ordered Brendan. "Failend saved you some corn cakes. You can eat them on the way."

Brendan scrambled to his feet. He rolled the single deerskin loaned to him by Deicola and tied it to the pack horse. When he had unhobbled Gray Streak, Failend handed him a small, deerskin bag containing the corn cakes. King Finian mounted first, the others followed and they were on their way again. By midday, they came upon a great rushing torrent of a river.

"Storms in the interior must have caused the river to swell its banks," Manchan commented to the king.

"What do you think? Can the horses make it?" King Finian asked.

"Not likely sire. Remember the trouble we had crossing two nights ago when we rode to the fair. The water was rising at that time," Deicola commented.

"Is there not a bridge near here?" King Finian asked.

"Yes sire, several miles upstream from here; but it hasn't been maintained since you vanquished the chieftain of this land. I don't know if it will support us." Deicola answered.

"Hmmm," King Finian pondered. Then he continued: "How long do you estimate before the river recedes enough to ford?"

"Two, maybe three nights," Deicola responded.

"Let's try the bridge," King Finian ordered and turned his horse to head upstream.

Failend, Deicola, and Manchan followed, with Brendan last, leading the pack horse. It didn't take long to reach the bridge. From the distance, it looked adequate enough, constructed of wooden timbers spanning between rock piers. The water was high though, nearly lapping at the underside of the bridge. As they neared, however, Brendan could see that the cross planks which formed the bridge deck were gray, indicating they were badly weathered, perhaps rotten. Some were broken in half and there were gaps where the planks were missing altogether. King Finian pulled his horse up just short of the entrance.

"We'd better do this one at a time," he said.

King Finian then rode up onto the bridge. He carefully walked the horse across the deck, the bridge groaning under the combined weight of horse and rider. All went well until he reached midspan. Then, reaching a gap, the king's horse apparently thought it was too wide to step across. The horse leaped, coming down hard on the far side of the gap. The horse's right foreleg broke a plank and stumbled, throwing King Finian from its back into the raging waters below. Failend shrieked. "Somebody help, Daddy can't swim."

# CHAPTER 21

Brendan dropped the reign of the pack animal. He raced Gray Streak downstream along the bank until he reached a point where he felt he had sufficient lead on the bobbing figure of the king to intercept him. Brendan then stripped off his belt and tunic, rode Gray Streak to the water's edge, and leaped from the horse's back into the raging torrent. Swimming head high, stroking like a frog as Dungal had once taught him, he swam across the river, keeping his eyes on the regal victim. Brendan swam cross current, making no attempt to swim against it. He knew it was useless to fight the river current, and he would need all the energy he could muster to deal with the king.

Brendan had calculated well. He reached a point about ten yards ahead of the king where the current would carry the king to him. Brendan swam against the current for a few moments to keep from being pulled downstream ahead of the body fast closing on him. Just as Brendan was about to reach for the monarch, the king disappeared below the surface. Brendan was on the verge of panic. He dove under the water; but the river was so laden with silt, he could see nothing. He swam back to the surface. The king's head broke the surface again, a little downstream. Brendan swam for him.

Swimming downstream, it only took a few moments to reach the king. Brendan caught him by the collar; but both were pulled under the surface.

"The sword, the sword," Brendan thought. Being unable to see, Brendan felt along the king's body until he found the buckle that fastened the belt which bore the king's sword and purse. He unbuckled the belt. Immediately they rose to the surface again. Brendan made for the far shore with the king by the collar in his right hand, swimming madly with his left hand, scissor-kicking with his legs.

When his legs finally struck bottom, Brendan stood up and pulled the limp body of the king by placing his hands under the king's shoulders. The water, although shallow, was sufficiently deep to buoy up the king's body. Although it used up Brendan's last reserve of energy, he managed to drag the king up on dry land. He examined the limp body before him. King Finian's face, where visible beyond the whiskers of his beard, bore a sickly hue of blue.

Brendan knelt alongside and listened at his nostrils. The king did not breathe. Brendan pulled back the king's jaw and looked into his mouth. There was nothing stuck in his throat. Desperately Brendan tried to think of something to do to revive the lifeless body.

*Perhaps if he could force air into the body,* he thought.

Brendan opened the king's mouth and held the king's tongue against the bottom of the mouth, leaving open the passage to the throat. Brendan took a deep breath and blew into the mouth. Immediately the king's chest rose. Brendan took another breath, but a gurgling sound from within the king told him something was about to come out. Brendan turned the king's body sideways. Water oozed from the king's mouth, followed by a violent fit of coughing. With the coughing, the king began to breathe again and the blue hue of his face gave way to a natural redness.

Brendan helped the king to a sitting position. The king coughed some more, then opened his eyes and spoke.

"Where am I?"

"On the far bank of the river you started to cross. Your horse stumbled and threw you into the river," Brendan answered him.

"Oh, yeah, I remember now. My whole life passed before my eyes. How did I get here?" King Finian asked.

"The young lad swam the river and rescued you, sire," Deicola's voice sounded from the bank above.

Brendan looked up to see Deicola sitting on horseback with both Gray Streak and the king's horse in tow. King Finian stood up, involuntarily coughing a couple more times.

"Are you all right sire?" Deicola asked.

"Yes, how is my horse? Where is my daughter?"

"Your horse appears to be fine, only a minor scratch on the right forelock. Manchan has your daughter under restraint."

"You restrain the daughter of your king?" King Finian bellowed.

"We felt we should determine your condition before letting her see you," Deicola answered.

"I understand, but we must go to her at once," the king ordered.

Deicola threw a cloth object at Brendan.

"Here put this on. It wouldn't do for the princess to see you in your undergarment," Deicola said.

Brendan recognized the garment as the tunic he'd hastily discarded. He put it on and Deicola rode forward and handed Brendan his belt also. At the sight of this, King Finian, now mounted, instinctively felt for his sword.

"What became of my sword and purse?" he asked.

"They're on the river bottom sire," Brendan answered. "I'm afraid I had to release your belt to save you. The weight was dragging us down."

"Very well, young Brendan. A dead monarch has no use for a sword or money," King Finian said.

The king mounted his horse. Brendan followed; but Gray Streak shivered a little once his master was on his back. Apparently he was not used to having a wet body on his back. Deicola led the way, a short distance, through the scrub oak and reeds to where Manchan waited with Failend. Manchan held Failend, her head buried in his shoulder, with Manchan rubbing her back in a consoling motion.

"Failend" King Finian spoke.

"Oh, Daddy! I was so scared," Failend said as she rushed to her father.

King Finian threw one leg over the horse and slid to the ground. Failend collided into his arms. She hugged her father hard, then looked up at him and said.

"I was afraid you'd drowned," she sobbed.

"Well I didn't, and we have young Brendan to thank for that," The king answered her.

"Brendan, Brendan rescued you?" Failend asked as though astounded.

"That he did, me dear. Now let's be on our way. I lost my sword during the ordeal. I don't feel like a proper king without my sword." King Finian urged.

"I would be honored if my king used mine," Manchan offered.

"As would I," Deicola added.

"Thanks men; but a man's sword is like a pair of shoes. It has to be custom fit. I'll have a new one forged at Dun Finian."

"Yes sire," both men said.

"Let's mount again. With luck we'll be home by dusk," King Finian commanded.

They rode hard the rest of the afternoon. The brush with death seemed to have infused in King Finian some new urgency of purpose. As he promised, they arrived at Dun Finian just as darkness began to envelope the fortress in gray shadows. The gate was open, but two soldiers stood guard, ready to close it at the sign of trouble. One of the soldiers, upon sighting the king and his party, shouted.

"The King approaches."

Brendan could hear echoes within the walls as others repeated the soldier's message. King Finian turned toward Brendan and spoke.

"Manchan, Deicola, and Brendan, your king invites you to stay at his house this night. The day has been long and we must eat and rest."

"Thank you, sire," Brendan answered first with Deicola and Manchan following in turn.

When they entered the main gate, Brendan looked around anxiously for some sign of Kaileen, Dungal or Uasal. He saw none of them. They rode to the entrance of the King's house where several soldiers took the king's horse as well those of Failend, Deicola, and Manchan. When one came for Brendan's mount, Brendan shook his head in refusal. Then he petitioned the King.

"Sire, I would prefer to look after Gray Streak myself, if you will give me leave to do so."

"Granted, but if you want supper, be not long about it," the king admonished.

"Thank you, sire."

Brendan then dismounted and followed the soldiers to a corral behind the king's house. The corral contained a large water trough as well as half a dozen feed boxes where grain could be placed for the horses. Brendan led Gray Streak into the corral constructed of sapling poles and took off his bridle. Gray Streak walked a few paces, snorted at the ground then lay down and frolicked in the dust. Brendan, in the mean time, followed the soldiers to a small shed where one of the soldiers handed Brendan a measure of grain in a wicker basket to give to Gray Streak. The horse, seeing Brendan return with the grain, ran towards him. Gray Streak nudged Brendan away from the feed box as he was pouring the grain in.

"Whoa boy, have a little patience now," Brendan chuckled.

When Brendan returned the basket to the soldier, he asked, "Have you seen anything of two women and a man, a mute, arriving these past few days?"

"Can't tell you, I'm afraid. The lot of us have been on patrol for the past seven nights. We just traded places with the guards within the dun this morning," the soldier answered.

Brendan shrugged and walked around front to the main entrance to King Finian's house. One of the two guards on the door opened one leaf of the door for him. Inside, King Finian was seated at the head of his table with Deicola and Manchan on his right hand and Failend on his left. On the table, next to Failend, lay a bowl, loaf of bread and bronze goblet.

"Come forward, take the place next to Failend," the king entreated.

"Thank you sire," Brendan said and sat down beside Failend.

"Why the forlorn face?" King Finian asked.

"I'm worried about Kaileen, Uasal and Dungal. There's no sign of them about the dun," Brendan explained.

King Finian had taken a spoonful of the stew set before them. He took a moment to chew and swallow. Just as he was about to answer Brendan, the sound of three knocks came from the entrance doors to the hall.

"Enter," King Finian bellowed, nearly choking.

One leaf of the door opened and a guard entered. He stepped quickly across the room, stopped short of Deicola and snapped a salute.

"What is it?" King Finian grumbled, obviously irritated at the intrusion on his supper.

"Sire, two women and a man with no voice just entered the dun. They beg audience with the king." The guard explained.

"Kaileen!" Brendan shouted and jumped up, then realizing he was in the presence of the king, slowly sat back down. "Beg pardon, sire, I forgot myself," he continued.

"Pardon granted," King Finian quipped, then addressed the soldier. "You say the man with no voice begged?"

"No sire." The soldier said, befuddled.

King Finian was obviously in the mood to have a little fun with the guard.

"So how many begged audience with their king?" he asked.

"Well only one spoke; but she said 'we' as though speaking for all three," the soldier hastened to clarify.

"And how would you describe this woman?" King Finian asked.

"Nearly as tall as I, red hair, quite pretty actually, more of a girl than a woman I guess."

"And the other woman; is she pretty too?"

"Yes sire."

217

"Then by all means we should have them in," King Finian ordered, winking at Brendan as he did.

"Father!" Failend scolded.

"And the dumb man?" the guard pressed.

"Well, we'll not be breaking up the trio. After all, I'm sure I could learn something from a man who can attract two lovely ladies. Invite them in," King Finan ordered.

"Father, you're terrible!" Failend scolded again.

The soldier bowed, and did an 'about face'; but before he took his first step, the King spoke again.

"One thing more."

"Yes sire," the soldier said, turning to face the king again.

"There is a woman who just opened a dress making shop within the dun. Do you know of her?" the king asked.

"Yes sire. She's very beautiful too," the soldier answered.

"Do I pay my soldiers to be eyeing all the fair ladies?"

"You pay us to be observant sire. The other comes as a natural consequence," the soldier snapped.

King Finian laughed. "Aye, you have me there lad. Go tell the three to enter; then fetch me the seamstress."

"Yes sire," the soldier answered; then rushed out, wanting to leave before the king decided to have more sport with him.

A moment later, the door opened again and Kaileen led the group of three into the room. They still carried the packs they were carrying when Brendan last saw them. King Finian, apparently noticing this also, spoke.

"Leave your bundles by the door and come be seated," the king ordered. He shouted: "Colgu, bring food and drink for four more."

The trio did as ordered. As Kaileen stepped from the shadows, she first noticed Brendan and involuntary shouted: "Brendan!" She rushed toward him, Uasal and Dungal following.

Instinctively Brendan rose to meet them. Kaileen collided with him first, throwing her arms around him and nearly knocking him over. Brendan could see tears in her eyes. Uasal and Dungal joined the huddle and they all engaged a moment in a group hug. Colgu entered with a tray of bowls. Seeing him approach, the group broke apart. Kaileen's face blushed as though she just discovered she was in the presence of the king.

"Excuse me, sire, it's just we thought the Vikings, the barbarians, had probably killed Brendan," she said.

218

"You are excused. But I am curious why the one who stayed behind to decoy the barbarians arrived at my estate before the three of you?" King Finian queried.

"As are we sire," Kaileen responded. "After all we were delayed some two nights because we encountered a river that overflowed its banks and we dare not cross until it subsided."

"Ah, yes, I know it well," the king mused. "Have a seat and supper and the three of you and Brendan can entertain your king with an account of your journeys."

Kaileen sat next to Brendan. Uasal and Dungal crossed to places Colgu had set opposite Brendan and Kaileen. Brendan noted with amusement that the three attacked the food set before them as though it were their last meal. As they devoured their food, there was a knock at the outer door.

"Enter," the king shouted.

One leaf of the door parted briefly and a tall, slender figure slipped inside. Even before the woman became visible beyond the shadows near the door, Kaileen bounded from her seat and rushed to her.

"Mother!"

"Kaileen!" her mother responded.

The two held each other is fond embrace. The sound of gentle sobbing emanated from the mother-daughter pair.

"Oh Kaileen, I thought I'd lost you to those vile, despicable, wretches!" Cummie sobbed.

"There were times when I despaired of ever seeing you again, Mother," Kaileen responded.

"Colgu," the king interrupted. "Fill the cups all round, I think it will be a long night.

A long night it was. Kaileen told all that she'd endured since she last saw her mother before the first Viking raid at Kilrush. Then it was Brendan's turn to tell of his escape from the barbarians, being befriended by Aiden, and the race at the fair. He left out the part about King Finian's near fatal crossing of the river; however, so as not to offend his host and benefactor. When, at last, all tales were told, Brendan was nearly ready to keel over from fatigue. The king noticed this and offered for Brendan and Dungal to spend the night in the hall. Failend offered Kaileen her old room within the house; but Kaileen asked that she might go and spend the night with her mother. Granting Kaileen's request, Failend made the same offer to Uasal, who gratefully accepted it.

The next morning, just after breakfast, Uasal and Kaileen drew Brendan and Dungal aside to talk of the treasure. They were reluctant to tell the king of it. They were afraid he would demand a large share of it as tribute. The four resolved that Brendan and Dungal would take it with them to the pasture and bury it. When they found an opportunity, Kaileen and Uasal would come to the pasture and they would decide how to divide and dispose of the treasure.

**\*\*\*\***

That had been almost four days ago and Brendan had seen nothing of any of the ladies, including Failend. Failend, he rationalized, was probably being closely watched by her father or his men. King Finian made it perfectly clear he disapproved of Failend previous visits to the pasture.

Even as he thought this, Dungal rushed up to him and tapped Brendan on the shoulder, pointing to a speck in the distance. The speck grew larger until Brendan recognized it as Failend, alone, riding Midnight, coming towards them. He thought the king surely did not know of this or Failend wouldn't be alone. When, at last, she arrived, she remained mounted and asked.

"Would you escort your Princess back to the dun?"

"Certainly. Would you give me a ride to my horse?" Brendan countered.

Failend held out her arm for Brendan to grasp. He took hold of it, and, leaping, settled on Midnight behind her. Her hair bore the sweet aroma of wildflowers. As they moved away from Dungal, Brendan slid his right hand around to hold Failend's slender waist. She made no attempt to resist his touch commented.

"A good rider needs not hold on to anything with his hands."

"I'm not as good as you," Brendan answered.

"Did you not beat me in the race at the fair?" Failend asked.

"Yes, but that was business. I felt obliged to Aiden and I had the prize of a horse wagered on the race," Brendan answered.

"And this is?" Failend probed.

"My pleasure," Brendan quipped.

"I thought as much," Failend responded; but made no attempt to remove his hand from her waist.

Once they reached Gray Streak and Brendan transferred to his own horse, they rode toward the dun, side by side. The two horses settled into a gentle cantor and seemed content to not contest each other as they had at the fair.

"Why haven't I seen anything of you these past few days?" Failend asked.

"I serve your father as a herdsman. My business is to look after his cattle. He'd not think well of me if he found me at the dun, would he?"

"I guess not," Failend answered demurely.

"By the way, does the king approve of you riding out here alone?"

"No, I'm supposed to have a soldier escort if I ride beyond a sentry's view of the dun."

"So where is this escort?" Brendan pressed, smirking to himself.

"Well, Father's away on business, so I relaxed the rule a little, being that I'm the heir and reigning authority while he's away," Failend explained, sporting a coy smile.

"Ah, so that's how it is?"

"That's how it is."

"I'm yours to command, my Princess," Brendan responded. As he spoke he waved his right arm and made an exaggerated bow which nearly caused him to fall off his horse.

Failend giggled. Then she continued. "In that case, I command you to have supper with me each night while Father's away."

"Your obedient servant. I just hope you point out to your father, you ordered me to dine with you. In case he is displeased when he finds out," Brendan responded.

As they continued their ride to the dun, Failend brought Brendan up to date on Uasal and Kaileen. Uasal was content to serve as Failend's new handmaid.

"I would have preferred that Kaileen returned to those duties; but she wants to help her mother with the garment business. In the short time her mother has been here her reputation as a seamstress has spread rapidly. Kaileen says her mother has far too much work to handle by herself."

"Oh, so that explains it," Brendan mumbled out loud.

"Explains what?" Failend asked.

"Oh, nothing. I haven't seen Kaileen or Uasal since I last saw you. I'd thought they might have paid a short visit to us in the pasture."

"You speak as though you missed one or both of them," Failend said with an air of suspicion.

"Not nearly as much as I've missed you."

"That's the proper answer," Failend answered him.

They had an excellent dinner of roast boar, bread, boiled garden greens, and turnips. Failend even provided a fine wine to compliment the meal. They ate alone, except that Colgu served them. Failend sat in the king's chair and Brendan in the one Failend normally occupied. After supper, Failend wiped her face with a napkin and pushed away from the table.

"I fear I've over indulged myself. How about a turn around the dun to settle our stomachs?"

"You only need to command," Brendan answered.

"I prefer to know your company is voluntary," Failend hinted.

"That it is."

Failend took Brendan's arm and they began their walk about the dun. They passed several servants huts built from ash poles and thatch, protruding from the massive dirt wall that created the fortress. There was little breeze and the smell of animal manure was powerful. When they came to a set of steps carved in the wall of the dun, Failend made the suggestion.

"Why don't we walk on top of the wall? I'm sure we'll find the air fresher up there."

Brendan followed Failend up the steps to the top of the wall. She was right; the air was much fresher up there. The sky had darkened enough that the first stars of the evening were now visible. A gentle breeze tossed Failend's hair about her face giving her an almost mystical appearance, like a fairy one would imagine from the stories told about the evening fire.

"I like it up here," she started. "In daylight you can see for a long distance. It gives one a feeling of power."

"Is power important to you, Failend?" Brendan asked.

"I'll not be denying my birthright, if that's what you mean," Failend answered.

"But is it really important? I mean if you hadn't been born the daughter of a king, would you desire to acquire it?"

"Well, Brendan, you were born without anything. Have you no desire for power?"

"I long for a house I could call my own. To know I will always have food tomorrow. But I've no desire to command other men to pay me tribute," Brendan answered.

"Is that the extent of your ambition, your desire for food and protection against the elements?" Failend pressed.

"Well, there's one more thing," Brendan answered.

"And what would that be?" Failend prodded, her face screwed up into a smug smile which suggested she already new the answer.

"You."

"Me?"

"Yes, you," Brendan insisted.

"Isn't marrying a princess just another method of acquiring power?" Failend asked.

"I would want you even if you were a poor as I," Brendan answered.

Failend moved closer, looking straight into Brendan's eyes.

"I think you speak the truth. I..."

Failend moved very close as she spoke, her lips were only inches away. Brendan couldn't resist the thought that flashed into his mind. He bent forward until his lips touched hers. She didn't back away. Instead, she reached both arms around his neck as though to hold him fast. Brendan responded by putting his arms around her shoulders and her waist. They remained motionless for a long time as Brendan absorbed the delightful sensation of her lips, inhaled the sweet smell of her body, and enjoyed the wonderful pressure of her arms on his neck. They might have stayed that way all night; but the spell was broken by the sound of a familiar voice.

"Are you all right, Princess Failend?" Manchan asked.

Obviously embarrassed, Failend broke the embrace and backed away.

"Yes, quite all right," she answered him. Then she looked at Brendan. "I think you should walk me back to the house now, Brendan," she said.

"Would you like me to accompany you?" Manchan said.

Brendan got the impression Manchan thought it his duty not to leave the two of them alone.

"That won't be necessary, Manchan," Failend answered in a regal tone.

"Very well, princess. I'll just continue my rounds then," Manchan answered. He then walked on down the wall.

Failend led the way back to the steps and began to descend them. Brendan followed. When they reached the bottom, neither noticed the figure who ducked back into the shadows. Nor were they aware this person had witnessed the whole incident on top of the wall.

# CHAPTER 22

Kaileen waited for Failend and Brendan to go some ten to twenty paces before she decided to follow in the shadows. Brendan was never aware they were being followed. When they reached the door to the King's house, one of the guards opened it for them. Inside, Failend turned to Brendan.

"You must go now. I don't know if Manchan will tell father what he saw; but the guard outside is under orders to report all who enter the king's house when the king isn't here. I don't think father will be too concerned about you coming for supper, but he will be concerned if he learns we've spent any appreciable time here alone."

"Okay, when will I see you again?" Brendan asked.

"How about coming for supper again tomorrow, same time?" Failend proposed.

"Done," Brendan answered.

"Until then," Failend said as she held Brendan's cheeks in her hands and drew his lips to hers.

A quick, but powerful kiss it was. Failend then spun Brendan around and pushed him out the door.

Brendan wasn't sure how he got back to the lean-to in the pasture. Apparently Gray Streak had learned the way to the lean-to in the short time his new master had kept him there. Brendan couldn't get his mind off Failend. He relived the kiss on top of the wall of the dun over and over again in his mind. Dungal was asleep when Brendan returned. He unbridled Gray Streak and turned him loose to graze. Brendan lay down; but he was so excited that sleep was long in coming.

During next several days, Brendan found the days too long and the nights much too short. Dungal asked why Brendan rode off each night. Brendan told him the truth; but only mentioned that he'd been invited to supper at the king's house. Dungal asked why he had not also been invited. Brendan only told him that he didn't know. Dungal did not appear contented; but he knew Brendan well enough to know Brendan would not lie to him.

It was now evening again. Brendan just caught Gray Streak, and was placing the bridle on the horse when he saw two figures approaching across the pasture. He mounted Gray Streak and rode to the hut where Dungal was roasting a rabbit over some coals.

"Looks like company coming," Brendan announced as he pointed toward the two approaching figures.

Dungal stood from his squatted position and turned to look in the direction Brendan was pointing. He put his right hand to his forehead as though to focus his gaze. A moment later, Dungal turned to Brendan and traced the outline of a female figure with his fingers. He then projected two fingers to indicate it was two girls.

"Do you suppose it is Kaileen and Failend?" Brendan asked.

Dungal pointed at Brendan and made a hugging sign with his arms and nodded, meaning "Yes." Dungal then pointed at himself, made the same hugging gesture, and shook his head, "No."

"Uasal, perhaps?" Brendan suggested.

Dungal took a second look then turned and nodded to indicate Brendan guessed correctly.

Brendan dismounted and hobbled Gray Streak so the horse wouldn't wander too far. By the time he'd done this, Kaileen and Uasal had arrived at the fire. Dungal reached down and pulled the spit containing the rabbit off the fire and presented it to the two ladies.

"No, thank you, Dungal," Kaileen said curtly. Uasal shook her head to indicate she declined also.

"We're here to discuss the treasure," Kaileen continued.

"Well, I was headed for the Dun Finian. I've been invited to dinner at the king's house. Will this take long?" Brendan responded.

"Did the king invite you?" Kaileen sneered.

"Not exactly," Brendan hedged.

A confused looked washed over Dungal's face. Kaileen continued.

"It's Failend you're going to see isn't it?"

"Yes," Brendan answered. He saw pain in Dungal's face. Dungal threw the rabbit into the fire in disgust.

"Dungal, I didn't know how to tell you." Brendan solicited his friend's sympathy.

Dungal pointed to his face and made the two finger gesture again. This time he was saying that Brendan was two-faced or a liar. Kaileen, appearing upset to be involved in the disintegrating relationship between two friends, spoke to divert their attention.

"We've come for our share of the treasure," she announced.

"Wouldn't you rather wait until we can trade it for something easier to carry about, like gold rings for instance?" Brendan asked.

"No, I want to see no more of you, Brendan," Kaileen spat the words.

Uasal was silent. She looked toward the ground as though she wanted to avoid being drawn into the conflict. Dungal slapped a hand against his chest and pointed first at Brendan, then in the direction of Dun Finian.

"You want to go with me to the King's house?" Brendan asked.

Dungal nodded "Yes."

"Okay, we'll go together," Brendan conceded.

"What about dividing up the treasure?" Kaileen began. "We didn't come all the way out here to go back empty handed."

Brendan pointed to the hut.

"It's buried under the straw bedding in the lean-to. Dig it up and take whatever you think is fair." Brendan sneered.

Kaileen looked at Dungal.

"What about you?" she asked.

Dungal shrugged his shoulders, then tapped his chest with his fingers and flipped his thumb towards Brendan.

"I guess he feels the same as me," Brendan interpreted.

"And you're not worried about the two of us cheating you!" Kaileen exclaimed.

Both Brendan and Dungal shook their heads simultaneously to indicate they were unconcerned about the ladies cheating them. This gesture seemed to infuriate Kaileen. She stamped her foot in disgust and continued.

"Aren't you the pair. Leaving a treasure you risked your lives to obtain to go chasing after a woman the king's not going to let either of you marry. It would serve you right if Uasal and I just divided up all the treasure between the two of us."

Brendan and Dungal looked at each other and smiled. Then they looked back at Kaileen and shrugged their shoulders together to indicate they didn't care. Brendan unhobbled Gray Streak and remounted. He held his arm out for Dungal to grab. Dungal took it and nimbly bounded up and lighted up on Gray Streak behind Brendan. Together they rode for Dun Finian.

When they arrived, Brendan tied Gray Streak in his usual stall in the stable and dumped half a bucket of grain in the wooden feed trough. Failend had given him permission to treat his horse with some of the king's grain whenever he paid her a visit. At the front door, the guards asked them to wait while one of the guards announced their arrival. A moment later the guard stepped outside again and reported.

"Princess Failend bids you both enter."

Inside, Failend sat, as usual, at the head of the table in the place normally occupied by her father. She looked up as Brendan and Dungal approached on opposite sides of the table. The candlelight reflecting from her golden hair created a special aura of beauty. She wore a gentle smile and spoke to Brendan as they sat down on either side of her.

"This is a surprise. I rather expected to see you alone, Brendan."

"Well, Dungal found out we'd been dining together without the king being present and insisted on me bringing him along," Brendan answered.

Brendan watched as Failend's eyes met Dungal's for a moment then quickly glanced down toward the table in a gesture of avoidance. This hurt. Failend obviously harbored some affection for Dungal. Then she asked.

"I thought our private dinners were private, Brendan. Who told him it was just you and I together?"

Failend's smile had disappeared and her voice sunk lower as her face reddened.

"Kaileen," Brendan answered.

"How did she know? And did she tell anyone else?" Failend demanded.

"I don't know how she knew. She came to our camp in the pasture late this afternoon. When she saw I was leaving to come to see you, she made a big fuss about it. She went on about the king now being away from residence."

"And what was Kaileen doing in your camp?" Failend asked suspiciously.

"She and Uasal came to conduct some business." Brendan purposely tried to stay vague.

"What sort of business?" Failend pressed for details.

Brendan fumbled with an empty goblet in front of him. He suddenly felt guilt at not telling Failend about the treasure earlier, even though he'd never had a reason to do so.

"To divide the treasure," he answered as though it was the most boring topic he could think of.

"What treasure?" Failend probed. Her eyes widened with excitement.

Brendan recounted the story of how they had taken the gold and silver paraphernalia from the Vikings and how Dungal, Kaileen and Uasal transported it to the hiding place in the pasture.

"You know, my father is entitled to tribute from any spoils of war," Failend said indignantly.

"We didn't know that," Brendan answered sheepishly.

Brendan was totally confused by Failend's attitude. He'd have never figured her to be so materialistic. This was a side of her personality he'd never seen before.

"Well now you know," she answered coldly.

"Failend, why are so upset that I never told your father about the treasure?"

"You never told me either. You wouldn't let me in on this little secret you and Kaileen shared would you?"

"I didn't see how it would matter to you," Brendan protested his innocence.

"What other secrets do you two share?" Failend questioned in a jealous tone.

Dungal pursed his lips in a mock kiss and made a hugging motion with his arms. Brendan knew Dungal made the gesture as a joke, suggesting Brendan and Kaileen were lovers. Failend, however, took it seriously.

"So you've been flirting with Kaileen, while you've been courting me have you?" Failend steamed. Her face was full flushed with anger now.

Brendan searched his thoughts desperately for something to say which would salvage the evening. He tried the truth.

"Failend, honest, this afternoon's the first time I've seen Kaileen since the night they arrived at Dun Finian after our escape from the sea warriors."

"I guess I believe you; but it hurts to know you withheld a secret from me."

"Friends again?" Brendan pressed hopefully.

"I suppose," Failend said with a pout.

Dungal took her hand and held it in his. He pointed to Failend and then touched his heart with his hand.

"You want to plead your cause too," Failend said. "Looks like you have competition, Brendan."

Dungal's gesture made Brendan angry. It just didn't seem fair that his best friend would vie for the same girl. Failend appeared to sense the growing hostility in Brendan and sought to quell it.

"Boys, let's all be friends tonight. I'm honored that both of you wish to woo me; but remember my father has the final say in whom I marry. Let's talk no more of love tonight. Colgu!"

Colgu appeared and Failend ordered he serve dinner. They enjoyed a wonderful meal of roast beef, onions and carrots, with bread and honey for dessert. To Brendan's amazement, Dungal was the life of the party. He told several tales of adventure. At first, Brendan interpreted the signs for Failend; but it took only moments before she read the gestures without any assistance. Dungal, for his part, relished in the fact that he could communicate with such a beautiful woman. As the night wore on, Brendan sensed a powerful force drew Dungal and Failend together. While Brendan had shared special moments with Failend, he'd never before seen the special sparkle in her eyes or delight in her cheeks that he saw now. He knew Failend would never love him like she appeared to love Dungal. This final thought depressed him. What only the day before seemed to be a blossoming relationship, now seemed doomed. Brendan was relieved when Failend finally announced it was time to say good night. Failend escorted them to the door, standing between Brendan and Dungal and taking both of them by the arms.

"Good night, boys, see you tomorrow night?" she asked, giving each of them a kiss on the cheek.

Dungal eagerly nodded, indicating he'd be there. Brendan merely stated, "Perhaps."

They rode in silence back to camp. It was impossible to talk to Dungal without being able to see him. The night was dark and the stars saturated the sky. When they arrived at camp, Dungal found a few embers and nursed them into a small blaze by adding some grass, twigs, and a few small diameter sticks. As the fire grew, Brendan made up his mind to discuss the thing which dominated his thoughts during the trip back from Dun Finian.

"Dungal," Brendan started.

Dungal turned his attention from feeding the fire and looked at Brendan.

"You love Failend, don't you," Brendan continued.

Dungan nodded that he agreed.

"It appears she prefers you," Brendan conceded. "I think I should leave and let the two of you decide your own fate."

Dungal stood up. He looked confused. He pointed at Brendan and drew his arm outward in a large sweeping motion. Then he upturned the palms of both hands, a gesture that asked "Why?"

"I like Failend too well. I will always be jealous of you two if I stay here. I have better clothes now, a horse, hopefully the girls left a little of the treasure for us to split. I think I will go to seek my fortune in another kingdom." Brendan explained.

Dungal put the fingers of both hands to his temple and drew them down along the side of his face. Brendan recognized that Dungal's gesture referred to long straight hair of Kaileen, an obvious reference to her.

"Kaileen? I think she made it clear earlier tonight she wants no more to do with me."

Dungal shrugged to indicate he didn't hold the same opinion; but Brendan changed the subject.

"Let's see if the girls left us anything," he said.

Dungal followed Brendan to the lean-to. They cleaned back the straw and scraped off the shallow dirt covering the treasure. Yes, there was still a bag left. Brendan pulled it out and dragged it to the fire. He spilled all the contents on the ground. One glance convinced Brendan the girls had been fair in dividing up the spoils. The only problem was that Kaileen and Uasal had taken nearly all the smaller items, leaving Dungal and Brendan the larger ones. These would be more difficult to carry and to trade.

"You first," Brendan addressed Dungal.

Dungal nodded and selected a dagger with a gold hilt, several gold goblets and a silver pitcher. Then he gestured for Brendan to take the rest.

"I will still have a little more than you," Brendan explained. "The weight of the metal in the remaining booty is probably a 1000 manns or more than what you've selected."

Dungal pointed his right index finger upward to signify, "But." Then he pointed to a gold goblet and his hair and traced a female figure with his fingers, and obvious reference to Failend.

"Okay, I guess you do have the better deal if you consider you'll get Failend," Brendan conceded.

Dungal smiled from ear to ear, apparently delighted to no longer be contesting Brendan for Failend.

"Let's get some sleep. I'll leave after breakfast," Brendan responded.

****

Three nights later, when the sun had disappeared from the sky and Brendan began to consider sites to settle for the night, he saw a settlement of some sort in the distance. "Good," he thought. He might barter for some fresh provisions. He only had one loaf of bread, a small round of cheese and a few chestnuts left. He'd eaten rabbit for three straight days and was longing for something else. Besides, if he set out snares now, it would likely be morning before he caught anything. He pressed on, passing acres of plowed fields, mostly planted in corn, wheat, oats, barley, beans and peas. The fields seemed to be free of weeds indicating they were meticulously cultivated. The ground rose slowly in the direction he traveled and he could now see the trail he traveled ended at a massive stone object. As Brendan neared it he saw that the object appeared to be a great rath, only formed of stones placed on top of each other rather than being constructed of earth. Unlike Dun Finian, there was no gate, only an opening where one would expect a gate.

Brendan passed through the opening, noting that there were no guards posted at the opening either. Inside, the first thing which caught Brendan's eye was a large building, with walls made of the same stones as the wall enclosing it. The building bore a roof of straw thatch and a large wooden cross towering above the wall containing the entrance. Brendan felt instinctively drawn toward this church, so much so, that he'd nearly reached it before he became aware that there were scattered about the inside of the perimeter wall dozens of little "beehive" huts. The odd thing was that Brendan saw no activity among these huts. About the same time, he heard the sound of many muffled voices coming from the church speak the words "Dominus Vobis cum." Curious, he headed for the church.

Brendan hobbled Gray Streak and went inside. When he opened the door, he saw the backs of nearly a hundred men in coarse brown robes. They knelt in nearly evenly numbered rows in pews made of roughly hewn wood with a wide aisle down the center. Realizing that Mass was under way, Brendan took a place in the pew nearest him.

When Mass ended. Brendan filed out with the rest of the monks. Outside, the gray bearded monk he'd knelt next to during Mass extended his hand.

"I'm Brother Matthias," he began. "Where do you come from?"

"My name is Brendan. I come from a land southwest of here."

"And what brings you to our humble community?" Brother Matthias asked.

"This fine gray horse," Brendan answered, walking toward Gray Streak and stroking the horse's neck.

Brother Matthias, a few inches shorter and much broader, both from shoulder to shoulder and front to back, than Brendan laughed heartily.

"Okay, it seems I'll have to watch how I put my questions to you. What purpose brings you to our monastery?"

"I, I thought I might ask hospitality for the night," Brendan responded.

"Ah, hospitality is it? Well I think we might scrounge food and drink for you, maybe even a bed for the night. I'll have to put it to the brothers. I think they'll agree; but they might want something in return," Brother Matthias said. He had a look not unlike the hawkers running the game booths at the fair.

"What might that be?" Brendan asked suspiciously.

"A story. We brothers rarely travel more than a few nights journey from the monastery. We thrive on travelers' tales, and you look as though you have a thrilling one to tell. Come. Let's join the brothers for supper."

Brother Matthias then took Brendan by the arm and lead him away from the church. Brendan stopped to take the hobble off Gray Streak, but Brother Matthias interrupted.

"You can leave your horse here. No one will bother it. After we eat I'll show you where you can stable..."

"Gray Streak," Brendan inserted the horse's name.

"Ah, Gray Streak is it?" Brother Matthais asked. "Suitable enough name. Is he fast?"

"Very," Brendan answered.

"I'm afraid fast horses have always been a weakness with me. My decision to join the monastery was in no small part influenced by my desire shun the temptation of gambling on the horse races." Brother Matthias confessed.

"And you're not tempted in the monastery?" Brendan asked.

"Oh, I'm tempted from time to time; but being at the monastery is a good cure."

"Why's that?" Brendan asked.

"First, there's rarely a fair close enough to here to be reached within a couple of nights journey," Brother Matthias explained.

"And?" Brendan pressed.

"And we take a vow of poverty here. Except for the clothes on our back, and a few religious articles we own no private property. So, I have nothing to use for a bet."

"Sounds like a rough life," Brendan mused.

"Actually, it's not. You'd be surprised how giving up material possessions frees your spirit."

"Well I've never had any material possessions, until recently; but I never felt that I had a free spirit. In fact, I've felt much freer since I acquired my horse. The horse gives me a mobility I've never known before."

"Yes, I noticed you have difficulty walking, were you born with the problem?" Brother Matthias asked.

"Yes, how could you tell?" Brendan asked.

"We brothers must care for each other and are sometimes called to care for the sick and injured on the local farms. Some of us have taken to the study of medicine and ailments of the body. One of our number has traveled to Rome and obtained manuscripts from a monastery there. One of these contains many of the ancient writings on the subject. Through the manuscripts and our corporal works of mercy we have learned much," Brother Matthias explained.

They entered a long building with walls of wood and a thatched roof. Inside was a long dining hall with two long, parallel rows of tables with an aisle in between. The hall rumbled with the resonance of many voices in conversation with one another as the monks took their places at the tables. Many delicious smells assailed Brendan's nostrils. Dominant among these was that of roast beef cooked in onions. Brother Matthias led Brendan to a line which filed passed another table at the far end of the hall. Here several monks served their brothers, passing out a flat loaf of bread, hollowed out, with slices of beef and carrots in dark gravy ladled into the hollowed space and a large wooden mug of ale. As they took their ration, Brother Matthias commented.

"We enjoy a rarity tonight, roast beef. We attended to the sick wife of a local farmer a couple of days ago. She was bedridden several weeks before she finally died. The farmer gave us a cow in gratitude. Unfortunately, the cow only outlived the farmer's wife by a few days. While the farmer's wife now has life eternal; I'm afraid the cow must be content to live on in us."

Brother Matthias grinned at Brendan, apparently pleased by his own witty remark. They found a couple of openings at the long table. Brother Matthias introduced Brendan to the brothers on either side of them and across the table. They sat and waited until all were seated. Then one of the brothers stood and said grace and they began to eat. During the meal, Brother Matthias pressed Brendan to tell about his journey and how he'd come to travel to the monastery. Brendan told the story of the Viking raids and all he, Dungal and Kaileen had endured. He omitted his real reason for leaving Dun Finian and its environs. He just told Brother Matthias that he'd decided it was time to see more of the world.

"Ah, the restlessness of youth," Brother Matthias mused pensively as though he'd discovered some great philosophical truth. "I expect you will be anxious to be off again tomorrow," he continued.

"Actually, I wouldn't mind staying for awhile," Brendan began. "I would be willing to work for my keep here and for six or seven nights' provisions when it's time to move on."

"Why don't you try living in the community with us?" Brother Matthias suggested.

"I don't think I care to give up my horse and few meager possessions," Brendan responded.

"I just said try. We have many lads try our life. Some stay; many leave. We just ask that you follow our rules while you're here. After a couple of years you will be asked to take vows of poverty, chastity and obedience for life. If you choose not to take the vows; you must leave at that time."

"What about Gray Streak?" Brendan asked.

"You may pasture him outside the monastery with the cows and sheep. You may ride him when you've completed your assigned duties. If you decide to take the final vows, you will have to sell him though," Brother Matthias explained.

"That sounds fair enough. I think I'll give your life a try," Brendan answered him.

"Good," Brother Matthias commented, "I will introduce you to our Abbot".

# CHAPTER 23

Four weeks had now passed since Brendan had been introduced to the Abbot of the monastery. Brendan found life here to be quite serene. He worked hard; but he had several things he never had before. First, he shared a cell with Brother Clement. This cell looked like a large beehive from outside; but it was well made with wattle wood walls and woven thatched roof which kept out the rain and wind. Brother Clement, a young man about Dungal's age, helped Brendan build his own chair and table and a straw mat bed. Next, the brothers were big on education. Brendan spent three to four hours of the day learning to read and write Latin and in the study of scriptures, mathematics and science. Finally, there was the food. The brothers worked hard raising their own crops and livestock. As a result, the dinner table contained an enormous variety of meats, vegetables, cheeses, breads, nuts and fruits. All of the monks took their turn at cooking, and some were definitely more talented than the others; but the food was always at least good and, more often than not, incredibly delicious.

The day began at dawn. After waking up and a brief wash up at one of half a dozen wells, the monks gathered for Mass at the Church. After Mass, they sat down in the great hall for breakfast. Following breakfast they worked at their assigned chores until the midday meal. Lunch was followed by classes. Even the older monks, the ones who didn't teach, engaged in study of some sort. Many read and discussed the scriptures or the classics from Greek and Roman authors. Some conducted scientific experiments on plants and studied the stars. The time set aside for classes ended in the early evening. The brothers then gathered for Vespers, an evening group prayer service or Benediction. Following this service, they went to the great hall for their evening meal. The time following the evening meal and before the brothers went to bed was free time, when the monks could meditate individually, join in small discussion groups or take walks in the woods or fields beyond the monastery. Brendan usually took Gray Streak for a ride during this time; but once in a while he went fishing with Brother Matthias. The brother had shown him the location of a small stream which teemed with trout. The two of them never caught less than half a dozen fish, although they often released the smaller half of their catch.

During one of these trips, Brendan decided to broach the subject of male-female relations.

"Have you ever desired a woman?" Brendan asked bluntly.

"My dear Brendan, taking the vow of chastity does not eliminate the desire. We are still men, you know. However, living here where we have only occasional contact with women helps; but there are times when the temptation is strong to renounce the vow," Brother Matthias responded.

"Have you ever loved any one woman?" Brendan asked.

"Love has a very special meaning Brendan," Brother Matthias began. "Often what a young man feels is a physical attraction or infatuation. Yes, there was a girl once I thought I couldn't live without."

"What happened?"

"She didn't share my feelings. She married a herdsman like you. I see them from time to time. She appears to be quite happy with him," Brother Matthias told the tale.

"And you don't feel bad she didn't marry you?" Brendan pressed.

"Oh, I did at first; but marriage is only one of three ways to spend your life. I found that committing to the discipline of monastic life and to God brings the pleasure that one gets from satisfying the inner longings of his soul. I would guess that this compensates adequately for not being able to enjoy the pleasures of sexual union. You also do not have the stress of having to care for a wife and any offspring resulting from that union."

"So you are happy?" Brendan asked.

"Yes, Brendan, I am," Brother Matthias answered.

Brendan could feel sincerity in Brother Matthias' voice. They continued on their way to the monastery. Brother Matthias had many stories to tell of his life as a monk. This evening he told Brendan the story of how he had been traveling home from taking the monks' tithes to the Bishop. On the way he met a woman who said her father was dying and asked him to come and give the last rites. Brother Matthias agreed and arrived at the woman's house to find her husband

and children gathered around the deathbed. Brother Matthias performed the last rites on the ailing man, shortly after which the man stopped breathing. The woman, who'd summoned him, placed a linen shroud over her father and ushered Brother Matthias and the others away from the deathbed. It being late, she offered Brother Matthias supper, and he, having not eaten all day, graciously accepted. The rest of the family, although understandably lacking in appetite, sat at the supper table as a matter of courtesy. The meal was disrupted abruptly when a voice demanded.

"Why wasn't I called to supper?"

All the faces in the room turned to see the former corpse standing, looking the pinnacle of health for his advanced years. The woman who summoned Brother Matthias was convinced he, (Brother Matthias), had raised her father from the dead. Brother Matthias immediately explained they had mistakenly proclaimed the living, "dead". The woman jumped up and offered her father her seat at table, then served him and set another place for herself. All present in the house had a good laugh and were still in high spirits the next morning when Brother Matthias departed after a hearty breakfast with all the family.

As they walked on, Brendan pondered his life at the monastery during the past several weeks. It had a hypnotic, calming effect. The hard work, good food, study of ancient writings, and best of all the conversation, yes even debate with the other brothers, all worked to put the mind at peace. At first he longed for the company of Failend; but gradually the desire lessened. The monastery provided adequate diversion. Where there were no woman; one didn't have to deal with that distraction. On the other hand, he didn't have to deal with the loneliness he felt when he tended sheep for Gall, the many nights in the pasture when the sheep were his only companions. These thoughts prompted him to ask.

"Brother Matthias?"

"Yes?"

"Do you think I would make a good monk?" Brendan asked.

"I think you would make a fine monk," Brother Matthias answered.

"Really?"

"Really; but..." Brother Matthias started to answer.

"But what?" Brendan asked, perplexed that Brother Matthias hesitated.

"Perhaps you should defer that decision until after you talk to the young woman waving at us before the monastery gate. I do not know her, and she clearly recognizes one of us," Brother Matthias explained.

Brendan looked toward the gate. He immediately recognized the lovely figure of Uasal standing before the entrance to the monastery. As soon as

Brendan waved back she came running toward them. Brendan watched in awe as her exquisite body sailed along the well worn path between them like an angel on the wind. She stopped so short she nearly stumbled and fell into Brendan.

"Oh, Brendan," she gasped, "You must come with me!"

"Why? What's happened?" Brendan asked.

"It's King Finian. I'm afraid he's going to kill him." Uasal burst out.

"Wait. Who's King Finian going to kill? What could I do to stop him? Take a deep breath and tell me slowly," Brendan directed her.

"King Finian caught Dungal and Failend kissing. He banished Dungal from his kingdom, sending Captian Kilian and some soldiers along to ensure the sentence was carried out. He told Dungal he would kill him if he saw him with Failend again." Uasal rattled off the story so quickly Brendan wasn't sure he'd gotten all of it.

"Well, I guess it was bound to happen. I doubt Dungal will try to defy the King. Why do you think the King is going to kill Dungal?" Brendan asked.

"Because Failend went after Dungal. She argued with her father. When he confined her to his house, she slipped out through the kitchen and found me. I tried to convince her not to disobey her father. She wouldn't listen. She went to Kaileen. Kaileen agreed to go with her."

"How do you know that?" Brendan interrupted.

"Because, when I went to Failend's room the next day and found Failend wasn't there, I first reported her missing to the king. Then, without telling the king what she told me, I went to see Kaileen's mother. Her mother was very upset. She said Kaileen agreed to help Failend find Dungal. The two of them set off some time that night. Failend has it in her mind that all she and Dungal have to do is find Father Sweeney, have him marry them and all will be all right," Uasal explained.

"She really must be in love," Brendan commented. "She's not thinking straight. Father Sweeney's sure to find out and interfere, even if they try to get married in another kingdom."

"I guess she thought she could bribe Father Sweeney into performing the ceremony immediately, without posting the Bans," Uasal suggested.

"Ah, yes that's how the rich think; but she doesn't know Father Sweeney. He's as dedicated and devout a priest as they come. He'll insist on the Bans and waiting the proper time for response to the Bans."

"That's what worries me," Uasal went on. "King Finian is sure to kill Dungal if he sees the two of them together. It won't matter to the king if Dungal came to Failend or Failend ran Dungal to ground."

"You're probably right there. King Finian does have a violent temper." Brendan commented. "But what do you think I can do?"

"I think he will listen to you Brendan. He seems to have a special fondness for you. He talks of you at table from time to time. I think you might talk him out of killing Dungal."

"I guess I should try. What do you think, Brother Matthias?"

"If you have a chance to save a life you should try, Brendan. You are always welcome to return here," Brother Matthias said.

"Do you think we can get to them in time?" Brendan asked.

"Yes, King Finian still doesn't know what Failend's plan is. Chances are good it will take him some time to locate them," Uasal explained.

"How will we find them?" Brendan interrupted again.

"Failend said that she heard Father Sweeney was headed for the burned out village at Kilrush to say a Requiuem Mass for those slain by the Vikings there. That's where we should go," Uasal suggested.

"And I think you should wait till dawn," Brother Matthias interjected. "You won't be able to travel very fast after dark, and a good night's rest will do more to aid your mission."

"I think he's right, Brendan. I haven't slept much in the past few nights. I could do with some rest," Uasal added.

Brendan turned to Brother Matthias.

"Can she stay at the monastery?" Brendan asked.

"No problem. I can shuffle some of the brothers around. We'll give the young lady her own hut."

They went into the monastery. True to his word, Brother Mattias got two of the brothers to give up their hut for the night. When Uasal was settled, Brother Matthias took Brendan to the kitchen and loaded him up with provisions for the journey. He placed food and drink into a pair of leather bags which Brendan could place astride Gray Streak's back. Brendan took the bags from Brother Matthias and slung them over his shoulder. Then Brother Matthias spoke.

"I imagine you'll be off at dawn's first light, so if I don't see you again, good luck."

"Thank you, but I sense you don't expect me to return," Brendan answered.

"I am afraid there is a young lady who will take your heart captive."

"You mean Uasal, the one who came here?" Brendan asked.

"Not necessarily, but you are going with her to meet two others. This is a strong temptation for one who has not yet taken vows. We'll see," Brother Matthias commented.

****

A week had passed since they left the monastery, but Brendan found traveling with Uasal so pleasant that he actual dreaded reaching their destination, especially since they were heading into impending conflict. Brendan loved the pleasant sensation of Uasal's embrace around his waist, as she held him during the ride. She also liked to talk a lot during the ride. Brendan couldn't think of a time when he'd heard the female voice for such a length of time. A couple of nights into the journey, as they sat by the campfire, they huddled together under a single blanket to cope with an unusually chilly night for the season. The warmth and delightful fragrance of Uasal enticed Brendan to the extent he tried to kiss her. She put her fingers on his lips.

"No, Brendan," she said.

That simple "No" hurt much more than if she had slapped his face. Uasal apparently sensed his hurt and continued.

"I am flattered that you have the impulse; but you are young and easily aroused by any woman. Perhaps I should sit apart from you?"

"No, I promise it won't happen again," Brendan answered her.

He kept that promise; but it was hard. Brendan interpreted any display of affection by Uasal as flirting. It certainly didn't help that she wasn't bashful about getting close. Her smile, too, always appeared an invitation to taste the sweetness of her lips. Even though he had to keep his emotions in check, Brendan delighted in traveling alone with Uasal.

They were now approaching the mill where Brendan and Kaileen had found the severely wounded Father Sweeney some months before. The water wheel of the mill rotated slowly as water passed from the pond to the tailrace below. There was a cart with a mule outside. Both of these signs indicated things had returned to normal here. Brendan rode up to the door which led to the inside. He and Uasal dismounted and Brendan tied Gray Streak to a bush by the stream where water discharged from the water wheel. They then walked to the door. It was slightly ajar, so Brendan and Uasal entered.

"Hello, is anyone there?" Brendan hollered, sure that the miller was somewhere within earshot.

"Brendan, is that you?" the familiar voice of Kaileen came back.

Brendan turned to the sound of the voices. Two figures came out of the shadows of the walkway which surrounded the large millstone. One he recognized immediately as Kaileen. It wasn't until the second figure was much closer, that he recognized him as the miller. Kaileen was decked out in a long dress of kelly green with white lace about each sleeve and a broad crescent-shaped collar made of the same lace. The collar lay above the green gown, gracing her breast and shoulders. Looking upon Kaileen reminded Brendan of the story of a fairy princess his father had once told him. To his utter amazement, she rushed forward and hugged him.

"Oh, Brendan, I'm so glad you are here!" she said softly as though she didn't want anyone to overhear.

Brendan looked into her eyes as she backed away a little. They were watery as though she were on the verge of tears and her face looked strained.

"I believe the last time you saw me, you said you wanted it to be the last time you saw me," Brendan responded.

"I was very angry with you; but Failend and Dungal are in trouble and I think you can help," Kaileen said sheepishly.

"How can I help?" Brendan asked.

"First, Failend and Dungal want to get married. They'd like you and me to be the witnesses," Kaileen explained.

"And?" Brendan prodded.

"I'm afraid sooner or later King Finian will catch up to them. He'll likely kill Dungal if you don't plead for him," Kaileen continued, tears now beginning to trickle down her cheeks.

"Where are they?" Brendan asked.

"Out by the mill pond, with Father Sweeney," Kaileen answered.

"Let's go talk to them. Maybe we can convince Failend that to return to her father for now it is the best thing she can do for Dungal. That should give us some time to think of a solution. Failend's got to try to change her father's mind slowly," Brendan explained.

"Okay, follow me," Kaileen entreated.

Brendan and Uasal followed Kaileen up some steps and through a door which led to the outside on the upper level where a great wooden gear was attached to the same shaft which caused the grindstone to turn. Outside, they quickly spotted Father Sweeney, Failend and Dungal. Dungal's rapid hand gestures indicated he was arguing with the priest. Although they were about fifty paces away, Brendan could hear Failend's voice also, indicating she spoke with a high level of emotion. When Brendan, Kaileen and Uasal drew near the group, Father Sweeney spoke first.

"Ah, Brendan, it's good to see you again. I was just trying to explain to your friends the Church requires certain procedures to be followed before I can administer the Sacrament of Marriage. We must of course announce the Bans of Marriage and conduct the prenuptial instruction."

"I guessed they hoped all could be done without King Finian's knowledge in the hope that the King would accept Dungal once he was Failend's husband," Brendan explained.

Father Sweeney opened his mouth as if to respond; but at that precise moment, the tall grass parted at a dozen different locations simultaneously. The first face Brendan recognized was that of Captain Kilian. Then Brendan spotted Deicola, Manchan and finally King Finian himself.

"So you defy your father and your king?" King Finian bellowed. "Get away from him, Failend and come to your father," the king commanded.

The King then looked at the two soldiers closest to Dungal.

"Seize him," The king commanded.

The two soldiers closest to Dungal each grabbed one of his arms.

"No, Father," Failend pleaded. "He can't communicate if his arms aren't free."

"Release him," King Finian conceded. "But seize him if he tries to escape."

When the soldiers released Dungal's arms, Failend strode to within a few paces of her father.

"Please don't harm him, father. I came to him he didn't seek me out."

"And what were the two of you doing with Father Sweeney?" the king demanded.

"They came to me for the prenuptial instruction," Father Sweeney butted in.

"Prenup... you mean the two of you were planning to marry without my consent?" King Finian steamed.

"Sire, I beg you calm down," Father Sweeney continued. "You know as well as I that I cannot administer the sacrament without publishing the Bans, so it is not likely that the marriage would be secret."

"So even you, a priest, are in on this conspiracy! I thought it was your job to discourage such matters," the king continued.

"It is my job to see that the sanctity of marriage is preserved. I believe these two are mature enough to consent to a lifetime of care and devotion to each other and any children they may have..." Father Sweeney continued.

"She can't marry a dumb man!" the king fumed.

"Why not?" Failend screamed.

"And raise a bunch of idiot kids? Your son, Failend will inherit my kingdom some day. Do I reward my faithful subjects by leaving them a dummy as their sovereign?"

"Our children will inherit my traits also, Father. He or she may well have all the faculities I have. Anyway, Dungal just lacks a voice. He's as intelligent, perhaps even more so, than any one here; and he fights like ten men on the battlefield!" Failend protested.

"Then perhaps he will fight me for you—to the death." King Finian responded.

The king then looked at Dungal, who had been listening intently to the angry exchange of words.

"Are you willing to fight me for Failend?"

Dungal nodded his approval.

"Do something," Kaileen whispered and punctuated her urging by digging her knuckles into Brendan's ribs.

"Sire, I ask you not to press Dungal into this fight," Brendan spoke up.

"And why not?" The king demanded.

"Well, sire, it appears that Dungal did not disobey your banishment order, and…" Brendan started.

"And what?" King Finian interrupted.

"Well sire, I've seen Dungal in action; I fear for my king's safety," the words tumbled from Brendan' mouth.

"You're saying I shouldn't fight him because he will defeat me?"

"It's very likely he will sire," Brendan conceded.

"I'm afraid, Brendan, you have just committed your king to the combat. King Finian cannot back away from a fight. My subjects would think me a coward. Manchan, loan young Dungal your sword and shield."

"Father!" Failend protested as she stood staunchly in front of him.

"Deicola, Manchan, restrain my daughter," King Finian ordered.

The two men grabbed Failend by the arms and removed her from in front of the king, carrying her, her legs flailing in the air, to where Brendan stood with Kaileen and Uasal. A large open area now existed between King Finian and Dungal. King Finian took his shield from his arms bearer, and withdrew his sword. Dungal, now with sword and shield, also advanced slowly toward the king. The king responded by moving toward Dungal. Both men bore the look of anger and determination.

# CHAPTER 24

When the two combatants closed to within an arm's length, King Finian struck first. He struck at Dungal's head; but Dungal dropped to his knees as the king did so, leaving the king to slice only air. Dungal then nimbly sprung to his feet again. The king swung again. This time Dungal parried the blow with his sword. When the king tried a quick follow-up blow, Dungal stopped it with his shield, a puff of chalk dust rising into the air.

The battle continued for a long time. Brendan noted that Dungal struck few offensive blows. He seemed to be hesitant to assault the king. This appeared to be a good tactic; however as King Finian's vigor seemed to wane with each blow. Dungal, however, showed signs of fatigue also. This was probably because he exerted so much effort in avoiding the king's mighty sword. Now, in an apparent effort to knock King Finian off his feet, Dungal ducked and swung his sword to that it caught the king behind the knees. The force of the blow knocked King Finian off his feet and flat on his back. The king impacted hard, clearly dazed. Dungal dove toward the king, his sword raised as though he sought to bring its hilt down on the King' head and render him unconscious. King Finian, although groggy, had enough presence of mind to throw his foot up, catching Dungal in the stomach and thrusting him into the air again. Dungal flipped over and landed flat on his back, hitting his head hard on the ground. Dungal started to sit up and passed out. The king, rising wearily, staggered over to Dungal. He stood for a moment as though trying to decide what to do next. Failend shook loose from Manchan and Deicola and rushed to her father.

"No Father, don't hurt him any more!" she shouted.

Manchan and Deicola rushed up and seized Failend again; but the king shook his head.

"Release her," he said; then he slumped to one knee.

Failend put her arm around King Finian, and exclaimed, "You're hurt."

"I'll be all right in a moment. Look to your young friend," King Finian ordered.

Failend moved to the motionless body of Dungal. She knelt alongside him and put her ear to his nostrils.

"He lives! Uasal bring water," she said.

Uasal yanked the pack off her back and pulled out a wooden cup. She ran to the pond, filled it and hurried to Failend. Failend took the cup and gently poured it over Dungal's forehead. Dungal stirred a little and sat up. Failend handed the cup back to Uasal.

"Please, some more, quickly," Failend asked.

Uasal returned to the pond to refill the cup. Manchan led the king to the side of the hill by the pond. Deicola started to assist but the king waved him off.

"See if you can assist young Dungal there," the king ordered.

Kaileen took a scarf from around her neck and went to the pond and she soaked it in water. She moved to the king and bathed the part of his head that had struck the ground.

"Thank you, my dear. You love your king more than my daughter, I think," King Finian responded.

"Now that's not true, sire. You saw how she turned her attention to your condition before she looked after Dungal, did she not?" Kaileen scolded.

"That's true, find me drink," the king commanded.

Brendan went to Gray Streak. He opened one of the bags of provisions the monks had given him. There he found the second wooden cup. He also saw that the brothers at the monastery had given them a bottle of wine. He grabbed the bottle also. He took the cup and bottle to the king.

"Water or wine, sire?" he asked holding the bottle for the king to see.

The King eyed the bottle.

"Where did you get that?" he asked.

"Some brothers I stayed with provided us with victuals for our journey," Brendan explained.

"Would these be the brothers who reside in the monastery some three to four nights journey north of Dun Finian?" The king asked.

"Yes, sire," Brendan answered.

"Let's have the wine then. Those brothers have some connection to a monastery in the land of the Franks. It is rumored that monastery makes some of the finest wine."

Brendan removed the cork and poured wine into the cup until it was about half full. He handed the cup to the king. King Finian took a sip, then held his head back and sighed.

"Ah, this good enough to bring the dead back to life," he said. He held the cup out for Brendan to fill it.

Captain Kilian came up to the king and saluted.

"Sire, may I dismiss my men to enjoy their midday ration?" Captain Kilian asked.

"Permission granted," King Finian replied. "Oh, tell Deicola to bring Dungal here," the king shouted after him.

A few moments later, Dungal, still weak on his feet, with Failend on one side and Deicola on the other, stood before the king.

"Sit beside me," the king ordered.

Dungal sat down on the grassy hillside a little distance from the king. King Finian offered him the cup.

"Take all you want," the king entreated.

Dungal took a sip, then another and another until the cup was empty, then handed it back to the king. The King, in turn, handed it to Brendan.

"Fill it up again," King Finian ordered.

The king then turned back to Dungal.

"Pretty good, isn't it?"

Dungal nodded that he agreed. A smile formed on his bearded face.

"Do you love my daughter?" King Finian asked.

Dungal nodded, "Yes."

"Well that leaves me with a bit of a dilemma. I planned for my daughter to marry another king or chieftain. Thus, my kingdom would increase in either size or stability. Now I have a daughter who loves a man who hasn't even a Bunne-do-at!"

The King the paused for a moment, staring off in the distance as though the answer to his problem would appear, then shouted.

"Captain Kilian."

Captain dismissed his men to eat and ran back to King Finian. He stopped and saluted.

"Yes, sire."

246

"Do you think you could make this man into an officer in the King's Guard?" King Finian asked.

"It would be difficult with the communication problem, sire. The men would have to learn his signs and I don't see how he could command the men in battle," Captain Kilian responded.

"That's true, but what about a trainer, to teach the men how to use the various weapons in close combat?" King Finian asked.

Captain Finian thought a moment; then answered.

"Yes, I think we can make that work." Captain Kilian said.

"That will be all, Captain. You may rejoin your men," King Finian replied. He turned to Dungal.

"Would you be willing to undertake officer's training under Captain Killian? It will take two to three months. You will not be allowed to see any women during that time?" King Finian put the question to him.

Dungal looked longingly at Failend. She smiled and nodded back at him. Then Dungal nodded his approval to the king. The king then turned to Failend.

"Are you willing to put off your plans for marriage until after Dungal completes his military training?"

"Yes, father."

"Well that leaves the problem of Dungal being unlanded. My daughter can't marry a man without land so I will have to include a parcel in her dowry. Dungal, give Failend a kiss and go report to Captain Kilian. I don't want to see you and Failend together again until the Captain says you are ready to assume your duties as his combat instructor."

Dungal stood up. Failend threw her arms around him and kissed him long and hard on the lips. King Finian cleared his voice loudly, indicating he wanted the embrace to cease. They broke and Dungal went over to where Captain Killian sat eating with his men. Failend watched longingly as he left. King Finian looked at Failend.

"Father, it looks like you can post those Bans after all."

Father Sweeney smiled, "If you so command, sire."

King Finian then lifted the cup of wine up to his lips and took a long drink. He gave Brendan a pensive look.

"And what of you Brendan? Are you to return to the monastery?" King Finian asked.

Brendan looked at Kaileen. Her eyes met his momentarily, then she glanced down and away, clearly embarrassed. The king glanced from Brendan to Kaileen and back to Brendan. Sensing Brendan was troubled by decision, the king decided to help out.

"I'll tell you what Brendan, if you are not committed to return to the monastery, I will grant you eighty acres of land, a cow now, and a male calf after next years calving season. In return, I'll ask that you graze part of my herd on the land I grant you until after calving season next year. What say you to that?"

"'Tis more than generous sire; but I do not understand why you should favor me so," Brendan responded.

"It's but a small repayment for the life of your king," King Finian answered him.

Brendan realized he referred to the incident at the river where King Finian nearly drowned. Before Brendan could answer, the king continued.

"Besides, I can't stand anymore unrest among the women in my kingdom."

When King Finian made the last statement he rolled his eyes toward Kaileen.

"Well sire, I would not want to insult my sovereign by refusing such a generous offer."

"Done. But I must warn you, owning land ties a man down. I expect you to work hard and make it produce well so that you can pay your King a generous tribute also!" King Finian admonished.

"Yes, sire," Brendan answered somberly.

"Kaileen, Uasal, will you accompany my daughter on our return trip to Dun Finian?"

"Yes sire," they answered together.

The King looked at Brendan again.

"Well, since we have business to attend to on my return to my house you might as well join the king's party too," the king entreated.

"Thank you, sire. Would the king be offended if I were to make the journey by horseback?"

"Not at all, Brendan; but you and I have the only two horses. Failend may ride behind me if she wishes. Do you wish to make the same offer to one of the other ladies?"

Brendan looked at Uasal, then to Kaileen. Decisions again. He wanted to ask Kaileen; but felt obligated to make the offer to Uasal since she had accompanied him to the mill. Failend looked at Brendan, winked, and spoke.

"If you don't mind, Father, I would prefer to walk."

"I would not presume to ride while my lady walks," Uasal responded.

"And neither would I," Kaileen concurred.

King Finian smiled at Brendan.

"I guess they made their choice," he said.

The king then stood up and threw his arm around Brendan's shoulder, starting for the mill.

"My boy," he said, "looks like you and I will have a long talk on the way home."

www.ingramcontent.com/pod-product-compliance
Lightning Source LLC
Chambersburg PA
CBHW020753250626
47155CB00003B/1046